MOURNING DE PACHMANN

The Quest for the Spirit of Chopin

Carl Abbott

Hamilton Books
A member of
The Rowman & Littlefield Publishing Group
Lanham · Boulder · New York · Toronto · Plymouth, UK

Copyright © 2012 by
Hamilton Books
4501 Forbes Boulevard
Suite 200
Lanham, Maryland 20706
Hamilton Books Acquisitions Department (301) 459-3366

Estover Road
Plymouth PL6 7PY
United Kingdom

British Library Cataloging in Publication Information Available

Library of Congress Control Number: 2011939285
ISBN: 978-0-7618-5745-7 (paperback : alk. paper)
eISBN: 978-0-7618-5746-4

"To all visually challenged keyboard artists, past and present"

CONTENTS

WHO'S WHO
IN
MOURNING DE PACHMANN

Dr. Charles Flemming—Professor of Psychiatry, Toronto University. born 1878, age 55.

Anne Flemming—His wife, deceased July 1919.

Simon Williams, FRCM—Music critic for the *Cardiff Western Globe,* on a Rome assignment for *The Musical Muse.*

Vladimir de Pachmann—1854-1933, recently deceased in Rome.

Marguerite (Maggie) de Pachmann/Labori—living in Paris. (Born December 14th 1864.)

Ferdnand Labori—former husband of Maggie. Died March 1917.

Francesco Pallottelli, Rome—Secretary and companion of Vladimir de Pachmann.

Richard and Mona Connelly—travellers, living in Dublin.

Agnieszka Lipska (born September 12th 1900)—Polish pianist from Kraków, Poland.

Alexei Lipski (1898-)—Her brother.

Nigel Billinghurst—Editor, *The Musical Muse.*

Lisa Johansen (1903-)—Wireless operator, *S.S. Montrose.*

A.K. Holland—Music critic of *Liverpool Post.*

Jacques and Jeanette LeDrew—Nice, France.

Paolo Volpe—Attendant at Hotel Splendide Royale, Rome.

Mr. Beretta—Manager, Hotel Splendide Royale.

Angelo—Clerk at Hotel Splendide Royale.

Leszek Janinski—Blind Polish organist from Warsaw.

Elizabeth Valentini—Secretary to Polish Ambassador to Italy.

Ambassador Radinski—Polish Legation in Rome.

Mrs. Radinska—Wife of the ambassador.

Angela Rossetta—Eight-year-old Italian piano student.

Sophie Rossetta—Angela's mother.

Bruno Garavelli—Music critic for Rome *Evening Post.*

Doctor Teresa Rockwell—Psychiatrist, from Boston, Mass.

Prof. Stapleton—Psychiatrist, from England.

Claudio Bianco—Attaché at Polish Legation, Rome

Miss Tamminga—Night clerk, Hotel Splendide Royale.

Inspector Roberto Olivetti—Of the Rome police department.

Claudio and Michael Tondo—Owners of the *Tiber Queen.*

Inspector Collina—Ostia police officer.

Mr. Minerva—Roman taxi driver.

Doctor Sheka—Attending doctor at the Ostia Hospital.

Nancy Holmes—Head Nurse at Ostia Hospital.

Mr. Mercanti—Manager, Hotel St. Regis Grand Hotel, Rome.

Sarah Flemming—Charles' deceased sister.

Janet Spalding—Secretary to Charles Flemming in Toronto.

Madame Giacomino—Roman tour director.

Miss Bernice Rosso—Concert agent in Rome.

Mr. deMilo—Concert agent in Rome.

Doctor Camillo Mazzini—Psychiatrist, from Napoli, Italy.

Inspector Arthur Bianci—Of the Italian OVRA.

Professor Maria Cagianno—Dept. of Ophthalmology, Misericordia Eye Hospital, Rome.

Marcello Gaddi—Owner of Centrale Roma Chemist Shop.

Alfredo Crepoldi—Attorney, Rome.

Renata—A receptionist, St. Regis Grand Hotel.

Elizabeth Lipska—Agnieszka's mother.

Adam Lipski—Agnieszka's father.

Clara Lipska—Agnieszka's young sister.

Kristian and Maria Morzychi—Lipski family friends.

Anna—Agnieszka's friend in Kraków.

Doctor Angèle Runowski—Kraków.

Maria Pilchner–Purser on *S.S. Scanyork*.

ACKNOWLEDGMENTS

Just as an epic novel requires an extensive cast of characters, so too does a novelist rely upon a large and varied group of friends, family and helpful professionals to ensure the plot develops into an interesting story.

I have been fortunate in that I was able to call upon the assistance of a great many people over the course of this project, including friends who read the manuscript and offered interesting comments and suggestions: Glenda McCarthy, Helen Taylor, Melanie Yuille, Gertrude Shane, Caroline Abbott, Françoise LeBlanc, Linda Cook, Mary Hann, Victoria Rosenberg, Karen Mann and Aubrey Shane.

Thanks also go to Jay Underwood for his patience in providing major editorial assistance, and to Doctor Agnieszka Zelichowska, who suggested the Polish family name Lipska, and whose own first name I borrowed for the heroine of this story.

Mirek Kapsa (of Polish origins) provided the helpful details on Polish train routes in 1933, which not only added an element of interest to the story, but accuracy that is so important in an historical novel.

Similarly I am indebted to Ms. Ewa Leszczynska, assistant to the Polish ambassador in Ottawa for referring me to Artur Soroko, current First Secretary and Press attaché, at the Embassy of the Republic of Poland in Rome, who researched the location of the Polish Legation building in Rome in 1933. It was Mr. Soroko who informed me that the Polish diplomatic staff in Rome in 1933 constituted a Legation rather than an Embassy.

FOREWORD

The idea of writing a biography of Vladimir de Pachmann (1848-1933), a famous pianist of the nineteenth century, occupied my mind for many years. I was first introduced to him—his art and his foibles—some twenty years ago when I discovered an obituary in a 1933 issue of the *Étude* magazine. The pianist had died on January 6th 1933 in Rome, where he had been living in retirement. What I read in that obituary aroused my curiosity. I had earlier become interested in the medical history of composers and musicians after buying the book *Creative Malady* by Sir George Pickering (George Allen and Unwin Ltd., London 1974) while I was on a medical visit to London. Pickering describes the careers of several creative individuals (Darwin, Freud, Proust and others) who maintained their creativity despite challenging medical problems. Vladimir de Pachmann was certainly different. He was very odd, as well as being talented. He was considered to be especially talented in his interpretations of the piano music of Chopin. His performances on stage often became displays of silly eccentricities and tricks—sometimes bordering on the bizarre. Both before and during his recitals, strange behaviour could be almost guaranteed. It included a predictable delay in starting to play during which he fiddled with the piano stool until he "got it right." He had a predilection to talk to his audiences while he played, sometimes accompanied by odd facial grimaces. Sometimes he reacted in an angry manner to the laughter that frequently followed his strange activities. The critics were unable to fathom the reason for his behaviour, and were largely intolerant and unsympathetic. On several occasions during interviews with the press, he explained that he spoke to his audiences because he believed they enjoyed it. After all, Liszt spoke to his listeners from the piano. There is no doubt that his popularity as a pianist was enhanced by his antics.

In the other obituaries, just as in the one in the *Étude*, writers often described similar interesting aspects of his stage performances. Off-stage, his personality was decidedly odd as well. The editor of the *Étude* described how he had personally witnessed de Pachmann's odd gestures and vocal grunting off stage, when the pianist was not aware of being watched. In 1989, I presented a paper at the History of Medicine Section of the Royal College of Physicians and Surgeons' annual meeting in Toronto, suggesting that de Pachmann might have suffered from Gille de la Tourette's Syndrome—a condition characterized by repetitive motor and vocal tics, usually beginning in childhood. My case was weakened by lack of reliable information about de Pachmann's early childhood in Odessa. The pianist himself was reluctant to reveal many details about his early musical life.

My ambition was to write a medical biography of this man, with an emphasis on understanding his psychological make up—an attempt to get into the mind of this unusual man—to explain his behaviour off and on stage. That required considerable research into his background, the opinions of music critics in Europe and North America as well as the public's response to his recitals. I had tentatively called my book *Understanding de Pachmann*. There was a plethora of newspaper reviews of his concerts and recitals to be found over the years, from 1880 to his final recital in London in 1925. The critics who reviewed his recitals often documented his antics as well as commenting on his performance. He was criticized for altering the scores with addition of chords, or for his unorthodox tempos. British critics were often more sympathetic to his foibles on and off stage than those in North America, where his erratic performances and his behaviour were considered unprofessional and unworthy of the standards established by other artists of his day. He was often criticized for his interpretations of the composers he included in his programme. This applied to his favourite composer—Chopin—as well as to his interpretation of Beethoven's sonatas. He travelled to North America and toured Canada on eight occasions. His marriage to a young Australian pianist, Maggie Okey, ended in divorce after eleven years.

My plans to write *Understanding de Pachmann* were easily derailed by the publication of a biography of the man in 2003 by Mark Mitchell (*Vladimir de Pachmann: A piano virtuoso's life*, Indiana University Press) and the knowledge that friends of mine, Ed Blickstein and Gregor Benko, were also preparing a more complete biography. I decided then to utilize the material collected over many years to write an historical novel surrounding de Pachmann's death in January 1933, and his legacy. It would be an interesting alternative since I claim no standing in the area of academic humanities such as music. Although de Pachmann, his wife Maggie Okey, his secretary Pallottelli, and others such as Benito Mussolini were real, other characters in this novel such as Charles Flemming and Agnieszka Lipska are fictitious, and hopefully bear little resemblance to anyone, living or dead. Some writers of fiction seem self conscious about the issue of maintaining a degree of *authorial absence*— but may ask themselves, "Does this fictional character *exist?*" Karel Čapek, the Czech author, journalist and playwright, has written; "If a man were to rummage in his past he'd find material in it for a whole set of lives," which makes it difficult for writers to avoid the autobiographic trait. Tolstoy was said to "walk through most of his novels."

All the quotations from the de Pachmann recital reviews quoted in the book are from contemporary newspapers, but in only a few cases is the name of the critic acknowledged. Most newspaper reviews were never signed during that period of music criticism.

An explanation is necessary for the alternating spelling of de Pachmann and Pachmann throughout the novel, as well as in direct quotes from critical reviews. The pianist always referred to himself and signed his name as *de Pachmann*, but the critics, especially the British, commonly referred to him as *Pachmann*, there being a suspicion that the alternative was an affectation of aristocracy.

Finally, readers will note that the spelling of Polish family names differs between males and females. Thus, you will find ambassador Radinski, Mrs. Radinska, Miss Agnieszka Lipska and Mr. Alexei Lipski.

Carl Abbott, Halifax,
November, 2011

CHAPTER ONE

"A great war leaves the country with three armies: an army of cripples, an army of mourners and an army of thieves." (German proverb)

Charles Flemming loved trains, but now he was feeling he had endured enough train travel. He looked at his watch, and was pleased to see it was almost 10:45 a.m. He had been making notes in his diary, and was relieved it was already Friday, January 13th but he was not superstitious about that conjunction; the new year, 1933, seemed to be off to a good start. The daily express train from Milan to Rome was moving at full speed along the remaining fifty kilometres of tracks towards its final destination. Flemming, professor of psychiatry at the University of Toronto Medical School, sighed with relief as the outskirts of the city soon began to emerge in the train's windows. Grey smoke from the coal burning locomotive drifted intermittently by the window, and he could occasionally catch a glimpse of the engine as the train navigated a sharp curve. He had examined these European locomotives carefully on several occasions when there had been an opportunity to leave the train and walk the platform. They had many features that differed from Canadian locomotives. One that had amused him on several occasions was the whistle — brief and high pitched. As he gazed through the window two young children waved to everyone as they leaned over the gate of a farm, one of the many he had seen flying by.

The sun was shining through low clouds, and the train interior felt decidedly warmer than on the previous day. He had become accustomed to the atmosphere in his compartment—the sounds and smells from inside and out. Outside it was a mix of coal smoke and the smell of farm manure. Ten minutes before he had become aware that someone in a nearby compartment had opened a package of ripe cheese, likely a *raclette*. It was still faintly obvious, but he loved cheese so it was not unpleasant. Since joining the train he had been served some French, Swiss and Italian varieties of cheeses that were new to him.

A fellow traveller passing by in the corridor, and pausing briefly to scrutinize the well-dressed passenger seated alone in the compartment, would describe a middle-aged man with a somewhat pale complexion, straight dark brown hair worn somewhat long on the sides and back. The early morning sun streaming through the carriage window highlighted in silhouette his pointed nose and a conventional chin. It appeared that he had not shaved for several days judging from his obvious dark stubble. When he was not occupied making notes with a pencil in a small notebook, he glanced out the window at the passing countryside. If an observer could have examined Flemming from outside the window his nearly transparent blue eyes encircled by dark shadows—giving the appearance of someone who had slept poorly—would have been seen closing briefly as if seeking sleep. When they were open and he was gazing out they would have displayed the typical rapid to-and-fro movements of railway nystagmus.

Flemming was coming to the end of a long and tiresome three-day journey from London. He had seen the progressive change in geography and climate as he watched the countryside pass by, through France and Italy. When he last visited Italy in 1926, he had taken a different route to Rome—through Switzerland. The landscape in both France and Italy no longer looked ravaged by the senseless war that had ended fifteen years ago.

He had not found it easy to sleep on the train—snatching only a few hours at night, trying to catch up during stopovers in Paris and Nice. He found himself dozing during the day, helped by the rhythm of the wheels on the tracks. The thought of a proper, comfortable hotel bed preceded by a long hot bath made him feel very happy. Time had passed slowly but he had not been bored. He had found time to revise the manuscript of his paper, *Psychiatric Implications of Tics and Obsessive Thoughts*, for presentation at the World Congress of Psychiatry on Tuesday morning. His interest in these disorders had developed after he had seen patients in Toronto with what had now become known as the Obsessive-Compulsive Disorder. He was coming to Rome primarily to present the findings of a personal study of twenty such patients who had shown strong obsessive impulses as well as compulsions to perform activities independent of their will.

Although the patients easily recognized these unnatural habits and phobias they found it very difficult to change. In his hands the disorder seemed refractory to treatment and in some cases terminated in psychosis. He had also worked on one of his hobbies: creating new palindromes but he had composed only a few. He had created one this morning while waiting for the dining car to open. It seemed to fit the occasion: *Roma te ecce et amor* (Rome we behold and love). He had never tried a Latin palindrome before.

Passing through France and now Italy, he had time to think about the current political scene in Europe. Not being political by nature, while living in Canada he had paid only scant attention to events that were unfolding in Europe since the end of the war in 1918, but he was now travelling through two countries which, like many of their neighbours, had been seriously wounded by that war. He had a sense that the optimism he and many of his friends at home had shared with most of the free world after the war ended was in danger of vanishing amidst emerging cynicism. He had read that Canada had lost more than 68,000 enlisted people in "The Great War," with 24,000 casualties in one battle alone. The battle of the Somme had been a slaughter. The British army, which was part of the Allied forces, in the first day of battle had suffered 50,000 casualties, either killed, wounded or missing. Italy, an ally, had lost more than a million and as many had been wounded. German losses had also been staggering. The war left many ex-servicemen unemployed, and Canada was no exception.

Back home, demobilized war veterans could be seen lining the streets of Toronto and other Canadian cities holding placards with messages such as: 'CONDEMNED TO STARVE IN A LAND OF PLENTY', 'WE WANT WORK AND WAGES', and 'SINGLE, UNEMPLOYED EX-SERVICE MEN: NO PLACE TO EAT. WHY?'

Newspapers were reporting an obvious military build-up in Germany, progressing at a worrisome rate despite that country's obligations outlined in peace treaties including the one signed in the palace at Versailles. Adolf Hitler's popularity in Germany was on the rise fuelled by his attempts to free the German people from the yolk of humiliation after their defeat in the war; from the constraints of the Treaty of Versailles, and supposed exploitation by minorities, including Communists and Jews. By promising a form of biological utopia, free of racial diversity, Hitler's party had the strong backing of many ethnic Germans and seemed likely to assume control of the government in the next elections.

Before leaving Toronto, he had re-read Erich Maria Remarque's classic novel of that war, *All Quiet on the Western Front*. The author had assumed a pseudonym after the death of his mother, whose name was Maria—so Paul became Maria and the family name, formerly Remark had become Remarque. The author had been conscripted to the German army in 1916 and after being hit by shrapnel while rescuing a wounded comrade, he spent time in a German field hospital. He tried teaching school after the war, eventually becoming a writer as well as a militant pacifist. *All Quiet on the Western Front* was about the horrors of war as experienced by soldiers in the trenches. "Every soldier believes in chance and trusts his luck," the author said later. In 1919, completely disillusioned, he renounced his medals, including the Iron Cross, and other decorations.

Published in 1929, the book was later denounced by Hitler as anti-German. Through this novel, Remarque had become a spokesman for a generation which—having escaped the bullets—was nevertheless destroyed by the war. In a similar way, Christopher, the young English officer in Rebecca West's *The Return of the Soldier*, arrived home from the war suffering from amnesia and shell shock.

Flemming had heard that Italy, like Germany, was also in trouble. It had found itself deeply in debt after the war and had soon become ungovernable. There was great resentment that the country—which had sided with the Allies against Germany and had expected more from the Treaty of Versailles, especially territorial gains—had been rewarded with so little. The Italians blamed the American president Woodrow Wilson. Struggles between right- and left-wing extremists had lead to civil war in some Italian cities. The rise of Benito Mussolini, and his Fascist party's assumption of power ten years ago was not a complete or universally accepted solution to the country's financial and economic chaos. Inflation was high, unemployment rates were rising, wages were low; but at the same time considerable order was said to exist.

He had heard that the trains in Italy were running efficiently and usually, but not always, on time. This train was already an hour late. He found the French and Italian railway personnel were generally pleasant, courteous and obliging. Someone in Canada had told him that steady employment in Italy could be assured as long as one carried a membership card of the Fascist party. The dining car meals were tasty. French and Italian wines had assumed a certain quality again. Prices for travel and commodities were very reasonable, with ex-

change rates advantageous to a Canadian traveller. The porter on the Italian
segment of his trip, whom he had begun to call Gino, had been very friendly and
attentive although he spoke very little English.

The chairman of the organizing committee of the World Congress of Psychiatry had sent a reassuring letter to members of the psychiatric community
months before Flemming left Canada, painting his country as an orderly, liberal
society, free of totalitarianism and having a progressive view of the management
of psychiatric illness. Some recent Italian immigrants to Canada that he had met
in Toronto had been less optimistic about the course of their native country's
government's plans.

One of the doctors he had met at a local hospital had described the Italian
medical community as generally disgruntled. Life in medical practice, once a
dream, could often be a nightmare. Compulsory membership in the Fascist party
was being considered for medical doctors. Another friend had suggested that
Mussolini himself might be a suitable case for psychiatric analysis. *Il Duce* (The
Duke) was authoritarian, vain and known to be a philanderer. It was well-known
that he had a mistress. Others had suggested that leisure time for the ordinary
Italian worker was under state control primarily to avoid useless and possibly
harmful freedom of thought. Recreational pastimes were encouraged, athletic
and sport societies flourished, as did choral societies, bands and night schools.

Although Flemming had met a few continental psychiatrists *en route* to
Rome, none seemed interested in discussing politics. Other travellers he met on
the train viewed him with interest, and without obvious concern that he and his
companion were English-speaking foreigners in their midst.

The journey had been made more interesting than Flemming had imagined
it would be as he had met a fellow traveller—Simon Williams—before they had
arrived at the Channel terminal, and as they prepared to leave on the ferry to
France on Tuesday. They had common interests and soon established a friendly
relationship. Charles, scrutinizing his new acquaintance, noted he was short,
lean and wiry—likely ten years younger than he—maybe in his mid-forties,
judging from his dark hair with lack of grey and his athletic physique. His distinguishing features were thick glasses, a well-trimmed beard, a Welsh accent, a
baggy, blue wool sweater and a limp, which seemed to favour his left leg. His
new friend seemed greatly relieved that the short train trip from London to Dover had come to an end and was not hesitant to talk about what had bothered him
on the train. Since his war experience in Italy in the Caporetto campaign in the
winter of 1916, Simon had avoided train travel as much as possible. His head
injury from a stray bullet had left him with insomnia, headaches and a weak leg.
One of the British field doctors had called it "shell shock".

The injury had eventually resulted in his being sent back to a Canadian field
hospital north of Ypres in Flanders, where minor brain surgery was recommended. This was the field hospital where Captain John McCrea from Guelph,
Ontario, was working at the time he wrote *In Flanders Fields*. Simon was later
sent back to Wales, where he spent almost six months at a convalescent hospital
outside Swansea. His flashbacks of the shock and horror of combat were blamed

on the consequences of psychological trauma. His horror of train travel had also been a curious sequel of this experience, and had remained a problem ever since. The medical explanation was that it was something akin to what was once called "railway spine" (or more accurately "railway mind"), a disorder which appeared in epidemic proportions in the late 19th Century, when train travellers developed complaints of mental anguish after experiencing terrifying railway accidents that had not actually resulted in obvious serious physical injury. Headaches, insomnia, anxiety, poor memory, backache, and weakness would plague some of these rail travellers some days after the derailment. Many of the crash victims subsequently engaged in compensation battles with railway companies.

While living in London in 1926, Charles had heard of the British surgeon, John E. Erichsen, who had made a name for himself at about the peak of the epidemic as a result of his interest in the emotional consequences of those accidents. Some began to refer to the problem as "Erichsen's disease." Since such accident victims did not die as a result of the accident there was no validation of Erichsen's explanatory theory of chronic inflammation of the spinal or meningeal membranes as an explanation for the symptoms.

The problem of "shell shock" during the war was commonly considered to be the result of an emotional disorder. It had not been restricted to British imperial troops. In Germany it was called "war neurosis," and was considered by medical doctors there to be a psychological reaction of frightened and weak-willed or "spineless" soldiers, who were blind to the national interest and had a selfish desire for compensation or pension. From a psychiatrist's view, such an array of disabling anxiety symptoms was likely the consequence of a poisoned memory that could persist in the wake of such disasters or as a result of the horror of combat in wartime.

Charles Dickens had been a victim of something akin to "railway mind." Always somewhat neurasthenic but having some genuine recurring physical ailments as well, Dickens was returning from France travelling on a train from Folkstone to London on June 19th 1865, with his mistress Ellen Ternan, and her mother when the locomotive derailed near Staplehurst. Ten passengers were killed and some twenty were injured when most of the first class carriages fell into a ravine. Neither Dickens, nor Ternan, nor her mother suffered any serious physical injury, so he was able to attend to some of the more seriously injured passengers, in some cases to no avail. Dickens never got over the shock, and for the rest of his life felt sick and faint when travelling by train. He avoided fast trains, and even at times felt terrified when travelling in hansom cabs through the streets of London. After more of such accidents, public alarm over the hazards of rail travel intensified. Charles had wondered how Simon would cope with the remainder of his train travel to Rome.

He found it curious that he was envious of Simon's beard. Flemming had grown a beard several times before and liked the change in his appearance, but he had met with opposition from his family who said it made him look old. His wife Anne had disapproved more than others, so he had shaved off his last growth just to please her. Since Anne's accidental death, he had frequently harboured a wish to grow a beard again.

The memory of Anne in that instant had filled him immediately with that same sense of sadness and emptiness in his chest, as if he had suddenly lost his ability to breath. At moments like this, after many years without her, he had developed what he thought were reliable coping skills to deal with his anxiety, but they sometimes failed. Most of the time his friends would not have noticed his reaction. Months after her death he concluded that he had likely been excessively anxious or perhaps had even dealt with his grief poorly.

Anne had died as a result of a major railway accident. On a night in July 1919, while travelling in a New York Central Railway sleeping car, she had sustained very severe injuries when the train—while stopped at a station—was hit in the rear by another passenger train near Buffalo. The cause was established as brake failure. Eight passengers and several of the train crew were killed, and more than one hundred were injured. Anne had survived for only two days.

Crossing the Atlantic on board the rolling liner—and even for a few days on the French trains—he had forgone shaving, wondering each morning as he gazed in the mirror just how a contemporary grey beard might look after so many years. But he had decided to shave every time after a few days of contemplating his somewhat dishevelled appearance.

Simon Williams' background was music, which had occupied much of his life except for the period of war service in the British army. He had hoped his studies would lead to a successful career in keyboard performance and teaching, but he had been left with the reminder of his injury: a weak left arm and leg leaving him with a limp, noticeable to others only if he was walking alone or when he was very tired. After the accident he often bumped into the left sides of doorways, and he never fully recovered his facility with the keyboard. For months he was unable to see the left side of the keyboard well, or read the left side of sheet music. It was as if he had been partly blinded by the head injury. The one redeeming feature of his service in Italy was learning a small amount of conversational Italian while resting in a military hospital in the north.

After discharge from the convalescent hospital in Wales, where he had met other soldiers suffering from shell shock, Simon soon discovered that employment opportunities were scarce after the war. He decided to resume his piano studies despite the problem with his vision and his left arm. It meant very hard work and practice, but he graduated from the Royal College of Music in 1923. He knew, however, that he would never have a career as a performer. Job prospects for a musician were poor in Wales, but he had been offered part-time work as music critic for the Cardiff *Western Globe* newspaper. This position had provided generous exposure to visiting artists and orchestras but a meagre income. Between teaching and writing he was able to travel to many music festivals and recitals in Britain and on the Continent, as his employer usually paid for a substantial part of his travel expenses. Before they had reached Calais, Charles and Simon had established a first-name relationship.

Simon discovered that they shared a common interest in the professional career of an unusual pianist, Vladimir de Pachmann, who had retired eight years ago to live in Rome. Before leaving England on Tuesday, they were surprised and saddened to see an obituary for de Pachmann in the January 10th issue of the London *Times*, which had included a photograph of the pianist taken from earlier times, seated at his piano, wearing his long grey hair neatly groomed, his stubby hands caressing the keys. The obituary had encapsulated many of the elements of the pianist's unusual life and career. He was eighty-four years old when he died of pneumonia in Rome on January 6th, after a long illness, suspected to have been prostate cancer. He had been living in retirement as an Italian citizen in Rome since 1925, with his long-time personal secretary.

When the subject of de Pachmann's death had come up in their conversation later in the ferry lounge, Charles and Simon discovered they had both been present at his last London recital at the Royal Albert Hall on October 21st in 1925. Charles had been working in London in 1925 and 1926 while on a sabbatical from the University of Toronto. That final recital was not one that demonstrated anywhere near the quality of piano playing for which de Pachmann had once been known. The conclusion of the critics was that he was much too old to be playing publicly at the age of seventy-eight, after such a long, successful career.

Vladimir de Pachmann had crossed the Atlantic to the USA for the first time in 1890, accompanied by his young wife, the former Marguerite Okey, herself an accomplished professional pianist. Charles, then not yet a teenager, had not heard their New York City recitals, but he and his mother, who had been visiting relatives in Boston, were able to find tickets for two of the concerts in that city a week later. Charles had developed an interest in keyboard music from his music teacher. They had especially enjoyed the performance and the stage manner of Marguerite de Pachmann, as had the Boston critics, so he was surprised to find no reference to her in the obituary. She was of course now his *former* wife, as they had divorced in 1895. It was during a later visit to Boston in 1912 that Charles had the good fortune to meet Anne, who would eventually join him in Toronto in 1915, but for much too brief a time as his wife.

Marguerite and de Pachmann had divorced after eleven years of marriage. She settled in Paris with their two sons and later married a French barrister, Fernand Labori, famous for his contribution to the defence of Captain Dreyfus. It was in Paris that she had established the Pachmann Piano School. Although Labori had died in March 1917—"after a long illness" his obituary had said — she had remained in that city, and had continued to teach, but had no longer given recitals. Her last recital in London was advertised using her former name, Marguerite de Pachmann.

That was on May 15th 1930 at the Aeolian Hall. Before leaving Canada, Charles had thought it might be possible to visit the ageing de Pachmann while he was in Rome, even though he had never had an opportunity to speak to the pianist on any of the occasions where he had heard him play, nor had he ever met his wife Maggie, as she was usually called. He had heard from friends in

Nova Scotia that Maggie's parents and two of her sisters had emigrated to Canada in the late 1890s, settling in Port Williams, a farming town in the Annapolis Valley of Nova Scotia. For years Charles had been curious about the circumstances surrounding the failed marriage as well as the nature of de Pachmann's odd behaviour on- and off-stage. The de Pachmann marriage was likely to have been troubled by his professional jealousy that was often apparent when they were sharing the stage, and when he was in the audience at her solo recitals. The marriage of two professional artists could be a problem and often lead to divorce, as was the case of the pianist Sophie Menter and the cellist David Popper. Popper's jealousy was such that he could be seen standing in the wings during her recitals – keeping a record of the number of her encores.

Several months before leaving Toronto on this journey, Charles had written a letter of introduction to Francesco Pallottelli—de Pachmann's secretary in Rome—signifying his interest in his aging companion's life and career, and to tell him that he had already written a significant amount towards an unauthorized de Pachmann biography. Charles' plan had been to concentrate on the pianist's interesting stage career, writing not as a musicologist but from a medical and psychiatric perspective. He had earlier negotiated with a Canadian publisher to review the first draft of the manuscript, but it had been rejected without a convincing explanation. The subject of the book was considered of little interest, and it would not likely sell except to a few musicians or music libraries.

From the beginning, when he was researching details for the book, even Anne had expressed reservations. "Why would readers be interested in the career of a cranky and somewhat flawed Ukrainian pianist, who lost his wife to a prominent Parisian attorney?" she asked him one morning over breakfast. "Fair question," he replied. But he had nevertheless pressed on with his writing in his spare time. He had decided to bring the almost complete manuscript to Rome so that some biographic details could be clarified, and with a view to obtaining de Pachmann's endorsement of the project. There had been hints that since retiring, the pianist had been writing his own memoirs. His secretary Pallottelli had already written and published a brief biography of de Pachmann in 1916. It was in Italian and Charles had never seen it. It was now out of print but he had been told a new up-to-date edition was to be published soon.

An Italian friend in Toronto, who had a relative living in Rome, had promised to arrange for a copy of the new edition to be left at his hotel in Rome, if it had been published by then. What Charles had heard about the earlier brief biography had reinforced his opinion that the pianist had suffered from an obsessive-compulsive disorder similar to the patients he had studied in Toronto. Charles had not received any feedback to his letter but still hoped that notes from the pianist's memoirs might be made available for his examination. He was told by someone that the failing health of the elderly pianist had precluded any significant personal writing during the past year.

Although he was a good sailor, Charles had decided to avoid food on the English Channel crossing and to spend most of the time on deck. He had eventually sought refuge in the ferry lounge, where he suspected the coffee would be weak and the atmosphere smoky. Searching for a familiar face, he had noticed Simon Williams engaged in conversation with another couple. He was introduced to Richard and Mona Connelly, travelling from Dublin to Paris, who had also just heard of de Pachmann's death. Mona was absorbed in reading the *Times* obituary. He joined the trio at their table, ordered coffee and soon found himself exchanging memories and anecdotes of the recently deceased pianist.

"Whoever wrote the obituary summed it up exactly," suggested Simon, "his eccentricities and antics did obscure much of his great artistry. But I disagree that these unfortunate characteristics were of little consequence. They may have seemed inconsequential to him and some critics but the world of music critics and his professional colleagues alike thought otherwise."

"I have read a lot about his odd stage behaviour and have a plausible explanation which I can discuss with you later," replied Charles. "Over several years, I have been working on a short biography of the pianist that I had intended to show to de Pachmann—regrettably that will no longer be possible. On Tuesday, I am presenting a paper at the International Congress of Psychiatry on a psychiatric condition that just might fit our recently deceased pianist. I know a lot of his fans will be mourning his passing and I am sorry I will not be able to meet the old man."

Mona Connelly, having just completed reading the obituary, turned to Simon and expressed a theory that professional music critics in many cities were too often inclined to find fault with musical performances and new music. "Their music reviews are often unsigned which in my view allows them to hide their identity. You are a critic—do you agree that critical reviews should not be anonymous?"

Simon paused before he replied. "Well, I have read and collected many British newspaper concert and recital reviews over the years and they are usually unsigned. Being a freelance critic, I like my editors to credit me with my reviews. Of course anyone who reads the same local or national newspapers with regularity should be able to identify the particular critic based on the writing style, or tastes in composers and individual biases. As a music critic, I am always aware of the influence of the more notorious of our profession. James William Davison of the *Times* is a good example. If he had still been around—I think he died in 1885—he would have had a field day with Pachmann (he used the shortened version of the pianists' name), especially if he devoted whole programs to Chopin, whose music Davison did not always greatly admire."

"Was he the critic who said that the entire works of Chopin present 'a motley surface of ranting hyperbole and excruciating cacophony'?"

"That's right," replied Simon.

Simon was travelling to Rome as well, on an assignment for *The Musical Muse,* a monthly magazine published in Wales. Simon had explained that the newly-appointed editor had seen fit to virtually adopt a young Polish pianist, Agnieszka Lipska, as he was convinced that she would eventually become the reigning queen of Chopin interpretation and a worthy successor to de Pachmann, as the authority in Chopin performance practice.

"I was pleased when my editor had a change of plans at the last moment and asked me to go to Rome in his stead. Have either of you heard of Agnieszka Lipska?" he asked. He seemed surprised when all three shook their heads.

"I heard her give a recital last Spring in Vienna, which was where we met. She had also made some recordings of several Chopin works for a Polish label in Kraków, which I later had an opportunity to review along with some of her earlier recording of the Mazurkas. So I was not a bit reluctant to accept Nigel Billinghurst's offer to send me to review these Rome recitals. As well as being a great pianist, she is also an exceptionally beautiful woman. She will be playing on Saturday afternoon at the *Reale Academia Filarmonica Romana* and in the evening at a private reception in the home of the Polish ambassador or I should say the embassy. I have to work out how I will manage to get an invitation to the second recital but Agnieszka's brother, Alexei, will likely be able to arrange something. I met him in Vienna as he frequently travels with his sister, playing the role of unofficial manager and guide even though he is a part time writer too."

"How did you rate her gramophone recordings?" Charles asked.

"As you might expect, a studio sound can be deceptive and be made to seem better than a live concert recording, but my impression was that her two records failed to transmit the magic I sensed at the Vienna concerts even considering the sounds of coughing from the audience. The flu season had been in full swing at the time. The programmes for the recordings and the recital were not the same of course. A friend suggested to me later that, because she is virtually blind, that fact may have added a new dimension to those concerts. That may have been so for the audience but not for me. I have heard other blind keyboard artists perform and have not felt that it was so important. The world of organists has included many who were blind; some are still alive and actively performing. The organist of a local church near my home in Cardiff is an excellent musician and has very poor vision. Excellent vision has never been a prerequisite for virtuoso keyboard talent. One advantage of a studio recording is that it facilitates the performer's focus on the music alone, allowing the removal of a barrier that sometimes seems to exist between the audience and the performer."

Charles was very curious to hear more details of the nature of this young pianist's blindness, as he had once presented a paper called *The Blind Musician* to the Ontario History of Medicine Society. He had read, in researching this lecture, that being blind seemed to heighten the sense of hearing in such musicians. He would have discussed Lipska's loss of vision further, but Simon had just looked at his watch and noted that the ferry would likely be approaching the harbour of Calais. In fact, some of the lounge crowd had already begun to move out onto the decks for a view of the French coastline. He felt he needed fresh air to clear his head after sitting in the smoky lounge. He could also feel the effects of the mediocre coffee.

"I suggest we continue this conversation on the train as I am very interested in your research," suggested Simon as they walked together towards the lower deck. "Are you taking the train all the way to Rome?"

"Yes I am. After a tedious and rough Atlantic crossing earlier this month and this almost equally nauseating crossing, I think the train will be my salvation."

"Well you know how I feel about trains," Simon replied, as he set off to find his luggage.

Charles' Atlantic crossing on the Canadian Pacific liner *SS Montrose* from Halifax in late December had been an unusually stormy one. The ship had left port on December 24th for Southampton. After arriving in England, he had read in a newspaper that a fishing trawler from Aberdeen had recently been wrecked when it struck rocks at Hole Head in the stormy seas with the loss of nine lives. A passenger liner had also been lost to fire in the Channel.

The boredom of the Atlantic crossing was helped greatly by a brief but exciting affair with a Norwegian wireless operator named Lisa Johansen from Bergen, with whom Charles had shared a dining table every evening, and, before long, her bed. It had been his first romance since Anne had died. Lisa was very keen and knowledgeable about the music of Edvard Grieg, and they had spent hours in bed discussing—amongst other matters—the composer's career and his poor health towards the end of his life.

"What are your plans?" he asked Simon as they prepared to step ashore.

"Apart from spending tonight in Paris, which is essential for us both to make train connections tomorrow, I am spending a day in Nice at the local Academy of Music with a sleepover there on Wednesday night but my schedule allows me to pick up another train to Milan the next day, with a sleeper from there in the evening. Would you be interested in exploring Nice while I am attending my meetings?"

"I don't mind changing my plans to suit yours, if you think that would be appropriate," Simon eagerly replied.

"I have friends in Nice with whom I worked with several years ago in our department in Toronto. Hopefully, they will not be too busy to see me and there should be no problem finding accommodation. I have a reservation at the Hotel Splendide Royal on Via Vittorio Venito in Rome. Where are you staying?" Charles asked.

"I don't know the name of the street but my hotel is the ... Hotel Bernine Bristol," Simon replied, after spending several minutes thumbing through a small black diary to find the name. Charles thought he remembered it. "I think it's on Via Barberini, which is not far from where I am staying." He had planned his travels well in advance, and felt some flexibility in changing his travel schedule. He would have to rebook a sleeper from Milan but it should not be a problem. The congress was starting over the weekend and he had already been assured that his hotel accommodation in Rome was secure even if he were tempted to take short diversions along the way.

Charles thought he would enjoy meeting the young, blind pianist. Simon had predicted that he would agree with him that she was likely the best Chopin interpreter of today, certainly in Europe. "If you have time to come to both the recitals I can see if it is possible to get you tickets for Sunday afternoon and an invitation for the evening recital too," he suggested. "You can see for yourself how beautiful she is. I know where Agnieszka and Alexei will be staying in Rome. Being a doctor you are probably curious about the cause of her blindness but I cannot help you. I have no idea about that. She might be willing to talk to you about it."

The recitals sounded like a great idea. Charles had just spent a week in London after his Atlantic journey, and had gone to two concerts including one that featured the music of Handel, with extracts from *Messiah*, as well as a performance of one of his organ concertos. The night before he had heard the brilliant pianist Frederic Lamond play Beethoven's Piano Concerto No 3 at a Promenade Concert at the Queen's Hall. On the same program he heard for the first time the symphonic poem, *Tabiola*, by Sibelius, whose music he had just begun to appreciate. The program notes said that the composer's music had caught on in England in the early 20th Century, first with his early symphonies and in 1907 with his violin concerto. The composer had been invited to England to conduct on three occasions, between 1905 and 1912. Initially, audiences had difficulty with the idiom, but by the 1930s Sibelius had become a popular composer in Britain.

The train journey from Calais to Paris had been very enjoyable as they had settled in a compartment with no other travellers, and had spent several hours discussing the world of music, music criticism and the maladies of musicians. The health of musicians and composers had become a hobby for Charles. Simon seemed much less anxious about this aspect of the train trip. Charles had promised to show him his manuscript and collection of de Pachmann reviews he had in his suitcase, once they had settled. His new friend had shown some interest in his comments about the possible explanation for the antics of the odd pianist.

Waking with a start—and briefly blinded by the strong sunshine—he realized he had been dreaming. The train was slowing and had jerked briefly as it approached the station. He gazed out the window; Rome at last! The eternal city—despite its ruins—looked splendid this morning. In one of his dreams since leaving Toronto, Charles had dredged up from his memory what Sigmund Freud had said about Rome, which he had loved to visit. He had compared the ruins of the old city to the human mind. Freud was convinced that nothing that had been formed in the human brain could perish—somehow being permanently preserved—and in suitable circumstances could once more be brought to life if regression could be taken back far enough. He remembered that John Keats had visited Rome and had died there from tuberculosis. Someone had told him that Goya, as a young man, had spent two years taking art lessons in Rome.

Some passengers were already collecting their luggage and had started moving toward the carriage doors. Was it the smell of coal smoke from the locomotive that had begun to infiltrate the train? Or was it another wedge of cheese next door? Thinking of the Canadian winter back in Toronto, Charles had no doubts that he could easily accept the climate of the south of Italy for the next week. Now he must find Simon who had not appeared.

CHAPTER TWO

"De mortuis nil nisi bonum"
(Speak nothing but good of the dead)

Charles had always been sceptical about the details he found in obituaries. Their theme too often seemed to be *"de mortuis nil nisi bonum."* It was therefore with wary interest that he had read the first of two other tributes to de Pachmann that he and Simon had found at a newspaper stand, prior to embarking on the Dover ferry. Both the *Liverpool Post* and *Scotsman* of Edinburgh had noted the pianist's recent death in Rome. Beginning in 1882, de Pachmann had travelled from London to Edinburgh and Glasgow for recitals and the local reviews had always been highly complimentary.

The Golden Arrow train of the French Northern Railway had already left Calais en route to Paris. Seated comfortably in the dining car with Simon, while awaiting the last dinner course, Charles had been reading A.K. Holland's comments in the January 9th issue of the *Liverpool Post*. Simon looked surprisingly relaxed so far—no hint of panic or anything like the way he had felt on the train from London to Dover. Simon now had a travelling companion who shared his interests, and he wanted to chat. Earlier he had volunteered his belief that he might feel better about train travel if he understood the psychodynamics of his anxiety.

The psychiatrists who had treated him in Wales had stressed the benefits of rationalizing the past. Charles' enjoyment of train travel was well known to his friends and family. Despite his personal tragic loss, he had never avoided train travel, and always felt confident the locomotive engineer would get him safely to his destination. Now he was settled in the dining car prepared to read what the music critic from Liverpool had thought of de Pachmann. Holland had observed the man at first hand on many occasions and had commented how, "the eccentricities of his platform manner" were "a source of diversion to the unthinking and of distraction to others."

Holland had summarized his memories of de Pachmann's recitals in Liverpool by noting the pianist's "infantile delight in teasing his audience. He would come on, acknowledge the applause, and at once begin to complain about the lights, particularly the light immediately over the piano, which it appeared was insupportable. This by-play would go on for a considerable time, while the old man steadily refused to play, sometimes retiring to the greenroom, where, no doubt, the discussions about the lights were continued. When finally induced to take his seat at the keyboard, he indulged in frequent asides to the audience in his immediate neighbourhood and would even break off in the middle of a group to deliver a speech that was totally inaudible to all but those in the front rows where he appeared to be explaining that he alone possessed the true secret of Chopin's style."

Holland had heard the de Pachmann performances of later years and seemed surprisingly tolerant of his odd stage behaviour:

"Whether these things were encouraged as being good showmanship or tolerated as the vagaries of genius is immaterial but it would be a pity if they were allowed to colour the memory of one who was unquestionably an exquisite artist. There was always sheer beauty of sound and loveliness of detail in the workmanship of Pachmann's playing at its best. Perhaps our view of his Chopin is too much coloured by his playing in later years, when its refinements had developed into something rather too precious and even spiritually a little *maladie*, according with Chopin's own last phase. But it is certain that Pachmann, purely as a pianist, suffered very little decline. It was part of his notion that practice makes perfect and that if Liszt had played a work five hundred times, and he (Pachmann) had played it a thousand times, he was so much the more likely to understand it better and therefore to play it better. His artistic ideals were pitched unusually high. Perfection—nothing less—both of technique and style, was what he aimed at."

There were further comments about de Pachmann's early years, which had always interested many of the pianist's fans—as well as the critics—who wondered where he had spent those early years of study. De Pachmann had steadfastly refused to answer that question when asked by members of the press.

Holland had noted:

"In his early years, after making a very successful debut at the age of twenty-one, he is said to have shut himself up for eight years and refused all engagements. He then made a second start, was not satisfied, in spite of the applause he won and again went back to study for a further two years."

That had always been a curious aspect of the young de Pachmann's career. It had been said that Franz Liszt and his student Carl Tausig had both done something similar; retreating from the concert hall in search of a higher level of performance and excellence. How well might de Pachmann have coped with the stresses of a piano competition? If performance anxiety had been the reason for the pianist's departure from the stage during his early years in Odessa, it would fit Charles' theory that he was a perfectionist with an obsessive-compulsive personality. Holland's theory was similar:

"Such rigorous self-criticism deserves remark in these days when young executants expect to jump straight into the limelight after three years at a conservatory. Even towards the very end of his life Pachmann had apparently not ceased to devote himself to problems of pure technique, such as fingering. It was his consistent absorption in the basic principles of his art and his instrument, the life-long search for a perfect pianoforte style, that lifted Pachmann above the rank of the common or garden keyboard virtuosi."

There were, however, doubts about the consistency of de Pachmann's piano virtuosity—a facility with which he was promoted in newspaper advertisements. Virtuosity was a word frequently used by music critics to describe performance style, but it was not easy to define. It was certainly an exceptional facility that allowed technical command of an instrument. It was a word not used solely for the piano or any other musical instrument, but also the human voice, as well as the art of conducting. Virtuosity at the keyboard meant the notes were played flawlessly, allowing for a degree of flamboyancy. At many of de Pachmann's recitals flamboyancy was very much in evidence, but not always flawlessness. Most musicologists felt strongly that the complete pianist should focus the attention of the audience entirely on the music and not on himself, as de Pachmann was wont to do, especially in his later years. Virtuosity, according to one writer, was "a blend of head, heart and hands."

The cheese and fresh fruit had arrived, so Charles and Simon concentrated on enjoying the final course and the remains of a carafe of 1931 vintage Bordeaux wine. Charles was interested in hearing Simon's reaction to the wine. The 1931 vintage in Bordeaux was not impressive, being reluctant to yield a substantial nose as well as being stubbornly tannic was Simon's view. The war had been a setback for the wine industry throughout Europe and the climate had not cooperated in 1931.

"We tend to drink non-vintage clarets in Wales," said Simon, "the blends are less disappointing. This one is poor in my view."

"I agree. In Canada, we are too far from Bordeaux to really have great vintages that arrive in good condition and are affordable," Charles countered. Eager to get back to the subject of de Pachmann and Holland's obituary, he changed the subject.

"You must have notice that Holland was obviously very tolerant of de Pachmann's stage behaviour. Concert audiences and many critics considered him to be a Chopin specialist, but by no means all of the critics liked the way he played the piano music of Beethoven or some other composers. Canadian music critics in particular, like Holland, were usually ready to praise the Chopin repertoire he played on tours there starting in 1891, but they did not always like the way he played Beethoven."

Charles paused to finish his wine. "He first played in Toronto in December, 1891, but I did not hear that recital. I must have been about twelve or thirteen years old. He had been invited to play at the annual convention of the Canadian Society of Musicians. By then he had spent many months in North America as he and Maggie had arrived in April of the previous year. She had returned to England alone in July of 1890, and later resumed her concert career in London. A few weeks after this Toronto debut, de Pachmann gave a second recital, this time for the visiting Mehan Ladies' Vocal Quartette of Detroit. The Toronto weekly magazine *Saturday Night* of January 9th published a review of that concert which I have here." He opened a file and read:

"A large string of Chopin numbers was played with lightness and elegance but with great superficiality. His renderings were more illustrative of technical facility than of artistic feeling".

"I first heard him play the *Moonlight Sonata* on his second visit to Toronto," said Charles as he looked up from the file. "That was in 1891 and the Toronto *Globe* critic wrote: "His playing of the Beethoven sonata was thoughtful and musicianly without showing any signs of greatness...."

"This was a concert he shared with the Canadian singer Madame Emma Albani and with a blind violinist, Ernest Willett from Chambly, Ontario. It was the first time I had heard a professional blind musician play. The critic who wrote under the name of Metronome in the April 16th issue of the *Saturday Night* wrote some interesting comments:

"De Pachmann played a liberal number of piano solos, opening with the *Moonlight Sonata*, of which he gave a thoughtful rendering but without great depth or power. In fact his playing is, as I have before indicated, polished and elegant to a degree, but to my mind, sadly superficial."

Charles looked up from his notes. "What do you think? Was that your memory of de Pachmann's playing?" He paused and added, "did he ever give up the inner self, to use Holland's expression?"

Simon thought for a moment. "I have been listening as you read these Canadian reviews. I heard him play numerous all-Chopin recitals in Britain, and he never seemed to play the pieces in the same style. In fact, he admitted the same in a several interviews. He was quoted as saying, 'I never play a Chopin piece the same way twice,' which is exactly what Chopin said about his own performances, so there is nothing inherently wrong with that. I read an article by Pachmann in *The Étude* some time ago, entitled *How Chopin played Chopin*. Wanda Landowska, the Polish pianist and harpsichordist, had written comments for the same magazine earlier and had suggested that as most of Chopin's pupils had died at an early age, an opportunity had been lost in having them pass on 'a Chopin tradition.' She was convinced that the concepts of his works,!! as presented in concert by Franz Liszt and Anton Rubinstein, had set the standard, even if Liszt himself had acknowledged of Rubinstein that no one could play Chopin's compositions as he could. Landowska felt that present-day interpretations of Chopin's works had absolutely departed from the intentions of the delicate, sensitive composer because of distorted romanticism and an acrobatic virtuosity."

Simon paused to gather his thoughts, and continued. "Despite what Landowska said about the Chopin legacy, we do have opinions from several of his students. One of them, Adolphe Gutmann, who studied with Chopin as a teen, said that the playing of his master was always 'very quiet...with seldom recourse to a *fortissimo*.' Friederich Streicher, another student, said that Chopin hated all exaggerations and demanded pianists always observe the strictest rhythms."

The waiter had come back to ask if they wanted coffee but they both declined. There was still some wine in the bottle. Simon resumed his comments:

"You mentioned Pachmann's Beethoven style earlier. Chopin seems to have had little admiration for some other composers. He loved Bach and Mozart, but Beethoven was one who left him cold. His last words were said to be, 'play Mozart in memory of me,' and they did of course, with the *Requiem* at his funeral in Paris."

"Yes, I remember reading that. It must have been a very moving funeral," injected Charles.

Simon had briefly turned his attention to the view outside the train window and seemed lost in thought. His gaze returned to his wine and he resumed his comments. "But to come back to the Pachmann style, the pianist had written articles about his playing technique over the years in a number of journals including *The Étude* and *The Strand Magazine.* You may have read some of them. The *Strand* article, *How to Play the Piano,* was published in November 1907 I think, and it was in that article he wrote that in Chopin's piano works, one could constantly find fresh points of view with different meanings and new beauties. In that same article he also boasted that although the public, for some reason, regarded him purely as a Chopin player, owing to the fact that his works figured so prominently on his programmes, he could, as he said, 'play all composers equally well'. "

Simon smiled as he paused to think. "He was very defensive about his interpretation of Beethoven's works and I must admit that he did play that composer's music well sometimes but more often he played it very badly. I have lots of examples in my article, *Vladimir Pachmann's Beethoven Performance Style: A Matter of Opinion.* You can read what I wrote later, as I have a copy of the chapter with me. After many years, I can now see that this article was excessively critical. It was originally published in 1920 after Pachmann had retired and later became a chapter in the book *Beethoven Performance Practice in the 19th Century,* edited by a friend of mine, Hans Werth, from Germany. This simple article has left the world of music criticism with the impression that I did not like Pachmann and his playing, which is only partly true. After publication of the book, I received a number of critical letters from Pachmann fans living in Europe and America, including an especially bitter one from the president of the Vladimir de Pachmann Society of Naples. Even before he retired to Italy, Pachmann's fans and friends there felt they should form a society in his honour so several of them sprang up in Italian cities, including Rome. That was very kind of course."

Charles was curious. "But how do you explain that he was considered worthy enough to be awarded the Beethoven Medal by the Royal Philharmonic of London in 1916? The list of previous winners is very impressive—not only pianists but violinists, vocalists, conductors and composers."

"Yes, that's for sure," Simon admitted. "Pachmann's award happened in the midst of the war. He was then about sixty-seven years old, and by then was well known in Europe and America. He had continued to give concerts in London and in other British cities between 1914 and 1918 while the war went on, so it seems that his loyalty to the London music scene during those years was one reason why he was chosen for the medal. I doubt that it was his Beethoven style that influenced the committee. He chose not to play a Beethoven composition on the evening he received the medal from Thomas Beecham. Instead, he chose one that he knew very well, the second Chopin Concerto—a wise move I would say."

"I agree," Charles replied, warming to the tone of the conversation. "I remember the matter of the de Pachmann *Strand* article that was the cause of considerable public comment after he came to America for a third tour. You must have read that article. It was written while he was still in Europe. He claimed that certain effects in Chopin's music were difficult to reproduce on old pianos but could be easily accomplished on today's Bechstein. He added that the Bechstein was the piano upon which he always played, which was not true. His US tour had been sponsored by the Baldwin Company and he played a Baldwin exclusively on that tour—except in Canada, where he played a Heinzman—with Baldwin's permission, I would assume. He was obliged to write a letter to the *New York Times* explaining that he did not know that the *Strand* was sold or even read in America!"

Simon nodded. He had heard about the Bechstein controversy.

"His love of pianos led to many endorsements throughout Europe, in Canada and the USA. I should mention," Simon added, 'before I forget, that the war, not surprisingly, had taken its toll on musical activity throughout Britain. I think you must have seen a similar effect in Canada as well. In my country, funds for support of the arts were rationed and diverted to the war effort. The musical professions were restricted, concerts were curtailed and some, but not all, music festivals were cancelled. Many musicians, composers and conductors had enlisted for war duty, so orchestras and choirs were often depleted, especially of men. Many of those who enlisted never returned from the battles in Europe. I was obviously lucky to get no more than what I thought was a trivial head wound, and spent some time in an excellent field hospital—run by the Canadian army. Earlier I had spent a week or so in a field hospital in Italy where I learnt a few Italian expressions, which I have tried to preserve. Despite all those war troubles at home, the Queen's Hall Prom concerts survived, opera flourished and composers continued to produce music."

The two men had finished their meal, so they made their way back from the diner to their car, where they settled with an after dinner drink. Charles had bought a bottle of Johnny Walker in London, and decided to open it after he discovered that Simon shared his taste for Scotch. After a few drinks Simon seemed eager to resume his comments on Pachmann's piano style, while browsing through the manuscript that Charles had pulled from his suitcase.

"I did not hear his second recital in London on June 22nd 1882," said Simon, as he thumbed his way through the document, "being then only two years old, but in the reviews we get the first hint of his reputation as 'a very remarkable pianist.' That was the description in the London *Times* after his debut on May 30th of that year, when he played the Chopin F minor Concerto. I see the *Musical Times* called him 'a born Chopin player.' But there was a comment that this young Russian Chopin interpreter suffered from what that critic called 'want of vigour' and that he played with 'over-refinement.' I see the same reviewer wrote, 'we must, of course, hear him in a leading pianoforte classic before venturing to give a precise estimate of his powers.' Not everyone liked this so called 'very refined style'."

"Other critics were not impressed with the Beethoven they heard later, when he played the C minor Concerto, op.37 on June 17th. The *Musical Times* said: 'His style lacks the breath and vigour and his reading is deficient in the depth of sentiment required by the great master's works'."

"The London *Times'* critic's reaction was similar: 'It does not strike us that M. de Pachmann has special qualifications for dealing with Beethoven. His performance on Saturday was lacking in breath of style and in that grandeur of conception which the greatest of imaginative musicians exacts from all who would worthily interpret him'."

"I mention these reviews in my article on his Beethoven style," Simon added. Charles nodded. "I am looking forward to reading that article," and he continued, "It was at this debut concert on May 20th of that year that Maggie Okey first heard him play. I think you know that story. She was so impressed that she wrote him to ask that he take her on as a pupil. De Pachmann was slow to respond. Perhaps he was bashful but he did go to hear her play at a concert she had sponsored eleven days later. Maggie had already won the gold medal at the London Academy of Music in 1881, and had played at public concerts during her academic years at the academy. The press had always been impressed with her playing."

"This same London *Times* reviewer," continued Simon, "referred to the custom of playing without the book or score, which of course left the artist vulnerable to memory lapses. That is what happened to Pachmann at this particular Beethoven concert. He usually played without the book except when playing with orchestras and during his career had occasional lapses in memory—but so did many others. Consequently, he used the score when he needed to feel safe."

"So playing recitals without the book was considered adventurous and risky in those days?" asked Charles.

Simon smiled and replied, "Playing without the book was not new. Von Bülow came to London in 1873 and performed all his recitals from memory. Liszt had earlier established the practice as well. Other pianists performing in London such as Bonawitz, played five sonatas of Beethoven from memory at a recital in 1879, and Sophie Menter as well as Hans von Bülow were equally eager to do the same."

Charles was becoming more appreciative of Simon's expertise. "My initial reaction to your comments about the flaws in de Pachmann's Beethoven leads me to think de Pachmann had little talent for the composer," he suggested, and added, "but there is something before the end of Holland's tribute that suggests otherwise. I saw it when I read the article earlier. He said that when de Pachmann played a Beethoven work, he 'appeared at his best in the finale where light and sparkling passages abound' adding that he 'deserved admiration for excellent qualities'."

Simon shifted in his seat and replied, "In my article I mention that when Pachmann and his wife were on their first visit to the USA in 1890, considerable discussion ensued over the issue of how Beethoven should be played, especially when the critics began to comment on Paderewski's Beethoven playing. He had been touring the US in the same year as Pachmann and had been criticized by some critics for his Beethoven style." He paused to sip his Scotch. "What did you think of Pachmann's Chopin when you heard him play in Boston in 1890?" he asked.

"I was impressed," Charles replied and added, "but the antics on stage were hard to fathom. The New York and Boston critics' reactions to both him and his wife are interesting. That was likely the beginning of my interest in his behaviour on stage. His New York debut on April 7th 1890 was the first of three all-Chopin recitals."

"*The New York Times* described his technique as 'singularly well adapted to these compositions.' His range of dynamic effects was considered 'not large' and the reviewer was critical of his use of two pedals to produce a soft and sustained tone. His concept of Chopin's music was considered to show chiefly a mix of 'delicacy and tenderness.' At the conclusion of the review there is this comment: 'M. de Pachmann's demeanour at the piano is perhaps not a matter for consideration here, except in as far as smiles, nods and grimaces tend to distract the attention of his hearers from the music'."

Charles paused to top up his Scotch and to offer Simon another. "We have not discussed the obituary from the *Scotsman*, which I notice refers to his stage conversations or eccentricities as 'an important part of the entertainment.' The writer speculates on the question: 'was he a great artist, or was he a brilliant charlatan?' and concludes that there is no consensus. He writes, 'People sometimes felt that he was like a *prima donna*, more concerned with how he performed a piece, than with what he performed.' In the same article you likely noticed that he discusses de Pachmann's wide piano repertoire as well as his Chopin style and raises an important issue of how well he interpreted the composer. He concludes there are various opinions on the correct interpretation of Chopin."

Charles paused and yawned. He looked at his friend and suggested, "You can continue to read my notes while I take a nap. I seem to have become sleepy."

"Fascinating story," Simon thought aloud, as he read on, but he was also realizing he had already covered much of the same ground in his own article on Beethoven. "This doctor seems to need a lot of sleep," he said to himself, as he watched his new friend quickly pass into slumber-land. "Probably the Scotch," he thought as he poured himself another and lit a cigarette. The train would not arrive in Paris for another few hours, judging from the views from the window. His head was suddenly aching and his leg felt stiff. They were to spend a night in Paris before leaving for Marseille.

CHAPTER THREE

"De gustibus non est disputandum"
(There is no disputing about tastes)

Simon watched as Charles removed books and papers from his briefcase as the *Sud Express*, just out of the Paris railway station, rumbled onward towards the south of France. The journey was estimated to take about nine hours, so they would have lots of time to talk, which Charles had hoped might help his friend relax and avoid the railway mind that he had so successfully suppressed during the journey from Calais to Paris. "I see you have also brought along a small library with you," he heard Simon comment with a laugh.

"I always like to have lots to read when I travel, especially by train. I have two books that will interest you," Charles promised.

They were now waiting in their compartment for the dining carriage to open for breakfast. The overnight stay in Paris, in a hotel near the *Gare de Lyon* train station, had been quiet. The hotel had been modest, but they had enjoyed a typical French dinner with a French wine in the small dining room. *Moule marinair* had been on the menu, as well as *Coq au Vin,* followed by a selection of French cheeses. A half bottle of *Coté de Rhone* had been just enough, after a round of cocktails before dinner. Simon's experience with cocktails was limited, but he had enjoyed the dry Martini. They had not been in the mood to explore the city. Simon had decided to telephone a friend—another music critic—who wrote for a daily Paris publication, to discuss the local reaction in music circles to de Pachmann's death. Charles waited for his return, sitting quietly in the lounge sipping a scotch and water. Simon soon returned from his telephone call to report that de Pachmann had already been buried at the Campo Verano Cemetery in Rome on the eighth. In accordance with his wishes and despite the fact that he had seemed to practice the Russian Orthodox faith throughout his life—it seemed no religious ceremony was held prior to the trip to the cemetery, although a Capuchin monk had read prayers at the gravesite, and had sprinkled holy water over the pianist's body before the coffin was lowered into the grave.

"The hearse carried only three wreaths, which I assume represented the two sons and his secretary, Francesco Pallottelli," Simon told Charles. "His sons travelled behind in a private car. There appear to have been no friends of the pianist at the funeral, so I'm not sure who provided this information. Leopold Godowsky, who was travelling to Europe on the liner *S.S. Europa,* was quoted as saying that in the passing of 'my dear friend de Pachmann,' the world has lost its most unique artist. He added that he did not believe his eccentricities were affectations. Godowsky you know has retired since his unfortunate stroke, even though he is still only sixty-two years old. He was a great pianist." Simon paused briefly and looked at Charles. "Here is an interesting question for you: do you know who Capuchin monks are? I did not know myself so I had to ask Max."

Charles shook his head. "No, but I am curious."

"Max tells me that Capuchins are Roman Catholic monks who separated from the Franciscan order about four hundred years ago to better serve the edict of Saint Francis, which specified that his followers devote their lives to help the poor and helpless. They have churches throughout Europe, not only in Italy. They are distinguished by the fact that they wear a hood called a *cappuce*. I think there are also capuchin nuns. My friend tells me that cappuccino coffee is so called because its colour resembles their hood and the creamy topping looks like the bald spot of the Capuchin monk's head! I think he may have been joking. Are you interested in old crypts?"

Charles made a face and shook his head.

Simon was undaunted. "He suggested we visit the Capuchin crypts below the Capuchin Church of the Immaculate Conception in Rome, on Via Venito. There are also famous Capuchin crypts in Palermo. Like you, I would not make a special effort to visit a crypt containing the preserved bones and skeletons of long dead Italian monks."

"I agree," Charles readily rejoined, "but what you tell me brings back a memory of a book I read many years ago. It was called *The Monk* and was written by a chap whose surname was Lewis. I'm sure it was about the adventures of a monk, or an abbot, who forgoes his monastic vows while working in a Capuchin monastery in Madrid to chase after a beautiful woman."

"Well our Capuchin monk in Rome was hopefully not that type," replied Simon as he chuckled loudly.

They were to be up early the next day to catch the express train to Marseille, so they had decided to retire to bed earlier than usual.

The train was now up to full speed, judging from the rate the telegraph poles were whizzing past their window.

"I have two books here that may interest you, if you have not read them before," said Charles, returning to his former conversation as he showed them to his friend. "They both offer some insight into the type of opinions held by critics and writers of a time when de Pachmann was at his peak in popularity. They might appeal to you so you may borrow them. This one was published in America in 1913—James Huneker's book, titled *Old Fogy: His Musical Opinions and Grotesques*. It's an interesting book because it reveals the author's view of a number of pianists of his day, including de Pachmann and Paderewski. This other book is *Plays, Acting and Music: A Book of Theory* by Arthur Symons. I picked that up last week in a second-hand bookstore in London. It was published five years ago and it gives Symons' description of de Pachmann's piano style, as he heard it some years ago—obviously well before the pianist's retirement. The books are not long and you could probably read each book in a matter of a few hours."

Charles continued, "Symons apparently was not primarily a music critic but he seemed to have developed a special attachment to his pianist friend. Symons' sexual orientation was questionable and he perhaps sensed that de Pachmann too might also have similar sentiments. There had been rumours that after his divorce Pachmann had developed a close male relationship with his secretary, Pallottelli but no one seemed sure of that. You likely know about that story," he added.

Simon did not respond so Charles continued. "Sexual orientation is a personal and private matter anyway, so it probably should not matter." He paused before continuing. "There is an interesting story about Huneker, the author. He had once been an ambitious pianist who had auditioned for a position as part of Liszt's group in Weimar, but he did not receive a sympathetic hearing from the master, so decided to return home to the New York where he began teaching piano classes and became a successful music critic."

"Another failed pianist becomes the next best thing—a music critic," interjected Simon. Charles, who could not help missing the meaning of the comment, shrugged and smiled but decided not to respond, and continued his commentary.

"Huneker had a strange relationship with de Pachmann. For years Huneker wrote a column in the New York magazine *Musical Courier*, under the name of The Raconteur. As an example, a few months prior to Pachmann's arrival in New York in 1890, Huneker predicted that he would not make a hit because he was 'too effeminate and his style stilted', or something along these lines. He thought that Maggie was in reality a better pianist than her husband, whom he wrote, 'is as mad as a March hare when it is chased by the shadow of the festive ground hog'."

"Huneker had heard de Pachmann perform somewhere, likely in London, before this tour of America in 1890 and had found his stage and off-stage demeanour amusing. In this book, he describes him as 'the fat little blackbird from Odessa,' having got to know him considerably more by then. He also considered him to be 'a little wonder worker' and later referred to him — here on this page, as, 'a whimsical, fantastic charmer, an apparition with rare talents and an interpreter of the lesser Chopin without a peer.' That is genuine admiration! Would you agree?"

Simon smiled and nodded in assent as Charles continued. "It was Huneker who was given the credit for labelling de Pachmann, 'the Chopanzee,' because of his posturing and facial expressions at the piano. In the *Musical Courier,* he never hesitated to poke fun at him, especially regaling in stories about his off the stage behaviour. This book could not possibly cover all the Pachmann anecdotes. I am surprised that Huneker got away with some of the things he wrote about the man. I don't know if he changed his opinion about Maggie after hearing her play in New York."

"Neither do I," replied Simon, "since I have not followed his tastes in pianists at all. It does, however, illustrate how some music critics' early opinions and comments can flavour the public's opinion of an artist such as Pachmann."

Charles nodded in agreement and continued his spontaneous lecture. "Symons had a very personal opinion of de Pachmann, but also admired the talents of Leopold Godowsky, as well as Clara Schumann and Teresa Carreno. In this book, he devotes a chapter to de Pachmann's art. In his opinion, the art of the pianist lay mainly in one thing: *touch*. De Pachmann, he wrote, beyond all other pianists, had what he called 'this magic' so that he always played Chopin with an infallible sense of what Chopin meant to express.

"I find it interesting that Symons could rationalize some of de Pachmann's odd stage behaviour. He refers on this page to the pianist's attempt to 'humanize Chopin's music' and assuming the music 'can only be reached through some not quite healthy nervous tension.' He writes that de Pachmann's 'physical disquietude when he plays is but a sign of what it has cost him to venture outside humanity, into music'."

Simon was listening with rapt attention, nodding occasionally in agreement as Charles continued. "He also writes, in reference to de Pachmann's search for the best sound, 'you see his fingers feeling after it, his face calling to it, his whole body imploring it. Sometimes it comes upon him in such a burst of light that he has to cry aloud, in order that he may endure the ecstasy'."

Charles looked up from the book. "That is very flowery language. Does that explain de Pachmann's habit of speaking to his audience and occasionally shouting exclamations?"

Simon smiled as he listened to the quotations and considered his answer; "That is very analytical stuff. I remember that Symons had a nervous breakdown early in his career, and it may have been at a time when he was travelling in Italy because he spent time there. After that illness, his writings never seemed the same. His attempts at art and literary criticism suffered. I would be cautious in giving a lot of weight to these explanations. But I am always interested in these ideas, so tell me more. What did Symons have to say about Pachmann's manner with Bach and Beethoven?"

"Well, he did have an opinion here too. Let me see if I can find the quotation." Charles thumbed through the pages and finally found the spot. "He explains that in playing Bach, de Pachmann 'had the music before him that he might be wholly free from even the slight strain which comes from the almost unconscious act of remembering'. He did of course as you said earlier—perhaps more than other pianists of the day—rely considerably on the score being on the piano, especially when playing with orchestras. You mentioned that earlier experience with the Beethoven Concerto, when he lost his way. There is a surprise comment that the *Italian Concerto in F* was 'the greatest thing' he had ever heard de Pachmann play. I had always known that he had programmed Bach infrequently and Symons knew that too because he says on page 210, 'on the rare occasions when he plays Bach, something that no one of our time has ever perceived or rendered in that composer seems to be evoked'. His playing, he writes, 'reveals Bach as if the dust had suddenly been brushed off his music' and Symons continues further on, 'he cannot interpret every kind of music, though his actual power is more varied than he has led the public to suppose.' I can imagine his Bach interpretations were very romantic.

"In regard to your opinion about his Beethoven performance style, there is a comment from Symons suggesting a barrier between Pachmann and Beethoven because he is convinced the composer, as he puts it, 'hides himself in the depths of a cloud, in the depths of wisdom, in the depths of the heart'. One would assume he means that the composer is inaccessible to the pianist. That would fit your theory about the weakness of de Pachmann's interpretation of Beethoven sonatas."

Simon nodded his head in agreement. "You have a good point. You mentioned Paderewski earlier. I am interested in hearing what Symons thought of him."

"Paderewski figures prominently in the book," Charles replied, as he thumbed through the chapter looking for the correct page. "He writes on page 217, that Paderewski showed 'absolute mastery of his instrument,' playing, 'the most difficult things without difficulty, with a scornful ease, an almost accidental quality which, found in perfection, marvellously decorates it'. Regarding his performances of Beethoven he writes, 'in the playing of the *Moonlight Sonata*, there was no Paderewski, there was nothing but Beethoven'. On the other hand, he describes the pianist's performance of the Liszt *Sonata in B minor* as if Paderewski were playing his own music. He writes, 'If ever there was a divine showman for it, it was Paderewski. He was no longer reverential, as with Beethoven, not doing homage but taking part, sharing almost in a creation … a *tour de force*'." Charles paused and looked out the window, and for a few moments watched as a station platform went quickly past.

"Symons may have suffered some decline after his mental breakdown, but he could still write the following profound statement: 'Liszt is the test rather of the virtuoso than of the interpreter,' adding that this is 'why, therefore, it was so infinitely more important that Paderewski should have played the Beethoven sonata as impersonally as he did than that he should have played the Liszt sonata with so much personal abandonment. Between those limits there seems to be contained the whole art of the pianist, and Paderewski has attained both limits'."

"I can see that he thinks as we do about interpretation," said Simon, who had been listening attentively. "You said earlier that the performer must always thrust the composer, rather than himself, onto his listeners. Personal intrusions into the performance of the composer's work can be an insult to the composer, but not everyone agrees that only the composer matters. There must be some room for interpretation because it is very difficult to find a definition for the term 'standard performance' especially when we talk about traditional performance of Beethoven's piano works."

"I agree." Charles was now thoroughly immersed in his topic. "It seems to me that you, as the critic, have a duty to serve both the composer—if you are judging a new composition—and the performer, especially if you are judging young talent. The critics who arouse most controversy are sometimes not even trained as professional pianists, and do not always understand the composer's score. Symons was not a musician as far as I know, but Huneker was."

The train attendant could be seen moving through the carriage announcing breakfast was now being served. Putting away his books, Charles and his friend began to make their way cautiously along the wildly swaying corridor toward the dining car at the front of the train. Simon had not mentioned his fear of train travel since leaving Paris, but Charles had considered raising the topic at some stage, perhaps during breakfast. Despite his obvious leg problem, Simon seemed to be in complete control as he navigated through the corridor and over the moving floor plates linking the cars. Some privacy was assured as the waiter was able to offer a table set for two. It was a pleasant sunny day and the French countryside could be seen moving quickly by. They both chose a continental-type breakfast with fresh fruit juice, croissants, fruit preserves and coffee. Charles thought it was a good moment to introduce the topic of fear of train travel.

"When you were first evacuated to the field hospitals in Italy and France what was the conclusion of the medical team that examined you?"

"They knew that I had suffered a head injury from the bullet that had pierced the right side of my helmet," Simon recalled slowly. "I had a headache that would not go away and the doctors found my left leg was weak, and to a lesser extent my left arm, but I could move them both. Oddly, I seemed to be unaware that my side was weak. My head was buzzing, my vision blurred and I remember being very scared. It had been more than twenty-four hours from the time I had slept, and I felt exhausted. The noise of gunfire and explosives in the trenches had been terrific. In the beginning the medics were inclined to minimize the extent of my injury. Some of the other British soldiers there told me they had been labelled as having shell shock, which they had been told could be due to both physical and emotional factors. After getting back home to Wales, I could see that some patients in the hospital where I had been sent were suffering from obvious nervous breakdown, and in some cases were considered insane. The hospital was in some ways like a lunatic asylum.

"Some of the injured were obviously also mentally retarded or mentally disturbed—I would assume from the time they were conscripted. They should never have been allowed to enlist. I suspect you know that the term *neurasthenia* was commonly used to explain the lingering symptoms and one military doctor actually diagnosed me as having a functional stroke. I am sure he thought I was bluffing. A week following the injury there was discussion about arranging to transfer me to a Canadian surgical unit in France for another opinion, as there was a skilled surgeon there. My leg and arm weakness had not improved. I walked clumsily, bumped into doorways and my vision was still affected. They finally suspected a blood clot under my skull outside the brain. Eventually, I did get to the Canadian unit on the outskirts of Ypres. The field hospital was called Essex Farm. It was there I met an excellent Canadian surgeon, who, after examining me carefully, advised me that they would need to drill a small hole in my skull to look for a blood clot."

"And what did they find?" asked Charles, who—despite his curiosity—had not interrupted his friend's story.

"They found a sizable blood clot, which they removed. They had hoped the operation would correct the weakness, but as you can see I still walk with a limp which I expect will remain with me forever. I have learned to compensate for my clumsiness and difficulty with my eyesight."

"How long did you spend at the hospital in Wales?" Charles was becoming sympathetic.

"I was there about six months. During that time I learned to relax again during the day and to sleep at night. But I was told I would never be able to perform military duties again. I was told over and over again that discipline and courage were all I needed to recover from shell shock. We were kept busy during the day. The hospital kept a small farm with chickens, which we cared for—feeding them and collecting their eggs. I started to play the piano again, usually in the evenings. I discovered the hospital owned a marvellous Blüthner upright, supplied by a piano store in Cardiff called Dale Forty. They are still in business. The piano was not always in tune, but a friend and I managed to learn how to tune it! I learnt how to play all over again. That was when I began to take an interest in the Beethoven piano sonatas." He took a bite from his croissant and drank some coffee.

"When I was discharged from hospital, I was short of funds. I went to live with my parents—who are still living in the same home—but they also had limited means at that time. My father was only occasionally able to find employment in the mines. The war was still on, and I felt pessimistic about finding work. I also found that I was having recurrent headaches on the side where I was injured. I have one of those every few weeks. I kept in touch with the hospital staff, and through their efforts I was able to get a small pension through the Ministry of Pensions. Mind you, I was told that it was a privilege and not a right! It came to less than five pounds per month, but helped pay for cigarettes."

Charles sat in silence for a few minutes. "I am impressed with your frankness in telling me all this. I think your permanently weak leg, and your visual problems are a result of the damage to the right side of your brain from the expanding blood clot. The right side of our brain deals with where we are in space, whereas the left side deals with speech and dominant hand function, which for me, and I notice for you too, is the right side. That means when our right brain is injured we are unlikely to be fully aware of weakness in the left leg or loss of the left side of our field of vision. Feeling confused or clumsy is likely to be the only obvious symptoms. The right side of the brain is very interesting because human beings seem to be able to function well without it. That may seem hard to believe. A few years ago, Walter Dandy, a brilliant neurosurgeon from Baltimore, reported that virtually all the right side of the brain could be removed for treatment of brain tumours and the patients could survive with little disability. You know now that it was common for military doctors to quickly blame physical complaints on the effects of shell shock. There is, however, some residual memory of your experience in the trenches which surfaces occasionally, such as when travelling by train. Trains can make you feel closed in and fearful of lack of space. I am curious about your symptoms triggered by travelling by train. When did you realize you had a problem?"

Again, Simon thought for a while. "I was not aware of the problem until several months after getting out of hospital. I was able to get an interview for work at a small newspaper in Bristol. The train trip to Bristol from Cardiff caused many of my fears to return. I remember the train had stopped for about fifteen minutes in the Severn tunnel because of a switch failure. It was dark inside the tunnel, but of course the carriage lights were on. It seemed like hours before the train moved again. I felt I was back in the trenches again. Memories of the loud explosions, the cries of my wounded mates, the smell of smoke and the sight of blood in the trenches flashed back to me as I sat in that train. I felt I needed to get out, but couldn't of course. I couldn't breath; I thought my head would burst, and I was in a cold sweat. After that, and during the return trip, similar symptoms returned, so I avoided train travel for years."

Charles thought for a moment. "I have heard that Freud as a younger man had a fear of train travel as well. He was also very fussy about getting to the station well ahead of departure—to be sure he did not miss the train. It is hard to believe, but he seemed unable to figure the schedules. He made numerous visits to Italy and especially to Rome, always travelling by train, but the arrangements were usually made by his brother, his son or his daughter, who sometimes travelled with him."

The train was now noticeably slowing as it moved through the outskirts of a small city. "This must be St. Florentin," suggested Simon, as the train seemed to be approaching the station. They had completed their breakfast, and it seemed an opportune time to proceed back to their compartment. After a brief argument over who should pay both the breakfast tariffs, which Charles won, they moved toward the rear of the train, now slowing to a crawl.

"I think you have dealt with your injury very well Simon. With care and the right amount of preparation, train travel should not necessarily be the torture you imagine. Tell me more about those headaches which keep coming back." They had settled in their compartment again and Simon seemed more willing to continue the discussion.

"They are not at all like the headaches I had for many weeks after my head injury and before my operation. These new headaches are easy to describe. They start suddenly behind or near my right eye, never the left. There is never any warning, and they reach a peak of excruciating intensity within in a few minutes, lasting a few hours. The pain usually makes me perspire. My right eye tears-up, and my nose runs. They usually come on after dinner, especially if I have had been drinking wine or scotch—or sometimes they start while I'm asleep and wake me up. I never remember having one before noon. If one wakes me, I get up, walk around, take several aspirins and generally suffer it out. If I'm lucky it fades and is gone in less than an hour."

Charles was pondering the likely explanation as he listened to the description. It was not like the usual migraine headaches, which Anne had complained of for years. She always had a warning of sorts: she felt sick leading up to the headache, and sometimes had a sensation of flashing lights before the pain began. He had heard Simon's type of headache referred to by his neurology colleagues as migrainous neuralgia. Sometimes it was called ciliary neuralgia. He had never read an explanation for these headaches.

"Well I would say you have a somewhat rare type of so-called ciliary neuralgia. No one seems to be able to explain it. It may have some relationship with
your old head injury, as it is on the same side."

"That seems to be the name a neurologist, whom I saw in Cardiff, called it
too," Simon recalled. "They were looking for possible sinus problems, but X-
rays of my head were normal. I was warned to avoid alcohol if the headaches
were coming frequently in clusters but I do not always follow that advice. No
drug treatment seems to be better than aspirin and time."

"I am thinking of Dickens again," said Charles, "because he described in
some of his letters a very similar type of headache that would incapacitate him
for days—pain over the eye with runny nose and tearing. That type of headache
is much more common in men for reasons that are not apparent. When Dickens
had these he was incapacitated and found if almost impossible to write."

The remainder of the train trip to Marseille had been very enjoyable. After
Lyon, the train had followed the twists and turns of the Rhone, past empty vineyards and fruit orchards with mountains visible in the distance. There had been a
stop in Lyon, and later in Avignon long enough for them both to get out, stretch
their legs on the platform, and for Charles to examine and admire the stationary,
but constantly noisy, locomotive.

Back in their compartment they continued to discuss music criticism, teaching skills and the range of music performance practice. At noon they had a very
relaxed lunch with spaghetti and meatballs, followed by cheese and fruit. Simon
was looking very relaxed and they shared anecdotes about many pianists, including de Pachmann. In the afternoon, they both had naps to sleep off the effects of
the half bottle of red wine they had ordered. In Marseille, there was a short wait
to connect with the train to Nice. Simon took the opportunity to telephone his
friend with details of their arrival. He returned to say that Jacques LeDrew,
would meet them at the station and had offered both of them beds at his home.
In the train station they were also able to make reservations for sleepers on the
express from Milan to Rome for Thursday evening.

Nice was bathed in lights as they alighted from the train. LeDrew was waiting for their arrival and after a short drive from the station they were introduced
to his family, his wife Jeanette and two daughters. Jeanette had prepared a buffet
dinner, which was clearly the product of an imaginative cook: smoked salmon,
rare filet of beef, cured ham, escalloped potatoes, green salad and chocolate
éclairs. Jacque opened a bottle of '28 Chateaux Lynch Bage, which was ready to
drink and proved to be very popular. Simon made some necessary phone calls.
Charles fell asleep in his chair before he had finished his coffee. It had been a
long day. By eleven o'clock they were all settled in their beds and sound asleep.

CHAPTER FOUR

"The piano works are the best possible introduction
to Beethoven's music." (A.E.F. Dickinson)

Simon had planned to write his paper on Vladimir de Pachmann's Beethoven piano style in 1913. Controversies surrounding Beethoven performance practice had reached the American press after the debut of the young Polish pianist, Ignace Paderewski, in New York City in 1891. It was 1920 by the time he had the manuscript titled, *Vladimir Pachmann's Beethoven Performance Style: A Matter of Opinion,* ready for publication. The first rough draft had been completed in 1914, but war service had interrupted his writing plans and his enthusiasm for the project never seemed the same. The Paderewski issue had surfaced as de Pachmann was still in the midst of his first North American tour that had begun in 1890. De Pachmann returned to England in May 1892 after giving 130 concerts in the USA and Canada.

Simon had left Charles a copy of his article to read, but the route from Nice to Milan was providing some considerable pleasure. Views of the Mediterranean on the right side of the train with distant hills on the left, some covered in grape vines, were a more attractive distraction. There would be several more hours before they reached their destination.

The brief stay in Nice had been relaxing. In the morning after breakfast, Simon set off to meet his friends. Charles had opted not to call his friends, but to wander about the town and to seek out the beach. It was warm and sunny. There were lots of attractive women to be seen on the beach. They seemed to have no agenda—perhaps taking a day off from the office, or perhaps they were tourists from Germany or Switzerland? Charles found a kiosk that rented swimsuits and towels. The Mediterranean was warm, and he later found a small restaurant where he had a slow lunch. He was to meet Simon back at the LeDrew home at four; the train was leaving at five. He found a wine merchant and bought a bottle of wine for the family. By four he had returned and they both said goodbye and thank-you to their friends before setting off for the station.

By now he had found a comfortable section on his otherwise uncomfortable train seat, and soon lost interest in the scenery, becoming engrossed instead in the Beethoven article. Simon had gone to the dining car for a drink and a cigarette. Charles began to read the manuscript that Simon had left:

"A precedent for high quality piano performance had already existed in Britain before Pachmann's London debut in May 1882. Hans von Bülow, Clara Schumann, Eugen d'Albert, Anton Rubinstein, Maria Krebs, Agnes Zimmerman, Sophie Menter and others had already performed there. All had met with considerable critical acclaim. The critical view was that they played Beethoven very well. Von Bülow, then in his late 40s, with a prodigious memory that allowed him to play without book, was capable of rendering performances that allowed one 'to look into the very depths of Beethoven's genius,' said the

Times. Eugen d'Albert's interpretation of Beethoven, some years later, was felt by a critic in the *New York Times_* (January 4th 1890) to be 'more warm and poetic' than that of von Bülow. D'Albert was, in fact, described as 'a Beethoven player, the greatest now living, as far as we know.' Clara Schumann, always playing with book, had convinced the *Times* of London (March 5th 1884) she could 'play Beethoven in a manner which shows that classical dignity may co-exist ... with intense individual passion.' The critic said she could render the Beethoven sonata in E flat, *Les Adieux*, 'with poetic meaning and technical perfection.'

"Obviously popular with British audiences for his Chopin playing, Pachmann did sometimes venture to programme Beethoven. In fact, he did so for his second recital in London, again with the conductor, Wilhelm Ganz, with whom he had made his London debut earlier. On June 17th 1882, he played Beethoven's 4th Concerto in G major and the critics were not impressed. The *Musical Times* later said he 'did not altogether gratify his critical hearers. His style lacks the breath and vigour and his rending is deficient in the depth of sentiment required by the great master's typical works. At the same time, the finish of his playing cannot fail to make itself admired, nor does the fact that he is a refined artist escape observation.' The *Daily Telegraph* critic thought the same:

'It does not strike us that M. de Pachmann has special qualities for dealing with Beethoven. His performance ... was lacking in breath of style and in that grandeur of conception which the greatest of imaginative musicians extracts from all who would worthily interpret him.'

"Pachmann continued to play in Britain for the remainder of 1882 with solo recitals of Chopin and a wide range of other composers. His Chopin interpretations were considered outstanding but he played no further Beethoven works that year. After a period of months living and travelling on the continent, he was back in London in the Spring of 1883, again programming mainly the solo works of Chopin and Liszt—some Bach, Field and Weber. On June 2nd, at the Crystal Palace, he again played both Beethoven's Concerto No.4 in G major, with Mr. August Manns conducting, as well as the thirty-two Diabelli variations in C minor for solo piano. The variations were played "with exquisite refinement of style", said the *Musical Times*. A recital a week later on June 9th at St. James' Hall was not as successful. His playing of Beethoven's Sonata in A major, op.101 was described by the *Musical Times* as follows:

'The result was extremely unsatisfactory—the *tempo rubato* is not required in Beethoven's music and unfortunately the masculine breath of style which really is needed is not forthcoming. In its place we had exaggerated nuances and a dreamy sentimentality of style ill-befitting the Bonn master's utterances.'

"In 1884, at a January 12th concert, the *Moonlight* Sonata was on the programme. The *Times* reported: 'It is impossible to agree without reservation to his reading of this work, the sentiment of the first movement being exaggerated, while the treatment of the finale lacks breath and dignity.'

"His farewell recital on February 28th, before leaving again for the Continent, consisted of familiar works by Chopin, Henselt, Bach, Beethoven, Cramer,

Liszt, Brahms and Schumann. This recital was reviewed by the *Times,* with the following general comments about the programming: 'He deals with the so-called classical masters in a manner which betrays the thorough musician and as a matter of duty, adorns each of his programmes with the names of Bach, Beethoven and Mendelssohn. But with none of these composers does he betray that genuine sympathy which is the artistic equivalent of personal affection'."

Simon's analysis continued. "Pachmann played several recitals in Scotland and England in 1884 but only five in London as he and his pupil, the pianist Maggie Okey, were to be married there on April 30th. His recital on February 28th was a mixed programme that included a Beethoven composition. The London *Times* produced a lengthy review, which praised his playing of all pieces by nine masters including Beethoven, but the climax of the recital was said to have been the rendition of the Chopin Sonata in B flat minor, op.35.

"The Pachmann couple's honeymoon took them to the Continent and his London concerts did not resume until November 1885. They gave a series of successful recitals in Copenhagen in the spring of 1885, where he was awarded the Order of the Danebrog by King Christian XI. One of his concerts there included a short work by Beethoven, referred to by the Danish critic, A.H. Hammereich, as 'a funny and perhaps, for most of the audience, an unknown bourrée in B minor.' This bourrée was a fragment from the Diabelli Variations, op.126.

"Back in London, after a performance of Beethoven's sonata in D minor, op.31, No.2 on November 11th, *The Musical Times'* reaction later to the poor performance was to state simply that the Beethoven … 'should not have been selected (to play).'

"Critics do not always agree on the quality of a musical performance and they sometimes differed in their opinion of Pachmann whose interpretation of the Beethoven sonatas was unpredictable and rarely spectacular. This is illustrated by the review of an afternoon recital at St. James' Hall on February 2nd, the following year, when he played "two important works of Beethoven" reported the *Times.* It was noted that the entire programme was played without book and without any wrong notes or lapses in memory:

'M. de Pachmann's supreme excellence in rendering Chopin has been so frequently insisted upon that the idea has grown in the popular mind of his being unable to do justice to Beethoven, who in many respects is the antipodes of the younger master. If it was the artist's intention to dispel this prejudice he fully succeeded…the Russian pianist plays Beethoven well, sometimes, indeed, to perfection. The latter epithet applies, for example to his rendering of the thirty-two (Diabelli) variations in C minor, one of Beethoven's most famous and most successful efforts in this his favourite form of composition. It must be owned that the sonata in F minor, op.57, which followed was less satisfactory. Here also the technical part was beyond reproach, and a fine dramatic spirit pervaded the whole. But the grandeur of Beethoven's intention seemed occasionally marred by a want of breath and repose. This was especially noticeable in the principal theme of the first movement. Here also one observed certain effects of phrasing which seemed to belong to M. de Pachmann rather than Beethoven.'

"The subject of individual preference in Beethoven performance style was touched upon at the end of this review. 'We are the last to find fault with individuality of execution or to set up a so-called 'classical' style as final and immutable; at the same time it cannot be denied that subtleties of reading, which are allowable in Chopin or in Schumann, somehow seem to pervert the perspective of Beethoven's vast design.'

"The reviewer concluded with the comment: 'all this, however, is a matter of opinion.' The critic of the *Daily Telegraph* also commented on the 'hasty generalization' that Pachmann played Beethoven less well than other composers. The enthusiasm in the review seemed to go beyond that of the critic in the *Times* mentioned above: 'Because M. de Pachmann plays the music of certain masters superlatively well, he cannot give satisfaction with that of others ... But M. de Pachmann himself administered a corrective yesterday by performing Beethoven's sonata in F minor, op.57 in a manner qualified to set right the most prejudiced. His rendering of the first and last movements especially was admirable. In point of mere execution this will be at once understood because he is such a master of the keyboard that for him no such thing as difficulty exists. But it was admirable also as an interpretation. The sonata is not one that allows various readings in a broad sense. Various readings are only possible in respect of details, and it was just here that M. de Pachmann made his performance so interesting to persons intimately acquainted with the sonata.'

"Like the previous reviewer there was a concession that the "classic Beethoven style" was impossible to define: 'We do not bind ourselves to approval of all he did, but upon many minor points in the work he threw an unaccustomed light, revealing beauties before shadowed over or not visible at all. Very slight touches did this sometimes, but it is astonishing when Beethoven is the subject what a very slight touch will do.'

"What the *Musical Times* critic heard, and seemed to have missed, in the Beethoven pieces was different still. This publication's comments were as follows: 'That M. de Pachmann is unsurpassable in certain departments of pianoforte playing is as incontrovertible as his desire to gain equal recognition in others is natural, and to a certain extent laudable ... The greatest of all masters was represented by his thirty-two (Diabelli) Variations in C minor and his *Sonata Appassionata*. The rendering of the former did not call for adverse criticism, but the first and last movements of the latter were disfigured by effeminate tricks of style and a lack of masculine breath and vigour which the master-works of Beethoven demand.'

"What seemed to be one of the most favourable receptions of the London critics to Pachmann's rendering of Beethoven, since he began to play in London four years before, was again confirmation that the performances of any music will vary no matter who the composer or artist and in a manner that is often impossible to explain.

"Later, in February of the same year, Pachmann returned to his Ukrainian birthplace, Odessa, where he gave several concerts, one of which included the

Beethoven sonata, op.101. Critical reaction was guarded and it was said that the pianos used for his recitals were not of good quality.

"Franz Liszt was in London from April 3rd—20th of that year and not surprisingly his music dominated the concerts. It is worth noting that Bernard Shaw in the *Pall Mall Gazette* (August 2nd) reminded his readers that Wagner had once declared that Liszt's playing of Beethoven's greater sonatas was 'essentially an act of composition as well as well as interpretation.' Beethoven had been a great admirer of Liszt as a boy-pianist and was said to have walked on to the platform after a Liszt concert and demonstrated his appreciation with a kiss.

"Later, on May 3rd, again at St. James' Hall, Pachmann had chosen to program three major sonatas: the Chopin B flat minor, the Weber sonata op.49 and Beethoven's sonata in A major, op.101. The *Musical Times* critic was disappointed and commented that the Beethoven work was one of the three…'needing almost every quality in pianoforte playing for its perfect interpretation. We cannot say that M. de Pachmann was altogether successful, something of breath and intellectuality being missing.'

"In the summer of 1886, Pachmann left England for the continent and did not return until a year later to give a single recital in London on June 2nd. Expectation of finding Beethoven on the programme and apparent disappointment was obvious in the recital review in the *Times*: 'His programme, as is usual on such occasions, consisted of a miscellaneous selection, to the exclusion, however, of Beethoven or any so-called masters.'

"He made up for this omission on his return to London in 1888. For his first recital on Jan.16, he played Chopin's Concert Allegro in A, op.46, J S Bach's *Great Fugue in A minor* as well as Beethoven's Sonata in F, op.54. The London *Times* reported the next day that '… his touch seemed more emphatic, more marked, his reading broader and more developed, than they had been on any previous occasion. Bach and Beethoven decidedly gained by the change, and a finer performance than that of the latter by M. de Pachmann could not have been desired.'

"The *Musical Times* reviewer considered the last two works the best features of the recital. Pachmann had proved again that he could play Beethoven to the satisfaction of the London critics.

"At this time, when Pachmann was preparing to leave England with his wife for his first American tour in 1890, the London critics, as we have seen, had often expressed reservations about his Beethoven performances. He and Maggie did not programme Beethoven works in their initial New York or Boston recitals. He included Canada in this North American tour and on his second visit to Toronto in April, 1892, he shared a concert with Madame Mattia Albani. The concert was reviewed by "Metronome" in the April 19th issue of the weekly *Saturday Night*: 'M. de Pachmann played a liberal number of piano solos, opening with the *Moonlight* Sonata, of which he gave a thoughtful rendering, but without great depth or power. In fact his playing is … polished and elegant to a degree, but to my mind, sadly superficial.'

"The concert was also reviewed by *The Globe*, a daily Toronto newspaper, whose critic reported virtually the same verdict: 'His playing of the Beethoven sonata was thoughtful and musicianly without showing any signs of greatness'."

Charles paused and took a few moments to reminisce about that concert in Toronto, which he had attended in 1892. His memory was hazy, as he would have been no older than thirteen, but he remembered his mother reading the lukewarm newspaper reviews. He had been very curious about de Pachmann's style and his on-stage gestures. He looked out the window and noted the train seemed to be making good time. Almost an hour had passed since leaving Nice. He could see only a few boats and an occasional ship in the Gulf. He looked away and saw Simon approaching along the carriage corridor, holding fast to the backs of the chairs as the train swayed while navigating a curve. Charles stood up to stretch and waited for his friend to reach their seats.

"I hope you are enjoying the article and did not find it boring," was Simon's first comment. "I have had a few drinks in the bar and been chatting with some Italian passengers. I think there is food being served in the dining car. I'm hungry. Why don't we see what's on the menu?"

"I haven't finished the article yet," Charles responded, "but I am enjoying it very much—in fact it is much more interesting than some of the papers I read in my medical journals. Your concerns about it being too provocative are unfounded. We can discuss some details later over dinner but your research has been very impressive. I like it and I like the idea of dinner as well. Let's go."

The dining car was two car lengths away and they found there were several tables still unoccupied. They were soon seated comfortably at a table for two on the right of the train with a view of the Gulf of Genoa. They spent some time surveying the dinner menu. "Do you feel like a glass of wine Simon?" Charles asked. His friend looked up from the menu and smiled. He thought he would like another.

The waiter appeared and suggested a bottle of Italian wine, which was reasonably priced. He recommended *Osso boco* as the main dish, so they both decided that would be their choice. There was to be a forty-five minute stop in Genoa while they changed trains for Milan. Simon seemed to know something about Genoa. "It is a famous old city—the birthplace of several very famous people—Nicolò Paganini and Christopher Columbus. I gave a talk some years ago at the Cardiff Academy on Paganini's life as I was always in awe of his talent. He had a brilliant violin technique that has probably never been equalled. He toured Europe extensively and made a large amount of money. But he seems to have had a sad life, having contacted syphilis, which is thought to have been the cause of his death at the age of fifty-seven. He lived in Marseilles for a spell before moving to Nice where he died in 1840—I think it was."

"I have heard that story," added Charles, "and I also know something of John Cabot, another explorer who was born somewhere nearby Genoa. He was given credit for being the first European to discover the island of Newfoundland, off the east coast of Canada. He had sailed from Bristol in 1497 with the approval of King Henry VII of England. Some historians say he may have landed on the island of Cape Breton, Nova Scotia. There is a friendly dispute between Nova Scotian and Newfoundland historians about that point."

The wine had arrived and they spent some time discussing the scenery passing by the window of his carriage. It was a vista that any tourist would have paid a small fortune to see. The sun had begun to set. Details of the distant sea had become indistinct. The lighted windows of a few scattered houses flashed by and shadows had begun to encroach onto the railway right-of-way. The *Osso boco* with boiled potatoes had arrived and became the main topic of their conversation for the next twenty minutes. They decided to sample the cheese tray and soon finished the bottle of wine just as the train's imminent arrival at the Stazione Brignole in Genoa was announced.

"We have less than an hour to change trains", said Simon, as he looked at his watch, gathered his luggage and prepared to leave the carriage, which had now come to a complete stop. "I have never been to this station before so we shall have to ask directions for the correct platform."

There were a lot of people on the platform as they moved along with their luggage and Charles could see there were a number of armed soldiers wearing the black shirts of the Italian Fascist militia. "These must be the Black Shirts, Mussolini's special army," whispered Simon as they walked past, "they do look rather sinister." The departure time of the Milan express was well posted and after their tickets had been verified and their luggage stored they were soon seated in a comfortable, otherwise empty compartment. It was almost 8:30 pm and the estimated arrival time in Milan was 10:20 pm.

Simon was quiet and seemed to want to sleep. Charles decided he would find Simon's article on Beethoven and resume where he had left off.

Simon's review continued:

"The critics in Boston proved to be receptive and sympathetic to Pachmann's readings of the Moonlight Sonata and the thirty-two Diabelli Variations towards the end of that tour in 1892. His performance met with considerable praise from the music critic of the *Boston Home Journal*, where Philip Hale had been music editor prior to 1890. After a Chickering Hall recital on February 11th 1892 the current *Journal* reviewer wrote:

'De Pachmann's reading of the Beethoven sonata and the 32 variations must have surprised such musicians as have heretofore underrated him as simply within the confines and limitations of the Chopinesque art. Ease, fluency, grace, poesy, and correctness, all of which Mr. de Pachmann displays as probably does only one other pianist, would not of themselves prove sufficient to cause him to be rated as a remarkable artist; but he is possessed of far more transcendent qualities. This he proved Thursday by the breadth interpretation and well controlled feeling with which he approached Beethoven. A pervading sense of deep feeling and poetic thought, of religious fervency as well, were the characteristics of his performance. The variations especially brought out the very best qualities of the artist's individuality, the dignity, breath and masculine vigour of his performance affording splendid satisfaction.'

"Philip Hale, now with the *Boston Post*, also present at that recital wrote with considerable flourish of the performance as follows:

'Yesterday he played music by Beethoven and showed thereby that he was not merely the man of one book. His reading of the sonata was free from academic dryness; it was also free from the symptoms of modernization, the disease that attacks so many pianists with fatal results in these last, nervous years of the dying century. He treated the composer with respect; he did not slap him carelessly on the shoulder; he allowed him to speak freely, without interruptions and without corrections. Nor did he accuse him of paleness and of lack of strength, recommending with the same breath the operation of transfusion of blood and insisting that Chopin's vital fluid would renew his youth. No. He was content to let Beethoven be Beethoven. He used the indescribable beauty of his tone, the subtle potency of his rhythm, the infinite wealth of his tone gradations, all the resources, in a word, of his mechanism, vivified by poetic and passionate temperament, in the service of the composer, and not for the glorification of self. Even the thirty-two variations, which, interesting in construction, become too often thirty-two ingenious devices for torturing the listener, were yesterday like unto the varied version of some rapt improvisator.'

"One suspects that Pachmann may have been in a particularly good frame of mind on that day despite coming to the end of a very long tour beginning in 1890. He occasionally did appear on stage in a bad mood and the quality of his playing often suffered. In fact, a few days later, on February 13th he did just that. It was winter and cold outside so the overheated hall was an excuse for his exasperation and poor performance. One critic wrote: 'Mr. de Pachmann did not seem quite in the mood for playing at first.'

"Pachmann's critics had noted on many occasions that he took liberties with the scores of Beethoven and that he was dry, superficial, too feminine and lacking in breath, grandeur of concept, intellectuality and classical dignity. These were all considered to be important markers of a good Beethoven piano performance style.

"Ignace Paderewski's first tour of America had been sponsored by the Steinway piano maker. Prior to leaving England for his tour he was described as being 'in his best form,' according to the *London Musical News,* (October 30th 1891). His performance of the Diabelli Variations of Beethoven, received 'an exceptionally fine rendering, remarkable for intellectual grasp, delicate refinement and graceful fancy.' The *Waldstein Sonata*, however, 'suffered from too rapid a tempo in the first movement but the adagio and rondo were very finely played.' His reception in America was less enthusiastic. His debut recital in New York at Carnegie Hall on November 17th 1891 was lacking in praise from the *New York Times*: 'he began by disappointing his auditors—he is no ideal pianist,' it reported. However, after his second recital two days later the judgement of the *New York Times* was different: 'his success is assured.' Later that month, Boston audiences, for the first time, were able to hear Paderewski play Beethoven. For Philip Hale, what he heard was not his impression of how the composer's music should be played. His review in the *Boston Post* described the performance of the Sonata in F minor, op.57 as follows:

'He is apt to comb the mane hair of the lion of music that it may be the more pleasing to the sight. Not that his playing of Beethoven is effeminate or colourless; on the contrary, the contrasting qualities of tone are often exquisite and the reading is almost always free from sentimentalism; but that virility peculiar to Beethoven, which is so noticeable in the performance of Rubinstein and D'Albert is often missed when Mr. Paderewski plays. The sentiment of Beethoven appeals more strongly to this pianist than the ruggedness or the demonic passion of the composer's nature.'

"Hale's opinion of Paderewski's Beethoven style was shared by the critic in the *Boston Home Journal* on February 27th:

'Concerning the performance of op.57 by Beethoven, on Tuesday afternoon, at the first of the four recitals, there ought not to exist the slightest doubt that it fell short of the scholastic standard of excellence. One felt from it but little of that power which, as a great factor in musical history of the world, is sure to increase with each generation. Paderewski became himself the central figure to which all the artistic details of the work were subordinated.'

"Three days later when Beethoven's Sonata, op.53, the *Waldstein*, was on the programme, the same critic was now full of praise for Paderewski's playing, reporting on that occasion:

'His playing ... was notably admirable, as it was not only just to his reputation as a great master of technique, but it proved him to be an eminent servant of artistic truth whose interpretation had been conceived, systematized and regulated from the ethical and intellectual principles of his art.'

During his second North American tour Pachmann was again in Boston. In January 1894, he played Beethoven's op.57 at Chickering Hall. The critic for the *Boston Transcript* later wrote:

'It was plainly one of his 'good afternoons' for his fine playing began immediately and without any preliminary warm up. He played the great 'Appassionata' with electric effect and at the same time without indulging himself in eccentricities.'

"Another critic's impressions were different:

'The qualities in which Mr. de Pachmann is opulent are not quite sufficient for the lofty thoughts of the master. Grace, delicacy, dreamy sensuousness are all needed in the interpretation of Beethoven, but strenuous passion, magnificent virility, the deeper, graver qualities of mind and soul are essential to the adequate rendering of his inspired works, and in these respects Mr. de Pachmann falls short. He is inevitably pleasing, and at times even fine, but he is not great— when he essays to give us the thought of the musician who is the master of them all.'

"Critics, as has been said before, differ in their interpretation of performances. Pachmann concluded his American tour and was in London, England on February 3rd, where he played a mixed programme, which included the Beethoven Sonata in C, op.53. The *Times* reported:

'For those who had the self-restraint to keep their eyes averted from the performer, the recital given by (the pianist) must have been an occasion of enjoyment ... if he did not exhaust the emotional possibilities of (the sonata), he gave a far more sympathetic reading of it than usual, and the effect of the whole was so good that it was easy to forgive the momentary failures of memory, of which there were several.'

"In October and November of 1899, Pachmann was again in Boston as part of his third North American tour sponsored this time by Steinway. He had programmed the *Waldstein* Sonata, op. 53 for his recital on October 31st. This time the critics seemed pleased and the *Boston Herald* on the following day described the recital as follows:

'His reading and performance of the Beethoven sonata were wonderfully fine in their virility, their largeness and their beauty and propriety of colour. It is true that he gave a greater emphasis than is usual to the dynamic indications of the composer, and that the interpretation, as a whole, was more vigorously dramatic than has been the accepted rule for the playing of the work, but there was nothing for which full justification might not be given, and no liberties were taken that were in any wise in conflict with the character of the work itself. The reading was in some essentials a new one, but it was always strong, dignified and wonderfully effective. The phrasing throughout was of rare beauty and the manliness of the effort, as a whole, was as striking as it was gratifying.'

"The reviewer's final comment was of equal interest:

'One drawback to a complete enjoyment of the concert ... was the artist's lapse, now and then, into something of his earlier and silly eccentricities, the absence of which in his other appearances here this season had given reason to believe that he had reformed them altogether ... It is a pity that he cannot be made to understand the vulgarity of obtruding these irritating tricks of personality into his performances.'

"Philip Hale, who was eventually to become Pachmann's favourite amongst American critics, writing in the *Journal*, made no mention of the pianist's annoying stage behaviour. Hale wrote that he had:

'Proved beyond doubt and peradventure that he is on loving and intimate terms with Beethoven ... his performance of the well known sonata was distinguished by thorough musical intelligence. The sonata was not as is often the case, merely three sections, put together and called by courtesy one work. The movements were related to each other; each was an indispensable part of the whole. No episode, no phrase was dwelt upon to the injury of the composer's flow of thought, yet the sense of proportion was so keen that nothing was slighted in the desire to make one overwhelming effect. Passages that were peculiarly Beethovenesque; passages that under the fingers and in the minds of others seem ineffective, grotesque, inexplicable, padding, were now full of strength, beauty, subtle suggestion, grandeur ... this man who is recklessly and ignorantly accused of affectation and insincerity played this sonata with a simplicity that was as noble as it was unusual, with a simplicity that is the flawless triumph of art.'

"The *Herald* had reviewed his first recital earlier in the month and had expressed relief that the '... eccentricities that diverted attention from his playing and rendered it almost impossible to take him seriously ... were no longer seen.'

"On October 21st, Pachmann was in New York City and played the same sonata at Mendelssohn Hall. After that recital, W.J. Henderson wrote in the *New York Times*:

'The pianist was heard to no advantage whatever in the Beethoven sonata, which he played in a very superficial and unmoving manner.'

"Although the Beethoven interpretations of both Pachmann and Padereweski had produced varying verdicts as to their merits, it was Paderewski style that had raised the most discussion of what constituted the proper 'Beethoven style'. James Huneker had written in the *Musical Courier* that Paderewski could not play that composer's works as well as Anton Rubinstein. W.J. Henderson in the *New York Sunday Times* felt that Paderewski had "disappointed his hearers" in playing Beethoven. Such remarks prompted the American pianist and teacher, William Mason, to write to the *Musical Courier* expressing his view of what constituted 'the Beethoven style'. Mason's contact with Liszt from 1853 in Weimar was considered sufficient reason to make him a good authority on this subject. Mason and many others who had heard Liszt play considered him to have been a great Beethoven player. Mason wrote:

'Whenever a pianist makes his first appearance in public as a Beethoven player he is at once subjected to strictness on all sides by numerous critics who seem to have been lying in wait for the particular occasion...There immediately arise two parties, each holding positive opinions, of which the one in the negative is usually the most numerous. Is the ideal Beethoven player a myth or does he really exist? If so, where is he to be found? In short, are we not looking for something that is much in the imagination?'

"Mason's conclusion was that, 'Paderewski's conception of Beethoven combined the emotional with the intellectual in admirable poise and proportion.'

"Back in London again in the summer of 1901, Pachmann played a recital at St. James' Hall on June 22nd, during which he included Beethoven's E flat Sonata, op.31, along with selections from Chopin and Schumann. *The Times* reported some surprise that he:

'Had so completely freed himself from all those regrettable affectations of manner which have been noticed so often ... and (it) may have made his playing of (the Beethoven sonata) a little stiff and unimpassioned.'

"In 1902, Edward Baxter Perry, the musicologist and pianist, published a book titled *Descriptive Analysis of Piano Works,* in which he devoted a chapter to the subject of 'Traditional Beethoven Playing'. He asked the same question as William Mason: "What does traditional Beethoven playing mean?" He pointed out that some pianists are considered to be "wonderful Beethoven players" whereas others were not. He noted that Hans von Bülow was considered to have been the representative Beethoven player of that period, despite his cold personality and otherwise uninteresting repertoire. Where he excelled was in technique and memory. In contrast, Paderewski was cited as playing Beethoven too warmly, too emotionally and too subjectively in the view of some critics.

"Perry examines the available but scanty evidence concerning Beethoven's method of playing his own works. He wrote that the composer's life was lived in some ways in open defiance of established tradition and his critics considered his music to be similarly flawed. He was a virtuoso pianist and played with warmth and intensity but lacked finish and precision. As was his nature, his music could be rough, stormy, energetic and impulsive according to Perry. 'With whom did the so-called traditions originate?' he asked, and concluded that it was with Liszt, who adored Beethoven, his music and ceaselessly promoted his piano works throughout his career as a performer. Over-editing of scores was also partly to blame for the current critical views of performance practice according to Perry, and concluded that there is no absolute correct traditional rendering of any of Beethoven's works!

"It would not be difficult to imagine that Beethoven in his early years was able to sway an audience by the force of his presence and personality as he sat at the piano. He had come to Vienna from Bonn as an unknown virtuoso and there were critics who found his style rough and his music compositional forms eccentric. Haydn had once warned him that an early Trio from op.1 might be found too difficult for most of the public and might not be well received. For years Beethoven had excelled at playing his own works.

"As noted, interpretations of virtually all piano repertoire could differ between pianists and differ from one recital to another for individual artists. It was true of Pachmann, Paderewski and is also true amongst today's pianists. Wilhelm Kempff is worth mentioning. He has not yet performed in Britain. Since his professional career, beginning in 1916, he has acknowledged his reputation for inconsistent playing. He could play something once but could not repeat it. He claimed to be a different person every night, responding to his inspiration for that moment and that can be said for many current artists.

"Despite Pachmann's statement to the press after his arrival in New York for the start of his fifth tour of America in the summer of 1911: 'I don't enjoy playing Beethoven — his music is not sufficiently … pianistic!' He never gave up playing the composer's music. A few years earlier during a final recital in Boston (on March 28th 1908) during his forth tour his playing was a great success. He played the *Waldstein* sonata, as well as a selection from Chopin, Schubert, Mendelssohn and Liszt. The *Boston Globe* compared his interpretation with Madame Teresa Carreno's, heard several weeks before:

'Where Mme. Carreno was virile, de Pachmann played the Beethoven number with infinite delicacy, with much more clearness and cleanness, and with far less fortissimo effect. His marking of the theme was clever and the ensemble was more a mental treat than a tour de force.'

"As an introduction to the review, the writer also commented on the prevailing sentiment of Boston's audiences towards de Pachmann:

'Except for one solitary number, never has the artist, better loved than any-body except Paderewski, and better appreciated by music lovers, perhaps than even that player, given Boston a greater treat.'

"At a Carnegie Hall recital on April 14th, he played the Sonata in C major op. 53 and *The New York Times* reviewer wrote:

'To those who had heard this sonata before, the music coming from under the pianist's fingers must have sounded like a novelty. In fact Mr. de Pachmann almost composed a new andante movement out of the rondo.'

"Later in the year, the *Musical Courier* on November 8th reported as fol-lows:

'De Pachmann's rendition of the '*Waldstein*' sonata was not according to the German traditions concerning Beethoven, but no one can account for the moods of a virtuoso like de Pachmann. If his interpretation of the opening sonata was original, it had moments of compelling beauty, and let all be thankful for that. Any pianist who can hold the attention of an audience for nearly two hours and a half, as de Pachmann did last week, needs no apologists. The smooth pas-sages of the *allegro con brio* could not fail to instruct in the performance of such a number, for throughout the tone was marvellously beautiful and not the tenth of a tone was blurred.'

"Pachmann was in America again in 1911 for an exhausting tour during which he played very little Beethoven. After he did play the *Waldstein* sonata in New York on November 4th, the critic in *Musical America* reported as follows:

'It cannot be said he did full justice to the *Waldstein* sonata. Although it was a beautiful performance tonally, it lacked the essential element of breath and dramatic force.'

"He played the same sonata in Boston on November 13th as well as in Providence a few days later. The local critic in *Musical America* thought he, 'played in a masterly manner.'

"Beethoven's works were uncommon choices of the pianist for the next few years. He did play one of his favourites, the Diabelli Variations, in London in October 1916. *Musical America* reported:

'... after a long introductory speech before playing which led his listeners to expect something stupendous in his performance of them, and, just as character-istically, so he played them in a manner that was by no means impressive.'

"Another similar example is a critic's response to a recital in Manchester, England. In November of 1920, he played the Sonata in D minor, op.31, No.2 after warning his audience that all the changes of pace in the performance were exactly "those of Beethoven himself' as the composer had played it for the pian-ist's father many years ago." The critic commented that Pachmann was probably more capable of restricting the energy of a piece in a way that is acceptable to the listener and added:

'The sonata in his hands was hardly more than a shadow of its full self and yet a piece of exquisite refinement and beauty.'

"Pachmann was back in North America for his final visit in 1923. He was seventy-five years old. At Carnegie Hall in late October he played to a packed house. The *Pathetique* sonata was on the program and Deems Taylor of the *World* described how the pianist smiled, gestured, made funny faces and giggled with almost continuous monologue between movements 'beating time as though he were conducting a band.' Lawrence Gilman of the *Tribune* described it as 'a one-man vaudeville show.' Only two critics defended Pachmann in their reviews.

"In Boston, on October 21st, he again played Beethoven's *Pathetique* and the *Boston Herald* critic wrote:

'His eccentricities of demeanour have gained upon him. Whatever his motives may be, he does not observe the usual etiquette of the concert hall ... Persons who demand above all that a performer shall show forth the inner meaning of a work, can have found little in Mr. de Pachmann's playing to admire. (The) pathetic quality (of the sonata) escaped (him).'

"The critic of the *Transcript* concluded that:

'Mr. de Pachmann is neither the pianist nor the musician of his prime. In flashes but only in flashes, both occasionally return. (He) played Beethoven's *Pathetique* Sonata in the veritable manner of the dry, desiccating, meticulous Rachmaninov whom he professes to abominate. '

"As has been said before, definite characteristics of the pianist's style have included idiosyncrasies such as clowning in a variety of ways, complaining of the central heating, claiming his performances had the composer's seal of authenticity while proceeding to deliberately tamper with the composer's tempos. Consistency was not a feature of his Beethoven style, nor was it always found in his rivals such as Paderewski. Pachmann occasionally played Beethoven well but he was never consistent. Often he was said to lack "breath and dramatic force", characteristics that Beethoven himself likely displayed. British critic always looked for the masculine, strenuous passion and virility which Pachmann seldom produced even in his early professional career."

Charles had come to the end. He laid the manuscript aside and again looked out the window. He was envious and at the same time impressed with the amount of time his friend had expended into researching de Pachmann's recital reviews. Simon was still sleeping. It was now 9:15 PM and the train was moving swiftly through an invisible and black countryside. The carriage temperature had dropped noticeably as they moved further north. Charles was reminded that it was winter in Italy and sometimes snowstorms and freezing temperatures could be encountered. He was feeling sleepy as well. The wine at dinner had helped. He stretched his legs under the seat ahead, found a soft pillow for his head, closed his eyes and was soon asleep.

CHAPTER FIVE

"Varium et mutabile simper femina"
(Woman is ever changeable and inconstant)

The Rome railway station platform was crowded on Friday morning. Friends and relatives had gathered in large numbers to greet the arrivals with hugs and kisses, chattering loudly and helping with luggage. A number of young-looking soldiers in black shirts carrying rifles over their shoulders could be seen, and were trying to avoid making themselves obvious. Simon had disappeared into the platform crowd, but he soon came into view some fifteen meters ahead. Progress along the platform was slow, and Simon's limp seemed more obvious today. By the time Charles had almost caught up, his friend had stopped briefly and appeared to be disengaging himself from an encounter with two short, middle-aged males, dressed in light-weight suits and wearing Panama-style hats. He caught what sounded like a shout of defiance in Italian from Simon as the two men turned away and quickly moved on down the platform unencumbered by baggage.

Charles was curious about the strange episode. "Who were they? Some friends of yours?"

Simon did not respond immediately as he resumed his slow pace towards the gate. "No, not at all!" he eventually replied with obvious annoyance, "just two Italian blokes whom I have never met before, speaking poor English, and telling me what I already know: Pachmann has died and the funeral service has already been conducted at the Campo Verano Cemetery—and also warning me about repeating what they called 'Pachmann insults'. Total rubbish!"

"What did they mean? Surely this could not be about your Beethoven article on de Pachmann? That was years ago!"

"It could be that," Simon admitted, "but I would be very surprised if that was the case, and I am also annoyed because it was such a trivial issue. That article came out years ago and I thought by now it would be water under the bridge. There was enough discussion about it after it was published to put the matter to rest and in the end I thought I was being fair to the man."

"Members of the de Pachmann Society of Rome perhaps, or the Italian secret police?" Charles suggested.

Simon shrugged as they continued their slow walk to the end of the platform. "Who knows? If so, it is hard to believe that two Pachmann fans would make a special trip to the train station just to tell me that he had died."

"How could they have known you would be arriving on this train? Did one of your newspaper friends who knew you would be coming on this express to cover Agnieszka Lipska's recitals tell them?" Charles was becoming more intrigued by the intrigue.

"I don't remember telling anyone other than Agnieszka and her brother. But remember—the train personnel did have our papers and passports long enough to notify contacts in Rome." Lowering his voice, Simon whispered, "you never know what sort of information network on visitors this Italian Government has in place these days."

Charles decided to make light of the event. "Do you think I'm safe travelling with you?" and added, "it seems like the type of mystery Sherlock Holmes would enjoy. After all he was a musician too. Is he still in the detective business or is he spending all his time minding his bee hives in Scotland?"

Simon took the bait. "I'm not sure, but wasn't he born about the mid-eighteen hundreds? That would mean he is now close to eighty years old. By the way, it was not to Scotland that he retired but to Eastbourne near the Sussex Downs, sometime about the turn of the century, I think. I expect he spends his evenings playing tunes on his violin—if he is still alive! I don't think you should have any concerns about travelling with me. We are staying at different hotels so you should be safe if there is more trouble." Simon managed to maintain a straight face. They had emerged onto the sunlit platform. "I don't think we have to be careful when we meet again. But now we must find a cab. I suddenly feel very tired and my bags are far too heavy."

The demand for taxicabs was brisk outside the exit from the station, so they waited in a queue for almost ten minutes. Simon had strolled off alone, away from the crowded platform to smoke a cigarette, leaving Charles to watch the baggage. The queue moved quickly, and they were soon settled in a comfortable Fiat taxi heading off in the direction of the hotel section of the city. The moan of the car engine and noisy rumble of tires on cobblestones coming through the open windows made conversation difficult. This driver obviously liked to drive fast in second gear. Over the din, Charles did discover that Simon's strategy was to contact Agnieszka Lipska and her brother at their hotel soon after checking in. He had told Charles earlier that she and her brother had asked him to speak briefly before the start of her Sunday afternoon recital, which was to be dedicated to the memory of de Pachmann.

"What are your plans for the rest of the day?" he asked.

"First, I plan to run a bath, soak for an hour and then catch a nap. Call me later if you find your friends or have specific plans for the evening," Charles replied, handing Simon a card. "I have written down the hotel phone number so you should give me yours in case you have trouble reaching me. Are you interested in meeting for dinner? There is a good restaurant nearby, or at least it was good when I was here before. That was a few years ago. The dining room in my hotel might also be a good bet, but it would be the first time for me."

They were soon at the Hotel Bernine Bristol, the closer of the two hotels. After saying goodbye to Simon, Charles continued on to Hotel Splendide Royal. Within a few minutes Charles was able to take a critical look at the hotel, which was new to him. Inside he was greeted in very good English by the desk personnel and concierge, and made to feel like an old friend. His passport and visa papers were examined and surrendered. Although he had never met his Roman contact, he had been promised that a copy of the new de Pachmann book or manuscript, recently republished by de Pachmann's secretary, might be left at the desk. The hotel concierge could find no trace of it. One of the clerks was sure she had seen something of that description earlier in the morning, but no one else had. Charles asked the clerk if he could look again, and also to transfer any outside phone calls to his room even if he was sleeping. An attendant, introduced as Paolo Volpe, was very soon escorting him with minimal formality to his room. The elevator was swift, quiet, and otherwise empty. They emerged into a corridor on the third floor that smelled fresh and pleasant. It looked as if the hotel had recently had a fresh facelift. He was soon settled in Number 332, a spacious, well-furnished room with an equally spacious connecting sitting room. The ceilings were tall, and the walls looked like they had been recently papered. Two windows overlooked a walled garden covered in green foliage, with many flowerbeds, fringed by tall cypress trees. A dog was barking intermittently in the adjacent garden. Charles opened the window, and could hear children's voices coming from what looked like a school play ground in the same direction. The bathroom was large and bright, and the bathtub generous. Forgetting about his unpacked bags, he was soon immersed to his neck in a hot soapy bath. It was the most relaxing moment he could remember since leaving London.

He found himself rehashing the events of the past three weeks, beginning with the stormy Atlantic crossing from Halifax, his brief but exciting shipboard romance with Lisa, his enjoyable stay in London, the discovery of de Pachmann's obituary, his meeting with Simon and hearing about his friend's musical mission to Rome; the unsettling encounter between Simon and the two strangers on the station platform, and the absence of the manuscript. He could not believe that it had been delivered and had disappeared. He was sure that his friend in Toronto had been given the correct hotel address.

Charles had invited Lisa—perhaps in haste—to join him on his travels to Rome and when they parted in Southampton she had seemed mildly interested. She told him, however, it depended on getting leave from the ship, and added that she had a habit of missing train connections. He now knew that to be true, as she had been nowhere in sight at Victoria Station three days ago—nor had he heard from her at his London hotel. Perhaps she had been unable to get the extra time off. He was not disappointed as it had been no more than a brief fling, although an interesting one. As wonderful as the experience had been, he had occasionally felt that his original wish for solitude onboard the ship had been interrupted. Lisa seemed to need to monopolize every moment of his time. Now his solitude had again been interrupted by his meeting Simon.

He did not know what to make of Simon. His new friend had a limp, which was likely the result of his brain injury in 1916. But Simon had also been left with the psychological consequences of shell shock. Although there had been earlier concern that the long train journey would have a disastrous effect on his friend's nerves, there seemed to have been no obvious incidences. Erich Maria Remarque's book *All Quiet on the Western Front* flashed into Charles' mind again. The author had been injured during the war, but had not suffered from shell shock. His novel was about the constant horrors of serving in the trenches. He was also a good pianist who gave lessons in his teens for pocket money and played the organ on Sundays in an insane asylum. Psychiatrists were beginning to appreciate the value of music therapy for their patients.

Charles had been surprised that Simon had spoken Italian to the two strangers on the platform, so he likely could speak enough Italian to have been asked to say a few words about de Pachmann and Chopin before the recital on Saturday. Perhaps he would speak to the audience totally in Italian. That would be interesting. Charles had seen an announcement of the Sunday afternoon recital in the hotel lobby. Agnieszka Lipska was to play an all-Chopin programme to include several mazurkas and nocturnes, a polonaise, the *Berceuse*, the *Fantaisie-Impromptu* in C sharp minor and the second sonata—the type of programme that de Pachmann might have presented.

Earlier his plan had been to contact de Pachmann's secretary after he had given his presentation on obsessive-compulsive disorders on Tuesday, which would be in five days. He needed to spend further time going over the manuscript before the meeting. It was still too long for the fifteen minutes he had been assigned. He was sure there would be no time for questions if he did not trim the text. Questions and discussion were as important as the presentation itself.

He had anticipated seeing several of the European pioneers in psychiatric treatment at this meeting. Some of them might be presenting papers.

Manfred Sakel of Vienna, whom Charles had never met, would likely be attending the meeting. His work on insulin-induced coma was currently of great interest, as it suggested a potential cure for a variety of mental disorders. Charles relished the opportunity of discussing the treatment with him. During his year in London in 1925, Charles had travelled to Vienna where he had meet Professor Julius Wagner-Jauregg, who would be awarded the Nobel Prize two years later for his work on fever therapy for general paralysis, a complication of syphilis infection. Although the professor had since retired, it was possible that he too would be coming to the meeting.

Would an earlier phone call allow Charles' de Pachmann contact more preparation for his visit? The deceased pianist's two sons, Adrien and Lionel, would likely still be in Rome to finalize legal matters in settling their father's estate. Charles did not wish to intrude on their grief, so he decided to delay any calls to the villa until after the weekend. Adrien de Pachmann was a Paris attorney who had spent a few years in New York after the war, as legal counsel with the French High Commission. Charles had heard that he was also a veteran of the 1914-18 war, having served with the French army and afterwards being awarded the *Croix de Guerre*. His father's estate would be well managed with his talent. Charles also wondered if Lionel de Pachmann—the musician—might be interested enough in the Chopin recital in memory of his father to attend Agnieszka Lipska's recital. Pallottelli would likely have been aware of the concert.

Charles could not decide what to think of Simon's article on de Pachmann. It was difficult to imagine that devotees of the pianist, and members of the de Pachmann Society in Rome, would feel strongly enough about their hero's reputation to threaten a music critic in public. There was also a similar society in Naples and in some other Italian cities. It was true that critics too often wrote with a sense of superiority about performers, and sometimes even the composer's music. Criticism could be easy, public performance was more difficult, and the critics' assessment could sometimes be determined by an excessively personal concept of how the performance should sound. Consensus seemed to be that de Pachmann's interpretations of Beethoven's sonatas were often—but not always—flawed. But was it really any different from that of other similar pianists over the last fifty years? Every performer seemed to have his or her own ideas about how Beethoven's piano music should sound, displaying his or her personal style, sometimes overruling the composer's authority for the thrill of interpretive individuality. But who could be certain how Beethoven himself played his music? William Mason was right—there was likely no such person as the perfect Beethoven interpreter. It would be no surprise to see a considerable number of loyal fans from the Italian de Pachmann Societies waiting to hear Simon's comments at the recital on Saturday. He would be wise to avoid controversy, such as references to the pianist's frequent failure to respect the dynamics of many composers, even of Chopin, his favourite. A certain amount of *tempo rubato* was usually tolerable, but passion and precision were the essential elements in any recital. Charles was curious to hear how the blind Polish pianist would approach Chopin. She came with a reputation for being a great artist.

He had become aware that the tub water was decidedly cooler, and a sense of weariness had settled into his consciousness. With some effort Charles emerged from his warm environment, found a bath towel and was soon debating whether he should shave now or after his nap. The nap was given priority but he conceded to hastily unpack one of his suitcases and hang up a suit for dinner. Evening shadows were already obvious as he climbed under the covers and fell quickly asleep.

Charles dreamed the Italian train was impossibly late because of a serious derailment just outside Milan. Shaken by the derailment, he had taken a long time to find Simon, and because of this delay there was serious concern and anxiety about missing his turn at the podium at the congress on Tuesday. Moreover, Charles' manuscript on obsessive-compulsive disorders, which he had been reviewing before the derailment, had disappeared and he was frustrated that the only extra copy, which he had packed in his suitcase, was nowhere to be found. Why were so many Italian police wandering through his bedroom and annoying Simon with questions about the missing de Pachmann manuscript? It was really none of their business. He was about to ask the police to leave, but he could hear a telephone ringing somewhere in the room. He set off to look for it and was surprised to find himself awake and reaching for the bedside phone.

His voice was croaky as he answered, "hello?"

"Hello Charles, this is Lisa."

He could never have mistaken the voice—her Norwegian accent. "I'm here in London. You sound sleepy. I finally found the hotel telephone number you gave me and decided to call."

Struggling to wake up, Charles responded; "Yes, I was asleep and you did wake me but I don't mind at all. It is nice to hear from you. What happened to our date in London? You didn't call and you missed the train."

"I'm sorry about that. I was asked to stay with the ship, so I didn't even get back to London after we parted. The alternate wireless operator was not coping well and head office wanted me to stay. I did not call because I forgot the name of your London hotel. I should have written it down; my memory has always been bad. It would have been wonderful spending the time with you in Rome. We will have to think of another time. When are you booked to return to Halifax and how is Rome?"

"The return reservation is open at the moment. I decided not to book until I saw how much progress I would make on the manuscript I told you about. The pianist I was hoping to interview has died—a week or so ago. That complicates matters, but I will now have more time to spend on my paper, which I will give on Tuesday. Rome is wonderful. The weather is warm and it is sunny. How can I contact you in the future?"

Lisa gave him a telephone number for the Canadian Pacific marine office in Southampton, where messages could be forwarded, and after a few polite remarks they said goodbye and rang off.

As soon as he had hung up—and before he could fathom the significance of the call—the telephone rang again. It was Simon.

"Hello Charles. You did ask me to call if I had news. With the help of the concierge here I have spoken to Agnieszka and Alexei. They are in a nearby hotel, the St. Regis Grand and are prepared to join us for dinner. Are you interested?"

"Of course, but I have been sleeping and this all takes time to sink in. Let me call you back after I have shaved and dressed. It should not take more than fifteen minutes."

"Your telephone line was busy when I tried a few minutes ago," Simon noted. "Were you talking to Pallottelli?"

"No, Lisa Johanson called me. She found it impossible to get away from the ship and didn't come to London. I feel now that it is all water under the bridge. I'll call you back after I get dressed."

CHAPTER SIX

"Fososa facies muta commendation est."
(A pleasing countenance is a silent recommendation)

When Charles first heard Ernest Willett—the blind musician who had shared the stage with de Pachmann in Toronto in 1891—he had been impressed with his apparent ability to play from memory, without being able to see the strings of his instrument. Years later, in medical school, he had known a senior student, an excellent amateur pianist, who frequently practiced in the dark. This fellow could commonly be heard playing Bach, his favourite composer, on the piano in the hospital auditorium—the room in complete darkness. Charles' clinical experience in neurology and psychiatry had made him realize that people who were totally blind from birth did not always feel a sense of being in darkness. They had never seen light, and had never had visual dreams for the same reason.

On the evening of their arrival, Simon had found Agnieszka and her brother at the nearby St. Regis Grand Hotel. They had agreed to meet at a nearby hotel dining room for dinner. Simon had been able to book a vacant table for four, and Charles was soon introduced to Agnieszka and her brother, Alexei; both had arrived a few minutes earlier and were waiting in the hotel reception area. She and her brother shook hands all around. She was tall and wore thick dark glasses. She moved with care to the table with the help of her brother, who was almost her height. Charles was surprised to see how pale she looked in the dim light. If she were wearing makeup it was not obvious in the somewhat dark restaurant, and he concluded she did not need to, as she was indeed very attractive. Simon had said so earlier. Her closely-cut dark brown hair was swept well back from her face, and she was wearing a plain low-cut black dress.

She had accepted his hand with enthusiasm and with a strong warm grip. Simon had not mentioned her age but she looked about thirty. Alexei, who had brown hair, was the quieter of the two and although both spoke good English, he had been content to allow his sister to monopolize the evening's conversation. He had a full beard similar to Simon's. Agnieszka was curious to hear about their train travel from London, and spent the first ten minutes enquiring about Simon's health: Were his headaches better? How was his weak leg? Was he still enjoying his work? She enquired about his editor, Nigel Billinghurst. She wanted to hear about Canada, the Atlantic crossing, and the winter weather, which she had heard was not unlike the climate in Poland.

Obviously proud of her fluency in English, Agnieszka told them she had learnt it from her mother, who had been educated at a school for girls in Bristol. She seemed keen to talk about de Pachmann, whose death, she said, had left her feeling very sad. "After I heard the news I decided to dedicate my Sunday afternoon recital to his memory. Before we left Poland we had heard his health had been fading, but we did not expect to hear that he had died."

She told them about her program for the recital of Chopin music on Sunday afternoon. The waiter, meanwhile, had arrived and was suggesting that veal was this evening's popular menu item, and veal scallopini was the dish he recommended for all. It seemed to suit everyone's taste. A bottle of Chianti was consumed while they sampled *antipastie*, and waited for their main course. A second bottle of wine was soon ordered. Agnieszka was seated between Charles and Alexei, and continued to be talkative as they ate. She commented on her poor vision and was not at all reluctant to talk about it—how being almost totally blind influenced her piano playing. Simon mentioned the subject of blind musicians, troubadours and their music, so she began to tell them about her memories of blind musicians she had seen while growing up in Poland. "When we were teenagers it was common to have blind musicians visiting from Ukraine—singing and playing the *bandura*, a stringed instrument from their country. It looks and sounds somewhere between a lute and a harp."

"I remember them very well too," added Alexei, nodding as he sipped his wine. Simon wanted to know the type of songs they sang.

"Songs of various kinds," she replied, "often with religious or moral themes, especially during Lent. I did not know the words but their music was always an inspiration to me. Perhaps it was because I could not see them in detail. Have you noticed how blind people are portrayed in paintings? There is a famous one by Brueghel hanging in a gallery in Basel. Alexei will remember it because we saw it a few years ago. It is called *Die Blinden* or *The Blind Men*. Some doctor in Poland claimed a few years ago that the men all had different types of blindness and he claimed he could identify the cause in six of the seven men—all except the one who has fallen into the ditch. If you have seen it you will remember that man's face and eyes are not visible in the painting. I did not notice that myself, but Alexei described it to me at the time."

"I remember seeing a picture of the Brueghel you describe, somewhere in a book," said Charles, "but I have never tried to identify the causes of blindness in every one of the men. I am sure I couldn't. I suspect you have not seen the painting by Domenico Fiasella called *Christ Healing the Blind*. I saw it several years ago in the Ringling Museum of Art in Sarasota, Florida."

"None of us has been to America except you," added Simon, "but tell us about it."

"I saw it once on a visit to Florida. I was told that an Italian man named Fiasella painted it sometime in the 17th Century. Ringling must have acquired it in his travels, perhaps in Italy. The interesting point is that the young man whose sight is being restored is a violinist—no less!"

"I didn't know that Christ had healed a blind musician," said Agnieszka.

"I am not an expert on *Bible* lore," Charles replied, "but there are a few blind people whom the *New Testament* says were cured by Jesus. In *Matthew* there is a story of two blind men being healed, but it doesn't say either was a violinist. In the painting I saw in Florida, one of the two men was certainly blind—the one whose violin was nearby. The *Bible* also mentions a blind beggar who was cured by Jesus. Bach wrote a beautiful cantata about that story. In that cantata, I think it is called *You, True God and Son of David,* Bach emphasizes how Jesus actively sought the sick and handicapped and healed them, but the blind person who was cured was not likely the blind violinist in the painting."

"But you cannot be sure!" interjected Agnieszka. "In the past, blind musicians were often forced to beg for money in the streets. My mother told me she had seen a 18th Century French print of a Paris street scene in which a crowd of onlookers were ridiculing the performance of a group of blind musicians who were dressed in grotesque clothing, dunce caps and donkey's ears. During antiquity the blind were regarded as an economic liability, and treated with utmost scorn. Begging on the streets became their traditional form of livelihood. Some but not all became wards of the church. Here we are this evening eating in a dining room in Rome, a city where not many years ago there was no official state aid for the blind.

"There is another painting that I remember in Florence," said Agnieszka, who seemed to be fixed on the topic of paintings of blind musicians, "It is by a 16th Century painter, Barocci, who once lived here in Rome. It is sometimes referred to as *The Painting of the Blind Man,* and he happens to be playing a hurdy-gurdy. I was not able to see all the details. Blind musicians were obviously a popular theme for some painters."

"Agnieszka, you must have read about the blind pianist for whom Mozart wrote a piano concerto?" commented Simon. "She seems to have been unusually talented, having learnt some sixty piano concertos despite her handicap."

"When I was a teenager she was my idol, and so was Thérèse Adèle Husson, who was a great French writer—also blind. That pianist friend of Mozart was Maria Theresa von Paradis. She lost her sight at age three. I have no idea if the doctors then knew why she became blind at such a very young age, but she came under the spell of Dr. Anton Mesmer, who tried to correct her vision with his magnet treatments but did not succeed."

"I think she was also a composer and organist. Was she not?" asked Simon. "Did she also devise a system for notation of her compositions involving a peg board?"

"She did," answered Agnieszka, "she also met Valentin Hävy when she lived in Paris and discussed his ideas for a system by which the blind could read. He was the one who established the first school for the blind in Paris—in 1785, I think it was."

The main course had been finished, and a tray of cheese and fruit had arrived. The wine had seemed to help everyone relax and stimulated conversation. It seemed to Charles that they had known each other for years. He was beginning to feel weary despite his afternoon nap. The wine had also made him sleepy. After a cup of coffee, he suggested that he was prepared to walk back to his hotel, but said he would like to continue their conversation the next day. He rose, said goodbye and excused himself.

Looking his way, Agnieszka spoke up, "I have a question before you go Doctor Flemming. Would you and Simon be interested in attending an organ recital with me on Sunday morning? Alexei cannot go because he has to complete arrangements at the legation for my recitals. The organ recital is in a local city church and will be given by a blind organist from Warsaw who received his training in Paris. I have never met him, but I heard about this before leaving home. I was told by one of my music teachers that he will be playing an unusual program — only the work of composers who were blind. They include compositions by Stanley, the English composer, as well as Langlais, Vierne and Augustin Barié from France. Barié was a student of Vierne. We can discuss the details later. Meanwhile, if you would like to meet us in my suite at our hotel tomorrow after breakfast I will play you some of my program that I have chosen for Sunday afternoon's recital."

She seemed delighted when Simon and Charles both expressed interest in the organ recital and the next day's meeting. After making his excuses, and shaking hands all around, Charles again said goodbye. On the way to the door, he saw the waiter and asked the cost of the meal. He said he wanted to pay for everyone and discreetly did so before departing for his hotel.

Before heading to his room he asked again at the reception desk about the missing manuscript. "No, the missing document has not turned up, but you should check again in the morning," was the response from the receptionist.

*** *** *** ***

On the next morning, Saturday, they met as arranged at Agnieszka's hotel to listen to her play some selections from her recital programme. Alexei had left them while he continued to make her recital arrangements and to meet the Polish ambassador to discuss the Sunday evening recital at the legation. So the three spent time discussing Chopin, his taste in pianos, de Pachmann's performance style and how musicians coped with blindness. The hotel had arranged for a Pleyel piano to be brought to Agnieszka's suite, which meant that she could play as they talked. She admitted from the beginning that she was prepared to have the two men carry the conversation. She said she would play parts of her program when it seemed appropriate. Charles had noted the previous evening that her hands were not large, but her fingers were long. This morning she was looking very casual, wearing dark glasses, a plain black skirt and red sweater.

She looked at Charles. "All of us appreciated the fact that you paid for the dinner last. Thank you very much. It was very generous."

"Yes, I agree," added Simon, "I should have remembered."

Agnieszka wanted to talk about Chopin. "I have loved his piano music from the days that my father allowed me to expand his assigned exercises to some of Chopin's earlier and easier pieces," she said. "From the beginning, I was not allowed to take textual liberties with Chopin's score. Some of the local Polish professional pianists who played the composer's music were often criticized for addition of cadenzas, octaves and thickened chords, changes in tempo and so on, although some teachers I know tolerated it. I have to admit it was tempting to change some melodies and harmonies. When I heard de Pachmann play Chopin in concert, which was only twice, and when listening to his recordings, I sometimes felt he used excessive *rubato* and softened Chopin's dynamic marking to fit his own taste. He liked to play Chopin in a free style, and he justified it by emphasizing that Chopin himself did the same. Listening to his recordings again recently confirms what I have been saying. He may have been uncomfortable in the recording studio. I don't know. James Huneker, the American critic, was convinced on hearing him play in private, that his playing was better in that setting than when he was on stage. He may have suffered excessively from that common malady—stage fright. If he did, he was not alone.

"The French music critic Ernest Legouvé wrote in the *Gazette Musicale* of the time that Chopin reserved his great genius for an audience of five or six. Of the few recordings I have made, I felt very little different when playing in the studio than in front of an audience. When it comes to the score, I try to be more committed to the markings but you may know there has been considerable editing of some Chopin editions. I do not believe that pianists should always put in what they think the composer, especially one like Chopin, left out. Of course I have always had considerable difficulty seeing any scores with facility and now it is utterly hopeless. So I rely on my memory and consistent practice."

"I sensed last night that you feel very comfortable discussing your blindness," said Charles. "Some have spoken about an inner vision that the blind person develops or perhaps has from the beginning, especially if they have been blind since birth. As you no longer see well, are you better able to concentrate on your music, with less distraction from visual images?"

Agnieszka remained silent for some time before replying. "I am sure I have inner vision, if you mean a special sense or appreciation of not being totally blind. I also think of blindness metaphorically, as being blind—politically or morally. I am not blind to the present political climate in this country for example—it is not what the people would likely choose. But it is probably better than what the Germans are facing. You, in the seeing world, know how much more dependent a blind person can be than you—communicating mainly through conversation and touch—needing help to get around. One adapts of course. I have been told that Beethoven felt that having inner deafness was far worse than deafness itself. He likely could hear and feel the music as he read the score and played the notes by sight, while being totally deaf. It is somewhat different than the experience of a blind person. I was just a child, maybe about five, when my vision began to fail. There is blindness in our family—a condition called retinitis pigmentosa, and there are other family members, including my father, affected like me. I wear shaded glasses in the daytime partly because I react badly to strong light, and I can actually see slightly better but in a blurred and tunnel fashion when there is scanty light. That is why I insist on the least amount of light on stage when I play. I could never use a score. Because I did have vision for a few years, I retain a feeling of space, distance, perspective and colouring in contrast to some of my friends from blind school who were blind from birth. I also dream in colour.

"Blind people often make excellent musicians, as well as piano tuners, because they frequently have a keen ear. There are many examples from earlier times. I mentioned the Ukrainian singers last night. Blind bards and minstrels moved around Europe visiting royal courts commonly playing the harp but also the violin and shepherds' pipe. There was a famous Irish harpist, O'Carolan, whom you must have heard of, who used to say, "my eyes have been transplanted to my ears." I understand what he meant. My father made a living and paid for my piano lessons as a piano tuner for years despite being virtually blind himself since childhood. For some reason, the blind keyboard musician is often drawn to the organ and there are lots of examples, especially among graduates of the Paris schools. The young man from Warsaw we will be hearing tomorrow morning is a good example. I have never played the organ but I would like to try some day. Some schools of music for blind people concentrate in their keyboard teaching on mastery of the organ and also now teach the Braille musical alphabet."

Charles was curious to hear more about the cause of her blindness, how the diagnosis had been confirmed and what prognosis had been suggested, but Simon changed the subject by interjecting with a question about musical style.

"What do you think of pianists who break the musical line by not playing the two hands together?" he asked, "de Pachmann was guilty of that in concert and in his recordings too."

"It is a device which others as well as de Pachmann have used. I have tried it on occasions and sometimes, if it is subtle, it can sound very attractive. Let me give you an example."

She played a brief passage from the Chopin E flat Nocturne, exaggerating with breaking of the hands, so that both Simon and Charles simultaneously broke into laughter. "I loved that," said Charles, applauding, "now I know why the audiences were approving."

"But also, I hope, why the critics disapproved!" added Simon.

"I know that today's critics are not tolerant of the habit, so I always keep the hands together when playing in public—and of course when critics are listening," Agnieszka concluded, with a smile. "Now if you will be patient, I should play some of the programme that I have chosen for tomorrow's recital. It is almost all Chopin. If you wish to stay I don't mind. You can leave and come back later if you wish."

They both decided to stay and listen. They seemed equally enthralled by the atmosphere and by her poise. Between selections she paused to ask for comments. Simon avoided commenting on her choice of music or interpretations, but was curious about her choice of piano for the recitals.

"I like the Pleyel piano best," she replied, "which is why I have chosen it for this tour. Of course this one is of a different style from the pianoforte that Chopin used. I know he also used the French Erard, but his favourite was the Pleyel because it seemed to produce the exact variability in volume that he wanted. However, it did not have the double escapement mechanism of the later Erards, and did not produce the volume needed for large venues. Chopin thought of the Pleyel pianos as having a light and elastic action. He did not wish to play loudly and he was often criticized for this. As he spent most of his life in Paris, the Pleyel Company must have doted on him and catered to his every taste. Even when he was vacationing, and also composing, in Majorca he requested an upright Pleyel, although it arrived late—just before they were ready to return to Paris. I believe he owned three Pleyels in his lifetime."

"De Pachmann used numerous pianos and endorsed just as many too, sometimes to his embarrassment because his tours to North America were always under the sponsorship of a major piano maker, such as Chickering, Baldwin and Steinway," added Charles. "He did not always use care in endorsing pianos of rival companies even when he was under contract with another."

They sensed that Agnieszka was more interested in practice, so after saying goodbye, her audience of two quietly left the room, and decided they should seek lunch downstairs in a café off the hotel lobby. They invited her to join them, but she was not in the mood to eat.

"I feel I should wander down to the convention hotel after lunch to investigate the registration for my meeting, and to look at local arrangements," said Charles, as they settled in the hotel café over a glass of wine and a light lunch. This time they decided to try a local regional house wine, which was very acceptable. "I seem to have lost sight of the fact that the main reason for my coming to Rome was to attend a psychoanalysis convention and to give my paper. Here we have spent the morning listening to wonderful music, but I do have to organize myself for this presentation on Tuesday."

The convention location was about a kilometre away, but Charles decided he would walk. The weather was balmy, and he discovered Simon was also interested in coming along. With a city street map, they were able to reach the Michelangelo Hotel, only once having to ask directions from a policeman who was able to point out the locale on the map. The meeting and presentations were to begin on Monday. Thumbing through the conference program he noted his paper was slated for presentation on Tuesday morning, in the section devoted to chronic anxiety states, and was to be chaired by a Professor Stapleton from London, whom he had never met. Simon had earlier decided to leave and continue his own exploration of the nearby city sites. He would find his way back alone. Seeing no one he recognized amongst the attendees, Charles soon returned to his hotel taking another route.

On arriving back he enquired again at the desk for the de Pachmann manuscript. No one had seen it, so it was suggested by the hotel manager that he call the local contact to explain the situation, if he could recall the name. Despite a search in his luggage he could find only a number for the de Pachmann Villa. Returning to the reception desk, Mr. Berretta was soon on the telephone speaking to the person who answered. There was a brief conversation, and after hanging up Mr. Beretta explained that he had spoken to someone who may have been the cook, and who reported that her employer had gone out and was not expected back until late in the evening. He said he would call back.

Charles had earlier discussed with Simon his plans for the remainder of the day. His new friend had not seemed eager to explore the city further, or have another late night. He was relieved, as he knew it would give him an opportunity to work on his talk.

Settling in a comfortable chair, he soon found the excitement of Rome was greater than that generated by reviewing the manuscript his secretary had typed so carefully. The references to Sigmund Freud in his discussion had awaked a memory of Freud's attraction to the statue of Moses at the Church of Saint Peter in Chains. He had heard about it when he was in Rome in 1926. Freud had visited Rome seven times, and loved the city. He was especially attracted to the statue of Moses, which had been crafted by the thirty-year-old Michelangelo on commission from the then Pope, Julius II. Charles felt a strong urge to visit the church again. He decided to forget the editing of his paper.

Descending the stairs to the lobby, Charles made some enquiries from the clerk about directions, and was advised that it was within walking distance. On emerging from the hotel he saw a taxi idling nearby, and quickly changed his plans. He would not get lost taking a taxi, and would have more time to spend at the church as well as having time after to see the Coliseum, which he was told was not far from there.

The Church of Saint Peter in Chains was made more impressive by the massive statue of Moses, which dominated the façade. Freud was fascinated by the powerful figure, the serious-looking face with a flowing beard, and had speculated on why Michelangelo had given the statue what appeared to be horns. Somewhere Charles had read that Michelangelo—in adding horns—had misinterpreted a biblical description of Moses. He would have to look that up some time. He decided to return to the statue later for a more careful scrutiny. He was told by a tour director moving about inside the church that the church was 1,500 years old, and contained the chains that had bound Saint Peter while he was imprisoned by the Romans in Jerusalem prior to his persecution. Charles could see there were many people in a long queue to see the chains, so he decide not to wait, but to move outside again where he found his way back to Moses, flanked by Leah and Rachel, the two wives of Jacob. He was aware that the statue had fascinated Freud who had spend hours visiting and viewing it whenever he was in the city, but as he viewed it himself today, he was unable to fathom the reason. Moses was depicted while seated and holding the tablets of the law under his right arm. The character of the biblical Moses had obvious importance for Freud as a Jew, despite what seemed common knowledge that Freud himself was not religious. In fact, Freud had made it obvious in his writings that he was not sympathetic to any religions. He saw Rome and the Vatican as the centre of the Roman Catholic Church, as well as being an archaeological treasure. It was the latter aspect that attracted him more. Yet it was interesting that Freud had written extensively on the subject of Moses. Charles decided he would have to look for English translations of these writings when he returned to Canada.

After another hour of wandering through the church and noting it was close to six o'clock, he decided to walk back to his hotel. He knew it was not far. Emerging from the church he took a few minutes to orientate himself—it was beginning to get dark. His walk back was enjoyable as he could see the sights in greater detail than earlier in the taxi.

He had made no firm plans for the evening and after a brief wash in his room he decided to have a light meal downstairs in the dining room. There was only light dining activity and the waiter had no difficulty finding a table where he could eat alone. A course of spaghetti with meatballs and a glass of red wine was enough to satisfy his appetite. A cup of coffee was just right to finish the meal and he returned to his room. He retrieved his manuscript for the meeting on Tuesday and after making some minor changes decided to turn in early. He fell asleep quickly thankful for a comfortable bed without the monotonous rocking of a sleeping car on railway tracks.

CHAPTER SEVEN

"Dies dominicus"
(The Lord's day)

Charles and Simon had arranged to meet Agnieszka on Sunday at 9 a.m. at her hotel, and to go to the Church of Mary Magdalena together. Charles had awakened early, taken a long bath, shaved, and enjoyed a slow casual breakfast. He was missing his morning newspaper. In fact the realization had only just dawned on him as he sat waiting in the dining room for his breakfast to arrive; he had not seen a newspaper in English since the British ones he read on the train. He seemed to have lost interest in the depressing news of the world, and Canada too seemed a very distant place. It was a beautiful sunny day as he set out to walk.

The sidewalks were already crowded with well-dressed Italians and children of all ages probably heading to Mass. When he arrived at the St. Regis Grand, he spotted Agnieszka seated alone in the lobby. Rather than approach her immediately, he paused deliberately just inside the main door, and took stock of this interesting and attractive blind pianist from a distance. She was seated alone, again wearing dark glasses, a white cotton dress, extending just below her knees, and matching hat with yellow trim. Her hair was swept back as he remembered from the night before. He noticed for the first time her attractive legs. She recognized his voice as he approached and sat down beside her. "I recognized your voice," she said. "Isn't this a wonderful Sunday morning?" He was curious to hear how she had spent the night.

"I practiced for several hours, and Alexei and I went to the dining room here for dinner. We had some wine, which made me sleepy, and I was in bed by eleven o'clock. The wine helped me sleep. I was awake early this morning and found the sunshine was so glorious this morning that I had trouble finding my way about the room. That happens when the sun is bright."

"Any word from Simon, or has he arrived?" asked Charles, looking about the lobby.

"He left a message for me. He will not be coming," Agnieszka said. "He says he is sorry to have to miss the recital, but he had one of his nasty headaches last night and he hasn't recovered! So we do not need to linger for him. But I think we do have some time before the recital—it does not start until ten. Why don't we have a coffee in the dining room? I have not had breakfast have you?"

He pretended he hadn't either. The dining room of the St. Regis was busy with breakfast, but the headwaiter recognized her and offered them a table overlooking the gardens. Charles held Agnieszka's arm as he followed the waiter, navigating their way through a line of tables.

"I am glad we have some time to talk. I feel I do not know much about your life in Canada, and you know very little about me. I have brought some photographs to show you and Simon. They go back many years. I hope you will not be bored. Some of my friends overdo this, I know."

Charles reassured her that he would love to see the pictures, and would not be bored. He saw she had brought along a small cardboard box of photos, which included many of her as a child—with her brother and her parents—playing at the beach, one of her seated at a piano in their home in Kraków. She would be about ten years old in that one, he thought. She was holding each photo up to her right eye as she attempted to identify each. She showed him a photo of her teachers. "This one is Madame Maria Zimmerman," she said as she pointed out a rather grim-looking middle-aged woman seated at her piano.

"She looks mean," he commented. She smiled at his remark. "She was my teacher at the academy of music. She was not as severe as she looks. Here is a picture of the main entrance to the school for the blind. This was taken about the time of my debut." She showed him pictures of her church in Kraków, a picture of her Pleyel piano, a birthday present from her parents when she was fifteen.

"There are a few more upstairs but that gives you a flavour of what my family looks like. People say I look like my father. What do you think?" Before he could respond, she continued, "you will notice there are no pictures of male friends. I had only one serious relationship, which did not last. I was a teenager and of course by then was almost totally blind. We were never close and my friend found my handicap too much to bear so we decided not to continue the relationship. He was not musically inclined and was bored when I played Chopin. We remained good friends for years. My life has been devoted almost totally to music."

A waiter had returned, and took their order of a black coffee, a double-cream coffee and toast. Charles was seeing Agnieszka in a new light. She was not as pale as he had thought last night. The bright sunlight had transformed her complexion, and she looked much more at ease. Although she was wearing a hat, it did not put her face in the shadows. He sensed she was eager to continue the story of her life.

"I feel I was left out of the important things over the years. Here I am thirty-two years old and what do I have? All I have is a competitive and sometimes precarious career in music. I would love to have had a stable and loving relationship with a man. Alexei's life has been very different, as you can imagine. He has had lots of female friends. He writes for a living, and is now working on a book. At times he has imposed his will on me — sometimes more so than my father. I think Alexei has deliberately diverted men away from my life, especially if they show too much interest. He has said many times that my being blind makes me vulnerable to men, but I have never felt that way. My father has given me the same impression—'too many obstacles in the way of a stable permanent relationship,' is how he expressed it."

The coffees had arrived with the order of toast and preserves, which Charles pointed out to her. He was curious about Alexei's book. He had not heard of it before now, and he wondered if Simon knew about it. He helped Agnieszka butter her toast, and he noticed she gazed intently at his face while he did. The dining room conversation was unusually hushed as if voices were being kept low.

"I want you to continue," said Charles in a whisper, as he leaned across the table. "I am a good listener. Keep your voice lower if you want to maintain some privacy in this dining room. You may have noticed the tables are very close together."

Agnieszka laughed and thanked him for his advice and said she would try to speak softly.

"I feel a need to talk frankly about my life Charles. I hope you will understand." Charles nodded consent. "Of course I do, and I am so very pleased you now feel free to call me Charles. But I do not want to become your professional adviser, your psychiatrist. I have taken a vacation partly to forget my work. I simply want to be your friend."

"That makes me feel better. I have never spoken to a psychiatrist or a psychologist before. But didn't you say last night you were giving a paper next week?"

"That is true," he replied, "and I still have some work to do on it."

"I am sure it will be a great talk," she said as she resumed her story. "I must tell you that in my younger years, one of my teachers fell for me and wanted to take me to bed—I mean, to seduce me. I managed to put him off and soon changed teachers at the school. I certainly felt sexual urges in those days, and still do. They are probably no different than the feeling of other women my age. You may be surprised to hear me say that I have never kissed a man other than my father and Alexei, and with Alexei only when we were children. I have never seen a naked man—not just because of being blind, but because it has just never happened. So you can guess correctly that I have never slept with a man and am still a virgin." She paused and smiled. "I have to tell you that I have always been curious about a man's erection and how it happens." They both laughed at her last comment. Some customers at the next table glanced in their direction, and he noticed they were smiling.

He felt he had to say, "forgive me for laughing, but I see others understand English and have found it amusing as well."

"I will speak more quietly. I have not talked about sexual matters with anyone else, but you are easy to talk to. I wish I could have children, although I know the blindness in my family can be passed on. Doctors in Poland have discouraged me from having a family and I understand." She paused to collect her thoughts and sip her coffee. "Last night I mentioned Adèle Husson, the writer. She wrote a book called *Reflections: The Life and Writings of a Young Blind Woman in Post -Revolutionary France,* that I have not read of course, but one of our teachers at school told us that her view on marriage was that blind women should never marry. That was based on her own experience of marriage to a man who was also blind. She wrote about how blind persons walk, their joy of hearing, how they respond to a sweet voice, how they eat and the importance of touch. That is why I rely so much on touch."

"When Alexei and I first met Simon in Vienna last year, I had thought he might be attracted to me. After all, we did have music in common, and he was always very interested in my playing, came to my recital, wrote a review for his magazine and sat during the recording sessions. We talked about physical attraction and love on one occasion, but although we became friends we never had a sexual relationship. He admitted to me that since his accident during the war he had lost all sexual desire, and doubted he would ever have a permanent relationship. He told me frankly that he knew he wasn't the one for me. I wondered if he was able to have sexual relations. I think he may also have sensed that Alexei would not approve of any advances towards me."

After a pause she added, "I never thought I would like a man who wore a beard. Simon had one last year and still does. The headmaster of my school in Kraków had a long bushy beard like Simon's which did not appeal to me."

Charles listened in silence. He would have to think twice about growing a beard. He felt privileged to be hearing her tell her personal secrets. He had not given a thought to Simon's accident having an impact on his libido, or rendering him unable to have an erection. He was now finding Agnieszka to be a surprisingly seductive woman. There was a strong sense of communication between them that he could feel across the table. He felt ashamed of a sudden temptation to take her hand and to hold it fast as she talked, but he suppressed the urge. What would she think? It was the first time they had been alone. She had been warned most of her life to be cautious with men. Was he any different from the others? But she did say how important touch was for a blind person.

"I sense you are a good listener. You likely spend hours in your office in Toronto listening to stories like mine. Isn't that what you do?"

Charles could not suppress a laugh, and then suddenly felt a sense of embarrassment, because Agnieszka did exactly as he had wanted to do himself a moment before. Had she read his mind? She reached blindly across the table and whispered, "will you let me hold your hand?" She paused as if waiting for his answer, and she seemed to ponder what she was to say next. "Because I cannot see you well across the table, I feel a need to be physically connected to you—to touch you when we talk about these things. I also hope you might want to hold me in your arms for a moment after we leave the dining room."

"Of course you can hold my hand," he quickly replied, as he reached across the table for hers. "Sometimes my patients ask for a hug before they leave my office. I usually comply, and have never felt threatened by it." He deliberately avoided the issue of holding her outside in the lobby.

Her hands were warm, and he could feel her strength as she gave him a long squeeze and held on. Charles was conscious that he was fixed in her gaze, but to her he would be little more than a blur. He felt flushed, but he was sure she could not notice. He was sure he heard her say something that sounded like, "Sometimes I feel I would prefer a strong permanent relationship with a man than my career in music."

He wasn't expecting that comment and was momentarily lost for words. He tried not to disagree with her and had thought of saying: "you should not say that! You are a great artist, talented, well-educated, and you have a promising future ahead. You are also very beautiful!" Instead he resisted, released his left hand and glanced at his watch. Agnieszka was still firmly holding his right hand

and seemed deep in thought. "We should find a taxi and go to the church," he suggested. She seemed reluctant to remove her grip, but did and began to rise from her seat. "I'll pay the bill," he said and left two lira notes beside his coffee cup. He held her arm as he guided her carefully toward the lobby. "Thank you for the coffee and toast," she whispered. "We have twenty minutes to get to the church," he told her. "You should leave your photographs at the reception desk. I will ask the concierge to find a taxi." He was promised that a taxi would be ordered immediately.

Agnieszka reached for his hand again as he returned from the desk. "Before the cab comes I want you to hold me," she whispered. He turned toward her, and before he could object they both embraced. He caught a faint scent of perfume as their faces touched. He wondered if she also wanted to kiss, as her embrace was very strong. He felt her breasts squeezing against his chest, and her thighs against his. Should they kiss? He hardly knew her and here they were standing in full view of the reception area. What would the staff think?

Later in the day, when he was alone, he could not understand why he had said, "I want to kiss you too," but he heard himself say it, as he guided her toward the lobby door. Did he know for sure how she felt? The doorman was nowhere to be seen. He noticed she had removed her glasses. They embraced again and he felt her warm lips against his cheek—it seemed for ages, but he had not been counting the seconds. He returned her kiss and was reluctant to let her go as he felt a warm, almost electrical, physical charge mixed with a hint of guilt. Now he was wishing they were not going to this organ recital after all. His thoughts were overwhelmingly on an organ other than the church variety, and he wondered if she felt it. He could not believe he heard himself ask, "do you still want to go to this organ recital?"

Agnieszka laughed as he finally, slowly released her. "The recital was my idea. We cannot hear an organ recital very day, even in Rome but we can kiss and hold one another anytime, can't we?" she whispered.

He was amazed at her frankness as he watched her staring upward toward his face, a smile spreading across hers. He noticed for the first time that her eyes were grey. He felt he could not respond to her comment, but he felt a wave of relief that she had made the right decision not to change their plans.

In the taxi he again offered his hand, which she accepted with some intensity. He kissed her several times on her cheek as she leaned back on the car seat. "You made the right choice. That was wonderful back there," he whispered. She was staring ahead and he heard her respond, "It was wonderful for me also. But I am sorry to have monopolized the conversation this morning, and I had very much wanted you to tell me about you and your life. Simon told me you were single again since your wife died. I was sorry to hear about that. It must have been a very sad event."

Charles was not prepared for this. He knew she would not have seen the tears well up in his eyes with the memory of Anne, and he hoped his voice did not betray him as it often did when this happened. He remained silent for a few moments and Agnieszka sensed his difficulty. She squeezed his hand. "Is it still very upsetting?" she asked, as his silence registered. "Yes, it can be," he replied, "but your question was appropriate and not in any way wrong. I will explain to you later when we are alone again. My life is not all a sad affair." She leaned over toward him and returned a kiss on his cheek.

He needed to change the focus of their conversation away from himself. "In English we have more than one meaning for organ. You may know that. A friend of mine told me an amusing story about an organist from Cardiff who was visiting London on business some time ago."

She looked toward him and smiled. "Yes, I know the two organs. Go ahead; tell me. I want to hear the story."

Anxious to break the awkwardness, Charles launched into the tale. "This organist needed to buy a spare part for the pipe organ in his church in Wales, and had been searching for a certain pipe organ work shop in central London without success. Finally, he decided to approach a man waiting at a bus stop. "Do you know Hardy's Organ Works?" he asked. The man looked puzzled, paused and replied, "I'm glad to know that and so does mine!"

Agnieszka broke into a giggle but regained her voice. "That's very funny. In Polish we do not have the same puns as you do in English. Did he eventually find the organ shop?"

"I hope so." Charles felt the relaxation returning.

She quickly added. "Are we almost there? This must be it." He realized she was right. The taxi had entered the Piazza della Magdalena but he knew she could not possibly see the approaching façade of the Church of Santa Maria Magdalena even as the taxi had now come to a complete stop. The fare was reasonable, and he added a tip, as he felt in a generous mood this morning. He felt an excitement that had been missing for weeks, as far back as the nights on the liner *Montrose*. Holding Agnieszka's arm tightly, he helped her climb the wide steps. "There are just a few more steps," he said, as they had almost reached the door. A cornerstone near the entrance read MDCLXIX. The church façade looked typically baroque with the entrance flanked by two large statues of unidentifiable males. An elderly woman, dressed in black, was selling tickets and passing out programs in the small entry area. She greeted them with "*buono mattina*" before he paid the admission fee. The program said the recital was sponsored by the Society of Blind Musicians of Rome. He noticed Agnieszka make the sign of the cross as she passed through the door.

"Let us walk to the front and examine the alter details," he suggested, as he led her by the arm. The air was cool, and smelled faintly of incense. He noticed there were still many unoccupied seats and the recital was not due to start for five minutes. Two sculptures of Mary Magdalene both by Pieta Bracci dominated both sides of the altar. One was of Mary Magdalene arriving at the empty tomb and the other was of her meeting the risen Christ in the garden. The church walls were decorated with many paintings with religious themes. They paused underneath a portrait of a seated young woman with bare breasts holding a cross. He leaned forward and read the inscription. "This is a painting of Mary Magdalene which is on loan from the Pinacotheca in Bologna. The inscription says

'Painted by Elisabetta Sirani of Bologna. 1638-1665,' so she had a short life. She must have died when she was ... twenty seven." He felt her squeeze his arm more tightly as they resumed their slow walk towards the front of the church. "How sad that Elisabetta Sirani had a regrettably short life!" she whispered as they found an empty pew.

"Please read me the program," Agnieszka whispered, 'I am interested in the Barié piece. I am looking forward to it. My friend told me that Barié was blind and died of a heart ailment at thirty-one—how sad. I think there is a difference in one's sense of loss when a young person is taken than when an old person like de Pachmann dies."

"They say it is even worse to lose a child," replied Charles in agreement. "So many children have died in infancy in the last century. Think of the Mozarts and also Mahler's parents. They lost a lot of children."

"Yes, I had heard that." she replied.

The program was printed in Italian. "I can read you only the highlights," he said as he scanned the program. "Leszek Janinski was born in Warsaw of course. He studied in Paris at the *Institute Nationale des Jeunes Aveugles* before returning to Warsaw last year. He is twenty-eight years old. He will be playing Augustin Barié's Toccato, op.7, No.3. It says here Barié was born in Paris in 1883 and died there in 1915, so he was only thirty-two. I have not heard this piece before, have you?" She had not either.

"The Barié piece is the last but one on the program. The first pieces are by John Stanley, Six Voluntaries, op.5. I think I have heard all ten of them played many years ago in Cardiff. It says here that Stanley was born in 1712, lost his sight at age two but lived to be seventy-four years old. Then there is a Prelude and Fugue by Jean Langlais, which he wrote in 1927. The program says he studied at the *Institution Nationale des Jeunes Aveugles* in Paris—as did Barié—but years later, under Vierne. Vierne's Fantasia for Organ, op.55, in six parts, is the last piece before a brief intermission. He will be ending the recital with his own *Improvisations on a Theme* by Caesar Franck. I think we are in for an enjoyable morning, don't you?"

"I like the program. I have not been to an organ recital for several years. I do not go to church often—I mean to worship. The last time I heard the organ played was in Kraków when we had a visit from a German organist who played an all-Bach program. I learnt some details of Barié from another organist, who said he had met him when studying in Paris. Barié was blind of course. My friend described him as a very tall man and highly intelligent. He was said to have had very large hands, capable of stretching an eleventh! He was extremely good at improvisation, which he learnt when he studied with Vierne."

Charles quickly scanned the notes before him. "Yes, here in the program there is something about his winning a competition for improvisation in 1906."

"I was told he was one of three first-prize winners in a competition," she added. "He died of a brain haemorrhage in August 1915, while on vacation with his new wife. I have a soft spot for him—as you say in English. I have been thinking of how much Simon would have enjoyed this program. Perhaps you should write down some notes on the program and show him when we return."

The church was beginning to fill as the time for the start of the recital approached. Charles wondered if Barié's might have been a case of Marfan's Syndrome, based on the physical description and his early death from a brain haemorrhage. He did not feel he should mention that, as Agnieszka would not be interested in those kinds of details. He was having a problem keeping his mind off the events of the last hour. He was truly surprised at the speed at which their relationship had developed. He worried that it had happened precipitously, and he felt some guilt that he may have taken advantage of her. Agnieszka had talked about her vulnerability, but she had also repudiated it. She was to give a recital in a few hours at the *Academia Filharmonica* and the last thing he wanted was for her to be to be distracted because of him. She had remained silent as he sat ruminating, but she had again sought and found his left hand, and was holding it firmly.

There was a sudden applause beginning from the front as Leszek Janinski was led into the church by a priest, or perhaps a companion. They disappeared briefly behind the altar to reappeared again as Janinski was seated at the organ. His companion also found a place to sit nearby. The organ, Charles had concluded from the Italian program notes, was very old; a tracker style, built in the 18th Century by an Italian builder, named Mascioni.

Janinski was a skilled organist, and the church soon reverberated with the Stanley Voluntaries. He could see that the assistant was helping with the stops, but there was of course no score, and there were no pages to turn. The other selections by Langlais and Vierne were received with generous but discreet applause. A short intermission followed, but they chose to remain in their seats. Agnieszka reassured him she was very relaxed and happy.

"This is what I needed to get my mind off the recital this afternoon. I do not feel nervous. Of course I feel some excitement just before. The Chopin pieces I have chosen to play I know like the palm of my hand. This experience makes me want to try playing the organ when I return to my country. There is a good one in our church, and I am sure the organist would be willing to let me use it. I shall have to go back to playing Bach again. I feel I have neglected him as Chopin has begun to dominate my repertoire."

"You cannot see the organ but the program notes say it is very old. From here it looks old with the pipes well hidden from view," Charles added. "Would you like to meet Janinski after the recital? I can take you up to the front, and ask someone if he might agree to meet another musician from his homeland."

"I would like that very much, but I will not say I am also blind," she replied.

When the audience who had left their seats had begun to return, Charles saw by his watch that it was almost eleven o'clock. They could still be back at the hotel by noon, even if they were to spend time with Janinski. He did not want them to be late because of her afternoon recital. The Barié toccata seemed to be the audience favourite, judging from the applause. It was certainly Agnieszka's. The final Improvisation was his favourite because the composer had allowed himself full vent to demonstrate the organ's range. No encores were forthcoming, and the church was soon empty except for a few folks who seemed to want to sit and ponder, or simply to bow their heads in prayer. He decided to speak to a priest whom he could see moving through the pews, picking up programs that had been left behind. Was Mr. Janinski willing to meet a Polish tourist?

"Yes, I am sure," the priest replied in good English, "let me see if he can meet you now," as he disappeared through a side door. In few minutes he had reappeared with the organist holding his arm. Speaking in Polish, Agnieszka introduced herself and Charles, and carried on an animated conversation. "I have told him how much we enjoyed his playing," she said turning to Charles. "I invited him to my recital this afternoon, but he is booked to leave in the late afternoon. We promised to contact one another in Warsaw when I am there next, which will be in another month. I did not tell him I was blind and he did not say he had heard of me. Now we can go," she added and turned to say good-bye to her new friend—in Polish.

CHAPTER EIGHT

"Credo quod habes et habes"
(Believe you have it and you do)

The return trip to the hotel was delayed somewhat because they were not able to find a nearby taxi, but Charles was able to hail one as they walked together along the main street behind the church. "I will help you up to your room," he said, as they reached the hotel lobby and called for the elevator that was very crowded. They were standing very closely together and he held her hand again. "Can you see if Alexei is back?" she asked, as they left the elevator. "He is down the hall in Room 250." There was no response to his knock so he returned to the door of Suite 258 and she gave him her key. He helped her find her way in. "I know where I am now," she said. "I have memorized the plan of the room. We have a few minutes to spend together don't we?" she asked as she turned to embrace him in the hallway outside the bedroom. They kissed again. "Now I have to visit the washroom," she said suddenly. "It has been ages since we left." He waited to hear the toilet flush as he walked into the adjoining room, and admired the Pleyel piano. He heard her walking toward him. She was in her bare feet.

"Now, give me a minute," he said as he turned to enter the bathroom. Inside he was surprised to see she had dropped her stockings and white underwear in a heap on the floor.

When he returned he was not surprised this time to see she had removed her hat and glasses and had settled on her bed. She was waving for him to join her. "Must you go? Stay a few minutes," he heard her say. His throat felt dry and he wished he had a glass of water. He wanted to slow things down, but he found himself sitting beside her on the bed despite his doubts. He leaned forward and kissed her again.

"I want you to touch me," she whispered. "I have never had a man touch me."

He was aware of his breathing, and despite the stupidity of it he felt he had to say, "you have a recital in a few hours. We will have time together later."

She reached for his right hand and held him in a tight grip. He wondered if she might direct his hand under her dress. Her other searching hand had found his erection as she turned toward him. "And what is this?" she laughed. He could not speak for what seemed like minutes. The best he could say was, "You are a very attractive woman in many ways," as he pulled away, "and I know now that we are of the same mind."

Agnieszka turned back and lay still, with her eyes closed, her arms now above her head. He thought of reaching to touch her breasts but his good judgement prevailed. "Will you be all right now? Do you want me to order you some lunch?"

"Alexei will be here soon and he has arranged for a car to take us to the auditorium. I will be fine. I never eat before a concert. I will look forward to meeting you there at intermission or after."

He bent towards her, whispered, "good bye" and gave her a brief kiss. "I must find Simon. I know you will play well. I'm leaving, but I would rather stay here with you."

The last he heard was, "I wish you would."

*** *** *** ***

Three hours later Charles was seated comfortably in Row A of the *Balcones* in the *Academia Filharmonica Romana* auditorium on *Via Flaminia*, awaiting the start of Agnieszka's recital. He was feeling emotionally exhausted from the morning experience. He had been very tempted to go further, but even touching her briefly seemed wrong. She had removed her panties and stockings for him too. It all seemed too fast. He knew his confusion and guilt would disappear, and he was slowly becoming convinced that there would be another and better time. After lunch he had met Simon, whose headache had finally gone, and they had taken a taxi from his hotel to the hall where they had eventually found the manager, Mr. Tramonti, backstage. Simon decided he would listen to the performance from the wings after his introduction, and would not need a seat. On their way, he had decided to ask Simon about the book that Alexei was writing. Simon could add very little except he knew it was on "some music theme—maybe a biography of a Polish pianist or violinist." Charles had forgotten to ask Agnieszka more about it. He had had too much on his mind over the past few hours.

The printed program notes were in Italian and English. He was pleased to be able to read the details of her life that she had not told him. The notes briefly summarized her career, beginning with early music lessons from her father, an amateur pianist and piano tuner and more lessons later in the local school for the blind beginning in 1905, when she was five years old. She had already lost much of her sight. Her talents were soon apparent, and within a year she had moved on to lessons at the academy of music under Madame Marina Zimmerman. By age ten, she was considered prepared for her local debut, where she played a programme of pieces by Liszt, Chopin, Brahms and the contemporary composer Karol Szymanowski. She included as an encore, one of her own compositions called *Polonaise*. The music critic, writing in the local newspaper, had predicted a successful career. In the years that followed, Agnieszka and her family had lived in Kraków, where she received instruction from several other Polish teachers of high repute. Her Vienna debut had been in 1932, which was the recital Simon had reviewed. She was said to be very much against piano competitions, and has spoken out against them, which did not make her popular with the committee for the Chopin Competition in Warsaw. In 1932 there were two competitors who obtained equal marks for the first prize in Warsaw, so the winner was chosen by tossing a coin. Hardly a fair way to decide the winner, she had suggested in a recent interview. A year later she was awarded the coveted Chopin Gold Medal from the Polish Friends of Chopin.

Charles had limited exposure to patients who were blind from retinitis pigmentosa. He knew the trait was carried in their families, and that it affected persons at different and variable ages. There was no reliable or recognized treatment that he had ever heard of in Canada. Not all children of families were affected or developed blindness, as her brother, fortunately, seemed to have excellent vision. Charles found it difficult to keep his mind off this unusual woman, who was ready to give herself so early and easily. She said she had had no sexual experience, but her eagerness was curious. Was he really the first man who had come this close to touching her the way she wanted?

He found his way back to the printed program, and could see that it was challenging:

Frédéric Chopin (1810-1847)

Mazurka in A minor, op.68, No. 2
Mazurka in B minor, op.33, No.4
Mazurka in D flat, op.30, No.3
Nocturne in D flat major, op.27, No.2
Nocturne in G minor, op.37, No.1
Fantasie-Imprompu in C sharp minor, op.61

Intermission

Berceuse, op.57
Ballade No.1 in G minor, op.23
Sonata No.2 in B minor op.58

The auditorium appeared to be filled to capacity. He found himself seated between two elderly gentlemen who were speaking Italian to their neighbours, and he was surrounded front and back by Italian chatter as the audience settled into their seats in anticipation. The lights had finally begun to dim as the stage curtain was drawn back to reveal Simon and the manager standing next to the Pleyel piano, especially chosen for this occasion. Mr. Tremonti moved forward and spoke briefly into the microphone in Italian, with a welcome and an introduction of Simon. Although he had debated reading his introduction in Italian, Simon had decided earlier in the morning to speak in English and to provide Mr. Tremonti with his notes. The congenial manager had agreed to provide appropriate translation for the audience. The applause had died down, and Simon began his introduction with Mr. Tremonti providing the translation in Italian.

"Good afternoon and a warm welcome to this afternoon's recital, a tribute to Vladimir de Pachmann, who died here in your city just seven days ago. Miss Lipska had asked me to make a few comments about the significance of this occasion.

"I do speak some Italian, which I learnt during the war, but I have decided to speak to you in English, and your manager, Mr. Tremonti, has kindly agreed to translate from my prepared English notes. I know some of you will understand English. (applause)

"As you heard, I am a music critic from Cardiff, Wales, where I work for the magazine, *Musical Muse*. Many of you will know that Mr. de Pachmann rarely considered music critics to be his friends. (Laughter and some applause) In fact he often said he hated them. (Moe laughter)

"I feel honoured to have been asked to make a few comments about Mr. de Pachmann, the pianist, whom I have heard perform many times and of course to introduce Agnieszka Lipska. I will not repeat what you have already read in your programmes about her early musical talent. Today you will hear Chopin's piano music played in a manner that some have suggested rivals de Pachmann's style. (Brief applause)

"I do not know if Mr. de Pachmann's sons or his private secretary are in the audience. If they are, I want to express to them, on your behalf, our sympathy on their loss. (Prolonged applause)

"What is there about a concert pianist that causes a stir in a city like Rome? Talent and reputation are important of course. Many celebrated pianists of the past—I am thinking of Liszt and Chopin—but there are many others who have played here and all had a certain charisma and appeal that was peculiar to each.

"In the case of Liszt, his virtuosity was said to be a demonic force. With Chopin, his poor health with physical frailty was a constant intrusion, so he seemed to avoid brilliant virtuosity. The styles of Liszt and Chopin could not be more different. Liszt was the dramatist, Chopin the sentimentalist. De Pachmann was somewhere in between. He worshiped them both.

"Unlike Liszt and Chopin, de Pachmann had few pupils, and created very few new works for the piano but he could recreate Chopin's style as well as, or better than, other artists.

"A friend of mine heard him play an original composition, a ballade, many years ago at a recital in Winnipeg, Canada, but I do not think he ever played it again in public. The manuscript has not survived, as far as I know.

"Towards the late period of his professional career he seemed to assume some of the persona of Liszt even with his hairstyle. He loved stage pranks, and at times he may have overdone some of them. (Laughter and a few hisses and boos)

"The forces that made his career a success were different than either Liszt or Chopin. Although he adored Liszt's talent and programmed his music, it was Chopin's music that he promoted and with whom he will always be most associated.

"Today you are about to hear a pianist who is possibly de Pachmann's logical successor—the next champion of Chopin's music. How appropriate that she was born in the same country as the composer! (Prolonged applause)

"You will witness and hear a pianist of exceptional talent, whose rise to the level of excellence has been possible by overcoming a major challenge to a successful musical career. She follows in the Chopin and de Pachmann tradition, which we remember today. (Applause)

"De Pachmann's success was derived from a combination of head, heart and hands, with a generous measure of antics and chat. (Laughter and some hisses)

"Agnieszka Lipska also has this unique ability to use her head, heart and hands, with appropriate virtuosity, but without that precious gift of perfect sight. You will perhaps wonder how it is physically possible.

"De Pachmann was able to charm his audience, especially women, no matter where he played. I guarantee both men and women here will be charmed by what you hear this afternoon. Ladies and gentlemen, I present Agnieszka Lipska." (Prolonged applause)

In anticipation, Simon and Mr. Tremonti had moved their gaze to the stage door, which was opening slowly. Agnieszka, with her brother taking her arm, walked slowly toward the piano amidst louder applause and some whistles. Simon and Mr. Tremonti spoke briefly to the couple, and after bowing to the audience, she settled at the piano as the others made a rapid exit. She was exquisitely dressed in a floor-length pink dress. She was wearing shaded glasses. The stage lights were dimmed so that she and the Pleyel piano became merely a silhouette. How very much like the atmosphere that de Pachmann used to promote, Charles thought. De Pachmann often made a fuss about the stage lights, which he thought were usually too bright. Sometimes he made a big issue of this, as he did with the height of his piano stool. During one of his recitals in San Francisco, he walked off the stage in anger over the bright lights, and returned only after he made sure that they were dimmed to his satisfaction.

Had Charles been a music critic he would have made much more sense of the recital. By the first half of the recital, his response was not at all intellectual. Although he was very interested in de Pachmann's musicianship, he readily admitted he was no expert on music analysis and interpretation. He could never explain why he liked some music more than others. There was obviously some unconscious and therefore hidden perception of what constituted beautiful music and it likely formed the basis for his tastes. One acquires an intimacy with pieces of music you love. The Freudian view of unconscious perceptions was very popular in the psychiatric literature. About all Charles knew was Agnieszka had excelled in having an exquisitely light touch; her *pianisimos* were magical and her *rubato* was consistent, and seemed to him just under enough control. But did she play loud enough for everyone in the audience? He had detected no wrong notes, even in the virtuoso passages, but he may have missed some. Simon would know. The audience response to each piece was electric. Agnieszka did not retreat backstage between pieces, but after standing and acknowledging the applause, returned to her piano stool—remained fixed in thought for a few minutes before resuming.

After a brief intermission, she was back to play more Chopin. Charles found that remaining seated during the break gave him an opportunity to dwell on the music and to think about his morning experience. If she had not told him of her innocence he would have concluded she was a very experienced lover. Thinking of it had made him tingle. He was fighting to think about something different. "I wonder what criteria the critics used to measure the quality of performances," he thought, "likely a mix of empirical and rational reasoning." He listened intently as she played the sonata, which was followed by continuous rhythmic applause and shouts of "*encore!*" It was obvious that an encore was expected, and she was ready to oblige. Returning to the piano from the wings, holding her brother's arm, she seated herself again at the piano and announced in Italian and English, "I will play for you a Study, op.4, No.3 by my countryman, Karol Szymanowski—one of the composer's tributes to Chopin. I hope you enjoy it." The change in style was obvious and the audience response—although less enthusiastic—persisted. For a second and final encore she chose a Rachmaninoff prelude, which was also cheered and applauded, but by then she seemed to have reached the limit of her endurance, and to Charles' relief she saw fit to decline further encores, and did not return to the platform.

Making his way backstage, he found Simon in a state of considerable excitement and full of praise for what he had heard. Simon did not seem upset about the occasional negative reaction to his introductory remarks, and Charles decided to avoid discussing it, except to mention that he thought that the introduction had set the right tone for the afternoon. They made their way down a long corridor to the dressing rooms. Agnieszka looked exhausted and obviously less enthused than he expected her to be.

"You were wonderful!" said Simon, embracing her. "I agree," added Charles, nodding in agreement. He would have loved to have embraced her on the spot and felt her body next to his.

"I could have played better. I was nervous at first—the *mazurkas* did not come off as well as on other occasions. I also found the auditorium too warm."

Her brother offered his opinion. "Agnieszka is rarely fully satisfied with her performances, but her judgement never seems to fit with what the critics and her friends think—so we shall see. There may have been some critics in the audience." He gave her a hug and whispered in her ear, "we all thought it was a great success, especially the sonata." The complement was loud enough for the others to hear and Charles and Simon both applauded in agreement.

"Now you should return to the hotel where you can rest and perhaps sleep for a few hours," he suggested. "I have made arrangements with the Polish ambassador, Mr. Radinski, for the recital and reception this evening at the legation," he said turning to his two guests. "A small number of guests have been invited, and you are both welcome to join us at 7 p.m. You will not need tickets. I will notify the legation you will be coming. You should take a taxi, as it is too far to walk at that hour. It is in the Palazzo Caetani on Via delle Botteghe Oscure 32. I am sure the taxi driver will know it. I was told before leaving Poland that Mr. Radinski is an interim ambassador as the previous appointee, Count Jerzy Potocki, refused to take over the Mission because of his objection to the 'Pact of Four,' which he considered to be an attempt to bypass the conditions of the Versailles treaty. He believed that pact would be to the detriment of our country. Our government has already decided to appoint a Polish diplomat, Alfred Wysocki, who is also a lawyer and journalist, to the legation. I am unsure when he will arrive. In any case, Mr. Radinski seems a very cooperative person and is keenly interested in music.

"Agnieszka needs to rest for a few hours. She has agreed to play a number of requests, and there will also be a very young female pianist from the city playing some selections. She is the daughter of one of the secretaries at the legation, and we hear she is very talented. We are thrilled that we can contribute to the social and artistic life of the employees of our country's legation. The ambassador has already arranged for a Pleyel piano to be made available for the evening. Now we should find the taxi that Mr. Tremonti had promised to call." Alexei rose from his seat, and suddenly looked as if he had remembered something. "My sister and I would like to thank you Charles for taking the time to go to the church with Agnieszka this morning. She was thrilled with the organist." He turned toward Simon. "I am sorry you missed it, but headaches sometimes can be a curse." Charles could see a faint smile on her face, as he sensed she was trying hard to say good-bye.

Charles and Simon decided to walk part of the way back to their hotels together. The sun was beginning to fade behind the horizon. Simon continued to discuss the recital as they walked together. "I have to put together a review to send back to *The Muse.*" Charles noted Simon was limping more than usual and looked tired. A taxi soon appeared and they were soon back at the hotel. They decided to order an aperitif in Simon's hotel bar, where they found that the atmosphere was loud and smoky. Once they had found a quiet corner in the bar, Simon produced a notebook and pencil, and was clearly eager to discuss the recital, and seemed curious to hear another point of view.

"Why don't you tell me first what you thought," suggested Charles. "Did you find the hall overheated?"

"I know Agnieszka did, but I was backstage where it was cooler. I thought the piano seemed well suited to the auditorium, but again being backstage could have given me a different perspective. She does not play loudly, and overall seemed to lack power with some of the pieces. But she has made the point to us that it was likely the way Chopin himself played, so that should not be a criticism. I had intended to comment about this in this review — in my introductory comments, and also comment on the audience response to it. It really has little relevance though. I will introduce the review by discussing the effect of Pachmann's death on the choice of programme. She did not anticipate that her audience would be mourning his death when she planned the recital program weeks ago. The dedication would have been a last minute decision. You would have noted on the program that her recitals were both under the joint sponsorship of the government of Poland and the Pleyel piano company, who subsidized her travel and also provided an honorarium."

"Are you planning to mention the piano?" Charles asked. "I thought it was wonderful. So many critics rarely do comment on the effect of a great sounding piano and if the effect is wonderful I think it appropriate to do so."

"I agree. I do not want to appear promotional though." Simon was cautious.

Charles attempted to be supportive. "The critic's view of a performance is very important, not the least for the fact that it becomes a permanent record of the occasion, and is invaluable to the writers who years later undertake to become the author of a biography of the artist. The critic becomes an historian, describing not only the music but also the professional life of the artist — what he or she was like on stage, as well as the effects of the performances on the audience. Just think, if critics had not recorded their impressions of de Pachmann's many recitals, where would we find the material to write about? When the critic's view becomes too personal, the documentation may become inaccurate and unreliable. So your contribution to the Agnieszka Lipska saga will live for ever as a testimonial to her talent."

"If I were more modest I would argue that point ... but I'm not," replied Simon as he took another sip of his aperitif, and looked over his shoulder at the other drinkers. The noise level in the lounge had become higher since they arrived and it was obvious that serious discussion of the recital was near impossible. "I vote we leave this discussion to a later time, maybe in a quieter setting after the evening recital at the legation," suggested Simon, as he put his pencil and notebook away, and rose to leave.

"Why don't you go back to your room and I'll meet you later so we can go to the concert together?" Charles suggested. " I'll call you before I leave my hotel—and I'll also pay for the drinks." He could see that Simon was relieved that he did not have to pay. He had wondered several times about Simon's finances, but would never raise the issue. A freelance music critic would likely make a small salary from the *Cardiff Western Globe,* and the *Musical Muse* expense account would be small. He could certainly afford a bar bill better than his friend.

Before they parted in the lobby Charles remembered Agnieszka's comment about Alexei's book. "Agnieszka tells me that Alexei is a writer and is researching a book. Did you know that?"

He thought Simon had seemed surprised by the question, as he paused before answering. "He told me about it last year in Vienna, but I have not heard if he has made any significant progress. He has always been interested in Pachmann's life, and it would not surprise me if he may have chosen to write about it. It seems that Pachmann has become a popular subject. You should talk to him about it, and tell him about yours."

Charles found his way back to the Splendide Royale within ten minutes. He decided he would check with the concierge again about the missing manuscript that had as yet not appeared. Neither the concierge nor the manager was on duty, but Volpe was eager to help. "No, Doctor Flemming, it does not seem to be here. I could call the person who was to leave it here. It is easier for me to speak in Italian. Is your friend speaking English?"

Charles found the idea attractive, but he realized there was a problem. "That is very kind of you Mr. Volpe, but although I think this friend does speak English, I have no idea where he or she lives, or even the person's name! I will certainly let you know if I find the name in my room.'"

He thought he needed more exercise, so he decided to skip the elevator and instead mount the stairs to the third floor. The chambermaid had been in and had left Room 332 very clean and tidy. His shirt and shoes from the previous day had been put away in the closet. It seemed she—or someone—had left an unsigned handwritten note on his pillow but it was in Italian, so he put it in his pocket to ask the concierge to read it for him later. He had several hours to spare before the evening recital. Alexei had said there would be food served there, so having dinner was not an issue. He decided to find his notes for the lecture on Tuesday. Registration had already begun at the convention hotel and he was already feeling some anxiety over the fact that on Tuesday he was to give that paper. The final copy could still do with some editing. He poured himself a generous serving of Johnnie Walker and settled on the sofa to think. He wondered what the note was about—probably some housekeeping matter—where she had left his shoes or something similar. Taking it out of his pocket, he tried to make sense of it but the handwriting was not easy. It was clearly addressed to him but unsigned. "It can wait," he thought. He tried, but could not concentrate on his lecture notes. Somehow they had been reclassified in his brain as low priority. His mind kept wandering back to the recital, to Agnieszka and her frank display of sexuality, to Simon, Alexei and to de Pachmann—poor man, now cold and lifeless in a wooden coffin six feet under ground, at the Campo Verano Cemetery. He thought of Anne again, and her memory once more made him feel sad and lonely. He had not thought of Toronto often at all since his arrival in London, nor while travelling on the Continent.

He had seen no reason to call Jeanette, his housekeeper, who would be enjoying her break from the daily preparation of meals, the weekend entertaining, house guests and extra housework that went with his being around. She would take good care of Toby, his yellow Lab, who loved to run loose in the park even when there was a lot of snow. He was sure there would be snow to shovel, but he had contracted this chore to a local teenager. His glass was empty, but he decided against having a second Scotch, remembering he had already had a vermouth at Simon's hotel. He needed to have the good manners to stay awake at the legation recital. It was not unusual for him to nod during concerts, if there had been drinks before on an empty stomach. Simon would likely be writing his review of the recital. Charles had not asked what his plans were after today. He thought he remembered hearing that Simon might be returning to Nice on Tuesday, as he had said there was business he had not finished earlier in the week. "I wonder how he will manage on the train?" Charles thought. "I really should have another chat with him before he leaves." But at the same time, he was conscious that he was becoming Simon's therapist, and that was very presumptuous—something he wanted to avoid.

Charles began to sense an unfair ambivalence towards de Pachmann. The dead pianist's influence was pervasive not only at the concert hall but in their conversations. Yet he did not feel he was really mourning the man in the same way that others were. He suspected Simon was not either—not the way Agnieszka seemed to. The pianist's sons would be feeling the grief, but gossip had suggested they and their father had become alienated in his later years. De Pachmann had continued to be a touchy, cantankerous man. The sons had spent their younger years under their mother's care after the divorce, and they had also acquired a stepfather who was a famous French hero—and likely easier to live with than their own father had been. De Pachmann had been generous towards them in a monetary sense according to press reports, providing support for their education. Would Maggie Labori be mourning her ex-husband? She was said to be a kind and gracious lady so he was certain she would respect his legacy, but would she mourn?

The local de Pachmann Society members would have been at his grave for the funeral service if they had been allowed. But how would they now show their grief and respect? Surely not by irritating gestures such as the one he had witnessed at the train station. How would they keep his memory alive? Had they have been out in force at this afternoon's recital? There were some in the audience who were annoyed enough about some of Simon's comments to express their feelings, but Charles had not seen anyone suspicious and they were certainly not near enough to him to stand out.

He put aside the conference manuscript and being curious about the note, he decided to walk down the stairs to the lobby, after quickly swishing his teeth with toothpaste in the bathroom to disguise the Scotch on his breath. There was a queue at the reception desk so he found a seat to wait until the coast was clear. Before long all the guests had been dealt with and he sought out Paolo Volpe who was on duty, and who after hearing of the note was very pleased to attempt a translation. After a few minutes he looked up at Charles.

"Doctor, this is a strange message. It is not signed. The writing is familiar and could be the chambermaid's—the woman who cleans your room. Here is what she or someone wrote:

'To Mr. Flemming, Room 332. The book you lost was left at the desk a few hours before you arrived. I know because I was cleaning in the lobby when a deliveryman left it there. About an hour after I noticed it was picked up by another man I had never seen before. He came in from the street and I think he used your name. I hope this helps you'."

Charles could not hide his surprise as he listened to Paolo's translation. "Are you sure that is what she wrote?" he asked.

Volpe nodded his head. "I am sure but I can ask Angelo to translate it too."

The clerk named Angelo could be seen through a glass partition, seated at a desk inside the office. He was speaking on the telephone. "He is on the phone, but he will not be long. Is your book important Doctor Flemming? Why would someone steal it?"

"That is a good question. I wonder myself. It may actually be a rough copy of a book I need for my research for my own book I am writing. The notes are not likely to be in English, so I would have needed a translation. Can you tell if the hotel paid the deliveryman for the notes or book? Would you have a record of the delivery?"

"I do not think there is a record. On the day you checked in someone at the desk said a large envelope had been left here. You remember we could not find it. It is a mystery."

Angelo had by now finished his telephone conversation. Volpe knocked on the door spoke briefly to him and showed him the note. Reading the note aloud, he rose slowly from his chair and come into the reception area. He shook hands with Charles. He was young, well dressed and spoke good English.

"Dr. Flemming, my name is Angelo. We have not met before. I was not on duty when you came a few days ago, but I heard about your lost book or manuscript from the manager. Paolo read you the note. I agree with his translation. My guess is this note was written by one of the chambermaids. I do not remember seeing this handwriting before but someone else might. Leave the note with me and we will ask about it and let you know. I will also speak to the receptionist who was on call the day she mentions."

Thanking them both, Charles returned to his room deep in thought. He looked at his watch and noted he had an hour before they were to be at the legation. He would have time to have a bath and change his shirt and suit before calling Simon.

CHAPTER NINE

"*Carpe diem*"
(Seize the opportunity)

Simon was waiting outside his hotel when Charles arrived at the entrance at 6:30 p.m. Simon looked relaxed, and had changed into a navy blue business suit with white shirt and striped grey bow tie. "Here we go again on another music adventure! I know you both enjoyed the organ recital."

"Yes, we did, and I have made some notes and saved you the program. I have also had an interesting experience." He proceeded to tell the story of the mysterious unsigned note as they waited for a taxi to arrive. They had been told by the doorman that the legation was at least two kilometres away—too far to walk at this hour. The sun was already setting below the horizon, and the street lamps had been turned on.

"What do you think it means?" Charles asked.

"I have no idea because I really have not heard you say much about the manuscript or the book itself and its importance. Is this a revision of the book that was originally published in Italian with an English translation, in 1919 by Pallottelli and was to be reprinted this year?"

"Yes, that is right, but I cannot tell you how much more information it will contain or if it is in Italian or English. That is what I want to find out myself."

Simon was quizzical: "You told me the first edition had been little more than a somewhat brief summary of Pachmann's professional life and career and there might have been a careful avoidance of reference to the failed marriage and other sensitive subjects. Is that correct?"

"Yes, that sums it up. I assume de Pachmann oversaw the older version and censored the parts he wanted to keep secret. I had asked a medical friend in Toronto if he could ask a colleague of his living in Rome—I think a lawyer friend—to find a manuscript or copy of the new version, and to deliver it to my hotel before I arrived. I thought the new information would be useful in my conversations with de Pachmann himself, if I had been granted an interview, but as I told you that had not been guaranteed before I left Canada. Any new material in this manuscript would be an addition to the details I had already collected in my biographic notes, some of which I showed you on the train."

The taxi had arrived and they set off for the Polish Legation located in the west end of the city. The driver knew the address. They reached the legation in quick time as traffic was light, and they had a fast driver. Neither had seen this part of Rome since arriving, but the sun had set and it was now too dark to see much more than the city lights from the back seat. Nothing further was said about the missing book until they had alighted and paid the driver.

"I will tell you more about this book later," Charles promised, as they slowly climbed the legation steps. Simon seemed to have missed—or chose to ignore—the comment, as he was taking his time up the steps, attending to his weak leg, which seemed more bothersome this evening. The four-story legation building was situated on a quiet street with no front garden. A flagpole flying a large Polish national flag was visible above the entrance, which led directly into an open reception area. Orchestral music could be heard coming from the open windows on the ground floor. They were greeted at the door by two soldiers who—judging by their dress uniforms—were part of the legation staff. The guards were interested in their names, and asked for proof of identity. "This must be usual protocol—part of the security for any legation," whispered Charles, as he produced an Ontario driver's licence.

Further inside the open reception area they were met by a smartly dressed young woman from the legation staff who introduced herself in English as "Elizabeth, private secretary to the ambassador." She announced their arrival in a clear voice to a tall grey haired man of about fifty, clearly Ambassador Radinski, standing next to an elegantly dressed woman of similar age, also in formal attire. The Radinskis were standing near a large open door leading to a larger room where a small group of adults and children had already assembled. Greetings were exchanged; they shook hands and after a brief welcome in English by Madame Radinska, they were directed into an elegant drawing room, lit by crystal glass chandeliers hanging from tall ceilings. The walls were lined with large oil paintings, some obviously modern but most seemed to be from Italian masters. A faint buzz of conversation was competing with the sounds of a small string orchestra off in a corner playing the *William Tell Overture* by Rossini.

Waiters circling the room offered glasses of Asti Spumanti with a lot of bubbles, as well as an official-looking paper with the legation coat of arms—the programme for the evening's recital. Chairs had been set out in preparation, and at the far end of the room a Pleyel piano had been placed on a raised platform ringed by large vases of flowers. Agnieszka and Alexei were nowhere to be seen. The program said the recital was to begin at 7:30 with a welcome and introduction from the ambassador and Mrs. Radinska, followed by a selection of piano pieces by a young pianist, Angela Roscetti. That was to be followed by a selection of requests played by Agnieszka. Angela was described in the program as the eight-year old daughter of a legation research assistant.

"I think we should find a good seat, preferably up near the piano," suggested Simon, as he slowly made his way through the crowd, holding his glass of wine. Some guests had already found seats, but they were fortunate to find two unoccupied in the third row.

"I am reminded that Maggie Okey was only eight when she made her debut in London—I think in 1870," said Charles, as they settled in their seats. "Her press reviews always described her as being a year younger than she really was. I wonder if this girl's parents and her teacher encouraged this."

"Mozart's father, Leopold, did the same with his son when they were on tour during his childhood years, and he was not the only one to do that," replied Simon. "He likely believed if the young Amadeus appeared to be a year or two younger, the greater the public's interest—and the profits!"

Most of the audience had settled into their seats, the orchestra music has ceased and soon a round of applause was being generated by the appearance of the ambassador and his wife stepping onto the platform. Agnieszka and Alexei had found seats in the front row near the piano. The ambassador's opening remarks into a microphone were in Polish and Italian, and were followed by a brief round of applause. His wife summarized his comments in both Italian and English.

"We welcome you all here tonight," she said, "to hear two very talented people, one from your city and the other from Poland. We admire them both for their talent and are very proud to present them to you tonight. Their selections are listed in your printed programs. My husband and I hope you enjoy the recital and invite you to stay for a buffet dinner after. Now, let the music begin with little Angela Roscetti, who is only eight years old. Her teachers have predicted a promising future for her. Those who work with us at the embassy will know that her mother Sophie is employed in the research section of the commerce division. Before I forget, I want to thank the agent for the Pleyel Piano Company here in Rome, who has generously provided the beautiful piano for this recital. I thank also the government of Poland, which has been very generous in their support of this evening's event."

Her comments were followed by applause while the overhead lights were dimmed.

Angela was a smaller-than-expected eight-year-old, who seemed to appear out of nowhere, lost no time in mounting the steps, gave a quick curtsey, sat down and immediately commenced to play. She was wearing a delightful white cotton print dress that fell just below her knees. Her first selections were four of Mendelssohn's *Songs Without Words*, which were played with considerable grace. They were applauded with enthusiasm for several minutes. She was playing from memory, never once looking at her hands. Her last selection was a Bach *Prelude and Fugue* from *The Well Tempered Clavier*. Her finger work was very precise and confident. Charles felt she played better in the Mendelssohn pieces. He did not feel an overwhelming sense of awe that he had anticipated he might, and he wondered why—perhaps because precocious pianists come and go. Only a small number of them managed to fulfill their families' and teachers' expectations. Anton Rubinstein, and Josef Hoffman came to his mind as prodigies who had become successful virtuosos as adults. De Pachmann—as far as anyone knew—had not emerged upon the Odessa music scene as a young prodigy, and his eventual success was slow to develop, and did not appear until he was in his early thirties. He remembered that Agnieszka's program had said that her debut had been at a similar age to Angela's. Had her subsequent professional career been all that everyone, including she had hoped for? She had talked about this earlier and he suspected she would likely enlarge on that subject again when they had more time together.

Angela, having acknowledged her audience's prolonged applause, seemed not to have planned an encore and by now had left the platform taking a seat next to Alexei. An intentional pause seemed to have settled upon the event. Guests began to murmur amongst themselves—probably offering comments on the performance and the selections. Simon leaned over and made a quiet comment about Angela's prospects. "One could never predict her future success based on this brief exposure, but I did like her stage presence and self-assurance. She has talent, but I hope her parents do not publicly promote her talents excessively to her detriment. Her teachers will need to play the role of referees between possible conflicting influences—the temptation to promote her as a prodigy versus the realization that a sound foundation must be laid. There remains much more to be learnt."

The ambassador had again climbed the steps and was asking for their attention. He was accompanied this time by a formally dressed man, introduced as Claudio Bianco, a legation attaché. After a few comments from the ambassador in Polish and Italian, which were received with applause, the attaché summarized his comments in Italian and precise English. "I hardly need to tell you that Miss Lipska is one of Poland's prize possessions and some of you, like me, were very fortunate to have heard her superb recital earlier today. Here she is again, in what we have tried to make a less formal setting, to play a few requests that have come mainly from the legation staff. The selections are shown on the program." Turning to Agnieszka, he directed his comments to her in Polish and English. "We are grateful that you have consented to take the time to come tonight Miss Lipska. Thank you very much. We look forward to hearing you play."

There was a long period of applause as Alexei helped her to the platform to be seated at the piano. She was wearing dark glasses, and had chosen an off-the-shoulder, full-length dark red dress, fringed at the top and bottom with tiny sequins. Tonight her hair was worn loose to her shoulders, kept in place by a narrow band. She was smiling, and seemed very relaxed. The extended period of applause allowed her to settle at the piano. No one had mentioned in the introductions that she was blind.

Agnieszka paused for a few minutes in thought before turning to the audience. Speaking first in Polish and then English she thanked the ambassador and his wife as well as the legation staff for their kind welcome, adding, "I enjoyed your playing very much Angela. You have a lot of talent and I wish you all the success possible in the future." A brief applause followed, and when the hall was quiet again she added, "I love all the requests you have made. They are pieces I often choose as encores in my recitals. The Chopin *Berceuse* was on my program this afternoon but I never tire of playing it."

The program notes said she was to play six requests: the first four by Chopin: two *Preludes*, the *Nocturne op.27, No.2 in D flat Major*, a *Mazurka, op. 33,.No.2 in D* and the *Berceuse, op.57*. The last two requests were for music by Liszt: *Liebesträume* and *Concert Etude No.3*.

Each selection was received with prolonged applause. As she acknowledged the audience response to the final Liszt piece, which called for playing with crossed hands, she mentioned it was also known as *Un Sosper*. She remained seated and turning to the audience announced in Polish and English, "As an encore, I will play a special request from Angela and also one from a visitor from Canada, who is in the audience and whom I have only recently met. Angela has asked me to play Chopin's *Mazurka*, op.17, No.4 in A minor. I will then play one of my favourites—the brief Prelude, op.11, No.1 by the Russian composer, Anatoli Liadov, composed in 1885. I hope you enjoy them both." Charles felt his face become warm, and his forehead sweaty, as he glanced briefly at Simon who was nodding his head in approval. He wished he could remember the *Prelude* but couldn't. He was sure he had not requested the piece. "It is a beautiful gem," whispered Simon. The Chopin *Mazurka* was immediately recognizable and was followed by lengthy applause. After the opening chords of the *Prelude*, he remembered it but could not say where he had heard it before. She was playing the piece with great sensitivity. The audience response at the end of the recital was a standing ovation, which lasted for several minutes. The attaché, Mr. Bianco, had also again mounted the platform and after shaking her hand invited everyone the join the ambassador and legation staff in the adjoining room for dinner. Charles rose from his seat and feeling compelled to seek out Agnieszka to thank her for the kind gesture, he made his way in her direction. He knew that the special dedication meant more to them both than anyone else would appreciate. She had pretended that he had requested it. She had now navigated the steps and reached her chair again under her brother's guidance.

Before she could sit again, he had reached her, and was able to say in a voice loud enough to be heard above the background chatter, "Agnieszka, that was so kind of you! How did you know the *Prelude* was my favourite too? You played it beautifully and you must have sensed the enthusiasm of the audience." He embraced her, and felt her return his strong embrace. He heard her whisper briefly near his ear, "I played it for you because you are so kind." Had her comment been audible to the others? He did not care if it had. Simon had been following him, and also approached her chair, waiting to speak. He could see that Alexei had moved over to speak to Mr. Bianco. They soon found themselves moving slowly toward the dining area with Simon taking Agnieszka's arm. Charles was pleased things had worked out like that. It would have been his choice to escort her but he knew it might have been too obvious to the others.

The legation staff had prepared a spectacular array of food, presented in a buffet fashion. The orchestra had moved into the dining room and was playing a Mozart *Serenade*. Charles knew that Simon would help Agnieszka with her plate and drink, so he chose to linger before helping himself to food. He wanted to seek out Alexei to speak to him about his book project while it was still on his mind. He found him alone at the end of the room smoking a cigarette and drinking a glass of wine. "I thought your sister's playing was wonderful," he said, as an introduction. "Thank you," was Alexei's reply. "The *Berceuse* is my favourite, but I know the Liadov *Prelude,* which you requested is one of her favourites." Charles thought he should get to the topic of the book immediately. "Your sister tells me you are writing a book about de Pachmann, and I may not have told you that I am doing the same." He was watching for an expression of surprise on Alexei's face, but he did not see one.

Pausing to take a drink of his wine his friend replied, "actually, I did know you were researching details of de Pachmann's life. Simon and I were speaking on the telephone when you were both staying in Nice earlier in the week. We were discussing the recitals and he told me then he had met a Canadian psychiatrist on the train from London who was coming to Rome to meet de Pachmann about a biography. I was naturally curious." He raised his left hand with fingers separated and paused. "You need not be threatened by my book, as it will be published in Poland and in Polish of course. De Pachmann was Agnieszka's favourite pianist and it was she who inspired me to undertake the project. I was fortunate to receive a generous grant from the National Frédéryk Chopin Foundation to allow me to work on it. That was last year, before we knew that the pianist had become ill. I have written a considerable amount toward the book, and was aware that there were serious gaps about details of his early years and especially about his marriage and his sexual orientation. Rumours suggested he might have been homosexual, but it was not easy to get evidence that this was the case—least of all from him. I am not certain that it is anyone's business anyway."

Charles had been listening attentively and decided it was time to mention the missing book. He summarized briefly the events surrounding the request for a copy of the new revised book, the disappearance of the book or manuscript draft from his hotel and his failure to connect with his contact in Rome.

"I also knew about this book," said Alexei, as he extinguished his cigarette. "Simon told me about its existence on the telephone. I am sorry it is missing but I am sure it will eventually be found."

Simon and Agnieszka had quietly approached arm-in-arm, both holding plates of food. "We have been looking for you both. Are you hungry?" she asked.

"I have been talking to Alexei about his book and my lost manuscript," replied Charles, "he has had a glass of wine, but we both seem to have completely forgotten about food." Taking Agnieszka's arm, he suggested she come with him to choose what was available. "What have you had?" he wanted to know, examining her plate as they walked slowly towards the table. "I suggest the melon and pastrami, the shrimp dish with rice and the ribs," she replied. They had successfully separated themselves from Simon, who had decided to talk to Alexei, and to light a cigarette as they left. "I wanted to have a few minutes with you alone—to say again that I shall always remember this morning's outing together," Charles whispered. "You can help me choose what to try. I would also love a glass of wine." He had noticed she was not drinking. "Have you had a glass?" He could feel her holding his arm tightly. "No, but I will let you find me one. I wish you could have stayed longer this morning." He did not respond, but motioned to a waiter who was standing nearby and briefly surveyed the choices. "Will it be red or white?" he asked.

"I will have what you have," she replied, and he chose a Chianti. "Come with me while I choose those suggestions of yours from the buffet," he suggested. He heard her ask; "When can we meet again—alone, I mean?" He did not respond immediately. There was a small group of guests, some of them children, making choices from the buffet and producing a mix of both Italian and

Polish voices. Examining the choices he found the ones she had suggested. "Let us find a seat that is quieter." Balancing both their wine glasses and plates, he lead her across the floor to a group of empty chairs along the far wall. Spotting a small table nearby he suggested she use it for her plate and glass. "I can use my lap." He paused to sample the shrimp for a moment.

"I have been thinking we could meet tomorrow for lunch, or later for dinner in the evening. I will be attending meetings in the morning but I will be having lunch somewhere, and can think of no one I would prefer to share lunch with than you. What would you prefer, lunch or dinner?"

"I prefer an evening with you, so we can have more time to talk," she replied without hesitation. She reached toward him, smiled and gently squeezed his arm for a brief moment.

"Fine, I will call you in the afternoon and arrange to meet you, perhaps about seven o'clock or earlier, if you prefer. I will reserve at a restaurant that is not too far, or you may prefer to eat in the dining room at my hotel or yours. I feel like having fresh fish for a change, even though these shrimp are very tasty. What about you?" She nodded consent. He added, "let's not involve Simon and Alexei in this. They can find something to do on their own. I'm not sure that Simon will be staying in Rome longer than tomorrow. I have not asked him about his plans." He could see that she was pleased with the dinner plans. "I would love dinner with you and I would love to have fish too," she replied, adding, "but when are *you* planning to leave Rome?"

Charles suddenly realized he had not decided for sure how long he would stay beyond Wednesday, which was when the conference would end. He also realized he had not asked her or Alexei the same question. He sensed he was losing interest in his research on de Pachmann. In fact, he wondered if he even cared if the missing manuscript were never found. The prospect of competing with her brother for the same book material did not appeal either. "I do not know when I will be leaving, but my enthusiasm for writing my biography of de Pachmann has waned. Alexei should finish his book and it could easily be translated into English if there was enough interest. I will let him have my draft manuscript. If I drop the whole idea, I do not need to linger long in Rome." He heard himself add, "unless you were to stay as well." Agnieszka seemed in deep thought and he watched as she swirled her wine before responding.

"Poor Vladimir de Pachmann, if he only knew!" and added, "but about my travel plans—I know Alexei would like to return home via Paris, but I have no recitals planned for several weeks, so I would love to stay in Rome longer." She paused, looked at his face, tasted her wine and added, "I like the wine, don't you?" Without waiting for an answer she added, "I have been thinking. If I stayed after Alexei returned on Tuesday, you would still be here, but you would have to promise to help me find my way around, and perhaps even accompany me back to Kraków on the train!" That was not a request Charles had expected, and he quickly decided not to commit himself. He sampled the shrimp again and thought he should joke with her about it. "Are you inviting me to Poland to meet your family, or to listen to you play your next recital ... or both?" he asked.

"Only if you are curious," she replied as she removed her dark glasses and looked at him intensely. "I want you to know it would be more than mere curiosity," he whispered. Pausing, he added, "I have just realized that I like your eyes better without glasses, but I understand why you wear them especially in this bright room."

Other members of the audience carrying plates and wine glasses had moved into adjacent chairs. Agnieszka recognized a voice and introduced Charles to a Polish-speaking couple she seemed to have met earlier, and whose names he knew he would never remember. She continued to engage them in conversation while he concentrated on his plate. He had not planned to travel elsewhere in Europe but had allowed himself another week in Rome to research his book. The idea of spending more time alone with her was more appealing than working on a book in which he had lost interest anyway. He knew he would enjoy tending to her needs if they were on their own. But was this all the result of his below-the-surface passion for this beautiful woman with obvious physical dependency as well as possibly emotional needs? This did not seem the appropriate place or time to discuss the details of a change in his travel plans. Seeing an opportunity, he asked if she would like a desert from the table and a coffee. She passed on the coffee but the sweet was appealing. He stood to go back to the table; "Let me find something for you there." He offered to take their empty plates, but before he could, the plates were quickly taken away by a passing waiter.

He returned with a coffee and some small cakes, which they shared. The orchestra had changed to a Strauss waltz, but neither of them knew the name, or which Strauss. Agnieszka finished her wine, and passed him her glass. "What is the time?" she asked suddenly, "I feel tired, as it has been a long day." It was just past 10 o'clock and Charles noticed many of the crowd were already bidding farewell to the ambassador and his wife. "I agree. You have done a lot today," he replied. "Have arrangements been made to take you back to your hotel?" She told him the legation had promised to provide a car for her and Alexei. Charles stood and looked about. "I will see where he is, and speak to him." He found her brother and Simon still talking at the far end of the room, and he saw they had finished their meal. After a word with the attaché, Elizabeth the secretary was sent out to make the arrangements. Returning to Agnieszka, he saw the ambassador's wife had found her, and they were in deep conversation. "Arrangements are being made to take you both back," he told her as they rose from their seats. "Let me help you back to the entrance. Alexei will be waiting there."

Agnieszka accepted readily, and after saying good-bye to many of the domestic staff, they made their way to the main door with Simon, Alexei and the ambassador following. "Remember to get lots of rest tonight," Charles whispered, "I will be anticipating having dinner with you tomorrow evening." She squeezed his arm and replied, "I will be too. I am planning to compose a little Polonaise for you tomorrow while you are attending your meeting. I want to keep my piano until I leave, if possible. It has been a few months since I had the time to be creative. Mother is always reminding me to do more composing so I now have the opportunity." They had reached the door. The legation secretary had anticipated that Charles and Simon would need a drive, and told them an Italian couple would be driving in their direction and had offered to take them in their car, and to drop them at their hotels.

Simon announced he was tired as well, and wished to have an early night. Before leaving him at his hotel entrance, Charles told him of his plans. "I am going to be attending meetings for the next three days, we have not talked about your agenda." Simon was planning to stay one more night. "I will spend tomorrow morning working on my reviews of the two recitals, although I can easily do that on the train," was his reply. "I really should see more of Rome, and I have an urge to visit Pachmann's grave before I leave. But I cannot afford to stay longer than another day, or I will be missing some important concerts in Cardiff." The evening air was now cooler so they agreed to move into the lobby for a few minutes to finish their conversation.

"That is a very nice idea of yours to go to the cemetery," Charles agreed. "I had also thought of making the trip, but it will not be until after my meetings are over later in the week. I have been wondering how you feel about facing the long train trip alone?"

"Well, it appears I will not be alone. Alexei tells me he plans to return to Poland with Agnieszka on Tuesday via Paris, so he has suggested we arrange to travel together on the same train to Milan, and then to Paris. He has business there and wants to contact some sponsors for future concerts. If I have their company I will feel better—much less anxious, just as I felt when travelling with you. You have helped me tremendously to understand the basis of my reactions to train travel."

Charles did not want to mention the possibility of Agnieszka staying longer. "Simon, I have decided tonight not to continue my research on de Pachmann. I have lost interest in my book, so tonight I offered Alexei my notes, and he can also have my copies of the North American reviews as well. I am not even going to pursue a search for the missing de Pachmann manuscript. I am sure there will be another copy at his villa if it is never found, and it may be available to buy soon. I do not really care to know who picked up the package. When I see the concierge tonight, I will tell him to forget about the matter. Perhaps if it does show up before Tuesday it can be of use to Alexei in his research."

Simon was silent as he listened to the decision. "I am sure he will appreciate your offer. I am sorry you have changed your mind about writing the book. Some of the material you showed me was new, and should be published."

"Simon, I should also tell you that Agnieszka and I are meeting for dinner tomorrow evening. There are some things she would like to discuss—things that are of a personal nature."

Simon shrugged and turned away, "I understand. That is fine with me." Turning again to face Charles he said; "You have been very kind to have spent so much time with me from the time we met on the ferry. It has been a unique experience and I will always be in your debt. When do you plan to return to

London? We could meet there or in Cardiff if you have time to spend before catching your boat."

Should he tell his friend of his possible change in travel plans? A white lie popped into Charles' head. "I have become very interested in the subject of creativity in blind musicians since arriving in Rome. Perhaps it has been because of your introducing me to Agnieszka and having heard her play. I even have a yen to travel to Poland to study how she and other blind persons learn new music, and how they compose. That seems to be the neurologist part of me. It would take much more travel time, so it is impossible for me to predict when I would arrive in London, perhaps in a few weeks. Tomorrow, I will discuss my plans with her and her brother."

Simon seemed to accept his explanation. They shook hands and warmly bid farewell. "I am sure we will see each other before Tuesday. I know you will have a safe trip back to Wales. We must keep in touch and I will contact you when my travel plans are finalized," Charles promised.

The time was late, but as he walked the two blocks to his hotel Charles felt the need to find his manuscript on Obsessive-Compulsive Disorders for the meeting on Tuesday. Preparing to pick up his keys at the desk, he noticed the receptionist was a young woman whom he had not seen before. "My name is Flemming," he said as he approached the desk. "I am in Room 332."

"Yes sir, I will get your key," she said in English. Taking a few steps back to retrieve the room key, she turned to add, "there is an envelope here for you as well Doctor Flemming. Mr. Volpe asked me to be sure I gave it to you when you returned."

Charles examined the envelope, which was from hotel stationery. His name and room number had been typed across the front. "Thank you, Miss...." and hesitated as he did not know her name. "Tamminga, " she replied. "I was on duty the evening your package was given by mistake to the gentleman who requested it as he passed through the lobby. I simply thought I was giving it to you. I have been severely reprimanded by the manager for this mistake. The message is likely to give you more details."

His curiosity being raised, he opened the envelope and read:

"Dear Doctor Flemming; You may have already have met Miss Tamminga, the receptionist who was on duty on the evening your manuscript was lost. In fact, it was not lost at all but given to an unauthorized man who was impersonating you. Up to now we have not found the package but Miss Tamminga has provided us with a description of the man and so has your chambermaid who saw him as well. We feel confident he was not a native Italian from his accent. If you can find time to speak to me in the morning, I can provide you with more details. Yours very truly, H. Berretta."

Charles could not fathom who had been given the necessary information that would allow this unknown person to collect the manuscript on the day before he arrived. Perhaps it was a representative of Pallottelli, who had decided to retrieve the document. Had there been a change of mind about giving him—an unknown visitor—access to the draft? There was also the possibility the docu-

ment might now be considered an integral part of the pianist's estate, and re-
trieval was therefore considered important. He might learn more when he spoke
to Mr. Berretta in the morning.

The telephone was ringing as Charles unlocked his room door. As soon as
he had reached the telephone he recognized her voice on the other end. "Charles,
it is me. I know it is late but I wanted to tell you that since arriving back from
the legation, Alexei and I have had a discussion about our travel plans. He is not
against my staying longer here, but he is obviously worried about how I will
cope alone, and especially how I will get back to Poland safely. He would feel
better if he spoke to you about it. I know you would not mind. He is here with
me now. Can you speak to him?"

"Of course I can. Put him on," he replied without any hesitation. He was
pleased to be able to discuss the idea with her brother, who was in truth her
guardian.

"Hello Charles—I'm sorry for the late call. Agnieszka has told me about her
decision to stay longer in Rome. I have no objection, as I am sure you will give
her all the support she needs. She does not need to travel to Paris with me. But
she tells me you will be in meetings all day for the next three days. I know she
will be able to practice her piano here alone. She can find lots to occupy her
time. She even wants to do some composing which will especially please
mother," Alexei said with a laugh. "The big problem is her travelling back to
Poland alone by train. She could not do it easily without help. You are a doctor,
so you can provide in that way. She says you might agree to travel back with her
after your meetings are over."

Charles had been waiting for an opportunity to interject a comment, and this
seemed the appropriate time. "I would be very happy to undertake the responsibility of being your sister's guardian, as you have been, and done so well. I had
a sister myself who was disabled. She was younger than me, and after my
mother died I shared the responsibility of her care." He realized he had not told
his new friends much about his family in Canada. "Agnieszka may have told
you we are meeting for dinner tomorrow, and it will give me an opportunity to
hear about the challenges facing me! So rest assured that all will be okay. I can
deal with the travel plans, and look after the finances as well. We can return via
Milan and Vienna." The telephone was silent and he could hear both speaking
away from the telephone in Polish. "Wait a moment," said Alexei, and there was
another brief period of silence until Agnieszka's voice emerged again, "Charles,
I am sure this will work for everyone. I am thrilled you and Alexei are agreeable. I promise not to be a burden to you — honestly. We can discuss the arrangements together tomorrow. Now I will say good night and I hope you sleep
well. I know I will."

Charles wished them both a good night, and replaced the telephone. Now
that matters had been settled, he was convinced he had no doubts about the decision. The prospect of spending some extra days with this beautiful, talented
woman was beginning to be a distraction from his intention to re-read his talk
before going to bed. He felt aroused simply thinking of the brief time they had

been physically close earlier today. He knew that was just the beginning. There was both a strong physical and emotional attraction between them which he was convinced would translate into their eventually making love. His mouth was dry and he needed a drink—a glass of Scotch would help him relax. After a visit to the bathroom, and the usual preparations for bed, he settled under the duvet, with his head propped up with two pillows and with a large Scotch and water on the bedside table. He tried hard to immerse himself in the boring world of obsessive-compulsive disorders. He had two drinks from his glass and before he had read two pages of his paper he was sound asleep.

CHAPTER TEN

"Beati mundi corde"
(Blessed are the pure in heart)

Charles was awake before sunrise on Monday, with a full bladder and with sex on his mind. He was thinking of Agnieszka and her sexual advances. The room was dark, and sometime in the night he had turned off his bedside light and rearranged his pillows. His half-empty glass of Scotch was still sitting on the bedside table, and his conference manuscript, he discovered, had slid onto the floor. He found himself trying to put together fragments of a dream, which he was convinced, had been interrupted by his waking up. He tried closing his eyes, and thought he could remember Simon and Alexei had been smoking and discussing the world of music criticism. Agnieszka was there, but what had she been doing? Speaking a foreign language, likely Polish, but he was not sure. He remembered she also spoke German. She was playing a Chopin *mazurka* on the piano—at the Polish Legation. Somehow he remembered de Pachmann seated nearby, nodding approval as he listened to Agnieszka play. She had not been wearing her glasses, and he wondered if she had been crying, because he could see that she was continually wiping her eyes with a handkerchief. He suspected it had some meaning, perhaps the memory of de Pachmann's glory days. He felt it was hopeless to try to interpret it now. He was not in the mood. The meeting was on his mind.

Looking at his watch, he saw it was early—almost 6:45. His recollection was that the conference programme for the morning had said that the president of the Italian Psychiatric Association would be the first speaker at 9 o'clock. He was to welcome the visitors and would speak on the subject, *Mending Man's Troubled Mind: Psychiatry in the 1930s.* He wanted to hear that. Scanning the programme on his desk for the Monday morning events, he noticed he had earlier circled several short presentations that interested him. An American from Baltimore was speaking at 10 o'clock on *Psychological Trauma and Memory: a Precursor of Obsessive Ruminations?* This was to be followed by a paper from two pharmacologists from a university in Punjab on *Rauwolfia Serpentina as Treatment for High Blood Pressure and Insanity.* A Canadian from Vancouver—whom he knew—was presenting a paper on *Symptoms of the Ebbing Stream of Life: Menopause and Mid-Life Crisis* at 11:30. That would likely be enough for the morning, as he anticipated he might be meeting colleagues from Europe whom he had not seen for years. There were a number of concurrent presentations which were in German, and one in Italian. There was to be a symposium in the morning on *Progress of Psychotherapy in the 1930s.* One paper on that symposium that caught his eye was an annual report from the Berlin Psychoanalytic Institute, which was celebrating twenty-five years of consultation and teaching. Berlin he knew to be a rival of Vienna in the area of psychotherapy.

He had never been to Berlin, but some friends had told him it was now a tense city because of the political turmoil, and one of the friends had described the city as "ugly but stimulating." There was also a paper on the first twenty years experience of the Psychoanalytical Society of Budapest, founded by Sandor Fenenczi in 1913. He knew something about Fenenczi. After a bath, and as he shaved, Charles recalled hearing that Fenenczi and Sigmund Freud had once been friends, but had fallen out because of differences of opinion about the best management of patients with severe disturbances in early infant-mother relationships. Fenenczi had advocated the direct expression of loving feelings by therapists, which might even extend to kissing and other degrees of intimacy. Freud had called them 'erotic gratifications'—a distinct contrast to his strict rules of treatment neutrality. Freud's view was that emotional abstinence could stimulate the release of unconscious affects and memories on its own. Charles was of the same opinion, and it was a view accepted by other leaders in the field of analysis including Ernest Jones, who considered Fenenczi's approach unacceptable.

There was fear that all manipulations of the transference process could be experienced by the patient as seduction or coercion by the analyst. An episode that had been well-publicized a few years earlier had raised concern about Fenenczi's mental health. He had developed progressive neurological manifestations of pernicious anaemia, and seemed to be showing signs of early dementia as part of the condition. It was well known that he had been advised by Freud last year not to read a paper on deviations from traditional analytic techniques at the Wiesbaden International Psychoanalytical Congress, but had insisted on reading the paper anyway.

Charles finished his toilet, and as he dressed he found himself smiling as he considered the folly of open dissent over psychiatric hypotheses and theories amongst therapists.

Now he was ready for breakfast, and after collecting the conference program and his manuscript for tomorrow's presentation, he made his way to the dining room where he discovered there were only two others eating breakfast at that hour. He decided to order a simple continental-style breakfast, and as he waited for a coffee he tried to put together his thoughts on his telephone conversation with Alexei the previous night. He now felt relaxed about the plans for helping Agnieszka, and quickly decided it was best to suppress that topic and instead to concentrate on reading his paper. He had also decided to leave the issue of the missing de Pachmann manuscript until after breakfast. There was enough time to read the manuscript for his presentation completely through once, as he sipped his coffee and waited for his order of cold ham, cheese with toast and preserves. Timing with his watch he estimated the paper was the right length—just under ten minutes.

Perhaps he should ask Agnieszka to listen to him read it before they went out to dinner tonight. He could not remember telling her any details of the topic he had chosen for presentation. There was a need to spend more time preparing answers for hypothetical questions, especially those from the psychoanalysts in the audience, but that could wait.

It was not yet eight o'clock when he finished his breakfast, so he was surprised to find the manager, Mr. Berretta, already at the reception desk. Mr. Berretta knew he had seen his letter last evening. "Doctor Flemming, you must be totally frustrated with our efforts to solve the mystery of the missing book, and we are very sorry it has not turned up as we expected. Yesterday, we decided to report the loss to the local police, and a detective came by to collect details. We gave him a detailed description of the man who collected it from the reception area. Before he left we were told a follow-up visit could be expected today, if they had made any progress. The local police are very efficient." Charles found himself listening with some degree of impatience, and several times resisted the urge to interrupt the manager's long apology. Finally, he found an opportunity. "Mr. Berretta, I do not want to seem rude and ungrateful, but I think we should forget about this damned book. In fact, last night I decided I would ask you this morning to give up the search. I am asking you now. My interest is no longer there. Recovering it has no financial value for me, and I have a plausible explanation for its disappearance. My guess is that someone in de Pachmann's family wanted to protect some information disclosed in the new book. You can notify the police that I have no further interest in the matter."

The manager had been taking in his comments with intense attention, and Charles could now see an immediate expression of relief come over his face. "Well, I did not expect this development Doctor Flemming, but I respect your decision, and I feel relieved. The hotel was certainly ready to do everything possible to help you find the lost book. It really was our responsibility to keep it safe in the first place."

"Do not let it concern you further," Charles heard himself say. He wanted nothing more than to forget the matter. He could think of nothing better than the idea of he and Agnieszka spending what he knew would be a wonderful week together. But now he wanted to get to the convention centre to catch the first speaker. Shaking hands with the manager as they parted, he moved to the hotel entrance to find a taxi, or perhaps to walk. He looked out and was disappointed to see it was raining, so he asked the doorman to order a taxi, which arrived promptly. He was at the Hotel Michelangelo by 8:40, so he found a chair in the crowded lobby and sat down to review the presentations in the afternoon programme.

Four short papers were to be given in English, so he would try to attend. Another Canadian psychiatrist was speaking at 1:30 pm on *Constitutional Body Habitus and Affective Tendencies: Validity of the Apoplectic and Asthenic Types.* Charles had heard variations on this theme before from this doctor, who worked at the Montreal Institute of Psychiatry. There were other topics he thought were worth hearing: *Verbal Tics as Kinesthetic Hallucinations,* which might have some relevance to his talk tomorrow, *De Clérambault's Theory of Mental Automatism as Precursors of Delusions and Hallucinations* seemed relevant as well. Before the afternoon coffee break, he would try to hear *The Madonna/Prostitute Dichotomy: A Risk in Middle Aged Men* to be given by an Australian analyst, whom he did not know. The time for the first presentation was approaching, and he decided it was time to move to the convention hall. As he walked the stairs to the second floor he estimated there were several hundred attendees in the lobby, with an equal mix of men and women. He recognized none of his Canadian or European friends. The lecture hall was already partly filled and he found a seat near the front.

The president of the Italian Psychiatric Association was introduced, and in English and Italian was very warm in welcoming everyone to Rome and to the meeting. In his presentation he briefly reviewed the history of psychiatry, beginning with early Roman and Greek thought. He reminded the audience that whereas Roman physicians had no definitive system of classifying mental illness, the trend by 500 AD was to separate philosophy and magic from medical science. Plato was given credit for anticipating Freud's concept of childhood experience having an important influence on behaviour of men and women. Aristotle's view was that human emotions were the causes of pain and suffering. Hippocrates was given credit for the term *hysteria*, which was due to a wandering womb, and he had believed it could be cured by sexual intercourse. Celsus and Galen had put both forward theories for the cause of melancholia and mania. Cicero had first used the term *libido,* which he believed to be the strongest physical urge in men and in women.

Much of these scraps of history Charles had forgotten. Progress in psychiatry was eventually traced to the present. The president believed that patient management in psychiatry was in a state of flux at this time in history. Restraining patients, hydrotherapy and other treatments were not always effective. Many patients in mental asylums throughout Europe were suffering from general paresis, a neurological complication of syphilis. It was easily recognized and diagnosed, often progressing to insanity. Although malaria fever treatment had seemed hopeful, no conclusive proof had been provided of long-term benefit in general paresis. There were hopeful signs that insulin induced coma or induced seizures might be helpful for some patients.

Leaving the conference venue at noon Charles noted the rain had stopped and the sun was shining. The bells from several nearby churches were pealing the hour, as they did daily at noon. He asked at the convention desk if his friend Professor Wagner-Jauregg had been registered, and was told he was not, at least not up to that point. He needed a walk after sitting much of the morning. Judging from the numbers exiting one of the venues, many of the delegates had been to the symposiums on psychotherapy. He had decided the most interesting paper of the morning he had heard was the one from India. The use of *rauwolfia serpintina* in almost one hundred psychotic patients—some with concurrent hypertension — was usually associated with a drop in high blood pressure to normal. Side effects, such as diarrhoea and stuffy nose, were significant but could be controlled by adjustment of the dosage. The day was so pleasant he decided to seek out a café to have a quiet lunch and read his manuscript again. It did not take long to find a quiet bistro several blocks away, where the menu was attractive and the clientele seemed to be locals. He ordered an aperitif, and decided on a green salad and pasta with a half bottle of 1930 Villa Lafaggio Chianti. He had been shown a table before he had noticed an American psychiatrist, Teresa Rockwell, at an adjacent table. Seeing her, he immediately registered where he had met her from the past. Teresa was from Massachusetts. They had met at a meeting last year in Toronto.

She recognized him when he called her name above the background noise. He rose and walked to her table. "I am glad to see you. I did not see you this morning at the meeting. Are you alone?"

"I missed the first half of the programme and also missed breakfast, so I am trying to catch up," she responded with a smile. "Will you join me? I am alone. Are you having lunch?"

"Yes, I am. I see you have already ordered but first I feel like having a drink." He moved over and settled into an empty chair.

"I have ordered," she said. "I was wishing there was someone to talk to. Isn't Rome a fabulous city? I seem to remember you told me last year that you were here some years ago. I see you are giving a paper on tics and Obsessive Compulsive Disorder tomorrow. I will be there to hear you. I have seen a few similar patients myself."

Teresa was a petite woman with red hair, who looked to be in her early forties. He now remembered that she practiced in a rural area outside Boston. He suddenly thought it might be therapeutic to talk to another psychiatrist about his new friend Agnieszka, and to see if her impressions of the development of the new relationship were like his. He was sure what he wanted was reassurance that the undertaking he had promised her brother was not out of line with professional practice. The idea of Agnieszka's vulnerability and the proper way to respect that was still on his mind. The opportunity to bring up the topic presented itself at the end of the lunch, after they had each had several glasses of wine.

"Teresa, I am sure I can trust you to keep what I have to say confidential. It is an interesting story that involves me and a younger woman."

Teresa looked puzzled but was quick to respond. "So you want a psychiatric consultation Charles? This must be serious." She smiled and paused to assess his expression eventually adding, "you can trust me, even though I have never had a shrink as a patient before!"

They both laughed at her humour, and he began by telling her of his dual intent in coming to Rome: To attend this meeting and give a paper, and secondly to research a book he was writing on a famous pianist who unfortunately had died a week before he arrived. He summarized the details of the train trip, his friendship with Simon, and his introduction to Agnieszka—who was virtually blind—and to her brother. He mentioned the subsequent developments that had almost resulted in their having sex yesterday. He explained how the de Pachmann book he had ordered had disappeared from his hotel, and why he had lost interest in that project.

"What has surprised me most is my commitment to look after her for the rest of this week in Rome after her brother leaves for Paris. Her vision is very poor, and she will need help in getting about. I have also promised her brother that I will personally escort her back to Kraków by train. What I have not told you is that it was her idea to stay in Rome with me during the next week, and I certainly did not put up any resistance. I said earlier that we almost made love, but this woman is somewhat naïve Teresa. It seems she is a virgin, but it makes me wonder how fair it would be to go all the way with someone so potentially vulnerable. What do you think?"

Teresa had been listening with rapt attention, and he could see she was watching his facial expressions as well. "Is there anything else that is important?" she asked. "I seem to remember that when we met last year you were still a widower and free to look at other women. Is that still the case?"

Charles nodded and added, "That's correct. I am still single but have had another relationship—not serious. On the ship from Halifax, I had a brief fling with a woman who was also lonely. In fact, she was to come to Rome to spend time with me here but she changed her mind at the last minute. Maybe she found someone else in London." They both laughed at his suggestion. "She did not turn up at the train station as I expected, but later called me here in Rome to explain why. So you see where I stand as far as relationships go. Now I seem to have fallen for this beautiful blind pianist from Poland, who lives thousands of miles from Toronto. Did I tell you she was in her early thirties? I have now lost interest in my book project."

"Charles, you have forgotten that the blind try very hard to be 'normal' like us. They try not to look for sympathy, and they sometimes resent those like us who are sighted treating them differently. There are likely more thirty-year-old virgins in Poland than you think! She happens to be one, and is also blind. The church in Poland has a very strong influence on morals just as it does in other countries. Is she Roman Catholic?"

"I think so, as I saw her cross herself as she entered a Roman Catholic church yesterday."

"But you cannot be sure. You likely know that members of the Russian and Polish Orthodox churches also make the sign of the cross. I suspect her family and her church placed a lot of emphasis on maintaining virginity before marriage." Teresa paused and added with a smile; "It is obvious she is attracted to you very much. Maybe it is not too early to suggest she has fallen in love. Of course, transference may be at work here, if she considers you have become her therapist, or even if she merely thinks of you as a good, trustworthy friend. I am sure you know there is evidence that transference can happen in life, with friends, not just in the psychotherapeutic clinical setting. If she is using transference, it could be for a number of reasons: unmet emotional needs, childhood neglect, early attempts at seduction, or even sexual abuse. You know what I mean. Over-attachment is a danger with erotic transference and when carried to extremes, obsession may be the worst outcome."

Charles was aware that she had paused, and was looking intently at him, awaiting his response. He took another drink from his glass and turned away to give himself some time to think. He had taken in all she had said, but his mind had kept wandering back to yesterday's events at Agnieszka's hotel and their breakfast together. That was when she had told him of her frustrations and her secrets. He refilled Teresa's empty wine glass.

"You are right about our attitude to the blind. I am as guilty as anyone. I have always considered they were struggling to survive against the odds, and usually felt pity for them. That is wrong. Of course musical talent is very easy to admire in a blind person, but one does not need to see to play a keyboard instrument. I had thought about the issue of transference, and I did point out to her from the beginning that I did not want to be her therapist but to be her friend. It remains to be seen if she wants only a close friendship or something more."

"I hope your relationship develops the way it should, if you love each other." Teresa sounded genuinely sympathetic. "Your friend sounds very interesting, and making love together is not wrong. You are both adults. Love is as much an art as musical talent. I feel privileged to be able to listen to your story. I will keep it confidential. But tell me about your paper. Is it ready?"

"Well, I think so. I happen to have it here." He glanced at his watch. "Would you like to read it, and give me some feedback? We have time. This is the first chance I have had to show it to someone who understands the problem." He pulled the manuscript from his briefcase and looked at her in anticipation.

"Of course I would love to read it," she replied looking at her watch. "We have about half an hour before the meeting starts."

Charles reminded her that he would go through the usual "thank you for asking me to speak and so on." He pointed to the first page. "Here is where it begins." Teresa began to read in silence.

"Most of you would agree that personality traits such as dedication to work, aiming for perfection and the need to be in control would be considered worthwhile characteristics in many avenues of life and work. Unfortunately, people like that often believe there is only one way to do something right. It can be very irritating if that person happens to be your boss. An obsessive-compulsive boss can rob his or her employees of any independent freedom and initiative because of extreme orientation to detail. If one combines preoccupation with detail and order, with reluctance to delegate authority or responsibility, some of us would likely consider that person to be very stubborn and rigid. If the person were ungenerous with money and miserly in spirit, it would fit a picture that is not rare, especially in some cultures. Some of these traits we see in ourselves and colleagues, especially in those who had make a success in administration (the deans and department heads of our medical schools for example); we see it in many of our best teachers and clinicians, as well as in some of our political leaders and government officers. If you need examples, certain police and customs officers come to mind. These criteria apply to persons who have what can best be described as obsessive-compulsive personality traits. There are also others who have the much more serious and problematic Obsessive-Compulsive Disorder, which I would like to discuss in more detail today.

"These patients have a lifetime pattern of recurrent, unpleasant thoughts, which drive them to perform ritualistic tasks. It is a disorder, commonly beginning in childhood, with a background of chronic anxiety. Simple tics of childhood, such as blinking and facial movements of the eyes or mouth, are early manifestations. Sneezing, coughing or hiccups are tics that may be heard. The thirty patients, who were referred to me with an Obsessive Compulsive Disorder for advice about management, have been primarily professional musicians, music teachers and managers of large companies. More men than women comprise the group. I have an interest in music and am familiar with a large circle of musicians who live and work in the Toronto area. All the musicians or teachers have been pianists or string players, but there have been three male conductors. For reasons that are obscure, no wind players or timpanists have been seen.

"Possessing the obsessive-compulsive trait would be expected to facilitate the development and the careers of talented, ambitious professional musicians, and it does. Some overlap of these traits with the more serious Obsessive-Compulsive Disorder is sometimes seen. Music performance is demanding and preparation for a professional career is stressful. Music critics will give credit and praise for the perfectionist who plays with a flawless technique. Discipline and perfection in performance is what they expect to hear and is what they report. When features of the Obsessive-Compulsive Disorder make their appearance in their professional lives problems occur.

"The common characteristics that were found in the group of solo musicians while in the public eye, usually on stage, included a form of performance anxiety or stage fright. This is not unusual in professional musicians who do not necessarily have the O-C Disorder. In some individual solo performers there is sometimes over-concern about fine details such as lighting of the stage. Is there too much light or too little? The height of the piano stool—which may have to be adjusted over several minutes—or even the height of the piano itself may be causes for concern and attention. Performance anxiety impairs concentration often leading to lapses in memory and playing of wrong notes, so use of a score becomes a partial solution even if it distracts from the musician's reputation for possession of an extensive repertoire. Several pianists habitually found latecomers to their performance—once it had begun—to be a major source of annoyance. Insistence on seating latecomers only after an appropriate break in the music should become a rule that every theatre manager should soon learn. Applause between movements of a piano sonata or a symphony—common in the past—is considered disruptive, inappropriate and annoying by some of today's solo performers as well as conductors. Audience noise, especially coughing, can be very annoying. Rigidity about imposing limits on the playing of encores can be a problem too. Facial and verbal tics, some of which have persisted from childhood are occasionally seen in these patients. Facial grimacing with some pianists and violinists, unconscious humming and singing with the music may be a compulsion and a source of annoyance for the audience. Some famous pianists from the past have a compulsion to talk to the audience as they play. Some examples include pianists Vladimir de Pachmann and the French pianist Francis Planté. There were others.

"On- and off-stage, the musicians who suffer from this Obsessive-Compulsive Disorder report intrusive and inappropriate thoughts or impulses that recur and persist to such a degree as to produce considerable anxiety. Efforts to suppress or ignore these impulses involve strategies such as repetitive, compulsive behaviours or mental acts that sometimes follow a rigid pattern. Repetitive bathing or hand-washing to remove germs is common. Washing or cleaning of dinnerware and cutlery before eating to ensure hygiene can be time consuming. When eating in public, or with family, such rituals may be embarrassing to spouses and more so to dinner hosts. Hoarding and collecting odd or very valuable objects can be part of the syndrome.

"Whereas some of these patients do have the O-C personality traits mentioned at the beginning of my talk, their problems of obsessions and compulsions go beyond personal acceptance, and are viewed by them and their families as troublesome and undesirable. They become a source of anxiety and distress. They may result in marriage break-up. This is in contrast to persons with simple obsessive-compulsive traits, who do not consider themselves in need of medical help. In fact, these individuals rarely accept medical advice and may resist any attempts to change.

"Freud has opened the door to an explanation for the obsessive compulsion traits. Transition from the oral to the anal stage of development may not have occurred in such persons, and this leads to anal fixations. These personality traits of perfectionism, lack of flexibility and excessive control in dealing with others likely arise from arrested anal development. There is a common belief that the O-C disorder develops differently and is a product of an anxiety neurosis. This is where therapy must be focused.

"Supportive psychotherapy remains the most effective tool, but it is by no means always successful. The details of such therapy are well-known to most of you here in this room. I have found it helpful to explore with the person the thoughts and feelings before, during and after compulsive rituals, as patients must not believe that such compulsions are injected by some exterior force, but are a product of their mind, the so called 'inner voice.' Some strategies I have explored include recommending extended breaks or holidays from teaching or from concert performances. Extending the time between engagements to weeks instead of days to provide temporary respite from the stage may be acceptable. If part-time teaching is an enjoyable experience for the performance artist, and as free from excessive expectations for perfection as possible, it can provide more time for regular psychotherapy and provide needed income. The same strategy has been applied to those in managerial positions. The addition of a spouse to the therapeutic process is advisable on occasion. Obsessions and rituals which cannot be suppressed may lead to resistant depression and unfortunately sometimes to suicide.

"In summary, the Obsessive-Compulsive Disorder presents a challenge to both patient and therapist. I do not claim to have come near to success in probing the causes or helping all my patients I have discussed. In a way, the patients I describe are unique in constituting an unusually concentrated and focused group of musicians, who also possess, in varying degrees, the O-C traits, which are so often seen in the professional musician.

"Mister Chairman, I welcome any comments and suggestions from the audience and would be pleased to respond to any questions. Thank you for listening."

Charles was watching her as she came to the end. He was awaiting Teresa's reaction and her response. "There are some loose ends that I myself can see," he admitted, "but please feel free to comment."

"I think you have not clearly distinguished the O-C *traits* from the *disorder* in your population of musicians. I know there is sometimes overlap. You said that. I would also have spent more time on management and outcomes, which seemed too brief. For example, you did not say how many of your patients were helped by your management strategies, which treatment you consider best and how many failed to respond to therapy—perhaps how many committed suicide. Do you have time to expand on that?" Charles could see Teresa had paid close attention to the manuscript and had given thought to his premise.

"I do. Thank you for your suggestions Teresa. I will think about how these ideas can be incorporated. Hopefully, if you hear it tomorrow, you will think it is better. Now it is time we got back to the conference. You have been very helpful and kind. Let me pay for lunch."

CHAPTER ELEVEN

"Tu ne cede malis sed contra audentior ito"
(Yield not to misfortunes but advance all the more boldly against them)

Some of the afternoon topics were of mutual interest, so Charles and Teresa both sat in on the presentation on the relationship between constitutional make-up and affective tendencies. Doctor Guy LeBlanc, a psychiatrist from Montreal, whom neither had met, had devised a classification of affective disorders based on physical appearance of his patients. There were two main types: those with a so-called *apoplectic habitus* and those with an *asthenic habitus*. The *apoplectic habitus* persons were not very tall, had short necks and extremities with broad, short hands and feet. They often had round faces and a high colour, with a tendency to obesity and high blood pressure. "These are people who family doctors should realize may, one day, have an apoplectic stroke," said Dr. LeBlanc. He was of the opinion that these people were "extroverts" and "good mixers," with degrees of mood varying between elation and depression, constituting a description of "cyclothymic" persons.

The second physical type was different. Those persons with the *asthenic habitus* are tall, thin, with a long neck, long arms, flat chest and long fingers and toes. They sometimes have low blood pressure and have a tendency to develop tuberculosis. They are "introvert" and tend to be "loners." They are sensitive, delicate, easily offended and shy. He referred to these people as "schizoid" in personality. These two types of physiques and temperament tend to follow a familial pattern but offspring of two parents who do not posses the same *habitus* will, of course, produce a mix of characteristics with variable presentations. Treatment approaches were discussed for the syndromes of alternating elation and depression in those with the *apoplectic habitus*.

Neither Teresa nor Charles was convinced that a good case had been made for this classification. It was obvious that the two affective disorder types constituted only a fraction of the population seen in a psychiatric practice. The next paper Charles had chosen was on verbal tics and kinaesthetic hallucinations, but it was to be presented in German, so he decided to wait for the paper on Clérambault's Syndrome. Teresa had decided to return to her hotel.

His interest was stimulated by the excellent, gripping presentation about Gaëtan de Clérambault, a French neurologist, who had described a syndrome of mental automation, with unpleasant feelings, which he thought were caused by the influence of someone else. In 1927, he had called the delusion *"psychose passionelle"* or delusion of passion. The patient was usually a middle-aged woman, who had a delusion or belief that a man whom she did not know or whom she had only recently met, was in love with her. Such female patients were usually living in some isolation, often having few social contacts. Their victims had usually done nothing to encourage the delusion, and were usually unaware of the woman's beliefs. The victims—who were sometimes prominent public figures such as politicians, priests or doctors—although inaccessible to the patient, become a love object. De Cléramault considered it to follow a bi-phasic course: first with a period of hope and later of resentment, sometimes leading to harassment of victims. Most of patients were resistant to exploring the reasons for the delusions. Schizophrenia was an important differential diagnosis in every case.

Charles was fascinated by the presentation. His first thought was of his relationship with Agnieszka. To make a case for this syndrome made no sense to him, but it was possible to make a comparison. Agnieszka was a seemingly well-adjusted talented woman—facing and dealing well with the challenge of blindness—who had met a Canadian psychiatrist two days ago, and found a common bond. She would hardly have had time to develop such a delusion about him. Although he was curious about why their relationship had developed quickly, it seemed to be a mutual feeling. He suspected their relationship would develop in the next week, and he had an open mind as to where it would go. He was determined to make the relationship as non-clinical as possible.

His interest in the paper on *The Madonna/Prostitute Dichotomy* was such that he had decided to wait until 3:45 and listen. It was scheduled after a coffee break, which he knew he needed. The coffee in the lobby was superb. He had heard of this psychiatric syndrome during his years in training, but he had never encountered a situation where the concept seemed a likely explanation for sexual problems in a marriage. He noticed there was considerable interest in the talk as it was not easy to find a seat in the small conference room. Dr. Stanley Graham was a wiry, grey haired character from Sydney, Australia, with an accent that was distinctive and a good sense of humour. He had been introduced by the chairman as "a semi-retired" clinical psychologist. Charles found the talk somewhat uninteresting. Perhaps he was he looking for something that had relevance to his practice, or to him. The case for the Madonna (or virgin) and Prostitute (sinful woman) dichotomy was based on the idea that the male psyche tended to divide women into two types, or categorize both mutually exclusive. The contemporary view was: there were good women (who were not 'easy' to seduce) and sexy women (who were 'easy'). The dichotomy developed in middle-aged men, who idolized women (usually wives) as virtual virgins to be respected, left alone and serving only to satisfy their loneliness. In contrast, the other women served to satisfy their erotic lust. Graham believed that there was really no distinct separation of women who were 'sexy' or those who were not. The presentation stimulated a lively discussion, but Charles felt he was ready to leave before the end, and decided to walk back to his hotel.

Agnieszka had left a message for him at the reception desk, suggesting he meet her at 6:30 because she wanted him to hear a new composition. It made him smile to think of her writing a polonaise dedicated to him. He enquired at the desk about restaurants in the area that specialized in fish dishes, and was told that *The Roman Fisherman*, in a small hotel nearby, had the best reputation and was within walking distance from her hotel. The concierge offered to call and reserve a table for two at 8:00, and departed into the reception office to make the call.

"Yes, they have reserved a table for you," she reported after hanging up the telephone and returning to the desk. "You may not have heard that the police were here in the morning about the manuscript matter. They have several suspects, who are tourists or visitors, but they also know that you have withdrawn your complaint. The police here can be very determined, and may not simply drop the matter. They consider theft a serious matter and were very curious to know why you wanted to drop the search."

"Thank you for making the call," Charles replied, "let me think about the matter of the police." She was able to exchange some money, and he noted the exchange with Canadian currency was still favourable.

He was looking forward to an hour of rest in the quiet of his room. First, he should call Agnieszka to confirm the times. She answered the phone, and seemed exited and very eager to talk about the fish restaurant and her new composition that had taken most of the day to complete. He decided to tease her. "Is it a polonaise or perhaps a sonata? How many movements have you written?" he asked.

"You can guess yourself when you hear it," she replied. "It is not a polonaise. It could be a romance. After all, I have written it for you."

"*Touché*. I will be there about six. I was told the restaurant is not fussy about dress code, so you can judge that casual attire would be okay but I plan to wear a tie. I remember telling Alexei yesterday about our dinner date."

Agnieszka assured him that her brother did know. As she had expected, Alexei and Simon had decided to have dinner somewhere to discuss their travel plans. "I am very pleased we will be spending the evening without them," she added.

After he had hung up, Charles realized how much he was feeling the heat. The room was very hot, and he felt uncomfortably sweaty. He decided to take a bath, and change into more casual clothes. He knew he would then have to try touching up the presentation. He had some relevant numbers with statistics, which he found amongst his notes, so he added them to the manuscript in pencil. He wanted to time how long it would now take to read the paper with the new material, and found it was still close to ten minutes. That would do. He was getting very bored with the paper, and he was finding Agnieszka was intruding pleasantly into his thoughts. There had been no strict adherence to time in today's talks. There would be about five minutes for questions and discussion, which would be enough. He saw it was 5:45, so he decided to set off to meet Agnieszka. He had thought he might bring the manuscript of his talk for her to hear, but he had heard it enough already. The sunlight was fading, and the evening was cooling with a light wind. The sidewalks were crowded with strolling couples, some with children and dogs on leashes. He felt very relaxed. He arrived at the hotel within fifteen minutes and found the lobby was very quiet. Agnieszka answered her doorbell so quickly he wondered if she had been standing just inside. She looked wonderful in a white, lightweight blouse with a long navy colour skirt and flat shoes.

"You are right on time! I am glad we will have some time together before dinner."

"You look wonderful," he replied, and she laughed as she removed her glasses. He put his arms around her and added, "you look beautiful tonight—but not just tonight—you always do. Why have I never told you that before?" They held one another for several minutes in the hallway, and he kissed her neck.

He heard her say, "What a lovely compliment. I wish I could see what you mean when I try to look in a mirror. I miss so much when I look at myself. Come in and take off your jacket. I want to play you my new composition before we go to eat. Help me to the piano. I have had a very enjoyable day — not as lonely as I had thought. Alexei spent a few hours here, and we discussed my plans for the rest of the week as well as the finances. I will tell you more about that later. His train is not leaving until tomorrow afternoon, so I hope you will find time to see him before, to talk about how you should deal with his little sister." She laughed as she took his arm and they moved into the studio. She settled herself on the piano stool and he squeezed alongside.

"You have never heard any of my compositions, so you may think they are too modern. However, I tend to favour the classical style so let us see what you think. I did not write a sonata with several movements because of time constraints! It is simply a brief romance, as I said on the telephone. I have tried to make it a happy piece as that is my current mood."

"I like that," he responded, "I can tell you are happy. It makes me feel happy too."

Agnieszka's romance was a very seductive work in C minor with some virtuoso flourishes toward the end. There were some 'modern' aspects, but they did not distract. She had played it from memory, but Charles could see she had made notations on a score, which she had left on the piano. He knew she would not be able to see the score well in this light.

"I think it is a lovely piece, and I will always remember that melody. It sticks in my memory. It is a unique piece because it is your creation and you composed it just for me." He kissed her on the cheek and gave her a squeeze. "Can you play it for me again?"

She did, and said she now wanted to play some Chopin preludes, which she did as he listened with obvious enjoyment. Finally, she suggested they find more comfortable chairs. After they had settled, she changed the subject.

"Now I would like to hear you talk about your life. We have some time before the dinner reservation. I feel very selfish not to have let you talk about yourself before this. You know something about my family and me. But first tell me about your day. How was the meeting?"

He gave her a brief resumé of the day's activities, and a description of the papers he had heard. "I had lunch with another psychiatrist from Boston and she was kind enough to read the paper I have to give tomorrow. Yesterday, I had thought I might have you listen to it tonight, but now you have been saved from the task. You would have been bored."

"I would not, but you can read it to me another time—I know it would not be boring."

He thought for a few seconds, pondering how he would tell her the essence of his life. Where would he begin?

"We were a small family. Our home was outside the city of Toronto, Ontario, in a farming town appropriately called Farmington! Our school was only a four-classroom affair even including high school students. My childhood had been reasonably happy until my mother became ill, and died of the effects of a stroke when I was fourteen. We were devastated. She had been told years before that she had high blood pressure, which did not respond to many treatments. My father never remarried. I had a sister who was ten-years old then and had always been disabled by cerebral palsy, yet always seemed very happy. Without a mother our household changed completely. I felt I must assume a larger part in my sister's care, which I accepted without complaint. The two of us became even closer as a result of that. The tragedy is she developed meningitis during an epidemic that year, and died when she was only twelve. I can still remember how she looked in her coffin, so pale and so very cold when I touched her hand, even though it was in the middle of a July heat wave. I had been tempted to kiss her cheek as I had seen father do before the casket was closed, but I decided not to. I wish I had. I had never seen a dead person before, and I was very sad for months after the funeral.

"My father, not surprisingly bore the brunt of her death the longest, and I suppose the most. I never knew then why that was, but now I can see that my mother was the tougher one over the years I was growing up. He could cry whenever Sarah's name was mentioned, and afterward he made a point of making himself more available for me. It was in high school, years later, that I realized I did not want to be a farmer like my father, but a doctor. No one had told me at that time why Sarah had died. The doctor had been coming to the house almost daily for weeks before the end. It was a few years later I found out she had died of meningitis. There was no cure then and there still isn't.

"I studied medicine in Toronto after getting a BSc degree at the university and always found studying tough going. I had done well in my small rural school but in university I was on my own, and I had not learned good study habits in my school. I drank too much beer, and smoked cigarettes. I played hockey and basketball, but was never a star. I was lucky to get through medicine with reasonable marks. I took over a general practice in another small town west of Toronto, where I stayed for three years before deciding psychiatry was for me. I had some very challenging psychiatric problems to deal with in practice, so it was likely the stimulus for me to apply for a position in the Toronto training program. I had studied music of course, and maintained my interest well into my years in university. I learnt to play some simple Chopin preludes reasonably well and I developed an interest in the maladies of musicians, especially composers. I found the topic of creativity, not just in music but also in art and literature very interesting. I married my wife, Anne, when I was thirty-five years old. By then I was a psychiatrist with a university appointment. We met in Boston and at first we did not expect marriage would work. She was American. She had a very good job in business there, and did not seem to be interested in moving north to Canada. But she eventually did. You know she was killed in a train accident—not immediately—but days after, as a result of her serious injuries. We had no children, so I have no descendents. Anne did not want children perhaps because she had witnessed the hardships her parents had experienced bringing up seven children on a limited income. You suspected yesterday in the taxi that I was upset talking about Anne. It is difficult to understand, but sometimes merely thinking about her premature death makes me feel odd. It seems to take my breath away, and I am temporarily useless." He paused to take a deep breath. "My father died of natural causes about five years ago, and I can talk about him and my mother without any difficulty. Memories of my sister Sarah will live with me forever. Sometimes, when I remember her, it makes me feel the way I do when I think about Anne."

"Do you want to change the subject?" Agnieszka asked gently.

"No. I feel fine. It isn't always that I get that way. I now live alone and work in a downtown Toronto home. I have a very friendly Labrador dog named Toby, who is almost six years old. I have bought a small farm in the Muskoka district, north of Toronto, which is where Toby and I spend weekends doing nothing except hiking throughout the woods. Sometimes I fish for trout, but I do not hunt game or birds. I must admit, though, I enjoy eating deer and pheasants very much. Someone else has to shoot them for me."

He paused and kissed her on the cheek. She was holding his hand and he could feel her warmth. He continued, "I think you were brought up in a religious home as you mentioned your church yesterday. My family was Methodist but we did not go to church often. The problem was there was no Methodist church in our town, so we did not often take the trouble to travel twenty miles on Sundays to do so. My parents obviously did not have the commitment."

He paused and gave her hand a squeeze. "Perhaps some day you will come to visit Toronto and stay with me—perhaps to give some recitals. I would speak to someone about tour arrangements if you were interested."

He was aware she had cuddled up to be close as he told his story. She spoke; "Now I understand you better. I was wondering if you have had a strict up bringing like me. My parents were always ambitious, promoting my career and they still are, especially my father. Our family are members of the Orthodox Church, which was somewhat like the Russian version. My father's grandfather's family was Jewish but they died in Russia where they lived and their religion died with them. I do not feel very religious either, but I love church music and choral singing that has been inspired by the *Bible*. I live at home and because of my blindness I depend on my parents to a great degree. My mother and a servant woman prepare the meals. Because of his blindness, my father is also dependent on her like me, so my mother carries a large burden. She drives us around in the family car. Much of my day, when I am not playing the piano, is spent alone which is so often boring. I listen to the radio. I often feel a sense of emptiness—perhaps partly from being blind. My life can be a prison. Alexei now lives alone and is very independent. I am fortunate I have lost no one in my family except elderly grandparents. I am fascinated to hear you took music lessons. How long did you study piano?"

"First of all, my parents seem to have been less strict than yours. I did get an occasional clout from my father if I was bad," Charles replied, ready to continue until Agnieszka interrupted to ask what a "clout" was, and he had to explain.

"My first piano lessons began when I was about eight, and I have to admit I hated it. My first teacher was a Miss Mildred Roberts, who lived in an adjacent town. She was a spinster and somewhat cranky, like one of your teachers. I would bicycle to her home twice a week after school. She had a good reputation and seemed an excellent player. I loved it when she played for me after the lessons. She produced many excellent pupils but I was not one of them. I was never prepared to practice daily, and my mother eventually suggested to my teacher I should take up the violin, which was a mistake as I never liked the sound of the violin as a child! I must have heard someone play a violin at some time and hated the squeaky notes. Needless to say, violin lessons were a failure too. Now, at this time in life, I wish someone had suggested the cello because I love it. One embraces the cello with your arms, like a lover and hold it between your legs." Agnieszka laughed at the analogy.

"You are right, there is something sexual about it."

"Sometimes, I think it is still not too late to take cello lessons," Charles continued. "A good friend of mine has taken up the cello in recent years and now plays reasonably well."

"It is so nice to hear you talk about your younger years. Do you also teach medical students as well as see patients?"

"I do and enjoy it a lot. Several years ago I was given an award for being the best teacher of the second-year medical class." He paused and realized he was boasting—so unlike him. He changed the subject. "Have you ever given music lessons?" he asked.

"Never. I do not have the confidence to teach—being a blind person. It would present problems for me and for my parents. I would have to teach from home and the comings and goings would likely frustrate my mother."

He looked at his watch and suggested; "Let us plan the arrangements for getting to the restaurant. It is not practical to walk, even if you have comfortable shoes. I think the best idea is to take a taxi. Do you need to make any preparations before we leave? I see the time is about 7:45."

"I will go to the bathroom and then I will be ready," she replied.

He helped her turn off the bedroom lights and lock the door. They set off down the hall arm-in-arm to call the elevator, which arrived empty. He stole a kiss as they descended to the ground floor. The doorman was eager to call a taxi and soon they were at the *ristorante* called 'The Roman Fisherman,' which as he had been told was nearby. The waiter was very efficient in getting them settled at a secluded table. Charles wanted to sit next to Agnieszka, instead of across the table, so they would be close. The clientele was small in number but somewhat noisy. They soon realized there was live music in the background — a pianist, part of a four-piece band, was playing popular music that sounded suitable for dancing. Charles wondered if she liked to dance but he did not immediately ask. Would being blind be an obstacle to dancing? He decided to find out—but first there was the menu. He felt an aperitif was the first order of business.

"I am going to order a martini cocktail, if they can make one here," he announced. "Have you ever had one?" She hadn't and was curious to know what type of drink it was. "The basic ingredients are a British gin and dry vermouth, which in Italy means Martini and Rossi vermouth from Turino. The vermouth is mixed with the gin usually in a 1:4 ratio. If you like it drier, meaning less vermouth and more gin, the ratio can be 1:6 or better. Let us see if they will make it for us."

The waiter arrived and was certain the experienced bartender knew how to make one with the suggested ratio of gin to vermouth. He promised there would also be the traditional olive. To be safe, Charles asked for the 4:1 ratio for Agnieszka. Meanwhile, they were promised the traditional wine and bread would be coming. "*Bianco o Rosso?*" the waiter asked. They chose a *litro* of *Bianco*, as they agreed they were likely to have fish.

Agnieszka was looking very relaxed and he found she wanted to hold his hand. He could feel her thigh exerting a slight pressure against his, and he responded in a similar fashion.

"You will have to read the menu for me," she whispered. "Tell me what fish dishes there are tonight. I cannot help you with the Italian translation."

"I may need some help from the waiter although there is an English translation," he replied. "There is *Storione in Fricondo,* a sturgeon stew, served with *pisselini*, which I think is fresh peas and there are other fish that he can tell us about. Meanwhile a *pasta e ceci*, pasta with chickpeas, might be a good way to start or you might prefer a *risotto* with either artichoke sauce or with wild mushrooms. I think I would like the one with mushrooms."

He was realizing the challenge Agnieszka faced every time she ate a meal, and although he had observed her eating before, he was curious to learn more about how she coped.

"If there is good lighting, I can see well enough to find the food," she explained with a smile, when he asked. "If I cannot find it, I will rely on you to help me. Sometimes I can make a mess, but I won't tonight. It helps to be sure I know where my wine glass is on the table! I have learned not to impulsively reach for things, so I find things by touch."

"You will not leave a mess, and I know exactly how to make sure you don't," Charles assured her, and changed the subject. "I have been thinking about the next few days and how we will keep in touch. I hope you will be fine alone in your suite, and I know you want to keep the piano until you leave. I assume the Pleyel dealer has agreed to that?"

She nodded, "Yes, they have, as Alexei checked with them today." She paused and squeezed his hand. "You might have some reservations about this idea, but I have been thinking it would be sensible for you to move to my hotel—perhaps to take Alexei's room so you can be nearer. You can keep in touch better. It does not seem logical for you to be so far away."

The waiter had arrived with the two martini cocktails, so she dropped the subject to talk about the drink. "I will be interested in your reaction," Charles said as she took a sip. He saw she made a face and felt he had to say, "It is an acquired taste. Take your time."

"I can see the interest," she commented, "but I think it will take me a while. It will be a learning experience," she said as she took another sip.

He suggested, "There is wine to come, of course. I can finish your martini cocktail if you want to leave it. But do you have any favourite items for dinner?"

The waiter had come back and was helpful in suggesting choices. Charles considered *lumache,* which they were told were snails, as an appetizer but in the end Agnieszka chose the *risotto with artichoke* and he *with mushrooms.* They agreed on the sturgeon stew as the main course, and *zabaglione* for desert.

"Have you danced much, and are you interested in trying?" he asked between courses. The music was slow, and he thought she would manage. It was a dance by Carl Fisher that he remembered from the past.

"In the school for the blind the teachers tried to teach us to dance, and you can imagine it was not easy. The dances we learned were slow and uncomplicated. If you chose a partner who had some vision it was better, as he would be less likely to step on ones toes! I would love to try now. It has been years and I am not good so you will have to be patient with me."

The dance area was not crowded, so there was room to dance without constantly avoiding others. He found she moved with the rhythm of the music very easily and she wanted to be held close. He was glad the music was not loud enough to preclude conversation. "You are a perfect dancer," he whispered, giving her a gentle kiss on her left ear.

"It helps to have someone who can see and can lead. Have you danced most of your life?"

"Probably since high school. In university we went to Friday night dances. Methodists are not supposed to dance, as John Wesley thought it was sinful. You may not know why Methodists are warned never to make love standing up."

"No, I don't. Tell me."

"Because it can lead to dancing!"

She giggled and moved closer. "I'm glad you are not a strict Methodist." He whispered in her ear, "I am being aroused, holding you so close."

"Yes, I know," she replied, "can you save that for later? But perhaps we should see what the waiter has for us next. I have enjoyed the food so far, and the wine is an ideal choice but I'm not convinced I should change to martini cocktails."

The waiter was preparing to bring the sturgeon stew, and it appeared within a minute, piping hot. "Do you think they catch this fish in the Tiber?" she asked, as she carefully examined the plate.

"I have no idea, but we can ask the waiter. Is there enough light for you to see?"

She said it was fine. She would manage. Charles decided to make another venture:

"While we are waiting for the stew to cool, we can think about some visits you might like me to arrange for us after tomorrow. I had thought of a visit to the Vatican to see Saint Peter's Basilica and Michelangelo's *Pieta*. Most tourists cannot leave Rome without having that experience. The present Pope is Pius XI, but I do not know much about him. He has had his problems dealing with Mussolini I think." He paused to try the stew and paused to get her reaction. "You can think about it later. I don't want to be too controlling. I suspect you do not always get the maximum benefit from these sight-seeing tours, but if we can find a good guide who can tell us what we are looking at, it should be better than trying to do it ourselves. I would think you might enjoy a guided tour of some of the fountains of Rome. There are many to see, but you can hear them too and stick your toes in the water. Any other ideas?"

Agnieszka was strangely quiet, and seemed to be looking at some space across the table. He squeezed her hand and knew immediately he should not have suggested she might not find tours rewarding. "I realize what I said was not appropriate—about you having troubles seeing the sights. You do not have to do any of these things but if the weather is fine, it would be nice to simply get out and wander. I will be with you every minute." He suspected she was crying, as she wiped her left eye with her napkin.

"I'm sorry to seem like a baby but it is at times like this when I realize just how much I miss by being blind. Sometimes I feel I really am in a prison. It makes me feel angry that I could be a burden to you. I am sure you would prefer to explore the sights of Rome like the other visitors without having to lead a blind woman over steps, through doors and around obstacles!"

Charles was unprepared for her outburst, her reaction, but he was not surprised either. He did not respond immediately, but held her hand tightly and leaned over to wipe away her tear, and to kiss her gently on the cheek. "I am enjoying the fish are you?" He could see she had not made much progress. "Yes, it is as nice as I suspected. Thank you. Can you help me to the toilet? I have no idea where to find it."

The waiter was helpful and directed them to an area at the far end of the dining area. "You are never in a prison when you are sharing life with someone you love," he whispered to her as they moved across the room. He was not sure how she would find her way around the unfamiliar toilet. He decided to wait and was surprised how quickly she reappeared again. "I feel much better," she said, "now I feel like finishing my dinner."

He wondered if she would prefer to return to the hotel, but she assured him she would prefer to stay. "I do not want to miss the *zabaglione!* And I also want to have a coffee. You are right. We can discuss our tour activities later. I feel very happy you are prepared to spend the next week with me." She squeezed his hand. "If you kiss me, it will make me feel better."

He did as she suggested and could see she had recovered. "We can leave as soon as we have that dessert. We do not have to stay late. What would you like to do after dinner? We could go back to my hotel or to yours?" She was squeezing his hand tightly. "I think I know what would happen in either case," she replied, "I want to give myself to you—to have you feel me naked, and for me to feel you too. I can almost imagine what it will be like already. It would be safer to go to your hotel, as we would not be interrupted. I would love to see where you sleep."

CHAPTER TWELVE

"Nuda veritas"
(Naked truth)

It was raining again as they emerged from the restaurant and waited for the taxi to arrive. The temperature had dropped, and there was a cool breeze. Agnieszka was in an expansive mood as she clutched Charles' arm. Her verdict was that the *zabaglioni* was "very good" and she had been full of praise for the service. Charles could tell she had enjoyed the wine too. He was feeling a sense of excitement. The decision had been for them to return to his hotel. There had been no debate, and it made sense to them both. His hotel was not far, and the taxi was swift in getting there. They navigated the route from the lobby to the elevator with surprising speed. He was getting used to the tricks that seemed to help her find her way. In the elevator, she kissed him and said, "thank you very, very much for the dinner. It was the highlight of my visit so far. It may take me some time getting used to martinis."

"It was the highlight for me too but your recital came close," he replied, as he returned the kiss. The elevator door opened at the second floor and he took her arm and walked her to his room.

"It is 10:30 already," he said, glancing at his watch. "So we will have at least an hour or so together. I hope you are not tired. I must get you back before too late, and I have to give my presentation at nine tomorrow."

"I am not tired," she replied, glancing around the room.

"You can sit here," he suggested, as he led her across to the sitting area and threw his jacket over another chair, "I will be only a few minutes in the washroom. Do you need to go?" She shook her head and stretched out in the chair. "No I'm fine."

"Let me try your bed," she suggested, when he returned, "It will be more comfortable."

"Fine, but do not go to sleep!" he replied, as he took off his shoes. She reached out her hand and he took her by the arm. He removed the bed covers as she kicked off her shoes. "I want to lie here and have you kiss me," she said as she stretched out on the edge of the bed.

"You will have to move in and make room for me if I am to lie down. This room can get too hot," he commented, as he walked over to open the window and pull the curtains. "I hope you will not be cold." She had edged further into the centre and he heard her mutter, "It is fine. Come and join me." She turned toward him and reached out her left arm and wrapped it around him as she searched for his lips. "I want you to hold me close," she whispered. He could feel her breasts pressing against him and the weight of her left leg crossed over his.

He fumbled to unbutton her blouse. "Do you want some lights turned down?" She replied, "If you do that, I will never see you—and I want to—as much as I can," she replied with a laugh.

"Your breasts are beautiful," he whispered as he kissed them, gently biting her left nipple.

"You can help pull down my skirt." Her white panties came off as well, as she lifted her bottom off the bed. He was surprised to see her pubic area without hair, looking as bare and pale as a child's. It had been a long time since he had seen a woman without pubic hair and he was curious. "You look as smooth a baby!"

"'That's because I shave—I always have. Perhaps Canadian women don't do that. In Poland, I think it is common. Mother was the first to suggest I do that, for cleanliness, she said. She told me she always did."

He could not help feeling amused by all this. He thought of the painting of Venus in Agnolo Bronzini's *Allegory of Venus and Cupid,* that he had seen at the National Gallery in London. Bronzini had chosen to paint her nude, and without pubic hair or—as was later suspected—Vatican authorities had quietly ordered someone else to paint over her pubic area to remove the hair and avoid disturbing local sensitivities.

"But it must be difficult for you to see to do that—to shave I mean," he suggested with a laugh. "Do you ever nick yourself?"

She laughed as well. "I have had a lot of experience. It is usually a task that takes only a few minutes once a week in the bathtub. It seems I have surprised you! Now you must get undressed." She needed some help removing his trousers, but it took no longer than a minute to complete, as he snuggled in closer beside her. Later he remembered how curious she had been exploring his body. Her hands loved to touch and explore.

"We will have to do this slowly," she said. He knew what she meant, and it was no surprise to him that she needed reassurance.

"I will be careful," he replied, as he continued to caress her.

He heard her whisper; "You have already brought me very close to an orgasm. I feel the build up is so much better than solitary sex." The comment and the thought that she might masturbate had never entered his head before. But why would it, and why wouldn't she?

"I am ready for you now," she whispered.

She was very relaxed and wanted to help him. Later, he remembered how easily it had happened. She was very warm, and was quick to have an orgasm, crying out briefly. He wanted to stay longer and heard her say, "stay inside, the pain is nothing, less than I expected and I think there is another orgasm coming!" He hadn't thought about pregnancy or birth control until this moment, but it had suddenly flashed into his mind. It was hardly the time to ask but he had to. "Are we safe tonight? I mean, when was your last menstrual period?"

"I think we are safe. I finished three weeks ago," she replied breathlessly.

He knew *that* was no guarantee. Women could ovulate at any time in the cycle, but he didn't want to say. He did not want this consideration to spoil the climax. Now, if they could only coordinate the two, and have one together...

Without any suggestions or instructions from him, they did. Later, as they lay quietly, each catching their breath, she told him, "I felt your orgasm almost the same time as mine, and I was sure you had one, because you laughed. Did you find it funny?" They lay close together in silence, and he wondered if he should tell her he always laughed when he had a special orgasm. He had never been able to explain why, perhaps for the same reason some women cried.

"The French call it *le petite mort,* and in psychiatric lingo we say it represents a release from the prison of self—a sort of driving out of all thought—if you can believe it. A psychiatrist would say, 'the ego is displaced for a short spell'."

Her hands continued to explore. "I do not understand the id or the ego, but I was warned by my mother and others that giving myself to a man like this should mean that you love him or he loves you ... otherwise, it seems too much like mere lust."

He did not feel he should interrupt. She was analyzing her reaction to their having intercourse together, and he thought it was a good idea for her to do so. He was willing to listen. He was tempted to say: "A question that sometimes comes up when this happens is: Will you be sorry or have regrets tomorrow?" but he decided against it.

She seemed to read his thoughts. "I thought this was a wonderful experience—one I will never regret. I hope we will have other opportunities again in the next few days. It would be nice to say 'I love you' but I do not know yet if I do. I know I trust you. Do you understand? Do you think love should come before having sexual intercourse like this?"

She was putting him on the spot. He knew what to say, because he had thought about it before, and had talked to his patients about the same issues. "I understand completely," he replied as he stroked her breasts and kissed her lips. "There is an inclination to want to say, 'I love you', after people give themselves to one another under circumstances such as we have tonight. I do not think a physical relationship needs love to be meaningful although some think that intercourse is more meaningful if you love the person. When we made love tonight, I wanted to do more than satisfy my own desire. I wanted to satisfy you— us—both. I tried to be as tender as possible in the way that I became part of you." He paused and added, "Do you know the English word *'tender'*?"

She nodded and continued, "I think I know what it means." There was a pause as she thought of what to say. "You have so many nice features, not just physical, that attract me to you. I felt it when I first saw you, even if dimly, and heard you speak on Friday evening in the restaurant, but of course what I saw was through tunnel vision. I knew after yesterday morning's recital that we were destined to have a strong relationship, and I wanted it to be a physical one. I have to admit there was an erotic element to it but isn't that an essential part of passion?" She waited for his response, which was not immediate.

"You cannot see me well at all, and perhaps if you did you might feel differently about me. So much of personal attraction is what one can physically see."

She was listening attentively and he knew she was ready to respond. "It is true what you say. I do not see you well, neither your good features nor your flaws, but it does not matter to me. Since losing my vision, I have learned that there are other ways to evaluate or judge people. I liked your voice when we first met. You are also a good listener. Perhaps it is part of being a psychiatrist—listening and talking to people. I can also tell a lot about you from the way you touch me. You may laugh at this comment but I like the way you smell too. I rely on hearing, touch and smell. Making love tonight was wonderful. You have a wonderful touch. I have never had two orgasms like that before—one after the other. I will never have regrets about giving myself to you because I wanted to show you how I felt. Is it love? I do not know but it had a strong erotic element, whatever that means. Later tonight, in my bed, as I continue to be aware of some discomfort, I will think of it as a trivial matter and an important reminder of you—which reminds me … about tomorrow. Do you know what time it is? I really should go back to my hotel. It would be wonderful to stay here and go to sleep in your arms but that is not practical."

Charles searched for his watch, which he remembered he had removed at some stage after getting in bed. It was on the floor and he could see it was late.

"Let's get dressed and I will see you back to the hotel," he suggested. "I will help you to the bathroom, so you can get organized." Gathering up her clothes and his own, he escorted her cautiously to the bathroom, where he pointed out the essentials. She seemed confident she could cope with the strange surroundings.

With his help she soon emerged looking as radiant as before. He called the reception desk and asked for a taxi, which was guaranteed to arrive in about ten minutes. "I promised I would give you Simon's article on de Pachmann's Beethoven style," he said as he searched trough a dresser drawer. "I have it here so you can take it back with you if you wish. If not I can read it to you later." She decided to leave the article until later.

The taxi ride to the St. Regis Grand Hotel was quick, and before long they had found their way to her room. He sensed she was tired, and he also could feel the combined effects of an evening of wine and love-making too. She was willing to be directed to the bathroom and then to her bed, where he helped her into her nightclothes. He lay down beside her and kissed her on the cheek.

"I wish you could stay," she whispered. "I wish I could too—perhaps tomorrow night," he replied. "I am not sure the bed is large enough." She laughed. "We will never know until we try!"

"I will come back from my meeting after lunch, and we can plan for the rest of the week. Perhaps Alexei will be available to talk about loose ends. Will you tell him that tomorrow? I also would like to see Simon before he leaves."

"Tie up loose ends?" she asked, "what does that mean?"

"It simply means making sure all arrangements are finalized and nothing is left to chance." He kissed her again. "I have to go. Sleep well and have sweet dreams." He gave her a long hug before getting up. "I'll turn off the lights and lock your door."

He heard her shout, "Thank you again, for a wonderful evening!" as he closed the door.

In the lobby, the receptionist at the desk looked up from the book she was reading as he approached. He introduced himself as a friend of the Lipskas. "I am enquiring about the possibility of accommodation for tomorrow on the second floor, to be next to Miss Lipska, who will be needing my attendance when her brother leaves tomorrow."

The receptionist left him to check the hotel register and soon returned. "Yes, I see Mr. Lipska will be leaving tomorrow evening, but his sister will be staying longer. I know her sight is very poor. You can have his room, or perhaps another that may be vacated in the evening on the same floor. I will put your name on the list."

Charles thanked her and found the street, which was deserted. It was not raining, so he decided to walk back. It was not far to his hotel, and the air was fresh. He was beginning to know his way after four days. He would have time to think about the evening as he walked. He felt a sense of guilt because he found himself contrasting Agnieszka with the other women in his life, but he could not get around it. Love-making with Anne for the many years they had been together had always seemed sublime. They were very compatible, but birth control had always been uppermost in Anne's mind, and he had often wondered if it inhibited them in bed. More recently, having sex with Lisa on the ship had made him feel detached, and he had never thought about the issue of love. She had always been in control and supplied condoms. She made it exciting but they never discussed love. There was something special about the way that he and Agnieszka had met in Rome, and he was convinced her being blind and partly helpless was an important part of it. Yet he hated the idea that she was different and attractive to him because of her blindness. She had talked yesterday about the importance of touch, and he had discovered she loved to be touched in return. Thinking of her detailed exploration of his body brought back memories that he would remember for days. He found himself smiling when he remembered her bare pubic area, and was undecided if he preferred it that way or natural. By the time he had reached his hotel, it was almost midnight. He decided to ask the desk to call him at 6:30 to be sure he did not oversleep and be late for the lecture. After a hot bath, he was ready for sleep. Within minutes of his head touching the pillow he was asleep, but not before he silently whispered, "you would be so easy to love."

*** *** *** ***

The telephone rang much too soon, and Charles realized it was still dark outside as he groped for the receiver. He had asked for a 6:30 call, and wondered now if it had been too early. He had a mild headache, and felt groggy as he found his way to the bathroom. He found two aspirins, drank two glasses of water, and began to shave—trying to keep his mind on his talk—but his memories of the evening continued to surface. How would he best plan the rest of the week with Agnieszka? It seemed reasonable to spend it in Rome, taking a few conducted tours of the city, perhaps finding some concerts in the evenings and planning to leave for Vienna on the weekend, perhaps on Saturday or Sunday.

By 7:20 he was ready to go down to the dining room, but he decided to pull out his manuscript, and sitting on the bed read through the paper aloud. He felt satisfied. Teresa's ideas had worked well and he had put in more details of the management outcomes and a few statistics.

He found his way to the main floor via the stairs, and decided first to speak to the receptionist at the desk about his plans for moving to Agniszka's hotel in the evening. He promised to settle his account later in the afternoon. The dining room was open by the time he had completed his business there. His head felt better, and now he felt like having a full breakfast—a dish of stewed prunes, eggs and ham, toast, preserves and coffee. His usual waiter was off for the day, and he was introduced to Antonio, who was keen to offer a first class breakfast. Charles had resisted the idea of telephoning Agnieszka to say good morning before he left the room, because he though it was too early, and he was now regretting the decision. He suspected she might be awake early and be waiting for a call.

Before the arrival of the prunes he thumbed through the programme for the rest of the day. Apart from two papers in the morning he saw no reason not to leave the meeting early, perhaps before lunch. He had seen a tour guide working in the lobby of the Michelangelo Hotel yesterday, and she seemed a likely source of information about city tours. Agnieszka might enjoy a tour of the Tiber. If it were warm and sunny it would give them a good view of the Vatican and other sites along the way. He was aware of the need to avoid arranging difficult or dangerous tours because of the care needed in getting about. A boat tour raised in his mind the question of her safety. He could not remember asking her if she could swim, but he should do that. If she had ever read any of John Keats' poems, a tour of the flat where he died—even a visit to his gravesite in the Protestant cemetery—might interest her, certainly it would him. Or would she prefer a visit to the Verano Cemetery to see de Pachmann's grave? Simon might have already been there, and he would give some feedback about the ease of getting around there. It seemed that in ancient Rome cemeteries, tombs and catacombs were so much a part of the city. Thousands of people had come here over the years for health reasons or just to enjoy the sites and pleasures, and remained here to the end. Like de Pachmann and Keats, some would remain here forever.

Breakfast had arrived, and Charles decided to forget about tours and cemeteries for a few minutes. Antonio could speak good English, and despite his intentions, Charles soon found himself in conversation about the sites of Rome as seen from a local resident's perspective. There were certainly lots of choices, and enough to occupy a tourist for weeks. The fountains of the city would be a good choice, according to Antonio. After a second double-cream coffee he felt ready for his presentation, and after a visit to his room to get his manuscript, use the toilet and brush his teeth, he was on his way. He decided not to call Agnieszka after all. He would feel guilty if she had been asleep. It seemed sensible to take a taxi to the hotel and after a ten-minute wait outside on the street he was on his way. The morning air was cool.

The sun had only been up for an hour. He arrived at the Michelangelo by 8:40, and set out immediately to look for the assigned lecture room. Professor Stapleton was already there, and they shook hands and chatted about their respective careers. Stapleton looked to be in his mid-forties and Charles learnt he was the superintendent of the Manchester and District Mental Health Clinic. Stapleton had read Charles' abstract, and was keen to hear his presentation. Stapleton was an amateur violinist and played in a local band on weekends. He offered a brief resumé of the morning's proceedings, some of which Charles had already decided to skip. He was looking forward to getting his presentation over and to get away, but he decided to stay and listen to a presentation at 10:30 on *'Classic Graeco—Roman Sexuality and Reason'* by an Italian psychiatrist from Milan. He was feeling a little anxious as the deadline for his talk approached.

The lecture room was slowly filling as Professor Stapleton moved to the podium sharply at 9:15 to welcome everyone and to briefly introduce "the first speaker." Later Charles would remember his presentation moving quickly over the 10–12 minutes, but he had rehearsed it so often it was not entirely a surprise. He was able to present most of it from memory. There was moderate applause, and no questions were immediately forthcoming from the audience. He had noticed Teresa in the audience, smiling as she applauded. Stapleton—after a pause to wait for questions from the audience—asked him to speculate why there were so few musicians in his patient population who played other instruments than keyboard and strings. "Your theory is that there is merit in possessing some compulsive traits in the training of musicians, but why so few wind players and percussionists for example?"

Charles had been partly prepared for this question but his response was less than ideal.

"I have to admit I do not have a good explanation," he replied. "It is true that all musicians benefit from the dedication and commitment required, but there may be a difference in the personality of the two groups. String players outnumber other musicians in the orchestra of course—and, like solo pianists and conductors—are more in the forefront, more extroverted, and in the case of pianists are more often giving solo recitals. Other instrumentalists are less likely to play recitals on their own other than brief solos as part of a symphony or overture. Because of that, they might be better insulated from performance anxiety. But I realize that is not a good answer."

A male member of the audience stood and introduced himself as an American psychiatrist from Chicago. He wanted to know if hypnosis or self-hypnosis might be an effective way to counter some of the annoying on-stage behaviour and to manage stage fright. "Whereas inherent personality traits cannot be changed," the American had suggested, "is it possible that victims of the Obsessive-Compulsive Disorder might be helped by hypnosis?"

"I have had no experience with hypnosis as a management tool but several of my friends have—with variable results. Thank you for your question." Charles felt the answer had been less complete than he would have wished.

The allotted time had transpired, and the chairman—after thanking him for the "interesting presentation"—was ready to move on to the next speaker. A further brief period of applause followed as he made his way from the podium. He suddenly felt an urge to go to the washroom. He was feeling wound-up, and knew he would find it difficult to concentrate on the next speaker. He also wanted to check on the availability of tours during the break.

He found a washroom and on returning to the lobby found the Italian lady at the tour desk in the lobby was free and eager to show him what was available. He told her of his suggestions, and mentioned his friend who had very poor eyesight. He thought they would prefer a guided tour, with a private car if possible, rather than a crowded bus. He also was curious whether there were any concerts scheduled in the city over the next few days.

"I will have to research what guides are available and also the availability of private cars," the guide told him. "There are guides who do those types of tours." She promised to look at concert schedules, and suggested he return in an hour, which he thought was ideal. It would allow him time to hear the presentation he had chosen.

He found the presentation on sexuality and reason in the Greek and Roman past to be boring, so he left before it ended. Making his way back to the tour desk in the lobby, he was pleased to learn that Madame Giacomino had found an English-speaking guide with a car, who would drive them to any sites they chose, beginning tomorrow, depending on weather. She would also facilitate finding a cruise boat to tour the River Tiber on a day of their choosing. Her search for scheduled concerts was continuing but she was not optimistic. He decided to return to his hotel, to contact Alexei and Simon and to discuss the tour details with Agnieszka.

CHAPTER THIRTEEN

"Applaudieren Sie, Freunde, die Komödie wird beendet"
(Applaud, friends, the comedy is finished)
Beethoven on his deathbed, after last rites

Emerging from the Michelangelo Hotel, Charles decided to first return to his hotel to drop off his manuscript, and also to discuss with the manager, Mr. Beretta, his move to the St. Regis Grand hotel. The weather had improved and the sun was shining, so a brisk walk seemed in order. He had decided the presentation had been moderately successful. As soon as he had reached the podium he had shed his preliminary nervousness. The response of the audience was not enthusiastic, but it was over now, and he could see no benefit in ruminating over what he could have said and didn't. Perhaps he should forget about giving presentations at meetings, and concentrate on his main hobbies—the history of medicine, and creating palindromes. He was surprised he had found the medical history talk he had just left uninteresting, and he had not created a palindrome since being on the train from Milan. Could it be his mood? He did not feel depressed, but he was preoccupied and did not feel in the vein for thinking about his talk and the conference. Yet, he was happier now than he had been for months. Perhaps it was his new romance with Agnieszka. On the most recent occasion when he had thought of Anne, her memory no longer left him with the same sense of breathlessness and weakness, which was a distinct change.

The events in Rome since his arrival had been far different than he could have imagined. He had not anticipated becoming involved in a love affair, even less with a concert pianist who had virtually no vision, was considerably limited in her ability to walk alone, and to whom he had promised to act as companion for the next week, as well as accompanying her home by train to Poland.

The manager of his hotel was on duty, so Charles explained his change in plans and his planned move. Mr. Berretta was sympathetic, and said the hotel would prepare his bill so that it could be settled in the evening before he left. He also mentioned the case of the de Pachmann manuscript that had disappeared. The local police had agreed not to continue the investigation, but wanted him to prepare a typed statement—it had to be in Italian—an outline of why the search for the book should be abandoned, and absolving the police of further responsibility in the matter. Mr. Berretta kindly offered to have his secretary prepare a letter for him to sign later. Charles spent a few minutes writing the outline of the letter that he thought would be considered both honest and fair.

He found his room very tidy as always, but the chambermaid was nowhere in sight. He wanted to try to communicate his gratitude for her contribution to the manuscript mystery. Perhaps a generous tip would be all that was needed, but he could do that later before he checked out. Now it was time to meet his friends. A phone call would be appropriate to be sure he knew where to find them. Alexei answered the telephone immediately.

"Hello Charles, we are all here in my room, number 250, discussing plans for our leaving and for Agnieszka's next few days here and travel plans. Are you able to join us?"

He said he would be there within half an hour. Looking in the clothes closet, he realized there was packing to be done before he checked out, and it seemed appropriate to do that now. It took less than fifteen minutes to put most of his clothes and his shoes in the two suitcases, and he was ready to leave. He had not packed his manuscript and notes on de Pachmann. This would be a good opportunity to deliver his notes and the draft of his de Pachmann biography to Alexei, who—Charles knew—would continue to work on his own version. He found room in his briefcase for all the notes. The weather had continued to improve, so he set off to walk down the street to the hotel. Workmen were repairing a large stone building nearby, and he stopped to watch a mechanical crane lift a large steel beam across the newly repaired walls. He had noticed the repairs going on before on other days that he had walked by. There was a loud babble of voices in the background as a number of the Italian workmen shouted orders to the crane operator, with their companions standing watching the cranes' boom make its slow progress across the skyline. He looked at his watch, noted that it was almost noon, and reluctantly moved on.

Alexei, Agnieszka and Simon were waiting for him in Room 250. Agnieszka, wearing dark glasses, was looking relaxed in an easy chair, sipping a glass of red wine. Alexei and Simon were drinking beer, and offered him a choice. He felt very much like unwinding and accepted a glass of red wine — a Chianti, that he found somewhat tannic but drinkable.

"Now we should discuss the details of the next few days," suggested Alexei as he looked in Charles' direction. "Agnieszka and I have talked about her plans, and she is happy to stay a few more days in Rome, but thinks you should both plan to catch a sleeper to Vienna by the weekend. Leaving on Saturday would get you to Kraków on Monday, if you can make good connections in Vienna. We have discussed her finances and she has more than enough for the hotel here and for travel. There may be other expenses, but if there are we can settle later. Simon and I will leave on this evening's train to Milan, and will be in Paris on Sunday. Agnieszka knows where I will be staying if you need to get in touch. I know you will be an excellent companion for her, as you know so much about her needs, and I sense you are good friends and happy together. I hope you have an enjoyable few days here and get to visit some of the city highlights."

Agnieszka appeared eager to speak, and was waiting for the appropriate time. She was curious about how his talk had gone, and how he was feeling about the audience response. "I also have a surprise to tell you later about the possibility of another recital."

"I rarely come away from a lecture or presentation feeling completely happy with how things have gone,' Charles replied. "I will tell you more about the details later, but for now all I can say is that I am glad it is over. I cannot wait to hear your news."

Simon also wanted to speak. "I want to say a few words about my experience here, without being too sentimental," he said, as he looked in Charles' direction. "I have already told you how much I have appreciated our friendship Charles, and our conversations about music as well as your insight into my disability. I have enjoyed meeting Agnieszka and Alexei again, and will carry back to Wales the good news about her triumph here in Rome. I am still feeling sad about Pachmann's sudden demise. I have felt his presence often during our short stay in Rome – with Agnieszka's dedicating her recital to his memory and the many discussions about Chopin and Beethoven." He paused for a moment to gather his thoughts. "I think I have time to read you the reviews of her recital on Sunday as well as the organ recital, which I missed. Two reviews are from city newspapers. Our manager was kind enough to have his secretary translate them for us and there are some extra copies if you want them. I will read what the critic in *The Morning News* wrote about Agnieszka's recital." Pulling the reviews from his pocket he began to read:

'Despite little publicity, the *Reale Academia Filarmonica Romana* was filled to capacity on Sunday afternoon to hear the Polish pianist, Agnieszka Lipska, present a programme of Chopin in her own unique way — unique because she seems the most authentic current interpreter of the Polish master currently on the European recital circuit. Miss Lipska has benefited from excellent instruction in Poland. She has taken as her mission the authentic interpretation of the piano music of her fellow countryman, a task that has greatly benefited her listening audiences. Yesterday's recital programme consisted almost entirely of the master's best-known compositions. The impact of the afternoon's recital was felt even more by her decision to dedicate the recital to the well - known pianist, Vladimir de Pachmann, who died several weeks ago in our city. Mister de Pachmann, was not a teacher of Miss Lipska, but he was at one time considered the world's foremost interpreter of Chopin's piano music. There are some who feel that she may be the logical successor of his legend.

'The programme was well suited to Miss Lipska's talents, and she showed remarkable poise and stage manner throughout. Her manner is to play with an excess of *pianissimo* or lack of *forté*, which was said by some to be the manner of Chopin and de Pachmann himself. This attractive pianist was unfortunately deprived of her sight at an early age, and now has very limited vision, which may have increased the impact of her playing. Of course one does not need to see to play a piano, but her audience did not fail to admire the manner of execution of Chopin's most difficult music by this young woman. The mazurkas may have suffered most during the recital with some loss of authenticity in their execution. Miss Lipska has made several records of Chopin's music, including the mazurkas, which were well recorded for the Polish label, Melodica. Her recorded mazurkas seem much more to the composer's intentions. The audience on Sunday afternoon responded with enthusiasm throughout her recital, and was rewarded with two encores. Miss Lipska was scheduled to give a short recital of requests for the staff and guests of the Polish Legation last evening. Attendance was by invitation only'."

Simon paused for a moment and found the second review. "There is another shorter review from a rival newspaper which will take only a few minutes to read:

'Agnieszka Lipska, the Polish pianist from Kraków, gave a most delightful recital of selections from the music of Chopin on Sunday afternoon at the *Reale Academia Filarmonica Romana* before a capacity audience. The programme was introduced by the Welsh music critic, Mister Simon Williams, who announced the pianist's intention to dedicate her recital to the memory of Vladimir de Pachmann, who died in Rome earlier this month. De Pachmann, an eccentric pianist, has played in Rome before in the same venue. He was best known for his interpretations of Chopin's music. It was suggested to the audience that Miss Lipska has now been passed the Chopin torch, a commitment she seems admirably capable of carrying. Her technique is not unlike that of de Pachmann, who played with an emphasis on *pianissimo* but with more *rubato*. Miss Lipska never once went beyond the composer's notations, and remained honest and respectful of his scores. Virtuosity for its own sake did not override dignity and sensibility. We look forward to other visits from this fine artist. On a related matter, it should be mentioned that Simon Williams, the critic, has been criticized in the past in other circles for his excessively negative assessment of Mr. de Pachmann's facility with the piano music of Beethoven. He should never have been chosen to introduce this memorial program'."

Simon paused briefly anticipating some reaction from the others.

Charles was the first to respond. "I think those reviews are wonderful, very accurate and exciting. They will have a very positive effect on your career Agnieszka. But I thought it unusual and inappropriate for the critic to add the comment about your Beethoven paper Simon."

"I agree," replied Simon. "These are very good, honest reviews. I have not yet completed my own reviews for the *Muse,* but I had a similar reaction to the recitals as these critics. As for the final comment on my Beethoven paper, I think I can guess the identity of the writer, and have found him in the past to be brash and unsympathetic to my writing."

"I have already read these local reviews and fully agree with you both," added Alexei. "As you can imagine my sister is not completely pleased, and she never is." He looked in her direction but received no response. "Did you also have a review of the organ recital for Charles to hear Simon?"

"Yes, the hotel was kind enough to also translate the one review of Leszek Janinski's Sunday morning recital at the church of Mary Magdalene. Unfortunately, I could not be there, but I have seen the programme and am very envious. The review is from Bruno Garavelli, who is an organist and who writes reviews of organ recitals for the evening paper. Garavelli wrote:

'Almost two hundred privileged people had the pleasure of hearing a unique recital on Sunday morning last at the Church of Mary Magdalene, given by a Polish organist, Leszek Janinski, who is blind. I personally will not soon forget the impact of hearing this young organist's artistry, playing selections by John Stanley, Jean Langlais and Agustin Barié, as well as his own *Improvisation on a*

Theme by Caesar Franck. All these composers share with Janinski the fate of being blind. Fate may not be the appropriate word, as many of the greatest organists have been sightless, and yet have overcome the complexities of the organ console, with its many stops and multiple keyboards. Added to this is the fact that organ consoles vary considerably, which greatly increases the challenges. Improvisation as a creative keyboard exercise seems to suit this blind organist very well as he is free of visual distraction and likely finds it easier than learning a composition by dictation. The selections by Mr. Janinski were well chosen to illustrate the organist's virtuosity as well as the variety of the compositions and the unique character of the Mascioni Organ at the Church of Mary Magdalene'."

Charles was the first to speak. "After Agnieszka and I heard this recital she was inspired enough to decide she wanted to investigate the possibility of playing the organ at her church in Kraków. I think she should be encouraged to do that. Perhaps one of Janinski's organ friends in Kraków would be willing to help with lessons. I agree with the writer's reaction to the recital. It was a very enjoyable experience and Janinski is a very talented organist."

"I will certainly try to do that when I get back," Agnieszka replied, glancing in her brother's direction. "But now I think we need to finalize the plans for the rest of the week. Charles will be moving to this hotel to make it easier for us to deal with the realities of my situation. It is possible that the hotel may make this room available to him. I would like to keep the piano in my suite 205 until we leave for Kraków. This has the approval of the local dealer, and will not cost the legation any money. This morning I was surprised when a local promoter called me here at the hotel to enquire if I might agree to give another recital before I leave. We are to meet later this afternoon to discuss the details. I would like you to be here when they come Charles."

"Of course," he readily agreed. "I would like to very much. When did they say they would be arriving?"

"They were to leave a message for me with a convenient time. Perhaps we should consider having lunch now. Can we ask the kitchen to make us some light lunch items Alexei? I would like another glass of wine please."

"I will call the desk to enquire," Alexei replied as he rose to find the wine bottle on the dresser. He filled her glass and offered another glass to Charles. "Tell me what you would like in the way of snacks before I call."

The main desk was called, to enquire about room service, and said that the expected visitors had left a message to enquire if three o'clock was a suitable hour to meet. The receptionist promised to call them and confirm that was suitable.

Charles remembered he had brought his briefcase. "While we wait for the food, Alexei and I need some time to talk about the notes I have here in my briefcase. I do not mind leaving everything with you, Alexei, as I have copies back in Toronto if they should be lost or if you cannot read some of my hand writing."

The dining room staff had been eager to take their order for a light snack, and the food soon arrived with a tray of cheeses, bread, ham and cold meats. Another bottle of Chianti was opened, more beer was poured and by the time three o'clock had arrived, everyone was feeling very relaxed. The telephone call from the reception area announced that the visitors had arrived and were waiting in the lobby.

Alexei offered to go down to meet them. "Perhaps we should greet them in your suite Agnieszka," he suggested, "this room is not very presentable and smells of cigarettes and beer."

They all collected their apparel and prepared to made their way to Room 205, with Charles guiding Agnieszka, who was unsteady and obviously feeling the effects of the wine. "Are you feeling unwell?" he asked, "perhaps you drank too much wine. If you do not feel like talking to these promoters at this time, Alexei and I can deal with them, and present you with the details later." She was unusually quiet and did not speak. There was no activity in the corridor. A chambermaid's work wagon loaded with towels, pillows and sheets was parked near the stairs leading to the third floor. The chambermaid was nowhere to be seen. They had reached her suite and he unlocked the door. "Would you like to rest while we interview the guests?" he asked.

"That's a good idea. I do not want to make a fool of myself. I feel ashamed that you have to look after me like this," she apologized.

He helped her to the bedroom and settled her on the bed. She removed her glasses and he could see tears well up in her eyes. He decided not to mention the fact, or to ask for an explanation. "Now have a rest and perhaps a sleep. I will call you when we have some idea of their plans. Do you think you could prepare for a recital by Friday or Saturday? That would give you two or three whole days. We do not have many days left here in Rome if we are to leave on the weekend."

She was looking sleepy as she stretched her arms out toward him and encircled his neck. "I cannot make decisions like that now, but I would like to include a Beethoven sonata in the program, perhaps opus 31, Number 1 in G Major. I love it—it is so full of subtle humour. The other pieces could include a Haydn sonata—I think the key is C Major for number 60. It was the last piano sonata he composed. I learnt it years ago when I was studying at the academy. And I insist on including Schumann's *Kinderszenen*—with a selection of Chopin pieces at the end. Alexei can negotiate the fee. I trust him to make a satisfactory arrangement. I want to hug you before you leave!"

By the time Charles had moved back to the reception area, the visitors had arrived. He was introduced to Miss Rosso and Mr. deMilo. Miss Rosso appeared to be the person who spoke the best English, and she seemed prepared to introduce discussion of the arrangements for a recital. She was a surprisingly young woman—perhaps in her early twenties; well tanned, dressed in a formal navy blue suit and wearing high heel shoes. Her partner was older and casual, in an open shirt, light slacks and sandals. Charles avoided any comments as he sat listening to the discussion. Simon had departed to his hotel to finish packing.

Alexei was very experienced in these matters, and in less than an hour had worked out a plan to advertise a matinee recital on Saturday, despite earlier plans to leave Rome on that day. The seating capacity of the church was about 450, but a full capacity was not likely. Charles mentioned Agnieszka's choice of repertoire and all agreed.

Miss Bianco was making notes, and promised the printed programmes for the recital could be ready within twenty-four hours. They would have to show the programme to the censors at the Ministry of Popular Culture, but she seemed to think her contacts in their office would allow for speedy approval. She would make sure the proofs were available to be sure that details of the opus numbers, keys for the selections etc. were correct. Would Miss Lipska agree to play a major Chopin piece in the second half? Alexei assured her that she likely would. Miss Rosso suggested a recent photograph of Agnieszka seated at her piano would be desirable for the printed programme and Alexei was able to find one from his briefcase. A fee was negotiated after a few minutes, and Charles suggested they ask Agnieszka to meet the visitors and to confirm the programme, as well as to respond to their request for a Chopin selection.

Alexei left to find her, and after a few minutes appeared with a tired looking Agnieszka. Introductions were made and she apologized for her absence. Yes, she would love to play some Chopin in the second half, certainly two pairs of Nocturnes, op. 27: the first in C sharp and the second in D flat major as well as two from op. 32: one in B Major and the second in A flat Major. She would conclude with the *Fantaisie-Impromptu* in C sharp minor, op.66. There should be some programme notes, which she promised to have finished by the next morning. The necessary documents were signed and the visitors prepared to leave with a promise to return for the programme notes, and with the final programme proofs in twenty-four hours.

Alexei ushered them to the door, and on returning was the first to speak, "That went surprisingly well. I am sorry I will miss your recital Agnieszka but my plans have been made. It will mean you and Charles will not be able to leave until Sunday. Charles will make the train reservations for you. Simon and I will be leaving on our train within a few hours."

Agnieszka had been silent since the Italians left, and finally spoke. "Alexei, it would have been great if you were here but we understand. Thank you for making the arrangements. Charles and I will see that the recital comes off in the style you would like. I am pleased with the programme, but there is some preparation to be done. I still have my piano and will step up my practice in the next two days. Some of the city tour plans might have to be curtailed or changed depending on how the practicing goes."

"You will not need to spend all day every day practicing Agnieszka. I suspect you know the programme well already," said her brother, "so you two can plan to make some short excursions depending on the weather."

"I will call the tour operator and ask about available options," said Charles. "She had suggested that a drive to one of the towns of the Castelli Romani or the

Alban Hills would be a relaxing change from the city, but let me research it further."

Alexei excused himself and returned to his room to finalize the packing. "Do you need some help looking for the scores of the selections you have made?" Charles asked Agnieszka. "That would be a great help," she replied. "I have some idea where the Beethoven and Schumann are, but I have not seen the Haydn sonata for days. Try the bottom drawer of the dresser in the bedroom." After some searching through the two bottom drawers he eventually found the Haydn score. The other scores were found in the piano stool. "Are you in the mood to try some of the pieces while we wait for Alexei and Simon to call on their way to the train station?" he asked. Agnieszka still looked sleepy and he saw her stifle a yawn. "I would like to try the Schumann as I know it the best. I played it at a recital at the academy of music in Warsaw about three months ago. I hope I am not too sleepy to remember the piece."

She had made her way to the piano unassisted, and began to play without the score. Charles listened as he stretched out in an easy chair. He remembered his other music teacher, Helen Anderson, playing fragments of this piece many years ago. She also played the organ in the Methodist church, and had often chosen to play the two slow sections, *Träumerei* and *Der Dicter spricht*. Both seemed to have been easily adapted to the organ style. His thoughts drifted to Toronto and his department. He had been away almost four weeks, and would likely be another three—depending on the length of his stay in Kraków and his return trans-Atlantic connections. He had warned his secretary that he would not be back for about five weeks. Tomorrow he must telephone her to say that he would be away longer than he had planned. He realized how much he was missing a good newspaper in English, and wondered how much had happened in Canada since he left Halifax.

He thought of Lisa and wondered where she was right now—midway across the Atlantic perhaps? Perhaps she was still waiting in Southampton for the *SS Montrose* to leave. How would he explain to this vivacious young Norwegian woman, whom he had undressed and made love to almost every night on the ship, the turn of events since arriving in Rome? Had he made any reckless commitments to her? He had invited her to join him in Rome and she almost did. Suppose she decided to surprise him by coming to join him now—this week. The thought made his heart skip a few beats. Heaven forbid. Surely she would never do that!

"You have been very quiet while I played. Have you been listening?" he heard Agnieszka say, as the music came to an end. She would not have been able to see how he had been lost in thought as she played. "I have played enough for this afternoon, and am too tired and bored to continue. Can we do something else instead?"

"Why don't we go down to the dining room to have tea and a sweet?" he suggested. "I enjoyed the Schumann very much, and you seem to have remembered it well."

"A cup of tea would be the ideal answer," said Agnieszka, seeking an anti-dote to the wine. "Will you leave a note on the door so that Alexei will know where we are?"

The dining room was deserted, and the lone waiter, looking bored, was ea-ger to fetch a pot of tea and some freshly-made small cakes. "When I made en-quiries earlier about local city tours, I was told that the guide could drive us in his private car to the cemetery to see the site of de Pachmann's grave. We talked about it before and I think we would both like to do that," Charles told her.

"Yes, absolutely," she replied eagerly, "I had planned to mention it to you again—maybe tomorrow afternoon? I would like to spend tomorrow morning practicing. We could leave after lunch. Before Simon leaves, we must ask him what he found when he visited the cemetery. I am not certain that he did in fact visit the grave, but he had said earlier he would like to. Perhaps you feel differ-ently but I am overcome by a sense of sadness when I think of de Pachmann and his legacy."

As if they knew they had just been discussed, Alexei and Simon suddenly appeared at their table. Charles noted again how much alike the two were. They were virtually the same height, and both had beards. Simon had gone to the cemetery on the previous day and had experienced problems finding the grave. "The caretaker was not able to understand English, and did not have an up-to-date list of the recent funerals, so I wandered around and came away with-out seeing the Pachmann grave site. If you take a local guide with you it might be easier."

"We are ready to leave," said Alexei, glancing at his watch, "our luggage is being put in a taxi, and the train leaves at 1700 hours. We must say goodbye." He moved to Agnieszka's chair and embraced her, leaving her with a long kiss on her cheek. "I know you will take good care of my precious sister," he said, glancing at Charles, who was standing having shaken hands with Simon. "I will try to contact you both when I am in Paris."

"For me it has been a very unusual visit," Agnieszka said, as they found themselves sitting alone. "I will miss them both, but the most exciting aspect of my visit was meeting you and getting to know you." She reached across the ta-ble and searched for his hand. Her grasp was just as warm and strong as he re-membered it on Sunday. "Can we go back to my room so that we can touch and hold one another again? I have not forgotten how you felt and I want you again." He could feel an intense sexual attraction as she gripped his hand. He leaned across and kissed her passionately. "Let me pay for the tea and cakes and then I will help you to the elevator."

They found their way to Room 205, and embraced in the reception area. He could tell she was eager as she pressed herself into his body. "I would like to have a bath before we go to bed," she whispered, "why don't you join me? You can wash my back." She laughed as he briefly scratched her back.

"A great idea! Let me run the water. We will need an extra towel." He looked in several drawers and found one. She was already undressing, and he noticed she had already shed most of her clothes, and was sitting on the edge of the bath in her bra and panties. "Let me help you with those," he said, as he unhooked her bra. He had not started to undress, but she was working on his trousers, which soon dropped to the floor. Her nipples responded to being kissed as he felt her hand searching inside his shorts. He shed the rest of his clothes as she stepped out of her panties. "Let me help you in the tub," he offered. She carefully lowered herself into the water. "It's lovely," she said, "come and join me. You can find the soap and wash my back and anywhere else you wish."

Later in the afternoon, as he made his way back to the Hotel Splendide Royal, he retraced in his mind their playing at love-making in the tub, which became more focused later in her bed. They seemed so suited for each other, and he could see that Agnieszka seemed to reach an unusually high level of arousal. He was still feeling guilty about the risks they were taking, and he resolved to seek out a chemist in the neighbourhood who sold condoms. In Canada when he was a teenager they were called 'French safes,' but he could not remember why. He knew the last thing he wanted to face was an unwanted pregnancy. The memory of her bare pubic area was still a reminder of his ambivalence to her habit of shaving. He was beginning to wonder if he was too conventional in his tastes.

At the reception area the letter for the police was ready for signing, and Charles was surprised to find his hotel charges were not as much as he had anticipated. He arranged to have some change available to leave for the chambermaid. Mr. Berretta emerged from his office holding Charles' passport and visa documents. "Doctor Flemming, it has been a pleasure having you as a guest for the past week, and I hope the rest of your stay in Rome will be as enjoyable. There is a matter I should mention to you, but you may not wish to take any action now that we have relieved the police of their task." Berretta paused and Charles felt a brief moment of panic, realizing that the issue of the missing manuscript had surfaced again. He had lost interest, and would have preferred not to have to rehash the details again. Mr. Berretta continued, "the police officer assigned to the matter of the stolen manuscript has been here while you were gone. Our police have a reputation for thoroughness. Even petty crimes are not tolerated amongst our citizens. He has identified with certainty, based on the descriptions from our staff, the person who retrieved your book." He glanced at a paper he had been holding in his hand. "They were pleased to learn that the man in question was not a citizen of Rome but a visitor who has now left the city. His Polish passport seems to have identified him as a businessman and writer. He was staying at a nearby hotel but left Rome this afternoon by train. His name is Mr. Alexei Lipski of Poland."

In his lifetime as a doctor and psychiatrist, Charles had listened to startling revelations and confidences from his patients, but he was not prepared for this.

"I know there has been a grave mistake," was his immediate unspoken thought, but he replied, "the police must have identified the wrong man. I can believe they are efficient, but this man is a personal friend, and also the brother of a well-known pianist who has been performing here this week. You must have seen the lobby advertisements for last Sunday's recital at the *Reale Acade-*

mia Filarmonica. She is very well-known, especially in Europe. In fact she is giving another recital on Saturday afternoon. I know you will find this request unusual, but may I check the name?" He reached out and accepted the official-looking police document from Mr. Berretta, who was looking very surprised at the reaction the letter had generated. Charles knew it would be written in Italian, and that he would not be able to read it. But he saw immediately the name at the end of the paragraph; it was indeed Alexei's. He suddenly felt weak, and decided he needed to sit. He turned away from the desk and still holding the letter sought a nearby chair. "This is terrible and also impossible," he said under his breath. The manager had left the desk to join him and found an adjacent chair. "I assume you know this man well enough to vouch for his honesty?" he heard Berretta say, "the police can sometimes make mistakes."

Charles had to collect his thoughts for a minute before responding. "You would find it hard to believe what a shock this has been to hear this news," he replied, looking directly at Mr. Berretta. "It may not be a mistake..." he paused to collect his thoughts. "But I must tell you something about my relationship with Mr. Lipski."

Charles' summary of the events that had transpired since arriving, his introduction to the Lipskas and the revelation that Alexei was working on a similar book took only a few minutes. He did not mention his own relationship with Agnieszka. The manager was listening attentively. "There might be some merit in having you meet the police officer who signed this," the manager suggested as he reclaimed the letter. "Some of your concerns and doubts could easily be cleared away. He would likely be willing to show you the evidence they had collected."

"I would like that, but the meeting would have to wait until tomorrow as I have some urgent obligations this evening—and it is already almost 6:30. The officer is likely off duty. If you could arrange a meeting for tomorrow morning, here at the hotel I would be very much obliged. Perhaps you might agree to be present to help as translator."

The manager assured him he would be pleased to do so.

"Now I must collect my luggage," Charles said, as if to remind himself more than the hotel manager.

Mr. Berretta promised to arrange a taxi. The corridor on his floor was empty—the chambermaid had likely left for the day. His suitcases had been packed earlier, so he had little more to do before leaving. He decided to call the tour director at the Michelangelo Hotel and arrange a guided tour of the Campo Verano Cemetery. No one answered the telephone, and he assumed the office had closed. He would call in the morning.

"I would like to leave money for the chambermaid who remembered seeing the person who picked up the package before I arrived. It is a small token of my appreciation," he said as he handed an envelope to Mr. Berretta. "I had hoped to see her but she was not around when I collected my luggage."

"I will make sure she receives it. I am sure she will be very pleased," the manager promised.

He said goodbye to Mr. Beretta, and assured him that he would call in the morning.

He felt very depressed and let down by the revelation. A hundred questions seem to pass through his mind as he watched the driver load his luggage in the car, and as he sat in the back seat for the short drive to Agnieszka's hotel. The sun had set and the streetlights had been turned on. "What would be Alexei's purpose in stealing the de Pachmann manuscript?" Charles thought to himself. "Was it simply his keen competitive nature? Perhaps it was an attempt to delay my research into the de Pachmann biography. He would have known that the missing de Pachmann book would be published soon and be readily available. Had Simon known all along that Alexei was the thief? Simon had been the one who had told Alexei of the biography project when he had called on the telephone from Nice. I was a fool to pass over my manuscript and notes to a man who had acted so maliciously behind my back." There was one question that he found surfacing in a disturbing fashion, and he tried unsuccessfully to suppress. "How much does Agnieszka know about this? And if she does know, why has she remained silent? He found it impossible to believe she knew! Perhaps she was waiting to tell him after Alexei and Simon had left. But they had just spent the last few hours together, including a wonderful hour of fun and sex after their tub bath! It would have been an ideal time to tell him. She would never have forgotten to mention it. Had Alexei insisted that she keep the truth from him?"

The taxi had arrived at his destination and it was with a heavy heart that Charles collected his luggage and approached the reservation desk. His room was ready, and after signing the register, relinquishing his passport and collecting the key, he made his way to Room 250. The porter promised to deliver the luggage immediately. The room smelled fresh and cool, and he decided he needed to relax in a bath before contacting Agnieszka. He saw from his watch it was after seven. They had decided earlier to eat in the dining room on the main level tonight, but he was not mentally prepared for the evening. Before his suitcases and briefcase arrived he decided he needed a drink. He remembered there was some Johnny Walker left from his travels. As soon as the luggage had been delivered he poured himself a generous measure of Scotch with a touch of water. He started the bath water, adjusted the temperature and sat on the toilet seat as he sipped his drink. He heard himself asking the question he had been pondering earlier.

"Will I mention this tonight or wait until I examine the evidence of the police in the morning?" He thought for a few more minutes, and decided it was only fair to them both not to raise the topic at this time. It would save a lot of unnecessary worry and, perhaps, bad feelings. But he would have to bluff his way through the evening and avoid giving vent to his disappointment and anger. "I cannot believe Agnieszka would not have told me about this, if she knew. Our relationship is strong and it would be completely out of character. I will try to have faith in her." He finished his drink, debated if he should pour another, but decided against it. His bath was almost ready and he quickly shed his clothes. Immersed up to his neck in the warm water he was feeling much more relaxed.

He decided to try to erase the matter from his mind for the whole evening. Music, food and wine would be good agenda topics for the rest of the evening.

Agnieszka answered her doorbell, and he could see she was already dressed for dinner. "You look wonderful. I have not seen that dress before and the colour suits you perfectly," He held her close and kissed her for a few seconds.

"Thank you," she replied, "that is a nice complement." She drew back and smiled. "I think you have been drinking Scotch. Am I right?" He grinned and replied, "Yes, you are right."

"I like your tie but I cannot see much more. I have been wondering if you had been able to make the move without any trouble. Have you settled?"

"Yes, but I did feel like I needed a Scotch after the move. I am glad we are eating here tonight. I would prefer not have to go out again. Have you been playing any new selections for your recital?" His arm was still wrapped around her waist as he guided her into the sitting area.

"I have been playing the Chopin pieces, and would like to play them both for you before dinner. Come and sit next to me," she replied, as they moved toward the piano together. She seemed very relaxed and began playing with obvious ease. "I feel very happy about these pieces. They are old favourites," she said, as she played the last chords of the D flat Nocturne.

"How are you progressing with the Haydn sonata?" he enquired. "Do you feel like playing me the first movement? I'm sure we have time."

"I am not in the mood for Haydn now," she replied with a frown. "Let me play you some of the Schumann again. It is more to my taste at the moment."

She had chosen *Kinderszenen*, op.15 as her last selection for the recital program. Charles noticed she played it with more attention than earlier in day. He had been consciously trying to divert his mind from the disturbing news of the afternoon and succeeded as she reached *Träumerei*, his favourite of the lot.

"I sense you are playing it with more feeling tonight. You are well on your way to polishing the program for Saturday."

"I agree. One has to be in a special mood for Schumann or Haydn and for Chopin also."

"Have you thought about an encore for the recital?"

"I will likely play the Liadov Nocturne that I played for you at the legation and possibly a *mazurka* of his. If they ask for more, perhaps a Rachmaninoff prelude."

"I did not get through to the tour guide office earlier but have you had any new ideas for an outing tomorrow, perhaps in the afternoon?" Charles asked.

"I am prepared to leave the plans to you. Why not wait and see what is available. Perhaps a trip to the de Pachmann grave site in the afternoon, and if you think there is time, a cruise on the Tiber. But now it is time to think of exploring the dining room menu, don't you think?"

CHAPTER FOURTEEN

"Omnium rerum primipia parva sunt"
(Everything has a small beginning)

The hotel dining room was not busy. The lights were low, and a small band on a slightly raised bandstand was quietly playing dance music. Agnieszka had made a reservation, and a waiter offered them a choice of a table near the band or at a table further away. She said she wanted to sit near the band.

"I recognize that tune they are playing. It is by Victor Herbert and it is *I'm Falling in Love With Someone*. Do you know it?" she asked as she gazed at the assembled group.

"Yes," said Charles, "and it would make an appropriate theme song, don't you think? I also know some other songs he wrote. He wrote a lot of music, some in a classical style including a cello concerto, which I have never heard. Isn't the song *Ah! Sweet Mystery of Life* one of his? From his Operetta *Naughty Marietta?*"

"I don't know much about his music. Perhaps they will play that song if we ask ... but I'm too hungry to think of song requests right now. I also would like a glass of wine. Can you look over the list and tell me what there is available. I feel like having a white wine tonight for a change. And I forgot to say to you earlier: this dinner is on me as you paid for dinner last night."

Charles noticed how relaxed and very chatty she seemed. "We can debate the dinner bill later," he replied, as he glanced over the wine list. "There is less choice in Italian white wines than red on this list, but we can go for a French white. What do you think?"

"You choose. I'm sure I will like it."

Charles looked up from the wine list. "Here is a wine you may not have had before. It is not French. Have you heard of *Est! Est! Est!*, a wine from Montefiascone? The list says it is a town north of this city. It is not a fabulous wine, but if you like a wine with a legend, this is for you. I think we should try a bottle. The description here is of a semi-dry wine made of about sixty per cent of the Trebbiano grape and the other grapes are Malvesia and Roscetta."

"I know nothing about Italian grapes, but since I do not remember having it before, why don't we try it? Seems an odd Latin name."

"Someone told me the story ages ago but I have forgotten the details. The waiter will likely know. Do you have enough light to read the menu? Most of it is in Italian." Charles was trying to be helpful.

"You know how little I can see in this light and how little Italian I know. Why don't we simply ask the waiter for suggestions?" Agnieszka appeared to have overlooked what he felt would otherwise have been considered an insult to her.

As if he had been summoned, a different waiter appeared out of nowhere, obviously eager to help.

"Before we order from the menu we would like to start with a bottle of your best vintage of *Est! Est! Est!* My friend has never tasted it before. We are also interested in the Latin name and what it means," Charles quizzed him.

The waiter spoke broken English. "I will do my best to tell you. It is about a German bishop coming to Rome for some event, perhaps a church gathering. That was about nine hundred years ago. He loved wine, so he sent his lackey ahead to scout out the inns with the best wines. His plan was for the lackey to write in chalk on the inn doors the word *Est*, if the wines were good there. After he had spent a night in Montefiascone, he was so impressed with the local wine he wrote *Est! Est! Est!* on the inn door. It means: *It is! It is! It is!* I will see if I can find you the best vintage we have in our cellar—perhaps a 1931, as it drinks well when young." He paused and continued, "I want to suggest our specials for this evening, starting with a pasta dish, *Spaghetti alla Carbonara*, which will go well with the wine. The main dish tonight is Oxtail – Roman style, with seasonal vegetables. You will like it. I recommend a red wine with it, perhaps a half bottle of Barolo from Piedmont. We have some good vintages in our cellar. Finally, you should finish with a sweet or dessert. We have a very nice winter fruit salad with a mix of mangos, apples, oranges and lemons."

Agnieszka was nodding approval, and it was agreed that the waiter's suggestions were ideal for them both. "Why don't we try the white wine now," she suggested. The waiter agreed and walked toward the kitchen. The band was now playing some new songs that they did not recognize. "Probably some local Italian compositions?" suggested Charles, but he wanted to change the subject. "We were speaking earlier about an evening river cruise on the Tiber. The tour office at the convention hotel had offered several evening cruises with dinner and live music on board, so we can dance. But I did not put my name on the list without checking with you, so they may not have space for us tomorrow evening. I can try tomorrow. What do you think?"

The waiter had returned and offered a 1930 *Est! Est! Est!* Agnieszka seemed eager to try it as she waited for the waiter to pull the cork and pour a small amount in her wine glass.

She tried the wine, smiled and nodded her approval. She gazed in Charles' direction. "I like this wine very much … but about the cruise—you know I do not see well at all in the night, so the scenery would be lost on me, but the food and entertainment sounds like fun. I would like to try it."

"Perhaps we can arrange to go after we return from the Campo Verano Cemetery in the afternoon if it is possible to arrange that."

Charles found himself still pondering the question of the de Pachmann book, and how the police had identified the thief. It seemed a good time to introduce the topic, as he was curious to hear her reaction.

"Tomorrow, I am going back to the Hotel Splendide Royale to meet the police inspector who discovered the person who took the book manuscript before I arrived last Friday. I want to be absolutely sure they have identified the right person."

He could see the expression of surprise on her face. He realized that he had not mentioned this fact to her. "It seems I did not mention that to you earlier in the day." Agnieszka shook her head. "No, this is the first I have heard about it. Tell me more." Her face registered concern as he gave a brief summary of the information Mr. Berretta had passed on to him in the afternoon as he was checking out. He added, "my concern is that an innocent man may have been blamed for this, so I will meet the police inspector tomorrow morning to discuss the evidence." She looked puzzled and paused before responding. "You say it was a man. Do they know his name and why he did this?"

He was trying to choose his answers carefully as he did not want to cause her undue concern, and lead to wrong conclusions. But he knew his intent and where the conversation was leading. He wanted her to provide evidence that would remove the blame from her brother.

"The manager told me the man was not Italian. He lives abroad, and has since returned home so it is not likely he will be punished. It seems he was visiting Rome on business. The chambermaid at the hotel had seen him come into the hotel and pick up the package, so the police have an identification of sorts. I have not seen the evidence so it remains to be seen if the identification was accurate or not."

"I suppose the meeting may be totally unnecessary Charles, as you would not likely lay charges against a tourist who stole something you no longer needed, and which it seems has such little monetary value. Of course it might be very valuable to someone writing a biography of de Pachmann. Do you know if Alexei knew of the book, or was interested in it?"

Charles considered his answer carefully. This could be an opening he was seeking, but he avoided it: "He never discussed it with me—but I agree, it would be helpful for someone writing a biography of de Pachmann, and that is why I had requested a copy before leaving Canada. A friend of mine in Toronto knew someone in Rome, whom she thought would be able to get a copy. She wrote the friend when she knew I would be coming here this month. She assured me a copy of the manuscript would likely be found, and said it would be delivered to the hotel before I arrived. My problem is I do not know the name of the friend or how to contact him—or her! I feel very stupid about that."

He was aware that he had offered enough information about the situation, and not being clear about the drift of the discussion he sought to change the subject. The arrival of the first course seemed a good opportunity to drop the topic. He wanted them to enjoy the meal while talking about other matters. "This is good," he remarked, as he tried the first mouthful of spaghetti.

"Promise you will keep me informed about the results of your meeting," she replied as she took another sip of the *Est! Est! Est!* "Tomorrow I plan to get up early and practice as much as possible. The organizers will be coming by as well and I need to edit the programme notes."

The topic of the missing de Pachmann book seemed to have been forgotten as they again returned to a discussion of the band and its repertoire. The band had decided to take a break, and the dining room was much quieter. The waiter had removed the plates from the first course. A pause in the meal gave Charles an opportunity to silently admire this beautiful woman seated across the table.

"You look beautiful tonight as usual, and I see you are wearing a beautiful necklace which I must have missed seeing earlier when I came to your room. It goes very well with your dress. Now I am wondering what it is." He leaned forward and gently lifted the necklace for close inspection.

"Do you know the stone?" she asked, "my mother's mother once owned it, and it was left for me when she died. I wear it on special occasions, such as tonight. I have a pair of matching earrings, which I did not bring this time. I seem to have packed in a hurry and forgot to put them in."

Charles was waiting to respond and decided to tease her for a few minutes. "Is it a ruby or a sapphire?" he asked with a serious face.

"I thought you would do better than that. It is neither," she chided him.

Charles relented. "Could it be an opal?"

The second course had arrived, and she waited until the waiter had left before responding.

"You have finally guessed correctly. I thought you would have known it because it was de Pachmann's favourite precious stone. I am sure you have heard that. He had a collection of stones, and boasted that he had invested large amounts of money on his hobby. It seems next to reading philosophy and scientific works, his pet hobby was collecting precious gems. He never wore them, and said his love for them was abstract. He was an expert on their details and he gave his best stones the names of composers. His most flawless diamond was christened Bach, his dusky emerald was Brahms."

She paused to sip her wine and try a sample of her vegetables. "The most poetical stone in his collection was the opal. Can you guess the name he gave to this stone?" Charles shook his head. "No, tell me."

"He called it Chopin, being his favourite composer. His ruby, full of scintillating colour, was dubbed Liszt."

"That is very amusing. What stone did he choose for Beethoven?"

"I have never heard. Perhaps he felt ambivalent about giving him his own stone."

Charles thought for a moment. "He considered Beethoven to be one of his 'invisible audience,' or so he said in an article in the BBC *Radio Times* about seven years ago. People often wondered if some of his inaudible conversation at the piano was directed to someone who was not there. He said in that article that when he played he would close his eyes and could see them nodding, smiling, advising, praising and encouraging him! He referred to Beethoven as one of the invisible spirits — his real audience, gathered around the piano. Beethoven to him was a "gentle soul of soaring inspiration", so he did give the composer his due, even though his interpretations of the composer's piano works were often severely criticized." He took another mouthful and paused before continuing.

"You have not read Simon's article on de Pachmann's Beethoven performance style but I will read it to you soon. The critic who reviewed your first recital mentioned it."

"I remember the reference to his article. Perhaps it would be easier for me if you read it to me."

"I will do that. Meanwhile, I am finding my appetite is less than I had thought. I will never get through this course, and I think it unlikely I will finish it all. There is also a lot of red wine left," he said as he refilled her glass. "I think we should pause for a while before dessert. Incidentally, I read somewhere that de Pachmann made a great deal of fuss about his food. But he also had most unusual and rude table manners. In my research, I found some very amusing stories about his antics in restaurants as well as at private dinner parties in friends' homes. James Huneker described how de Pachmann lost his temper at a private party at the critic's home—in New York, I think. It was all because he took a dislike to the man waiting on the table! Sometime before de Pachmann retired, he boasted in an interview he was, as he said, 'Pachmann, the musician when at the piano, but Pachmann, the gourmet at the table'. He added that for diets and strict rules of feeding and living he had a 'monstrous contempt'."

"He also had a ritual of washing his cutlery at the table before eating. That fits my theory of his having an obsessive-compulsive disorder. He was likely fearful of germs. Some who have that problem cannot stop the compulsion to wash their hands. He also boasted that he smoked cigars every day, and paid no attention to advice from doctors! He patronized a German restaurant in Union Square, New York very often, usually eating alone, seated at the same table, while consuming numerous litres of beer! He loved to be the centre of attention in restaurants, grinning and bowing to the other guests, who laughed at his every antic. He enjoyed his intimate conversations with all the waiters, smoking and joking with them after the meal. He was quite an actor!"

Agnieszka was amused. "I expect you had planned to include these stories in your book. Do you think his seemingly reckless life style in eating, drinking and smoking cigars was harmful?" He was beginning to enjoy Agnieszka's curiosity about his research about de Pachmann. "I do not think so, judging by his longevity. He lived to be eighty-four, but at present we know very little about his health or his quality of life in his final years, and it is possible that privacy considerations will dictate what will emerge in the future. Later photographs show him with a paralysis of the muscles in his right eye that would suggest he may have had a brain aneurysm, or perhaps a diabetic condition affecting the muscles of that eye."

The waiter had arrived with the dessert dish, and as they sampled the mixture of fresh fruit they spent some time debating the health benefits of apples. The bottle of red wine had finally given up its last glass. Charles was starting to feel the effects of two bottles of wine, and he could see Agnieszka was as well. She did not seem in the mood to debate about who would settle the dinner bill. He asked to have the bill put on his hotel account, and they made their way from the dining room after leaving a generous gratuity and saying "thank you" and "goodbye" to the two waiters.

Agnieszka was grateful that the way back was only a short elevator ride, and seemed interested in bed and sleep. "I am going to hold you for a few minutes," she heard him say as he helped her undress and into bed. She yawned and said she did not want to wear her nightdress tonight. "I want to sleep naked tonight. I would love you to join me. I am so glad you will not have to get dressed later for out doors," she whispered, as she felt his naked body move close to her. He had thought there might be minimal sexual activity tonight but that was not the case. Her kisses were passionate, her hands very active. He already felt aroused and ready before his fingers began to explore her. "I am not too sleepy for you," she whispered. He was mindful again about protection—he had not had the time to look for condoms. "I will take care tonight as we should not take chances"'

Later, back in his own room, he marvelled that, as before, she had climaxed so quickly. He had been able to control his. She had fallen asleep in a few minutes. It was now almost midnight and he was anticipating a long day tomorrow. After asking the reception desk for a call at seven he too fell peacefully asleep.

CHAPTER FIFTEEN

"Campo santo"
(Holy ground)

Wednesday was another sunny day, and Charles was awake, out of bed and had shaved before the telephone rang to remind him that it was seven thirty, his wakeup time. He felt better after a hot bath, but he was not looking forward to the police interview. The tub was longer and deeper than the one in the Hotel Splendide Royale—he was able to stretch his legs out straight so his head was almost under water. Conscious of the time, he hastily washed, dried and dressed. He decided not to call Agnieszka. She had said she would wake on her own and have breakfast in her room. He listened outside her room door as he walked to the stairs and heard no sounds. She was likely still asleep, and had not yet begun practicing. He went downstairs to the dining room and asked for a light breakfast with orange juice, toast and coffee. Before he left for his walk to his assigned destinations he made two calls from his room—first to Mr. Berretta confirming the appointment with the police officer. He was told it was scheduled for eleven o'clock. That meant he would have time to visit the Hotel Michelangelo before then and arrange the tours.

The hotel telephone operator was very helpful in making a very clear telephone connection with his secretary at her home in Toronto. Janet Spalding was elated to hear from him, after reminding him that it was still dark and night in Canada, not quite five A.M! She was curious why she had heard no news from him for more than three weeks since he left Canada. He found a weak excuse, and apologized for waking her. He had forgotten the time difference.

There was a lot of snow in Toronto and the weather was cold. She reminded him of his teaching obligations—several lectures that were to begin in early February. After dealing with other necessary department business they discussed his short term plans to travel to Poland before returning to Canada. Janet promised to find details of Atlantic liner crossings from England to Halifax or Montreal, as well as schedules for the liner service from Poland to Canada. He knew the trip from Poland by sea would be slower, but more importantly, a less bothersome route than trying to make train connections back to the Channel ferry through Czechoslovakia, Germany and Belgium. She promised to find the local telephone number of the person who had arranged for the book to be delivered at his hotel. He hung up after apologizing again for the early call, and asking Janet to call his home to tell Jeanette of his change of plans and to say he was thinking of her and Toby.

The morning was cool, but he had enquired about the weather forecast before he set off. He was optimistic that the sun would warm up the day. The Michelangelo Hotel lobby was quiet, as many of those attending the conference had likely left to return home. The tour director was having a quiet morning, so Charles did not wait long. Arrangements were finalized for a driver to arrive at their hotel after lunch for a visit to the Campo Verano Cemetery, and later to take them back to their hotel, before joining the tour boat, the *Tiber Queen*, which was leaving at four p.m. for the river cruise. He was told a considerable number of psychiatrists and families had booked the tour. He decided to take a taxi to the railway station, to enquire about sleeper accommodations for the train to Milan and then to Vienna, *en route* to Kraków. A ticket agent with limited English referred him to a superior, who on scanning the possibilities informed him that the next available accommodation for two was on Sunday afternoon. It was ideal as the recital was on Saturday afternoon. Having paid for the one-way train tickets to Kraków, he set off for Hotel Splendide Royale, and arrived ten minutes before the appointed hour.

Mr. Berretta was occupied with a guest, so Charles found a seat in the lounge. He was surprised to find a copy of the London *Times* from earlier in the week. He scanned the world news section, found very little of interest from Canada, and within a few minutes Mr. Berretta arrived with the police investigator. Inspector Roberto Olivetti was introduced—a tall, efficient looking man with closely-cut dark hair, dark glasses and a prominent black moustache. Instead of a uniform, he was dressed in a dark blue suit with a striped grey tie—no black shirt or identifying signs of a police officer. Mr. Berretta explained that the inspector's English was limited, but he would act as interpreter for as long as it was necessary. A female kitchen worker had meanwhile appeared with three cups and a container of coffee. Olivetti had brought a brief case with papers pertaining to the case, which he spread out on a nearby table as he drank his coffee. Obviously having been warned by the manager that some doubt existed as to the evidence against Alexei, Olivetti began by assuring them that there was no doubt in the minds of the police that his officers were correct in their judgement. The evidence was based on the sworn affidavits of the chambermaid and the receptionist on duty, both of whom were able to identify Alexei from the photograph in his passport, which the police had examined on the previous morning. Miss Tamminga—who had been working on the day the package had been surrendered to the stranger—had described the accent of the man, who wore a beard and whom she said had come to the desk and identified himself as Doctor Flemming, a guest of the hotel.

He was not Italian in his speech or manner. No, there had been nothing else unusual about the man. Had other passport pictures been shown to the chambermaid and receptionist to examine? Yes, passport pictures of other male tourists registered in other hotels had been included—a number of psychiatrists enrolled at the congress, some well known local criminal types, all with beards—even a Mister Simon Williams from Wales, who had been staying at a nearby hotel, and had recently left on the same train as Mr. Lipski. The witness knew, however, that Mr. Williams and Dr. Flemming had not yet arrived from Milan when the book had been taken. The police had also known that Simon and Alexei were friends and had been spending time together. Olivetti said the police were now prepared to consider the matter as a common theft, and since the manuscript was not considered valuable and could be easily replaced, no further action was considered necessary. He acknowledged that Charles had signed a letter absolving the police of any further action, and showed him the letter for confirmation. Not having any particular talent for solving mysteries, and despite feeling depressed about the news, Charles was rapidly feeling resigned to the fact that the police were indeed correct in their conclusion. Now he was faced with the problem of explaining this to Agnieszka whom he knew would be upset and angry.

"Please thank Inspector Olivetti for taking the time to come here this morning and for showing me the evidence," he said to Mr. Berretta, who spoke briefly to the inspector. "My pleasure," replied Olivetti in English, as he rose and with a broad smile shook hands with them both and departed through the lounge door.

"Thank you for the time you have spent on this matter," Charles said to the manager. "Please thank your staff for their help—Mr. Volpe, Angelo, Miss Tamminga and the chambermaid, whose name I never did hear."

With a heavy heart he set off to walk back to his new hotel. His mission was becoming more complex with each new development. He was not at all certain that he should mention the police evidence against Alexei to Agnieszka. She was due to give a recital in three days, and this information could be a major distraction. Perhaps it would be best to mention it after the recital? Or did she really need to know at all? He had noticed a chemist shop down a side street on previous walks, and remembered his intention to look for condoms. He wondered if they were readily available in a Roman Catholic city like Rome. The Vatican was against contraception, and they might not be easily available. A few years ago Mussolini had succeeded in establishing a dialogue with the church, which reaffirmed the Roman Catholic Church to be the state religion. Now both church and state were opposed to birth control.

The shop was easily found, and the chemist was a pleasant middle-aged man who said he spoke some English, and was curious about why Charles was visiting Rome, and where he lived. He also knew immediately what Charles had in mind. He shook his head, "You may not know this, but the distribution of contraceptives has become a crime in this country. The fascist government, with the church's approval, has dictated that the main role of Italian women is to have children. The only people allowed to use condoms are men in the armed forces."

"I understand, but is there no place where tourists can buy them?"

Charles could see the chemist was thinking about how to respond. "There are some chemists who do sell them under the table, but only to trusted customers." He paused and added, "Did you say you were a doctor?"

"I am a doctor and you can trust me to be very discreet." Charles could see it was possible they could work a deal.

The chemist excused himself and disappeared into a back room. When he returned he saw that another customer had entered the shop. "Excuse me while I look after this woman. She has come to collect a prescription." Charles moved discreetly away until the woman had left.

"I do have a small number of what you need. They are made by only one factory in this country owned by Hatù and most of them go to the armed forces."

He presented a small package for Charles' inspection. "You can be sure they are very reliable. *Il Duce* would see to that!"

"You are very kind to do this, and I know it must be kept a secret. How much do I owe you?"

"There are six condoms in a package and they sell for fifty *lire*." After a brief conversation about life in Canada, travel in Europe, the psychiatric congress and Italy's unemployment problems, Charles paid the bill, shook the chemist's hand, and left to continue his walk to the hotel. He had used French safes infrequently—several times with Lisa on the ship—and remembered that they took much of the fun out of sex. He should have asked the chemist why they were called French safes, and what they were called in France.

Agnieszka was playing the piano when he approached Suite 285. The door was unlocked, and he crept inside to listen to the last movement of the Haydn sonata, which she finally concluded with considerable flair. She was surprised to hear his applause and turned to greet him with her arms outstretched. "How was your day?" he asked after they kissed.

"Sit with me," she suggested as she moved over on the piano stool. "My day was wonderful. The agents arrived earlier, and we signed the contract for the Saturday recital. I gave them my programme notes, which they took back for printing. The printed programme is very good, without any errors. A copy is sitting on the desk." He rose, crossed the room and retrieved the programme. "It looks very professional," he commented, thumbing through the pages. "I thought so too," she replied. "The organizers had to show the programme to the Government Cultural Censor, or Minister, or someone with a similar sounding name. They approved of the programme without any questions."

"The Haydn sonata certainly sounded polished, but I do not know the piece well. Are you happy with the other pieces?"

She smiled and turned to play a brief chord on the piano. "The Beethoven seems the best to my ear—as much as I love the Chopin. Now tell me how you did with the tour arrangements and the train reservations."

He briefed her on the arrangements for the tours but decided to avoid mention of the outcome from the police interview. She seemed to have forgotten that he had that appointment.

"Why don't we have a brief lunch before the taxi arrives to take us to the cemetery?" he suggested. "It is almost midday."

*** *** *** ***

The tour guide arrived on time. She was a middle- aged woman who introduced herself and the driver. She was Frances, and he was Aldo. She confirmed that Madame Giacomino had previously briefed her on the plans to drive to the Campo Verano Cemetery specifically to find the recent gravesite of the late Vladimir de Pachmann. They set off, and *en route* they were given a brief description of the cemetery's history and the number of people who had been buried there over the years. Along with de Pachmann were some very famous people. The entrance was quiet, and Agnieszka spotted a flower display just outside.

A bouquet of seasonal flowers was prepared by the florist, and they set off to walk to the caretaker's shed. It was a long walk, but Agnieszka had worn comfortable walking shoes, and seemed to be able to avoid the obstacles while holding Charles' arm. Frances spent a few minutes in conversation with one of the caretakers who looked up the names of recent burials. A map was provided, and the trio set off to find the plot.

"I continue to feel sad about de Pachmann," Agnieszka said, as they walked slowly down the path. "He had a very successful career and made a lot of money. I hope his final years here in Rome were happy for him. I wonder if he approved of the fascist government, or joined the party. Someone told me his secretary and wife were said to be party members. When I heard de Pachmann play just before his retirement he was past his prime. I did not hear him play Beethoven, but his Schumann always seemed full of new ideas. Of course his Chopin was the best even though he took liberties." She glanced in his direction. "Did you ever hear him play Bach or Scarlatti?"

"No, I didn't but he was said to have played them both well — romantically I expect. How about you? Have you played Bach in any of your recitals?" Charles was still glad of the opportunity to avoid raising the topic of the police interview.

"Yes, I have, and although I did not mention it, Angela Roscetti has asked me to play *Jesu, Joy of Man's Desiring* as an encore, and I said I would. It has been a long time since I played it, as an arrangement by Myra Hess. I shall have to trust to my memory as I do not have the score with me."

They were approaching a row of freshly prepared graves, and Frances had gone ahead to look for the one holding de Pachmann. She stopped, and pointed to an area freshly covered. "This is it," she said as she bowed her head, and made a sign of the cross.

"I want to get closer to see the message," said Agnieszka, "can you help me over the grass?" Holding her hand Charles slowly navigated her to the small sign that marked the grave. "Let me read it for you. It gives his name and his date of birth—July sixth, eighteen forty-eight. He died on January eighth. There is an Italian message underneath which I suspect is Rest in Peace." He could see she was crying as she wiped her eyes with a handkerchief. He remembered a story he had heard of de Pachmann frequently visiting Chopin's grave in the Wimereaux Cemetery in Paris. He quietly told her the story. "When de Pachmann visited Chopin's grave he was said to have silently asked the dead composer on each occasion to forgive him for all the wrong notes he had played!" Charles could see that she found the anecdote amusing, and seemed ready to move on. "That is so much like de Pachmann," she said. "I feel the same way sometimes—wanting to ask not only Chopin but others for the same reason—all those wrong notes. Sometimes I feel ashamed after a recital—to realize all the mistakes I made."

He was concerned that she was tiring. "We can leave your flowers at the top of the grave site," he suggested, "let me put them there for you. We have a long walk back to the car. Do you feel you should sit and rest? I see a bench ahead where you can sit for a little while." She seemed ready to accept the suggestion. He spoke to Frances, "if you would rather walk ahead, please do. If you give me the map we can find our way. I know the direction." His guide agreed and set off down the path.

They were silent for a few minutes. He was curious about the type of trees that were lining the paths. There were some pines, and he wondered if the others were cypress. Before he could ask Agnieszka if she knew trees by their smell, she asked him the one question that he had hoped she would have forgotten: "What did you learn from your meeting with the police this morning? Who was the tourist who was identified by the hotel staff?" He did not want to tell her the truth, and yet did not feel like lying. "The police feel that the man who best fits the description is someone we know. It is not Simon. They think the man was Alexei, based on the witnesses' descriptions." Charles felt he had to look away to avoid seeing Agnieszka's pained expression. Neither spoke for what seemed like a minute. He felt her reach out for his hand and she was squeezing it intensely. She edged closer and put her other arm around his neck. "I am so sorry. What can I say? I am so very angry with my brother for that. I was suspicious it was he who did it. He has let me down again." She lowered her voice and he saw tears in her eyes. "I will explain later," she added. She kissed him and suddenly stood. "We should be on our way back. I want to get the matter out of my mind." She held his hand and together they started walking silently in the direction of the gate.

CHAPTER SIXTEEN

"Culpa lata dolo equi paratur"
(Gross negligence is the same as intentional harm)

The *Tiber Queen* was one of two river boats that Claudio Tondo and his oldest son, Michael, had acquired about ten years ago from the former owner who, because of increasingly poor health, had felt that retirement was essential. For years the city authorities had imposed strict regulations on the operation of all cruise boats on the Tiber. In addition to catering help, there were to be at least two competent operators on board for each trip. Annual safety inspection of the engines and navigational equipment was a requirement, and adequate numbers of life jackets were to be easily available. Food and alcohol were permitted for sale, but intoxication was considered a valid reason to restrict the sale of wine and stronger spirits. Only once had a passenger come to grief over this issue. Two years before, a male tourist from Denmark had joined the cruise while already in a state of intoxication and had fallen into the river within an hour of departure from the wharf. Fortunately he had been rescued by the crew of another cruise boat following closely behind. The local authorities arrested him when he returned to Rome, and he was detained for several days before his release was negotiated with the Danish embassy.

The ancient port of Ostia, thirty kilometres downriver at the mouth of the Tiber, was the usual destination for the Tondo's river cruises. The journey took about two hours, with a one-hour stop in the port to allow tourists to explore some of the sites in the port, to visit the naval museum, buy souvenirs, and perhaps sample a dish of spaghetti with clams, a local speciality.

The interrogation from the police on this night of January 18th, following the disappearance of a tourist, who had fallen overboard in the vicinity of the dock in Ostia had left Claudio, Michael, and their passengers in a state of considerable anxiety and fear. The police officer, Inspector Collina, had arrived at the dock and had hinted that the boat's licence might be revoked if negligence was considered to have been a contributing factor. He demanded a detailed description of the journey from the dock at the Saint Angelo Castle embankment in Rome. How many passengers had bought tickets and had boarded? Unfortunately, Claudio had to admit that the exact number could not be provided—an estimate of seventy-five was the best he could do. The majority of passengers had been booked, and tickets sold, through the tourist desk at the Michelangelo Hotel and it was assumed that they consisted almost entirely of registrants at the recent psychiatric congress. There appeared to be equal numbers of men and women; some appeared to be couples. There was the usual loud chatter and laughter. The passengers were in a party mood, but had consumed no more wine or alcohol than any other group.

The majority were speaking German, French or Italian; but there were some English voices audible. Although a few had remained in the main cabin, dancing to the music of the small on-board band, most of the group had been on deck admiring the views of the city for the first part of the trip to Ostia. Yes, they had noticed the beautiful young woman who wore dark glasses, soon after she boarded. It was not difficult to notice her—she stood out from the others with her black cocktail dress. It was assumed she was the wife of the middle-aged man who accompanied her when they came aboard. He had been holding her arm as he escorted her when she moved throughout the boat, and also brought drinks from the bar in the rear of the cabin to their table. That she was blind made sense now, but it had not been obvious to either of the boatmen. Neither Claudio nor his son had seen the woman dancing, as she seemed to have spent much of the downriver voyage up on deck with her male friend and another woman, who also spoke English and who later had identified herself as another psychiatrist from Boston. She knew the male psychiatrist but had just met the blind woman at the dock before the boat left Rome.

Had the blind woman been drinking more than the others, or had she seemed intoxicated? The psychiatrist—whose name was Teresa—was suspicious that she had, and the male companion also expressed concern as well. The bartender was called, but could not express an opinion. As far as he could remember the woman had not been at the bar or bought drinks. Many men had ordered drinks to take back to the tables. Was she behaving normally? Teresa thought she looked and acted depressed. She had been seen by Michael making at least one visit to the toilet. The male doctor she was with had waited outside for her return and helped her back to their table.

The downriver part of the cruise had been uneventful and yes, all the passengers had disembarked at the port, and all had been accounted for when they returned an hour later. The blind woman and her companion had boarded, but she had not seemed in any way unusual—certainly not obviously intoxicated. A buffet dinner was always served in the cabin on the return trip, although some of the passengers had been permitted to take their food and drink to the upper deck. The couple in question had chosen to eat at a table with two other passengers, one being the woman from Boston.

It was about 7:50 p.m. when the confusion erupted. The boat had left the dock about ten minutes before. It was now dark. The band was playing, and the dance music was loud. The man who had been with the blind woman had suddenly appeared on the bridge demanding in English that the boat be turned around because his female friend had disappeared, and might have fallen overboard. He was clearly in a state of panic. He had already asked the band to stop playing. Other tourists were collecting on the bridge to offer advice. Yes, the engines had been stopped briefly while Claudio and his son both tried to make some sense of the story. Michael was able to communicate in English, and another Italian passenger helped with interpretation as well. Within a few minutes the engines were restarted, and the boat was directed slowly downstream again. The boat was searched, but the blind woman was not found.

It was a dark night, and although there were two spotlights on board, the river was as dark as pitch. It seemed the female psychiatrist—Teresa—had offered to accompany her blind friend to the toilet from the table shortly after they left the dock, while the others had remained eating. Having directed her to the door of the women's toilet, the psychiatrist had been assured by the blind woman that she would be able to find her way back to the dining area. She had not been seen since. No one on board had seen her emerge from the toilet, and no one had seen her on deck or heard a cry above the noise of the band and the engines. Her dark glasses had been found on the deck near the rear of the boat. Moving slowly with the tide, within twenty minutes, the *Tiber Queen* had again reached the dock at Ostia without any sign of the woman. Did anyone know if the blind woman could swim? Her friend, the doctor, who was not her husband, could not say. He said he had intended to ask her before they booked the tour. Obvious embarrassment and frustration was visible on his face, as he admitted the fact to Inspector Collina later at the port dock. His psychiatrist friend from Boston, and an Italian psychiatrist who was alone and agreed to stay, were very helpful, and able to inject some logic and reason into the turmoil. The police, after obtaining a list of those on board, their hotels and telephone numbers, released the boat and crew with the remaining passengers and they set off back up the river to Rome.

Teresa and the Italian-speaking psychiatrist had offered to stay while the police made arrangements for a further search of the river at dawn. Although there were two other cruise boats on the river that evening, none had reported seeing anyone in the water or seen a body. The stark realism of the police reports had caused Charles to recoil in horror and he had begun to weep. The police expressed surprise to learn that the missing woman, Agnieszka Lipska, was a Polish concert pianist and was scheduled to play a recital in Rome on Saturday afternoon. Charles found no comfort in being told that it was possible she had been able to swim ashore and seek help along one of the banks of the river. Others had fallen into the Tiber before, and had been rescued. That section of the river was a popular location for swimmers during summer months and the river banks were sandy. A police car that had been sent out to search the roads within reach of both sides of the river had returned to report that no trace of Agnieszka had been found. Finally, at midnight it was with great reluctance that Charles agreed to be driven back to Rome, with the others, in a police vehicle. There was nothing more to be done. He was numb and remained silent throughout most of the return journey.

There was a gnawing sensation in his gut that told of his anguish and guilt. He would have to find the telephone number of Agnieszka's parents in Kraków. It would be somewhere amongst her belongings at the hotel. Had she taken her passport with her? He had not taken his. They had been passed in at the hotel reception area but hers may have been returned. Her family would be horrified to learn she had fallen overboard and drowned while under his care. He found it difficult to imagine it to be true. In the morning it would be best to ask for help from the Polish ambassador who could communicate more effectively with her family. Charles remembered Agnieszka's consternation earlier in the afternoon when he eventually told her of the results of his interview with the police, and of their unconfirmed suspicion of Alexei as the person who had taken the de

Pachmann book. He could have lied to her about it, but she had raised the issue during the cemetery tour, and although he had tried to drop the subject, he found he could not dissuade her. She admitted she had a suspicion of her brother's guilt. The trip back from the cemetery to their hotel had been made in virtual silence. She could not be consoled. She did not want to see her brother again—ever. The news had ruined her afternoon visit to the site of de Pachmann's grave. It was with some persuasion that she had agreed to continue with their plans to join the others at the boat dock.

Could she have jumped into the river deliberately? Had she wanted to commit suicide? The questions left Charles with an even bigger ache in the pit of his stomach. He decided to speak to Teresa about it in private when they arrived at his hotel. The Italian psychiatrist had sat with them in the back seat, but had remained silent, and was thanked for his generous gesture when he was dropped off at his hotel. He promised to call in the morning to see if there was any news.

Despite the late hour, the bar was still open at Teresa's hotel where they were both dropped off by the police officer. "Come and have a drink at the bar," Charles suggested, "I need to talk to you about this disaster." The bar was still busy but they found an empty table and ordered drinks from the waiter. "I need a double whisky. What about you?" he asked. "I will have a small glass of red wine," Teresa replied. The waiter departed with the order, and Teresa—with a guilty look—again expressed her regret that she had not waited when Agnieszka was in the toilet—but Agnieszka had insisted that she could manage on her own.

"Agnieszka could have survived the river and swam ashore, in which case she will be found in the morning. She might have been a strong swimmer; we don't know that she wasn't," Teresa said consolingly. Charles was finding it impossible to be comforted by the possibility.

"You are very kind to say that, but she was almost totally blind, and would have had great difficulty finding her direction in the dark. My greatest dread is that she may have deliberately jumped overboard."

He proceeded to tell her of the events leading to Agnieszka's distress in the early afternoon. "I feel she may have also had more wine than I had assumed. Her glass was often empty and the others, as well as I, were often refilling it. It is possible she may have lost her balance from the effect of the wine and fallen into the river."

"I had not met her before but my impression on the cruise downstream was that she was very quiet and looked depressed," Teresa noted. "What do you plan to do now? I can arrange a taxi to take you back to the hotel. You should not walk back at this hour. And besides, the police will be calling you if they find her." He agreed to her advice, swallowed his whisky in one motion, and paid the bill.

They stood up and she gave him a long hug. "You look like you needed that. I will give you my telephone number here, so do not hesitate to call me at any hour if there is any news, or if there is something I can do to help. Be sure to get some sleep and thank you for the drink." He knew he wouldn't sleep but he tried to produce a brave smile as he thanked her again for being so kind.

The taxi drive to the hotel was brief, and as he entered the lobby he knew he needed to get Agnieszka's room key to look for her passport and her parents' address or telephone number; but he would not call them at this late hour. The receptionist was shocked to learn of the accident. No, there had been no calls from the police, but she promised to direct any messages to his room. No, Miss Lipska's passport was not in the safe. She found a key to the room, and he took the stairs to the second flood. He felt exhausted, depressed and demoralized. His mouth was dry from too much wine. Why had he been such a fool to allow her to be moving about alone on the boat? He knew he should have had less to drink too. He was ashamed to have to admit to the police he had not asked her if she was able to swim. His sense of guilt was overwhelming, and his stomach pain—which had abated somewhat during the drive back—had returned. It had not been helped by the whisky. He felt in his jacket pocket and found his own room key, as well as her dark glasses. He had forgotten that he had been given the glasses by one of the passengers as he stood on the port dock.

He wondered why he was surprised to find her suite so very tidy, as it had never been otherwise whenever he had been there with her. It registered as another realization of his obvious admiration and love for this woman, whom he had known for no more than four days. The challenges she dealt with did not appear an obvious obstacle to her coping skills. But was she able to swim? He turned on the light in her bathroom and glanced in the mirror. The reflection was not at all pleasant—his eyes were red and puffy, his hair uncombed. He inspected his teeth and concluded he needed to brush them. He found her toothbrush and toothpaste, and felt better in a few minutes. Leaving the bathroom after using the toilet, he began his search by opening drawers in the two bedroom bureaus. That was no help, but on the top of her dressing table were some envelopes, the contract for Saturday's recital, and a copy of the recital programme. Her photograph was on the front page of the programme.

He picked it up and gazed at the beautiful woman seated at the piano. The lump in his throat seemed larger. Impulsively, he placed her picture to his lips and held her there for several minutes. Agnieszka, where are you? And are you alive and safe? He could feel tears again, running down his face and he suddenly felt an impulse to do something he had not done since a boy. He walked back into the bedroom and slowly knelt by her bed. His mother had taught him to kneel at his bed before going to sleep and to thank God for his blessings. "I want to pray for her safety". He was out of practice but he closed his eyes and after a few seconds began.

"Dear God, please help us find Agnieszka. I want her to be found alive and unharmed. Be with her at this time of need and forgive me for my failure to protect her."

The lump in his throat would not allow him to go further. He did not want to get up and found himself staying on his knees, his eyes closed, his head resting on her bed, face buried in his sleeve. He remembered something from the past, a memory—probably from when he was a child, something that someone had said during a church service—a funeral perhaps? God always answers prayer but not always the way we want. His will be done. He could not remember if it had been Anne, his mother, his father—or perhaps his sister—for whom he had prayed, but to no avail. He had lost faith in the power of prayer.

He had been asleep on his knees for several minutes and awoke with a start. His watch said 1:35, and he knew he still had a task to complete. Scanning the room for another possible place to look, he moved to the clothes closet and began to search her pockets, which to his relief was where he found her passport. The hotel must have returned it after she had registered. The passport details were in Polish but there were two telephone numbers on the last page. Pocketing the passport, and turning back to take the recital programme, Charles turned off the lights and moved down the hall to his room. He felt he needed a bath, and turned on the water before he began to undress. His throat was still dry. He ran the cold water tap in the sink, and filled a drinking glass, which he emptied twice. The hot bath was what he needed, and he could feel some of his tension dissolve.

Before getting into bed, he checked to see if his telephone connection was intact and finally settled under the comforting duvet. He thought he should have a look at Saturday's printed recital programme but he was asleep before he could get onto the second page. His light remained on. The telephone rang in the middle of a dream just before dawn.

CHAPTER SEVENTEEN

"Erare est humanum"
(To err is human)

Charles realized the bedside light was still on as he reached for the telephone. The receptionist's voice was reassuring as he tried to wake up and listen to her message. The police officer, Inspector Collina from Ostia, was on the line and he had news about *Signora* Lipska. She was alive and well, and was a patient in the hospital in Ostia for treatment of exposure and abrasions. She had no serious injuries and would probably be discharged later that morning. The head nurse wanted Charles to come to the hospital to discuss Agnieszka's treatment, and her discharge, with the medical personnel.

"Please tell the police that I will leave right away. Is it possible for you to find me a taxi at this hour?" Charles' relief was instant.

The hotel receptionist reassured him she could arrange a taxi for the trip to Ostia. He could tell from his watch it was not yet six o'clock. It was still dark. His heart was racing and he felt an overwhelming sense of relief and joy. There was no time to shave. He used the toilet, splashed water over his face, brushed his teeth and quickly got dressed. His mind remained in a state of high excitement and relief. She was safe. So she can swim! She managed to swim ashore. He remembered his earlier prayer for her safety, and concluded it had been answered. Within five minutes he had descended the stairs on the run and arrived at the reception desk, where he was told the taxi should arrive at any minute.

The driver – who introduced himself as "Minerva"–said he knew his way around Ostia, having been to that hospital before, and estimated it would take about twenty-five minutes to get there at this time because the roads would not be busy. It was still dark and there was a chill in the air. Charles settled in the back seat and concluded he had complete faith in the driver, who had already set off at a fast pace, the beam of the headlights piercing the darkness. The driver was right. There was virtually no traffic on via de Mare, as Charles closed his eyes knowing he would not sleep.

A dream that was interrupted by the telephone call had surfaced from his memory: In the dream, he was alone on a railway platform, feeling out of breath from running to catch a train that always seemed to move away, faster and faster down the track. It is dark and he can see the red lights of the rear carriage slowly disappearing into the darkness. He stops because the suitcases he has been carrying are suddenly very heavy. They drop onto the platform and he slowly walks away. He is frantic because he is sure Agnieszka is alone on that train. He had promised her he would be back with the luggage in a matter of minutes—before the train was to leave. She is alone on the train and there is no one to guide her through the train carriages to the dining room. Why was he late? Had he spent too long gazing at the statue of Moses at the Church of St. Peter in Chains? Sigmund Freud had done the same on many occasions when he was a visitor to Rome. Like Freud, he had simply lost track of time but he knew that made no sense. The church was too far from the train station for that to have happened. He had been to the church before and he knew the distance so he must have been somewhere else.

The driver was making good time on the almost deserted highway. He had turned on the car heater, and the back of the car was now warm and cosy. Music and intermittent conversation was faintly audible from the car radio. Leaning forward, Charles could see that the speedometer, just visible from the back, was touching the 100 km/hour mark as the telegraph poles flew quickly by. Across the horizon the dawn was slowly breaking. Minerva soon turned off the main road and drove quickly down several deserted side streets. They were almost immediately at the entrance to a driveway on the left leading to the hospital grounds. The lights seemed to be turned on in all the rooms on the ground floor. After a brief negotiation about the fare and the return trip, Mr. Minerva agreed that he could find breakfast in the town, return within an hour and was prepared to wait outside until Charles was ready to return to Rome. It seemed to be a logical plan.

The hospital main door opened into a small hallway lit dimly by wall light fixtures. A middle-aged receptionist was seated at a small desk further down the hall on the right. She was talking on the telephone in Italian, and he waited until she had hung up. He introduced himself, and was told he was expected. "Doctor Sheka is expecting you and will be waiting on the second floor. Turn left at the end of this corridor and you will see the elevator at the end. Take it to the second floor, turn right as you get off and you should see the surgical ward straight ahead. I was told to tell you that your friend is doing well and not in any danger." She picked up the telephone and dialled a number. "I will call to say you have arrived." Charles was impressed with her English.

"Thank you very much. You are very kind and your English is very good," he told her.

The surgery ward was easy to find, and he could see the doctor dressed in white walking toward him down the corridor accompanied by a young female, whom he concluded was a nurse.

"I am Charles Flemming, Miss Lipska's friend, who was on the *Tiber Queen* last night when she fell overboard." They shook hands, and it was the nurse who broke the silence by introducing herself in perfect English. "I am Nancy Holmes, head nurse, and this is Doctor Sheka, who is from Ethiopia. He speaks very little English but you can see I do—I am an American living here in Ostia. Your friend is sleeping at present. She is very tired from her experience. We have examined her several times, and the doctor is pleased with the findings. There have been no serious injuries. She has some abrasions and bruises." Doctor Sheka smiled—showing very white teeth—and nodded in agreement, seeming to comprehend the message.

"I know you are eager to see her, and we can wake her shortly, but we should speak briefly about the events leading to her coming here. This is for the hospital record. Let us sit in the examining room for a few minutes," Nurse Holmes said, in a way that made the suggestion more like a command. Charles was used to this type of manner in some Canadian nurses. They moved into a room off the corridor, containing three chairs and an examining table. The nurse offered him one of the chairs. "Please sit here Doctor Flemming. We were told that you are a psychiatrist attending the psychiatric conference in Rome. Two of our consultants have been attending." Charles was feeling very tired and was glad to sit again.

"Let me tell you briefly about your friend's unfortunate adventure after falling off the tour boat last night," Nurse Holmes continued. "Fortunately she is a strong swimmer, and reached the beach despite the dark night. She had lost her shoes and glasses, but managed to swim to the beach on the left of the river. She must have used the direction of the boat's motor to orient herself in the water. She thinks she may have fallen asleep on the beach, and woke up feeling wet and cold, struggled up the riverbank and was discovered by the driver of a passing car, who brought her here at about 12:20 a.m. She had no identification papers or passport. She could speak very little Italian, and it was not until I came on duty at 6:30 this morning that she was able to tell us the details in English. In cases like this the hospital is obliged to notify the police. They have been here, recorded the details of her accident, as well as the medical report. They suspected she was the person who was missing after falling off the boat. Doctor Sheka had been called earlier and examined her. He found no serious injuries. She was exhausted and dehydrated, but her vital signs were stable. Her abrasions were cleaned and dressed, and she was admitted merely for observation. She was frightened, and complained to the doctor of a headache. We were surprised to discover she was almost totally blind, as she did not show obvious signs of that when she arrived. It seems odd to us that a blind person would fall off a boat at night, and could swim ashore and survive with so little in the way of injuries. The river is polluted, and few of the locals swim in the water in the winter – certainly not at night. She told me she had been drinking wine on board the tour boat and was feeling intoxicated."

Holmes had been speaking without any interruption, and Charles had been taking in every word. She paused to take a deep breath and to look him in the eye. "I suspect you have questions."

He hesitated briefly, as he had the same lump in his throat that he had tried to get rid of last night. "I want to thank you both for the care you have given my friend tonight. She has been very lucky," he paused and added, "and you will have guessed that I have been very neglectful. I feel ashamed and guilty". He decided he should give them more details about the background of their relationship. "We have been friends for only a few days. Because she is almost totally blind, I had promised her brother, before he left Rome yesterday, that I would be her guardian—her guide, and I have let him down—and more importantly, her as well. I had wondered if she had deliberately jumped from the boat because she had received some distressing news about her brother yesterday. I am hoping that she will be able to deal with that in the days ahead. She was obviously very upset about the situation with her brother but I am relieved she was able to keep her head above water despite her disappointment and to swim safely to shore. She would not likely have told you but she is an accomplished pianist. The police had already been told. In fact she was to give a recital on Saturday afternoon in Rome at the Church of All Saints. I am hoping she will feel well enough to go through with the recital. We shall have to see. It can easily be cancelled if she isn't. I should mention that her glasses were found on the boat deck. I was given them by the police officer. I discovered them in my pocket last night!"

There was a pause and Nancy Holmes spoke up. "I should mention that the doctor suspected she may have deliberately jumped from the boat. The cause of her blindness he could not immediately explain, and wrote in her records the possibility of a conversion reaction or hysterical blindness."

Charles shook his head, and could not resist a smile, as the idea seemed both absurd and amusing. "I can assure you her blindness is genuine, and is due to a familial disorder called retinitis pigmentosa. She has coped with it in a marvellous manner, and has become an accomplished pianist. Perhaps you should reassure Dr. Sheka."

"I will explain," Nurse Holmes replied and, turning to the doctor, spoke for several minutes in Italian.

"Perhaps this would be a good time to go to see her?" she suggested, glancing again at Doctor Sheka who nodded his approval. They left the room and moved further down the corridor passing other patients' rooms until they reached Room 2-36. The door was open and Charles could see there was a nurse seated in the dark at the foot of the bed. Agnieszka appeared to be still asleep. Nurse Holmes moved ahead after turning on the light over the bed, and looked at her sleeping patient. She was squeezing Agnieszka's hand as she leaned forward to whisper something in her ear. She motioned Charles to come forward. "She is almost awake." Agnieszka opened her eyes and smiled. "There is someone here to see you. Your friend from Canada has come down from Rome to see you," the nurse said as Agnieszka struggled to sit up.

"Is it you Charles?" Agnieszka asked as she turned her head to get a better sense of the room. He tried to swallow the lump in his throat. "It is me. I have missed you tremendously and I am ashamed at what happened." He moved closer to the bed and reached for her hand. He found her hands were cold as he felt her arms embraced him and her warm kiss on his cheek. "I came as soon as I received the phone call. I am very happy and relieved to find you safe and sound." His arms enclosed her, and he held her fast. "I love you and have missed you very much," he whispered. "We have been very worried that you were lost in the river. The medical staff here has been wonderful."

He released his grasp and stared at her face. She was crying, but had managed a smile. "You are as beautiful as always," he assured her, "... and your bruises will be gone in a week or so. I will never forgive myself for letting you go to the toilet without helping you find your way back."

"It was not your fault. I made a decision, clouded by the wine I had been drinking. Your friend Teresa did not understand how helpless I was. When I came out of the toilet I felt ill and needed fresh air. The engine fumes seemed to be strong in the toilet. After moving outside and moving toward the rear I must have tripped and could not stop myself falling over the railing. It was a big shock to hit the water but my first impulse was to kick off my shoes and swim toward shore on the left side. I could barely see the lights of the boat moving further up the river. I tried to shout, but I remember hearing no sound. I was coughing, and remember spitting water out of my mouth. When I reached shore I managed to get up to a grassy area and thanked God I had not drowned."

"Do not tire yourself," Charles consoled her. "You can tell me all about it later. Your doctor and nurse feel you can leave any time. Do you feel ready to go? I have a taxi which can take us back to the hotel if you feel you are able."

"I still feel tired and sleepy, but I can catch up when we get back. My headache has gone. Yes, I am ready to go"

"Doctor Sheka should check you again before you get dressed," Nurse Holmes suggested. "It should take only a few minutes. I think the laundry has washed and dried most of your clothes. Your beautiful dress will need more attention but it is dry." Agnieszka managed a smile. "The dress is not important. But I do not have any shoes!"

"We will let you have a pair of hospital slippers," the nurse replied with a laugh, "and you should also have a small breakfast before you leave. I will ask the kitchen to prepare you something."

Mr. Minerva was waiting in the corridor near the front door at the hospital entrance. It was almost daylight, and the port was beginning to come to life. Charles assured him that they would be ready in about thirty minutes, and returned to the surgical ward where he finalized arrangements for the medical bills to be sent to their hotel later in the day. He found Agnieszka had dressed, and was sitting by her bed. She had already eaten two slices of toast, and was drinking coffee. He sensed she was rushing to finish and reassured her. "You should not hurry—we have lots of time. The taxi driver is outside but is prepared to wait as long as necessary." He knelt beside her and reached for her right hand, which was still cold. She leaned forward and kissed him on the forehead. "You said you loved me—did I dream it?"

"'It was not a dream," he whispered, returning her kiss.

"That makes me very happy. I love you too. I came to that conclusion when I was lying here in my bed over the past few hours before you arrived. We have a lot of catching up to do, don't we? But I am ready to leave now."

They said their good-byes to the medical team, and headed for the elevator. He could see she was ashamed of her dress that seemed to have shrunk a few sizes, but her slippers were comfortable, and she said she was ready to get back to Rome and to her piano. He felt relieved that Saturday's recital seemed to be on in her mind.

CHAPTER EIGHTEEN

"Aequo animo"
(With equanimity)

The receptionist and manager broke into spontaneous applause as Charles and Agnieszka entered the hotel lobby. Agnieszka had slept most of the way with her head resting on his right arm and sitting on her tucked-up legs. Mr. Minerva, the taxi driver, had agreed to take a more leisurely route back to Rome, carefully observing the speed limits. The city looked distinctly more pleasant than yesterday afternoon. The sun was shining, and traffic was light. Charles felt tired, but it is difficult to sleep when one's mind is in a whirl. There seemed so many things that needed to be discussed, but he decided they should wait until later. He did not want to disturb Agnieszka's nap, and he was unsure how she would deal with the sensitive issues that were on his mind. If she were prepared—and able—to proceed with the recital, it would be preferable to leave unresolved matters until later.

He was relieved that the Polish ambassador had not become involved, and the thought of calling her parents in Kraków had played on his mind continuously. He had several people to thank, especially Teresa and the Italian psychiatrist, who had offered to stay with them last night in Ostia. He had forgotten his name. The police in Ostia had been very helpful.

The hotel manager was trying to be as discreet as possible as he took Charles aside to show him the news items on the front pages of two of the city's morning newspapers. He translated the headlines. "This one," he said, "says: VISITING BLIND PIANIST FALLS FROM RIVER TOUR BOAT: MIRACULOUS SURVIVAL and the other newspaper article: POLICE INVESTIGATE MYSTEROUS NEAR-DROWNING ON *TIBER QUEEN*."

"I would prefer that you not tell Miss Lipska about these articles Mr. Mercanti," Charles said quietly. "She has not heard what you said. Can I ask you to read the details to me later, or perhaps one of your staff could translate them, and type me a copy? Do you feel the police will need to investigate this further?"

"We can translate it and type it for you," the manager said, being his most helpful. "I do not know for sure, but I would not be surprised to see the police here to question you again. They are very much aware of the issue of safety on the river tour boats, and since the news has reached the papers they may consider talking to you both. If they do visit you, I can be available to help in translation. My guess is that some details in the newspapers were provided by the police as well as by passengers on the *Tiber Queen* as they came ashore at the Castel Sant'Angelo Embankment late last night. News travels quickly."

Agnieszka was looking very tired. She had been sitting in a chair near the reception area, and had dosed off briefly while Charles was speaking to the manager. It seemed appropriate to deal with her need to get some further sleep. She needed no encouragement to go upstairs to her bedroom.

"I can tell you are still very tired," he said as she rose from her chair. "You have a whole day that you can spend sleeping, relaxing or doing anything you want to do." They made their way to the elevator and to her room. She said she was interested in having a bath and a shampoo. He ran the bath water, and helped her get undressed. Her clothes were dry, but they showed signs of exposure to the river. He could tell she was not interested in spending a long time in the bathtub, and she was soon out and settled in her bed after he helped her dry her hair. She looked troubled, seemed unusually quiet, and did not seem interested in discussing the events of the previous evening. She wanted him to get into bed, but he said he should call Teresa first and give her the good news. He found the hotel telephone number and asked the receptionist to dial Teresa's room.

She was not answering her phone, so he asked the hotel operator to leave a message with the good news, and the operator gladly complied. As he hung up the phone, Charles remembered he should call the Polish legation as well to explain the events of last night.

The secretary, Elizabeth, was surprised to hear his voice; "No, the ambassador has not seen the morning newspapers yet, but I will pass on the news, and I am sure he or his wife will call Agnieszka later." The secretary knew about the recital and was curious if the accident might mean a change of plans. "Not as far as I can say," was Charles' response, "but I have not discussed Saturday's event with Agnieszka yet." He realized he had to do so soon. "The ambassador and several other legation staff had bought tickets," the secretary told him. She placed another idea in Charles' mind. "Can I suggest that you ask Mr. Radinski, or perhaps Mrs. Radinska, if either would be prepared to introduce Agnieszka before the recital?"

Charles had not thought of that detail. "That is a wonderful idea. Would you mind asking the ambassador first and suggest that his wife might also be willing? She seems to speak English very well, but they can decide." The secretary said she would ask, and would call Charles back in the afternoon. He realized he had not kept a telephone number for the very kind psychiatrist, who had waited last night and had returned with him in the car. Perhaps Teresa would remember his name.

He returned to the bedroom and was not surprised to find Agnieszka was sleeping deeply. He decided not to wake her, and returned to the sitting room area. His watch said it was almost 10 o'clock, and he was suddenly aware that he had not eaten since yesterday evening on the boat. Leaving a note on her bedside table telling her of his plans, he checked to see if he still had the room key, quietly left the suite, and headed down the hall to his room. He needed a wash and a change of clothes before going to the dining room. He passed the chambermaid in the hall and suggested she wait until later to tidy Room 205 because Miss Lipska was sleeping.

He telephoned the reception desk and suggested they hold any telephone calls to her room until he returned from the dining room. After a quick wash, a shave and change of clothes he was ready for breakfast. The dining room was open and breakfast was still being served. He ordered a larger meal than usual. The coffee tasted great, and he found the two soft-boiled eggs, toast and jam just right. He remembered that Agnieszka had eaten before leaving the hospital, but he decided to take a light breakfast up to her room nevertheless. Discussion of the recital plans was the most essential strategy for the rest of the morning.

As he approached her room with a tray of coffee, fruit, cheese and bread, he knew she was already up. He recognized the Haydn sonata she was playing. He let himself in and crept into the room where he found a chair off to the side. She was playing dressed only in her dressing gown. The sound of his applause as she finished the last movement startled her. She turned and looked in his direction.

"I did not hear you come in," she exclaimed with a smile. "What do you think of the Haydn?" He walked toward the piano and seated himself on the stool beside her. "What I heard sounds fabulous," he replied as he embraced and kissed her.

"I have had a very nice sleep with no bad dreams," she reported.

"I'm glad. Your hair is dry and you look much better after surviving the Tiber River. It does not appear to have affected your touch."

She turned back to the piano and ran her fingers of her right hand over the upper keyboard, producing a brief chord. "No, I feel fine. We have not discussed the concert. You must have had concerns about my ability to cope with the programme. It has been on my mind a lot, back at the hospital and between naps. I feel it will be a challenge but I am prepared to do it. I see you have brought me coffee and cheese. Let me drink the coffee before it is cold."

She ate a small portion of the cheese and drank some of the coffee. "That was just what I needed." She turned from the tray of cheese and looked at him directly. "Do you feel I'm capable of doing it?"

He smiled and reached to kiss her on her nose. "I am prepared to leave the final decision entirely up to you. We could cancel or postpone it to another day without a great deal of trouble. I have spoken to Elizabeth at the legation and explained what happened on the boat, and assured them you were safe. The ambassador had not heard of the accident. She agreed to ask him or his wife to introduce you at the recital. Many of the legation staff have purchased tickets. She said the ambassador himself would likely want to speak to you about it later. I presume he has not called?"

She shook her head. "No, the telephone has not been ringing." She paused and looked down at the pedals. "There are some things I want to talk to you about Charles. Now seems a good time to do that." She took another sip of coffee and stood. She reached for his hand. "Let us find a more comfortable chair." He offered his arm and they walked across to the nearby settee.

Her next comment surprised him. "What I have to tell you will be a shock. I am ashamed it has taken so long. You deserve better. But you must not think I have not trusted you with this information. I trust you fully and will always do so. As a psychiatrist you must be aware that exposing dark family secrets can be difficult. This is one of mine."

He reached for her left hand and kissed her on the cheek. "You know you can tell me anything. I am not easily shocked."

"I knew you would say that. What I have to tell you is the truth about my brother and your missing book. The news that Alexei was the prime suspect was no surprise. I was very angry and saddened as I'm sure you could see. It was a reaction to the realization that he had stolen something of yours. The truth is— he is what is known as a kleptomaniac—and has been since he was a boy. My parents became aware of it when he started school. He brought home books belonging to his classmates."

She took another sip of coffee and continued. "At first they thought he had borrowed them, but over time it became obvious that the owners were unaware of his having them. Over the years since, he seems to have restricted his stealing almost exclusively to books about music, musical manuscripts and scores. He is writing a book about de Pachmann. In his early teens he was banned from access to the school library, where security was very lax, and later to the city public library. My parents were very embarrassed when those restrictions were announced. Our family doctor referred him to the Warsaw Psychiatric Institute for Children where the diagnosis was confirmed. They were told that the condition was chronic and was sometimes triggered by stress and depression. He did not steal for financial gain, so the books and other materials were easily found and returned to their owners. I remember my mother, at regular intervals while he was at school, going through his bedroom book shelves looking for books he had taken. The books were quietly returned to the owners or libraries without a word to him about it. This is the first time in several years that I have been aware that he is back to his old habits. What has seemed odd to me and to my parents is his lack of remorse when the stolen property is discovered. I hope your book is the only thing he has taken since we left Kraków."

She paused to finish her coffee and fruit and Charles gave her free hand a gentle squeeze. "I have been listening, and am relieved you have told me the truth about Alexei. Do not continue to be angry or depressed about it. The book he took is not likely worth much—a hundred *lira*, perhaps—no more. If he finds the material useful it will likely help him with writing his own book. I certainly would never demand that he return it. We should try to forget about it. Kleptomania is not a rare problem, and can affect very proper and otherwise law-abiding people. I have seen several patients over the years of practice—not specializing in stealing books necessarily but being caught for repeated shoplifting. Many shops have a low tolerance policy for shoplifters, and will prosecute offenders. I think merchants lose a lot of money because of those people."

Agnieszka was sitting back with her eyes closed as he spoke. He sensed she was about to respond as she turned toward him. "I have been struggling to understand if I might have deliberately allowed myself to fall overboard last night. The nurse at the hospital asked me if I was trying to commit suicide and I answered with an emphatic "no!" I told her I was very frustrated with my brother and admitted I drank too much wine. It was very foolish and I am truly sorry."

She opened her eyes. "There is something else you should know. The doctor asked me if I could be pregnant, because he said he thought he could feel an enlarged uterus."

CHAPTER NINETEEN

"Vapora ogni ricordo che non sia d'amore"
(Any memory that is not love evaporates)
Sibilla Aleramo, Italian Artist and Poet (1876-1960)

Charles tried to smile as he absorbed the news. "You know that pregnancies in virgins are very rare. The Virgin Mary is the most famous! I suspect the doctor may have felt a full bladder or a benign tumour of the uterus — a fibroid perhaps. They are common benign tumours, and can be mistaken for a pregnancy if they are large enough."

"Well you can imagine I was shocked to hear the suggestion. I told him I had not missed a monthly period." Agnieszka was as frank about these matters as she had been about making love.

"You should have a proper gynaecologic examination when you get back to Kraków. Your family doctor can check it." She agreed. The discussion was interrupted by the ringing of the telephone. "Let me answer it," he offered, standing and walking across the room. It was Elizabeth at the legation. He turned to tell her the ambassador would like to speak to her. "I will go down to the lobby as I need to speak to the manager," he suggested. As he left he could hear her in an animated conversation in Polish, interspersed with laughter.

The manager was in his office and was curious to know if Miss Lipska was feeling better. "She has recovered very well and is presently speaking to a Polish friend on the telephone," Charles assured him. "Have you had an opportunity to have the two newspaper articles translated?"

"I think so, but I will ask my secretary." The manager left briefly and returned with two typewritten sheets. "Have a seat and have a look. If there are some sections that need clarification I can help. I will be in my office."

The first article was the longest: "VISITING BLIND PIANIST FALLS FROM RIVER TOUR BOAT: MIRACULOUS SURVIVAL, By M Legetti."

He read: 'If you believe in miracles you may consider the events of last night and early morning would qualify as such. Passengers on the *Tiber Queen*—mainly medical doctors and families attending the World Congress of Psychiatry—were shocked to discover that a young woman had fallen from the deck of the boat into the river soon after leaving the dock in Ostia yesterday evening just after dark. Sometime after seven the boat had left to return to Rome after an evening river cruise.

'The female passenger, who is almost totally blind, is a celebrated pianist from Kraków, Poland and had already given two successful concerts in our city. A final recital had been planned for Saturday afternoon at the Church of All Saints here in Rome.

'Police reports in the early morning confirm that the woman was able to swim in the dark, despite being blind and was later admitted to the hospital in Ostia for treatment of minor injuries. The reason for her fall into the river is under investigation. It is understood that the owners of the *Tiber Queen* have been absolved of any blame'."

The second article was shorter and unsigned: "POLICE INVESTIGATE MYSTERIOUS NEAR-DROWNING ON *TIBER QUEEN*

'The police of Ostia are investigating the circumstances which lead to a blind woman tourist falling from the deck of a river cruise boat, the *Tiber Queen*, last evening shortly after leaving the wharf at Ostia. Local authorities have always been strict about safety measures on river cruise boats. In the case of the pianist Miss Agnieszka Lipska, who was visiting Rome from Poland, police found she was unable to speak Italian when she was admitted to hospital in Ostia. Investigations into the cause of the accident are continuing. Fortunately, the woman was a strong swimmer despite being blind and was able to reach the riverbank, where she is said to have been found and immediately taken to hospital. Her injuries were not considered serious'."

Charles wondered if he should show Agnieszka the news items, or save them until after the recital? She needed to practice today, and it would be better if she had no distractions. If the police needed to interview them again, perhaps he should try to do that after the recital as well. He had no preconceived opinions about how the Mussolini government operated, but he was surprised so much weight was put on blame and responsibility in both articles. The guilt he had endured for hours before the news of her rescue had virtually dissolved — perhaps too lightly. He had been primarily responsible for her safety. He had made a commitment to Alexei before he left for Paris.

The feeling of guilt, and the need to insulate her from the newspaper articles, was suddenly pervasive again. It had been a frustrating and challenging week. His plans for a week of study in Rome had somehow been completely turned around since he had met Simon and the Lipskas. Simon's problem had been a challenge. Alexei, the kleptomaniac, was another issue, and now there was the challenge of explaining to the police how he had been so negligent on the boat last night. He decided to discuss his concerns with the manager.

Mr. Mercanti was obliging, and they sat in his office to discuss these concerns. "Thank you very much for the translations, which were ideal. I am now struggling with how to deal with the possibility that the police will need to interview us again. It would be nice to delay that until after Miss Lipska's recital in two days. I would like to keep the newspaper items from her as well. Would it be possible to contact Inspector Collina in Ostia and enquire about their plans?"

"I could certainly do that," Mr. Mercanti said happily. "I will stress that you would like to bring the unfortunate affair to a close. I must be diplomatic, because the police can be difficult. Leave it to me."

Charles found Agnieszka playing scales as he entered her room. She paused and told him about her conversation with the ambassador and Mrs Radinska, as he sat beside her at the piano. The Radinskis had said they were pleased to be introducing her on Saturday. They did not feel she should call her parents, as she was safe and her parents would likely worry if they knew she had almost drowned. Charles wondered if the ambassador had mentioned the newspaper items. He sensed she still knew nothing about them, so he decided to keep it that way.

He put his arm around her waist. "Have you had enough to eat? You had very little breakfast."

"I feel fine—not a bit hungry, but I am tired. I have a little more to practice and am planning to play the complete programme after lunch. If you have other things to do, I do not mind." He leaned over and kissed her. "I do have a few things I need to attend to, so I will leave you to practice alone. I am very happy you are safe."

She smiled, returned his hug and kissed him loudly on the cheek. "It is almost a miracle." He did not say he had prayed for her safe recovery last night.

"I will leave you for a few hours." He looked at his watch. "I should be back about twelve-thirty to have lunch with you. Perhaps we can go out to find a restaurant nearby for a change." She said she liked that idea. After another hug and a kiss, as well as telling her he loved her, he stood to leave.

"I suddenly feel tired again and would like to sleep a little longer," she sounded tired. He helped her back to the bedroom and saw that she was comfortable before returning to his room.

**** *** *** ***

Agnieszka was sleeping deeply when the telephone rang. She had been dreaming that she had been playing the second movement of the Beethoven sonata at the church recital. The telephone ring was a recurring E and E flat, and she thought she had played a wrong note. Lifting the telephone she heard a feminine voice speaking accented English. "Hello, Agnieszka—this is Sophie at the legation."

"Hello, Sophie. Thank you for calling. I have been sleeping."

"Sorry to wake you—Angela wanted to speak to you. My Polish is poor, so I will speak in English. Angela was upset to hear of your accident. It was in the morning newspaper and on the morning news from Radio Rome."

It took several seconds before Agnieszka could. "I hardly know what to say! I am feeling fine, but I am surprised to hear I was in the news. No one told me about that but I have recovered and am practicing for the recital. I would love to speak to Angela."

"Angela understands some English—if you speak slowly. I will put her on the telephone."

There was a brief pause before Angela's voice came through. "Agnieszka, we are sorry to hear about you. Get better soon. What will you play on Saturday?"

"You are kind to call Angela. I will be playing pieces by Haydn, Beethoven, Schumann and ... of course, Chopin. Do you have an encore request?"

There was a pause. "Let me think ... yes, will you play some Bach? Perhaps *Jesu, Joy of Man's Desiring*? I love it."

"I played it a few years ago at a concert in Poland, but I do not have the score here. I will practice it today", she said slowly, "but I may have to pretend I know it. It will be fun trying. Thank you for the call. I will see you after the recital" She paused before continuing. "Let me speak to your mother again."

Sophie came back on the line almost immediately. "Agnieszka, we are very happy now to hear you are well. We have tickets for your recital. See you at the church on Saturday. Goodbye."

She hung up after saying goodbye and realized the information had left her feeling depressed again. She felt ashamed and angry that the news of her accident was so public. "I wonder if Charles knew about it. If he did, he must have tried to keep it from me. Or was he planning to tell me after the recital?" she thought.

She glanced at her watch, and could see immediately it was not telling the correct time. It said 8:24, but it had to be later than that! She was puzzled and held the watch to her ear. It had stopped, and she knew immediately why. It was the twenty minutes or so of exposure to the water as she swam ashore last night. "I do have another watch, but where is it?" She suddenly felt hungry and concluded that Charles must be late. She walked across to her bedroom bureau and pulled open one drawer after another, searching with her free hand amongst the items of clothes. The jewellery box was the likely spot and there it was—it had also stopped but needed only to be wound-up. She called the desk and was told the time was 12:35. A call to Charles' room found him preparing to come to take her to lunch. He had been on the telephone speaking to Janet Spalding in Toronto again.

She had a quick wash, applied some lipstick, and thought of changing into comfortable walking shoes. It would be good to have a walk outside. She must have slept for hours since the river episode. She heard a knock, and the door quickly opened with Charles asking loudly, "Ready for a walk and lunch?"

She stuck her head out of the bathroom door. "I am starving. I had lost track of time but my empty stomach told me it must be noon or later. My watch had stopped after the swim last night!"

"We could walk for a short spell. It is too far to walk all the way. I reserved a table for one o'clock at a nice dining room near the Church of Saint Peter in Chains. I have visited the church before." Charles hoped his attempt at levity would not sound feigned: "I will introduce you to Moses who lives outside. We can pick up a taxi on the way if you get tired."

She laughed, "I see you already know Moses well! I do feel like a walk but I will put on comfortable shoes first. After that we can go!" Having found her shoes, she reached for his arm, and they walked toward the door together. "While you were away, I had a call from Angela and her mother. They had heard about my accident and were very concerned. They had read about it in a newspaper and heard about it on the radio. They were wondering if I had recovered."

He tried to hide his surprise. He had not anticipated she would hear about the newspaper reports from friends. "I did hear about the newspaper articles from the manager, but I decided not to tell you today. I did not want you to be distracted from the recital preparations. Did I make the right decision?"

They had reached the elevator and were waiting for it to arrive. She looked up toward him and did not answer his question. Instead he heard her ask, "Do you mean there was more than one newspaper that carried the story about my accident? I expect the ambassador knows by now and it makes me feel ashamed again." Charles did not respond immediately. The elevator door had opened, and he could see there was a family inside chattering in Italian. "We can talk about it in a moment," he replied as they entered.

They alighted onto the ground floor. He was feeling some guilt over his deception and lack of openness with her. Holding her arm, Charles directed her toward the reception desk. "I should speak to the manager about the possibility that the police will want to interview us again." He spoke to the receptionist and explained the matter; "Please tell Mr. Mercanti that we will be out for lunch for a few hours, in case the police call." The manager was not in his office, but the young woman promised to pass on the message when he returned.

The sun was shining intermittently as they set off in silence in the direction of the church. He could feel her firm grip on his arm as they crossed the street to the other sidewalk, dodging two bicycles, which had not stopped on the red light.

"Did you feel you needed to protect me from the newspaper articles so I would better concentrate on my recital?" she asked.

"I have to admit I did make that decision when we arrived back from Ostia this morning. Perhaps it was not the right decision. How do you feel about it now that you know?"

"It reminds me of my attitude in the past when someone, usually my mother or brother, read to me negative reviews after my recitals or concerts. In the beginning they tried to hide the reviews from me. They knew I was very sensitive and defensive. The critics were not often mean, but what bothered me was what they did not say in a positive way—in praise, as much as what they wrote in a negative way or criticism. I would have to hear what today's newspapers said, to be sure I could answer your question. Could you ask the manager to translate the articles for us when we get back?"

Charles recognized his dilemma immediately. Should he tell her the manager had already done so, and that he had not shown them to her? They were waiting again for another traffic light to change, and it gave him an opportunity to think about his response. How did he assess her response up to now? He had no sense that she was very concerned about the content of the articles or upset on hearing that the police were still interested in details. The lights had changed to green and they set off. "As no one has committed a crime, I suspect the police have very little to work on. But the manager warned me that the police are always curious when accidents like this occur. We can reassure them that no one pushed you, or you did not deliberately jump into the river."

"Well, we know neither of these happened, so they should be content with that," she replied. They were walking slowly along Via Torino, and he knew they would be late if they did not catch a taxi. There was still about a mile to walk. "Why don't we take a taxi the rest of the way? I will hail the first one that comes by." Agnieszka did not object, and before long a taxi pulled up. In a few minutes they had arrived at the dining room. "We can visit Moses later," he suggested. She laughed and responded, "you and Moses!"

"After lunch and Moses we should pay a visit to the Church of All Saints to be sure you are happy with the arrangements, and that the piano is properly tuned."

They had settled at a table near the window facing the street. "I think that would be a good idea," she said, "I have had bad experiences in some towns on tour with less than ideal pianos, but our organizers promised a good Pleyel for this one." She paused and added, "Angela has asked me to play *Jesu, Joy of Man's Desiring* for an encore so I must try to practice it this afternoon and tomorrow morning. It has been ages since I played it. I have the score of an arrangement by the English pianist Myra Hess but I left it at home."

The waiter arrived and suggested some items for lunch, and they decided on a half-bottle of white wine. A soup called *Stracciatella* was a menu special, and they both ordered a bowl. They agreed on a spinach dish, *Insalada di Pollo e Riso,* with chicken and rice, to follow. He noted she was looking more relaxed than she had earlier. "You look better after the brief walk," he said. He noted she was checking the time by holding her watch up close to her left eye. "I do not like this watch as much as my other. The dials are not as easy to read."

"I want to buy you a new watch to replace the one that was ruined by water," he said, "… maybe later in the afternoon or tomorrow before we leave we can find a watchmaker."

She smiled and reached for his hand. "That would be very kind. We can see how much time we have. What did you learn from your telephone call to Toronto?"

"My secretary was able to get me details of the American Scantic Line sailings from Gdynia. Their ships sometimes stop in Copenhagen briefly, and then sail non-stop to Halifax. That would be ideal for me. I did not fancy travelling through Europe just to pick up a ship in England. It is still winter in Canada, but by the time I get back I hope the worst will be over."

He suddenly thought of Alexei, and wondered what had happened to him and Simon since they left Rome. "I have been thinking of Alexei and Simon. Did you expect to hear from your brother by now?"

She looked surprised by his question. "No, he said he would call but I was not expecting him to. He was going to Paris for a week and certainly would have reached there by now. He had several contacts there and would likely call me if there were issues with the recital arrangements for next month. That is the way he operates."

She paused and added, "I am not sure how polite I would be with him if he does call. After the missing book affair, I am not exactly feeling a sense of brotherly love. What do you think? Am I being unreasonable?"

"Well at least you were not totally surprised by the news having lived with his problem so many years. But you know how little I feel about the loss of what is really a small item."

The wine and first course had arrived, and they were getting into their lunch. She had developed a more serious look, and he could tell she was preparing to make another comment. Instead, she kept her gaze on her wine, which she was sipping and savouring. He started his soup but remained silent and eventually he heard her say, "I was going to comment on the wine—which is very nice, but my thoughts are beyond that. Mentioning Alexei makes me think of my future back in Poland. In a few days we will be leaving Rome and it will be the end of an amazing experience for me. We have met—as if by fate. There have been so many crises, and you have been so generous in having me as your friend—and soon you will have me as your travel companion. I often wonder what the future holds for us after Kraków. You will meet my parents and likely experience a Polish family for the first time. I realize I have not spoken to my mother for days. She may not know that Alexei has gone to Paris alone, and that I will be bringing you back to Kraków to meet them, so I must call her later today." She was tasting her soup between comments, and he did not want to interrupt, even to ask her if it was to her liking.

She wanted him to butter her bread, and he did—taking an opportunity to tell her he thought the soup was unusual; to say he was enjoying listening to her; to say she was as beautiful as ever and that he loved her. She smiled broadly and said, "thank you—that is a wonderful thing to say. I love you too." She reached for his hand and held it tightly. "I like the soup, and I love Italian bread. I think my father and mother will like you as much as I do. Did I tell you my father's name is Adam and hers Elizabeth? My father likes to drink vodka before dinner—neat without any mix—cold, out of the freezer. My mother prefers to drink wine, but we serve it only occasionally with dinner. They live a simple life with regular unsophisticated meals at home compared to the life I lead when on concert tours. They do have a woman from the town, she comes in by day to help with the meals. The meals I have had in Rome have been wonderful and this lunch is no exception. I hope you will not be disappointed with Poland." She had laid her spoon aside and was gazing at him with a serious face. "I shall miss you a lot when you return to Canada—but I do not want to think about it now. Why don't we talk about Moses ... and Freud?" she asked with a grin.

Charles laughed at her last comment, but he could sense she was sentimental about their relationship. "There will be lots of time for Freud and Moses. I agree the last few days together have been fabulous, but there have been dark moments. It has not been long since I almost lost you and you eventually dragged yourself out of the Tiber. Do you feel any ill effects?"

"I do have some aches and pains where I bumped into the stones on the beach but they will be gone before long. I certainly feel prepared to do the recital—if I can manage to come up with an improvisation of the encore, for Angela. I have been thinking of the enlargement of my uterus, which was such a surprise. It was amusing really to be asked if I might be pregnant. Hopefully it will turn out to be nothing serious. So, overall, I seem to have escaped without much ill effects."

They had finished their soup course, and the waiter had brought the spinach dish. The young man was curious to know how they were enjoying the wine. Agnieszka said she loved it, and he nodded his approval.

It was two o'clock by the time they had finished lunch. Neither was interested in a desert or coffee, and after some discussion about priorities they decided to skip the visit to Moses and head for the Church of All Saints to examine the piano and the acoustics. The church did not seem far on the map, but they decided that a taxi was appropriate to save time. It was a smaller church than they had expected. It looked very old and poorly maintained. The corner stone read MDCLXVI. A few people could be seen entering and leaving through the front door. Agnieszka had hesitated and he could see she had been examining the Roman numerals carefully. "Charles, I do not remember my Roman numerals. Do you know how to translate them?" Charles walked back and re-examined the corner stone. "I'm not sure but I would say it means the church was built in 1666." He regained her hand and moved on. He could see four life-size statues of saints, two on each side of the main door, as part of the church façade. Arm-in-arm they walked slowly past each of the figures, examining their features. "They are the *New Testament* saints: Matthew, Mark, Luke and John. Here is Luke, who was known as the physician," he said, "but I would be surprised if he knew much about the causes of physical illness. My guess would be that he spent much of his day counselling patients about social and inter-personal problems, much as psychiatrists do today. Luke was not a Jew, nor was he a disciple of Jesus."

"I did not know that. I assume none of the physicians of that time were women. Do you know if they were?"

"I don't. But women played a significant role in the lives of the disciples. Remember Mary Magdalene? Some women probably had something to say about what happened in their men's lives. Let's go inside and see the church." They mounted the steps together and entered into a small vestibule, which lead into a dark and cool sanctuary seemingly lit only by candles. Someone was playing the organ quietly in the background. Charles could see through the door that the windows of the church were narrow, and of dark stained glass that seemed to admit very little light. In the vestibule was a large poster announcing the piano recital for Saturday afternoon, with a prominent photo of Agnieszka seated at a piano. There were also details of her programme and a short description of her as a YOUNG POLISH PIANIST AT HEIGHT OF HER CAREER in Italian, Polish and English. He pointed her toward the poster and read her the brief description of her career. "The tickets cost 100 *lira* which is a good price."

"That description is an exaggeration," she commented, after he read the description for her, "but the photo reproduced well—as much as I can see of it."

"I agree with you about the photograph, but not about the description. It is very accurate. You are too modest." Holding hands they walked towards the altar, and found a grand piano virtually invisible except for the three legs just visible under a canvas cover. A sign on the piano read *NON APRIRE PER PIACERE* (Do not open please). Agnieszka approached the piano, squatted to peer at the legs as Charles lifted the cover slightly. "In this light it looks like a Pleyel as the legs are characteristic!" She stood up and turned to him. "I do not think they will allow me to play. Besides I would be competing with the organ."

"I do not know for sure, but the sign seems to say 'do not open' or something like that. We would have to ask permission. Let me see if I can find the sexton or a priest who understands English. You sit down and listen to the organ music while I look for someone."

He set off to look, but returned after a few minutes to report that he had been told the agents had specifically insisted that the piano was not to be played as it had been recently tuned for Saturday's recital.

"Well, at least we know it has been tuned. How many do you think the church will seat? I cannot get an impression of the size," she asked.

"I remember Miss Rosso saying the capacity was about 450. Let us walk down the centre isle and I can do a quick count," Charles offered. She held his arm as they walked slowly towards the entrance. "I estimate more than four hundred, but we have not heard how many tickets have been sold," he said as they came to the last row of pews. "What do you think of the acoustics, based on the organ music?"

"I think the acoustics will be fine but I would love to try the piano an hour or so before the recital begins," she said, leaving Charles amazed by her attention to detail. "It is interesting that I find there is not the warmth here that one feels with some more modern churches. Perhaps it is because it is so dark and full of shadows. Now we should find a taxi back to the hotel, as I need to practice my version of the Bach if it is to sound authentic and not too much like an improvisation. The critics would have fun with that. For some reason improvisations seem acceptable for organists but not for pianists!"

Outside the sky had become overcast. A taxi was waiting for business around the corner not far from the entrance. They were back at the hotel within five minutes. The receptionist had two messages—both for Agnieszka—which were passed to him to read. One was in Italian and he knew he would need a translation. It looked like it might be from the police, judging from the letterhead. They were told the manager was available to help. "Let us find a seat and we can see what the second message says," he suggested. "The second is from the agency, from Miss Rosso. All arrangements had been made at the church for the recital at two o'clock on Saturday. She writes: 'Dear Miss Lipska, Mr. de-Milo and I will call for you about 12:30. That will give you time to try the piano and test the acoustics, which we have been told are very good. You may also be able to try the piano tomorrow before the press conference if it can be arranged. We are pleased that most of the seats have been sold as of this morning. Since Saturday is a holiday it is possible there may be a large number of civil servants and government officials here to listen. I will call you later this afternoon to discuss the possibility of arranging a short press conference before or after the recital, if you agree. It can be at any time of course, perhaps tomorrow or on Saturday morning. You may be asked some questions about your close call on the *Tiber Queen* last night, but we expect mainly music critics to be there and only a small number. I do hope you have recovered fully from your accident. Best wishes, B. Rosso'."

Charles looked at her to see if her face portrayed any doubts about the press conference. She was smiling as she returned his gaze. "I am amused by her suggestion that my swim in the Tiber would be of any interest to music critics or music lovers who read the newspapers." She shook her head. "Press interviews do not bother me in the least. I would be pleased to agree."

"I was hoping you would say that. It will add to your reputation in a positive way. I cannot see the Tiber episode being an issue of any significance— perhaps for the police, but not music critics."

He could see Mr. Mercanti, approaching to speak to them. The manager was holding the message that had needed translation. He sat down nearby and proceeded to look at the message. "This is a message for you Miss Lipska, from the local police regarding your accident last night. I will not read it all to you but give you a summary. They would like to speak to you and Dr. Flemming before they complete their report of the accident on the *Tiber Queen*. They want to know when it would be convenient."

She looked at Charles for his reaction. "Since I would prefer to practice this afternoon, I think tomorrow morning would be best for me. What do you think?"

"Yes, I agree," he replied. Turning to Mr. Mercanti he asked, "Would you be available to help with translation during the meeting with the police in the morning? That is, if the police officer can see us then?" The manager nodded and replied, "Of course. I am sure Inspector Olivetti, who signed this message, and whom you may have met before about the missing book, would come here rather than insisting you go to the police headquarters. I will call him and ask if that arrangement is satisfactory. You may not know this, but there was another short news item in this afternoon's paper about the river incident. Would you like me to read it to you? I can find it for you."

Receiving their consent, he returned to the reception area to find the newspaper.

Charles decided it was an appropriate time to mention that the manager had arranged earlier to have the previous newspaper articles translated. "I have them upstairs and will read them to you after this." She nodded but did not reply. He sensed she was not happy. Mr. Mercanti returned and sat down again. He had found the article on the second page.

"It is titled NEW INFORMATION CONCERNING NEAR DROWNING OF PIANIST ON TIBER and reads, 'Further information has been obtained about the accidental near-drowning on the Tiber yesterday evening. A tourist from Poland, Agnieszka Lipska, who is almost totally blind, fell from the *Tiber Queen* and disappeared despite efforts of the crew and passengers to locate her. The *Tiber Queen* had been chartered to take a large group of visiting psychiatrists and families down river to Ostia and back. As is usual on such tours, wine and food were available and it is said that Miss Lipska may have fallen overboard after wandering the deck unescorted and having consumed too much wine. The owners of the *Tiber Queen*, Mr. Tondo and his son, have been interviewed by the police and their licence to serve wine or alcohol is being reviewed in view of the near drowning. Miss Lipska is a well-known concert pianist visiting the city for a series of recitals in memory of the Ukrainian pianist Vladimir de Pachmann, who died here earlier this month. Police are continuing their investigations and interviews with witnesses as well as with Miss Lipska and her friend Doctor Flemming, a psychiatrist from Canada, who had accompanied her on the cruise. The misadventure ended without tragedy as the blind pianist is a strong swimmer and was able to reach shore near Via Falzarego on Isola Sacra. She was later taken to the *Ospedale GB Grassi* in Ostia, where her injuries were considered minor and she was released early this morning'."

`"I should mention," Mr. Mercanti warned, "that this news item is in *Il Impero,* the official newspaper of Mussolini and the fascist party. They print propaganda and only officially-approved news after significant censorship, but not all readers are aware of the control exerted by the regime. The hotels buy the paper and they know what matters are really like."

Agnieszka spoke up, "Thank you very much for taking the time to read the news item for us Mr. Mercanti."

The manager rose and returned to the reception area, promising to contact them when he heard from the police. They remained seated for a few minutes and Charles knew by her face she was troubled by the newspaper article. "Let us forget about the newspaper Agnieszka. Do you feel like playing the piano now?"

Before she could answer, Mr. Mercanti reappeared and announced that a Doctor Camillo Mazzini would like to speak to them. "He says he had met you, Doctor Flemming, last night on the cruise and came back to Rome with you in the police car later."

CHAPTER TWENTY

"Corruption optimi persima"
(Abuse of the best things is the worst of all abuses)

Doctor Mazzini—a short, dapper, middle-aged man with closely cut grey hair and a small white moustache—was wearing a well-fitted grey suit, white shirt and dark red tie. Charles realized he might not have recognized him unless they had been reintroduced. It had been dark on the dock in Ostia, and Charles was now feeling guilty because he had virtually ignored the man in the police car last night. He had been totally occupied with the tragedy and his memory was foggy for details of many of events over the last twenty-four hours. He rose to shake hands and introduced Dr. Mazzini to Agnieszka.

"This is the doctor who was very kind and stayed with Teresa and me in Ostia last night. Doctor Mazzini, meet Agnieszka Lipska, the pianist who fell into the river last night but who is now safe and sound. She is giving her final recital in Rome on Saturday afternoon." The visitor bowed briefly in her direction, "I am very happy to meet you and to learn you are safe. I read the news item in the paper this morning." She nodded and replied, "I was told how kind you were last night, and am impressed with your thoughtfulness. Charles told me about it. As you can see, I have fully recovered from it all." Charles could see she had frowned when Mazzini had mentioned the newspaper item.

Turning to Charles, Mazzini continued in his slightly accented English; "You must be very relieved and happy. Is there anything I can do to help you regarding the police matter? It was mentioned in the paper. I know how they work, especially the secret police, the OVRA—I live in Napoli. They are all the same throughout the country! The secret police can be very annoying."

Charles was surprised at the gesture. "That is a kind offer. We would like your opinion of our situation but we should find a more private place to talk." He looked about the lobby and saw a group of empty chairs at a far corner. "Those look private enough. Can we move over there?" He helped Agnieszka find her way and they moved into the new chairs. Doctor Mazzini produced a package of cigarettes, which he offered to them both before lighting his own. He continued his explanation after quickly blowing a cloud of smoke into the air above the table. He did not appear to inhale.

"I assume you have not yet met the police again to talk about last night? The newspaper said they wanted to be sure of the facts or something like that." They both shook their heads and he continued. "The *Polizia di Stato* are very pervasive in our lives. You can likely guess I am not a member of the Fascist party, although there is a rumour that all doctors employed by the ministry of health might be asked to take an oath of loyalty to the regime sometime soon. University professors already have been asked to take this oath of loyalty, and it is rumoured that school teachers may be next. You may be surprised to learn there are not a lot of party members. The vast majority of farmers do not belong partly because they cannot afford the fees. Few war veterans and members of the middle class have joined. In Rome there is a significant membership because of the large numbers of civil servants who are interested in protecting their jobs. An estimate recently suggested there were just over a million Italians members—out of a population of about forty million, so the party is not popular."

He paused to puff on his cigarette and again blew smoke out of his mouth without inhaling. "It is surprising that only a few creative artists and writers have left my country despite the fact that the regime does not tolerate their opinions, and the secret police have had them under close surveillance. There is a network of paid informants, often working in hotels and hostels. It is safer for those opposed to the regime to pretend to conform outwardly. They can then carry on with their work without constant surveillance. My family and I do that. I tell you this because it is important to know that there we have a secret police in Italy. I mentioned it earlier. It is called OVRA, which means *Organizzazione per la Vigilanza e la Repressione* or as some refer to it as *Opera Vigilanza Repressione dell'Antifascismo.* Whatever one calls it they are organized primarily to protect Mussolini but also to neutralize opposition with the aid of informers."

He paused and looked in the direction of the reception area, returned his gaze to his listeners, lowered his voice and continued; "Every hotel in the country sends the names of its occupants daily to the local police commissariats. This hotel would be no exception. The OVRA has served the party for the last five or six years under the control of a man called Arturo Bocchini, a very powerful and influential member of the Senate. He is in his early fifties and has the complete confidence of his boss, Mussolini. The police headquarters are here in Rome. They are responsible for patrolling our borders, the harbours, waterways and railways. They are interested in you because of last night's accident on the river. If you are lucky they may take into consideration that you are tourists and not Italians."

They had both been listening with some amazement. Several seconds passed before Agnieszka spoke. "Doctor Mazzini, I am sure you are right about the tactics of the OVRA, but why do you think they would be so interested in my accident on the *Tiber Queen?* I can explain what happened. I see very poorly and we had been drinking wine on the journey to Ostia. I had too much to drink—more than the others I think and I was intoxicated. No one pushed me and I did not try to commit suicide."

Doctor Mazzini smiled as he responded. "I believe you. I think it might be your friends rather than you who might have to answer the question of why they had not taken more care with your safety on the boat. I will try not to be judgemental, but Doctor Flemming seems to have been your guardian. The police could claim that he could have prevented this accident if he had been more attentive and not left you alone. Your other friend, the woman who stayed behind with us last night—the American psychiatrist—could also have prevented your accident if she had insisted on waiting for you. Being a woman is important in this country. Women have been elevated in status by the regime. Although they do not yet have the right to vote, they are promoted as custodians of the family and an important part of their mandate is to have children. Accidents like yours are considered an embarrassment, an indication of failure of the government to protect a woman—even though you are not an Italian." He took another puff on his cigarette, blew out the smoke before stubbing the end in an ashtray standing on the floor. He turned to Agnieszka and continued.

"I note in the paper that you have poor vision Miss Lipska—I hope you will forgive me for mentioning that fact. For the police, it makes a stronger case for suspecting negligence on the part of the cruise boat operators and perhaps your friends. I hope this tale has not been too depressing, but the reality is that this country is a repressive state under the *Polizia di Stato,* with control by fear. I have some friends in the OVRA in Napoli and would be pleased to contact them to ask if they could intervene if you should have problems with the local Roman agents. I will give you my telephone number as I am spending a few more days here before returning home."

He stood, scribbled his hotel and home telephone numbers on the back of an envelope and passed it to Charles. He glanced at his watch. "Now I must leave you with good wishes for a suitable settlement of the *Tiber Queen* affair, and of course a successful recital. I may be able to come to listen but I cannot promise. Please telephone me any time before I leave if you need help. My name is Camillo," he said with a wide smile.

They all rose and shook hands again. Dr. Mazzini smiled and paused before adding; "You may not know this, but the regime even frowns on people shaking hands now! We have been told it is a disgraceful gesture, a betrayal of fascist dogma. I do not understand it and so I ignore it. Now when we greet a friend or are introduced to someone new we are being told we should salute with the Roman gesture!" He illustrated dramatically the salute. "If you are curious about the way the regime boasts about its accomplishments and have the time it would be worth trying to see the large exhibition called the *Mostra della Rivoluzione Fascista* at the Palazzo delle Esposizione here in the city. You will get some idea of the way the country is run, and how much emphasis they place on their achievements. I was curious enough to go during this past week."

"I appreciate your candour Doctor Mazzini, and will call you if matters become difficult." Charles still did not feel he had fully expressed his gratitude. "We will think about the idea of looking at the exhibition. I want to thank you again for what you did to help us last night. It was not considerate of me to ignore you after all you had done. I take the blame for what happened last night. Fortunately, Agnieszka seems well prepared for her final recital at the Church of all Saints. We would be pleased to see you there."

"I understand why you feel guilty about the accident, but do not feel guilty about ignoring me." The psychiatrist from Naples turned and walked quickly toward the entrance, glancing briefly at the female receptionist and nodding as he passed.

Agnieszka looked tired. "I do not want to think any more about this issue Charles. I should go upstairs and think about preparing for tomorrow's recital. I need to work on the Bach piece. I would also like to call mother and explain what has happened. I would hate to learn she has been hearing this news from a newspaper or over the radio. Can you speak to the manager and arrange a time to meet the police tomorrow?"

"I think the phone call to your mother should be easy. I will speak to the receptionist and ask her to make enquiries about a long distance call which you can take in your room. I will arrange for tomorrow's meeting. We also have to think about the time of the press interview. But first let us go back to your room." Looking at his watch, he added, "I see it is already gone four-thirty."

They walked to the elevator, past the reception area. The concierge, a middle-aged woman with long grey hair, whom he had never seen before, was obviously interested in getting their attention. "Doctor Flemming," she said, in very good English. "I think you should know that your conversation was overheard by the hotel secretary, who has an office behind the chairs where you were seated. There is also a microphone that allows us at the reception desk to hear conversations from the lobby. The hotel was designed to allow monitoring of conversations."

Charles was speechless. He remained standing and listened as the concierge continued. He could feel Agnieszka's arm gripping him firmly. "Contrary to what your friend told you, many of us believe our Fascist state comes close to being the ideal—at least as good as many other democratic European countries. Some countries, including England and the United States, actually consider Italy to be a model for others. The natural greatness of our country and its people is no myth. That idea is considered to be essential to the plans of our government and our leader. It is entrenched in the hearts and minds of our people. *Il Duce* has proved he can get things done, to build a working, productive country without senseless strikes and labour unrest. In other words, he has put our house in order. You should try to visit the exhibition, which celebrates the ten years of our accomplishments under the rule of our leader Mussolini."

As she spoke Charles was debating whether he would retort with annoyance and anger. He hated the thought of someone eavesdropping on confidential conversations between him and his friends. Now that she appeared to have finished her lecture, he decided to terminate the conversation with a brief comment. "Our friend who was speaking to us was merely giving us an alternative view—one that seems to be more common that we had thought. But to change the subject, my friend Miss Lipska would like to make a long distance call to Poland. We will call you from her room to give you the number."

They proceeded to the elevator and pressed the button for the second floor. The elevator was otherwise empty. Agnieszka was quiet, but looked annoyed. He knew she was thinking about the conversations in the lobby, and decided to make no comment himself. As they alighted she whispered, "Now I know what is so wrong with this country's government. One cannot trust anyone. What a display of propaganda!" They had reached her room, 205, and he opened the door. "I agree, but it is not worth discussing now. I think the concierge is likely a well-informed member of the party. I hope our friend Camillo does not get a telephone call this evening."

After she had settled and given him the number of her home in Kraków, he called the reception desk and spoke to another clerk, who assured him the call could be made promptly. They would get a call soon.

Within five minutes, Agnieszka was speaking in Polish to her mother. She was very animated with what seemed to be stories of Rome, the fine weather, the death of de Pachmann, her recitals and her new friend, whom she said in English, had agreed to be her companion, when Alexei had decided to leave for Paris alone. They would be coming back to Poland together in a few days— leaving on Sunday. "Yes, he is here with me now and I want him to speak to you. You will love him as much as I do. But before he does speak to you, I want to tell you about my recent accident." The story of her mishap was abbreviated and minimized. "I fell into the river last night and had to swim ashore in the dark. I feel fine now." The story would have been curious to her mother, and several minutes passed as Agnieszka listened to the reaction on the other end of the line. "It was in the newspapers here, but I am glad you did not hear about it before and worry about it. Now here is Charles." She seemed to have success-fully diverted questions about the details of her accident and passed the receiver to him.

He found her mother easy to talk to. She was curious to know the details, which he also tried to minimise. He successfully diverted the conversation to Agnieszka's excellent recitals earlier in the week and her preparations for the recital on Saturday. He heard her mother say, "We will be pleased to welcome you to Poland next week. I hope you have a safe journey." He said goodbye, and Agnieszka had the final word in Polish before hanging up the receiver.

He sat down beside her on the bed. "Your mother sounds very nice. I know I will enjoy meeting your parents. Now I should leave you alone to practice. I must speak to Mr. Mercanti, and will come back in a few hours." Looking at his watch he added, "It is now almost five o'clock. Think about what you would like to do about dinner this evening." He gave her a strong hug and a kiss on her cheek. She returned his hug and they kissed with more passion. She fell back-ward on the bed pulling him over as well. He could tell she was passionate. "Get undressed," she whispered, "I want you now. It has been too long." He helped her undress, and she slipped under the covers. His clothes dropped to the floor and he was beside her in a flash. Their hands were exploring as they kissed, and he could feel she was ready for him. "You are very hard. It is amazing," she whispered, as she helped him find his way. His entry was easier than before, and they rapidly reached a rhythm. He heard her say, "Talk to me," as he was quiet and seemingly lost for words. "You are wonderful," was all he could think of saying as they reached a climax together. The thought of the recently acquired condoms in his bedroom flashed through his mind, and he briefly prayed she had not recently ovulated. Praying seemed to have become a coping mechanism in the last twenty-four hours.

*** *** *** ***

Details for the police interview had already been arranged by the manager. Eight-thirty on Friday morning had been suggested as a good time, as he knew that would suit them both. There been no call from the agency to arrange details of the press interview. Considering the available time it would have to be tomorrow or on Saturday morning before the recital. Charles returned to his room, listening to the sound of the Bach encore, as he passed Agnieszka's room. As he entered his room he suddenly thought of his own mother for the first time in days.

It was always a pleasant memory. He had long rid himself of the prolonged grief after she died. It had been the telephone conversation with Agnieszka's mother that had triggered a memory of his frequent chats with his own mother when she was very ill and close to death. His mother had devoted her energy almost totally to the family. Her life as a mother had been a true example of altruism. Sarah's death, several years after his mother had died, meant his mother had not shared the grief that he and his father had endured after his sister's fatal illness. His mother was sometimes quaint in her conversations and it made him smile just thinking about it. She liked to reminisce—often telling them about her early life in England before she came to Canada at the age of fifteen. She loved to describe how she had met his father—at a local art auction in Toronto. They were both bidding on an old watercolour painting. He had outbid her, and eventually got the painting. She had looked so disappointed as he retrieved his buy that he gave her the painting as a gift! He later admitted it had been love at first sight.

His mother had loved to read to him before he started school, and she later did the same for Sarah. His mother could ride a bike, drive the family car with great skill—sometimes over the speed limit—and she could change a flat tire without any fuss. She was a better driver than his father, who took very little interest in their automobile. His parents both loved card games: canasta, cribbage and auction 45s; but it was his mother who was the top player—she seemed to have a knack for getting the best hands.

He had often wondered if his interest in music had come from his mother or father. Although his mother could play the piano with some skill, she was reluctant to play in public or even for friends. The accordion was his father's instrument, and he never hesitated to get out his "windjammer" and play at house parties and for dancing. Charles wondered how his mother would judge the Italian cuisine, because she had been an excellent cook. He loved her pea soup, roast pheasant, leg of lamb and oatmeal cookies—and he remembered she loved olives.

He realized he had been seated in a somewhat dreamy state. His reverie ended abruptly with the ringing of the telephone. His first thought was Agnieszka as he walked to the bed, but the feminine voice was that of Teresa Rockwell. "Charles," he heard her say, "Tomorrow is my last day in Rome and I had to call to say I received your message and am overjoyed that Agnieszka is safe."

"Yes, she is, and I am negligent in not calling you again to say thank you for standing by me last night. We had a visit from Doctor Mazzini just an hour ago. He was the psychiatrist who stayed with us at the dock and returned with us in the police car. He painted a very depressing picture of life in Italy under the Fascists, and warned us of the tactics of the police. I am guilty for not acknowledging his help as we parted last night but he was very understanding."

"I hope you will be able to sort it out with the local police," Teresa sounded unworried. "I received a message today myself telling me that they were meeting you both tomorrow in the morning at your hotel. The police want me to be there as well—at eight thirty. I do not mind. I am not leaving Rome until the late afternoon. Someone at the hotel told me the river episode was in one of the local papers today. I assume the recital is going ahead as planned?" He assured her it was, and after thanking her for agreeing to come tomorrow morning, he hung up.

He remembered thinking at some stage during his return from Ostia with Agnieszka it would be an appropriate gesture to inquire if Nancy Holmes, the nurse at the Ostia hospital, and Doctor Sheka might be interested in having tickets for the recital. He needed to call Miss Rosso and discuss the arrangements for the meeting with the press and would ask for several tickets. He found the telephone number for the agency and rang. The telephone was answered immediately by Mr. deMilo, who said Miss Rosso had left, was already en route to the hotel and should be there soon. Agnieszka would want to be part of the discussions. He walked down the hall to her room and heard no music so he rapped and found the door unlocked. She was seated at the piano making notations on a sheet of music. She looked up and welcomed him with a "come in!" He bent over to give her a hug and kiss. "I am finishing some notes for the Bach encore which I think I have retrieved well enough from my memory. I would like you to sit and listen. Tell me what you think. I am glad Myra Hess will not be there, as she might be appalled by my memory of her arrangement."

"I came to tell you that Miss Rosso is on her way here to talk about the press conference, but we have time for you to play the Bach. She hasn't arrived yet. I remember it is a short piece."

"Yes, it is about four minutes with repeats."

He sat and listened to the familiar choral theme from the cantata, which he realized he could not name. "I think you play it with great sensitivity," he said as she finished. "I will go down to the lobby and look for Miss Rosso and bring her up here."

He found that his expected visitor had not arrived. He enquired for the manager but was told Mr. Mercanti had left for the day. His assumption was that the press conference could be held in the hotel, but he had not discussed it with Miss Rosso or Mr. Mercanti. After a few minutes, Miss Rosso appeared and apologized for keeping him waiting—she had problems finding parking space. They took the elevator to the second floor and greeted Agnieszka, who had changed into a skirt and blouse. She pointed to some chairs. "Please find a comfortable chair. We are curious to hear what plans you have made for the meeting with the press."

"There is considerable interest in the press conference," Miss Rosso replied, after she had found a chair. "The news of your recital has reached the office of the Ministry for Popular Culture. The present minister had received the notification from the group that controls cultural activities, the *Opera Nationale Depolavaro*. Our agency must clear music entertainment with them, and they in turn notify the ministry. You will be pleased to know that the minister himself has decided to attend with his secretary as he seems to enjoy music of German composers."

Agnieszka looked toward Charles, who obviously shared her surprise. "I am pleased of course. Perhaps I should have chosen some pieces by Italian composers such as Busoni or even Respighi."

"Please do not choose Respighi, as he has not always found favour with the regime!" Miss Rosso was quite emphatic. "Busoni might be better but you may not know that he became *persona non grata* in this country after he fled Italy for America during the war. We do not hear his music often and his mistakes and poor judgement may still be remembered."

"Well, I have chosen an encore by Bach that Busoni did not arrange. You may know he arranged many of Bach's themes."

Beatrice Rosso laughed and quickly replied, "I do not think the ministry staff would know a Busoni arrangement unless it was pointed out. They are not experienced musicians." She paused to look at the printed programme. "And besides, the encore has not been listed on the programme." She continued; "I also have some other news that you might interest you, but I will need your approval before it happens. The Ministry of Popular Culture has also offered to record your recital as part of their promotion of culture. They have said there would be no cost involved on your part. It would be done by Radio Rome whom I know have good recording equipment. The ownership and distribution rights of the recorded material would be yours. There would be a requirement for Rome Radio to consult with you about distribution or broadcast after you had an opportunity to edit the music tapes later. That could be done after you return to Poland." She looked at them both for their reaction. Charles was the first to speak. "Since the ownership will be yours Agnieszka, you should be the one to decide. If you decide the tapes are not to your satisfaction, you will have the right to decline publication and broadcast." Agnieszka was obviously deep in thought. Before she could respond he added, "you should also consider if the presence of a recording crew in the church would increase your anxiety level."

"No, I do not have any hesitation in saying yes," she replied with a smile. "The conditions seem fine, and it would be fun listening to some repertoire that I haven't yet recorded." Miss Rosso looked very pleased. "I will notify the radio station as soon as I return to the office. Regarding the press conference, I think it could best be held at the church—perhaps tomorrow at noon. The resident priest has given us permission to hold it in the Saint Paul room at the front of the church. Can we agree on twelve noon for the press conference?"

They both nodded agreement. "That seems suitable to us," replied Agnieszka, "but at some time I would like to spend half an hour trying the piano and the church acoustics, especially now that it will be a recorded. I am sure the radio crew will want to try the piano sound as well. Perhaps we could do that tomorrow before or after the press conference if it is agreeable with the others?"

"I am sure that will be possible but I will confirm that."

Miss Rosso rose to leave. "There is another issue that I want to mention. You may consider it an irritant. It is always an issue when a minister of the government attends a cultural event in this country. If he is present, concerts always begin with the playing and singing of our two national anthems. I am sure you have never played them Miss Lipska, and you may not even recognize them! We have the traditional *Inno di Mameli* or *Hymn of Mameli* first, followed by the new party anthem, *Giovinezza*. You can be sure the audience will sing them both with vigour! We have a pianist whom we regularly ask to play the piano part of both anthems if there is no band or orchestra present. She is prepared to accompany the singing. Do you feel comfortable about that arrangement?"

Charles gestured to Agnieszka for a reply. "It is your decision Agnieszka, but in my view one that you cannot easily refuse at this late hour."

"I have no difficulty with that arrangement. I am becoming used to the local party protocol. It seems that culture is not immune." Charles sensed some resentment in Agnieszka's response.

"I was sure you would agree. If you had not, it would be somewhat embarrassing," Miss Rosso replied.

"Can I ask a favour from you regarding some extra tickets Miss Rosso?" asked Charles. "We have two good friends, who work in Ostia, whom we would like to invite, if you have two extra available." He looked toward Agnieszka and added, "we haven't discussed it, but I think it would it be nice to invite the nurse and doctor who looked after you so well."

"I agree completely," she replied.

Their visitor smiled and replied; "Of course, we have several that have not been sold. I will save them for your friends, who can get them at the door. Now I must leave you and make the final arrangements. I will see you at the church tomorrow for the press conference and of course on Saturday for the recital."

They both followed her to the door and said "goodbye."

CHAPTER TWENTY-ONE

"Fide non armis"
(By faith, not by arms)

The reality that the day had been a long and difficult one for them both, had led to a unanimous decision to go to bed early to catch up on lost sleep. They had decided to have a light meal in the dining room with no more than a glass of wine each. Agnieszka in particular was exhausted, and admitted she was feeling the days ahead would be more demanding than any so far during their stay. She was complaining of a headache—a complaint she said was unusual. She had complained of a similar one when she was brought to the hospital in Ostia the previous night. She also felt an odd, nagging but intermittent lower abdominal discomfort again.

In the afternoon, Mr. Mercanti had called the hospital to speak to Nancy Holmes on Agnieszka's behalf. Nurse Holmes had left work for the day, but he was given her home phone number and found her there. She was delighted to accept the invitation to the recital. Could she also bring her husband? She knew Doctor Sheka was working on the weekend and would not be able to come. Mr. Mercanti said he was certain she could bring her husband. Tickets would be available for them at the church before the recital.

The Radinskis had telephoned before dinner, and later paid a brief visit to see that Agnieszka was well, and to bolster her confidence. They thought she might be in need of reassurance. Her headache had gone by then. They reviewed the recital programme together, and discussed the surprising news of the planned attendance by the Minister of Popular Culture. The Radinskis had met the current minister at least once, and reassured Agnieszka that he seemed interested in culture. They were not surprised to learn that the minister had asked for the singing of the national anthems. The ambassador and his wife were both willing to speak brief words of introduction. Before they left, they kindly invited Charles and Agnieszka back to the legation for tea after the recital. The diplomats were pleased there was to be an interview with the press, and promised to attend and make the introductions.

Over dinner, Charles and Agnieszka found themselves discussing the motives of the Ministry of Popular Culture in becoming part of tomorrow's recital. Charles was annoyed; "I think it is another example of a carefully planned and manipulative public display—a fascist spectacle promoting the party," he declared. "The anthems will be injected into the programme to extend audience participation, but also to boost the omnipotence of the party and its leader. The ministry will likely try to present the recital as an extension of the Exhibition of Culture with the promotion of party accomplishments that we heard about from Doctor Mazzini."

"You may be right, and the choice of a female accompanist to play the anthems is interesting," she added. "What do you think it means? Could it be an example of the promotion of women as cultural icons—an extension of their role as wives and mothers?" She continued without waiting for his response. "I wonder if the cultural bosses would be offended if I played our Polish national anthem at the beginning of my recital."

"Your theory about the woman accompanist is probably correct. I think it would be a very nice gesture to play your national anthem—but at the end—perhaps as an encore. It could of course dilute the impact of the Italian anthems, and it may not be diplomatically correct. You would be wise to speak to Miss Rosso and the ambassador first. You could do that tomorrow before we go to the church. I suspect you can play your national anthem very well—you must have played it a hundred times."

"You are right I have. It could be played without an announcement."

"I am glad you agreed to have the recital recorded," Charles was trying his best to be reassuring. "There seem to be enough safeguards to prevent the state from capitalizing on the project. I should ask Mr. Mercanti for an English translation of the national anthems. I have to say I've never heard them played or sung. Have you?"

"I have not, but I have played our anthem many, many times at the start of concerts and recitals in Poland. I haven't talked to you much about my country's problems since we met. I think our discussing national anthems has made me somewhat sentimental. I should tell you a little background." She seemed to be thinking about her next comment, and he did not want to interrupt. She had been staring at her wine glass and finally began.

"I was fourteen when the war began, but I have vivid memories of what terrible conditions we had to bear. Poland has had a very tragic history. At one time it was a great nation—I am going back several hundred years. The territory of the commonwealth of Poland and Lithuania at one time was very large, but at some time in the Nineteenth Century—after the defeat of Napoleon and by a decision of the Congress of Vienna, it became hopelessly partitioned, under Prussian, Austrian and Russian rule. There was a lot of internal bickering. The Russians were our worse enemy. In 1830, Polish nationalists in Warsaw rose against the Tsarist rule, but the Russian army put down the rebellion and a period of harsh suppression followed. Chopin decided to leave Poland the year before, first moving to Vienna for eight months and later to Paris. He had been disillusioned with the state of affairs in my country. Suspecting the worst, he left and never returned. I have never fully understood why he didn't return after matters improved. Part of him was French—his father I mean. His affair with George Sand was one reason why he stayed in Paris.

"After partition of my country, some Poles ended up in Germany, some in Austria-Hungary and many, sadly, came under the control of Russia. Fortunately Kraków was not in the Russian sector. In 1914, some Poles fought for the Allies and some for Germany. That war left the population in a state of extreme poverty. Our government was non-functional. Our train system was a mess. We had great expectations that the peace conference in Paris in 1919 would compensate Poland for its suffering and sacrifices. We had been promised territorial gains, and most importantly ready access to the Baltic. Unfortunately, there was constant disagreement in Paris about what we would get—how much of Ukraine, how much of Lithuania and so on. Many Polish people of influence were very frustrated. One of them, Paderewski, the pianist, had vowed he would never play in public during the war until Poland was free. After the war he became prime minister of a coalition government. He campaigned strongly for new boundaries that were determined on linguistic rather than religious grounds. He said famously, 'Poland cannot breathe without its window on the sea,' while campaigning for the port of Danzig, formerly part of Germany."

She paused and apologized for her long commentary. "Am I boring you with all this?"

Charles shook his head. "Of course not—I am fascinated. Please continue."

She drank the last of her wine. "Poland eventually did get to use Danzig, and it is now our major port, but the Germans have always regarded us with contempt since. Our other territorial gains made bad friends as well. We still have a difficult relationship with Lithuania. In 1920 there was more fighting—now with the Russian Bolsheviks, who were determined to take over our country—but we won, and as a result gained considerable territory from them. It all makes for a sad tale. Poland now seems to be making a good recovery, but we have considerable distrust of Germany, especially Adolf Hitler, who is clearly anti-Semitic, and unfortunately becoming very popular in Germany. The Germans are still licking their wounds over the settlements from the Treaty of Versailles. I think you will be surprised to see how we have managed to improve our lot when you come to Kraków."

"I am sure you are right. I will be interested to meet your parents and to see Kraków, which I know is a wonderful city. I was told before I came to Italy that the Italians were also bitter about their settlement decided for them at the Paris Conference. Someone suggested it was one of the many discontents that lead to the rise of Mussolini."

Charles stretched, stifled a yawn, and looked at his watch. "It is almost ten o'clock. Have you had enough to eat? Like some coffee?" She declined, and he decided to pass as well. Signing the dinner bill, he rose and offered his arm as they walked to the dining room entrance. She squeezed his arm. "That was just right. Thank you."

She had decided she needed a long bath before bed. It allowed him time to examine the bruises and scratches on her legs, and he noted they were clean and already starting to heal. Afterward he helped her wash and dry her hair. She had already chosen her wardrobe for the recital. She showed him the semi-formal dress that she had worn to the organ recital on Sunday but with a different headband and necklace.

He had wanted to spend the night with her, as he had not done that before. Helping her wash in the bathtub had aroused him. When he mentioned spending the night there was a brief discussion but in the end they knew they both needed uninterrupted sleep and decided not to do so tonight—but perhaps tomorrow night.

They hugged, kissed and said goodnight. She looked sleepy and relaxed. "Tomorrow I will call you, and we can have breakfast together before the police arrive. We can sort out what we will say about your adventure on the Tiber," he said.

In his room he could not help but ruminate about the suggested changes in her recital format. The fascist elements were obvious. The concept of the party organizational genius as being superior to the mediocrity of the ordinary people would likely prevail. He would never say so to Agnieszka, but he resented how she, and to some extent he, had been manipulated to be seen to endorse the fascist ideology. He could not see a way out. Before getting into bed, a brief word with the clerk at the reception area requesting a call at seven was the last he remembered after closing his eyes. That was not strictly correct. He did spend a few minutes fantasizing what it would be like if Agnieszka were there in his arms.

*** *** *** ***

He was awakened by the telephone. The night seemed to have gone by very quickly and it was Friday morning. His sleep had not been interrupted by dreams, as far as he could remember. He turned on his bedside light and noted his watch said six fifty-five. He could have gone back to sleep, but there was work to be done. A bath and shave did not consume a lot of time. As he prepared for the day he imagined what would happen at the police enquiry. The police would want to rehash his version of events on the boat, as well as those of Teresa and Agnieszka. The last he wanted to happen was an accusation that Teresa had been negligent in leaving Agnieszka alone while she was in the toilet. It had been his idea to take the boat tour. Agnieszka had been very upset about Alexei's behaviour. After the cemetery visit she had been very quiet, looked depressed, and had been drinking more wine than usual on the trip down river. He had also had more wine than usual, and had not paid enough attention to her comings and goings. He rehearsed his story as he shaved.

A telephone call to Agnieszka's room produced a sleepy voice asking the time, but she was ready to get up—she felt hungry, and told him she could be ready in about twenty minutes. She was ready as promised, and they headed downstairs to the dining room where a large number of hotel guests had already gathered. The hotel seemed to have acquired more guests overnight. "Do you have your appetite back?" he asked as he looked over the menu.

"I feel like having a good breakfast, because I do not usually eat much immediately before a recital. Tell me what you see that is interesting."

"Would it help if I told you I want a grapefruit, followed by a hot cereal and an order of fried bacon with toast?" Despite his earlier misgivings, he found he could manage a smile.

Agnieszka found a smile of her own; "That would suit me, but I would like a croissant instead of bread."

A waiter was soon heading to the kitchen in search of coffee and the grapefruit. Charles decided to wait until after breakfast to discuss the Tiber details. He reached for her hand, and she smiled again and squeezed his in return. "You look lovely this morning as always," he whispered, "do you feel relaxed about the recital?" They were sitting close to a family of three who had been speaking Italian, but the trio seemed very quiet as they ate.

"I am relaxed and I had a good sleep. I decided to dress casually and also as conservatively as possible for this meeting. I wondered if the police would pay attention to how we dressed."

"Well, I did not dress up either. I though a light sweater and casual trousers would be suitable." He paused, as the waiter had arrived with coffee and the grapefruit. "What questions do you think you will be asked at the press conference this afternoon?" he asked as they both sampled the coffee.

"I have been wondering that myself. I suspect they will want to hear about my early piano teachers, my interest in Chopin's music, what it is like being partially blind and its challenges. They will possibly ask my opinion of de Pachmann and his piano method. I can speak to that. I expect they will want me to discuss the choice of repertoire for the recitals—why I chose Haydn, Beethoven and Schumann for today. That will be easy to explain. Do you think they will be curious about my falling into the Tiber, as Miss Rosso suggested?"

He decided upon caution. "That seems quite a good list of topics. I can only guess about the Tiber experience but it has been in the newspapers. What would you say if they asked you about the political situation in their country?" She laughed. "I will think about that carefully. We are leaving Rome on Sunday, and I do not want to say something offensive that will annoy the police. We may never be able to leave. You would be unable to go back to Canada and I would have to give recitals for the Minister of Popular Culture in Rome for the rest of my life!"

He laughed, squeezed her hand and quickly replied, "That would mean we would be in Rome together for the rest our lives. It could be much worse."

"Do you think so? I sometimes wonder where our relationship will take us. You and I live such different lives— thousands of kilometres apart." He could sense her intense gaze, and he was struggling to say what would seem appropriate. "These questions will be easier to answer when we settle the current Roman issues with the police, and you have given your recital. We will have a lot of time to talk about our future on the train going back. I am optimistic. If we are meant for one another, it can happen. We will have to be very honest with your parents, because their opinion is important. That reminds me: I wonder what Alexei has been doing in Paris."

She had begun to eat her grapefruit and paused to reply. "I have lost interest in his whereabouts and if, and when, he will call. If he has an issue to discuss he will call me. He may be back in Kraków already."

Charles chose not to reply and began to eat as well. The hot cereal had arrived somewhat earlier than anticipated, so they ate their grapefruit in silence for a few minutes. She finally spoke. "I would like to speak to Ambassador Radinski and Miss Rosso about my playing of our national anthem tomorrow afternoon. If they feel it is appropriate, I shall need to practice it, as I haven't played it for weeks. Do you mind calling the legation and Miss Rosso after breakfast?" The toast and croissants had arrived, and he helped her find the butter and preserves. He looked at his watch and mentioned it was almost eight o'clock. "We can go back to your room and call from there. There will be time before the police arrive at eight thirty."

Back in Agnieszka's room, telephone calls were made to the legation and Miss Rosso. Elizabeth answered the legation phone, and after hearing of the question of the national anthem said she would discuss the matter with the ambassador after he was finished attending a staff meeting, and call her back. She offered to be an interpreter at the press conference in the afternoon, an offer Agnieszka gladly accepted, adding, "Miss Rosso said she was uncertain about official protocol regarding the Polish national anthem and wished to leave the decision with the legation. So the ambassador should know the best course."

Agnieszka hung up the receiver. "I feel better about the day now. Let us go down stairs and wait for Teresa."

They walked down the stairs arm-in-arm. To their surprise, Teresa had already arrived ahead of time, as had Inspector Collina from Ostia. Introductions were made and Charles set off to find the manager. Mr. Mercanti had already reserved a room off the lobby. He had been called earlier and been told that Inspector Olivetti of the Roman police would be joining them along with an Inspector Arturo Bianci from OVRA. Charles was surprised to learn that someone from OVRA would be there, but he said nothing. They moved together down the hall and found seats in a room that seemed to be designed for small parties. The walls were lined with hunting scenes from the past: wild boar hunts in Tuscany seemed to predominate. Charles mentioned to the manager that they would like a copy of the Italian anthems—in English. He was assured it could be done.

Within five minutes the remaining police officers had arrived and were introduced. Collina was the first to speak, with Mr. Mercanti translating in short paragraphs. The Inspector, reading in Italian from notes, summarized the details of the events leading to his investigation of the *Tiber Queen* "accident," as he called it. The officer from OVRA was making notes. The statements of the captain and crew, the bartender, other tourists who had seen Agnieszka on board— as well as the statements of Charles and Teresa—were summarized. Collina's comments concluded with a summary of Agnieszka's medical examination, and looking in her direction, he asked if she had fully recovered. She replied with a smile, "thank you for asking. Yes, I have fully recovered and am well enough to play a recital tomorrow afternoon." Collina replied with a comment about her remarkable fitness as a swimmer. "Accidents like this on river tours are very rare, and when they occur they come under the jurisdiction of OVRA who are responsible for the safety of harbour and river traffic. This is why I requested Inspector Bianci to be present today. He has already read this report."

Inspector Collina asked for any comments that might shed any new light on the reason for the accident. Teresa was the first to speak. She spoke slowly, to allow Mr. Mercanti to keep up with the translation. "I had not met Miss Lipska before we arrived at the boat, and at the time did not guess that her behaviour during the cruise was any different from usual. Dr. Flemming, whom I had met in Canada, had told me earlier in the week that her vision was very poor. We were all having fun and drinking wine down below deck. Other passengers had moved to the upper deck to see the views. I later concluded that Miss Lipska was unhappy, maybe depressed. She seemed detached and less amused by the conversations." The manager, who had been making notes, interrupted to ask for another word for "detached," and "absorbed in thought" was offered as an alternative. After a brief translation for the officers, Teresa continued. "I know she has admitted to you since that she drank more than usual. When I accompanied her to the toilet facilities, I was prepared to wait for her, but she was insistent that she would find her way back. She did not want me to wait."

She paused for a few seconds and listened to the Italian version. "I did not sense she was intoxicated, but we went to the toilet arm-in-arm. The river was smooth and the boat was not rolling. I feel a major part of the blame for her accident should rest on me." Collina and Bianco were both writing notes as Mr. Mercanti interpreted her comments. Collina looked up; "Thank you Doctor Rockwell." Turning to Charles, he spoke in English, "Doctor Flemming. Can you add anything?"

"I have already given you my version Inspector Collina, and I agree with your summary of my statements given to you on the dock at Ostia. Doctor Rockwell is prepared to take the blame, but Miss Lipska's safety on the boat was my responsibility. It was my idea to take the tour. I knew her vision was not good, but I had not even asked her if she could swim! I expect Miss Lipska will not agree with either of us, and want to accept total responsibility herself. I think that is not appropriate, but I will ask her to speak to that point."

Agnieszka sat straight up in her chair listening to the translation. She leaned forward toward the Inspector. "I do accept total responsibility, yes. My poor vision has always been my own personal challenge, and this is not the first time I have slipped or fallen and injured myself. I have to admit it is the first time I have fallen overboard in the dark and had to swim." She laughed and they all smiled. "I cannot, however, recommend that type of swimming at night for other tourists." She paused and rubbed her nose. "You have not said in your report what great care I received at the hospital in Ostia and I would like you to record that Doctor Flemming and I were very impressed and naturally are very grateful. I am referring to Doctor Sheka and Nurse Holmes. I also want to mention Doctor Camillo Mazzini, a psychiatrist from Naples, who was a passenger on the boat and who stayed with Doctors Flemming and Rockwell well into the night, long after the *Tiber Queen* had returned to Rome. So, as an investigator of such serious events, you likely do not often have three persons ready to confess guilt as you have today!" Everyone eventually laughed as Mr. Mercanti finally caught up with his translation.

"I think Inspector Olivetti would like to speak," Collina suggested.

Olivetti stood as he spoke. "I have listened to the comments and I have also read the report. I was brought into this case because of Miss Lipska's brother's involvement in a minor crime at the Hotel Splendide Royale earlier in the week.

We are convinced he was the person who stole a book, the private property of Doctor Flemming, from that hotel's reception desk, before the doctor arrived in Rome, by impersonating the doctor. We are curious about a possible connection between that event and his sister's accident. It is uncommon for the police to be called to investigate two separate events like this where the same people are involved. I would like to hear Miss Lipska's comments about that."

Agnieszka looked flushed as she sat thinking of her response. She began slowly, looking in the inspector's direction. "It is true that there is a connection. It involves only me and my brother, no one else. My brother is a pathological thief—also known as a kleptomaniac—stealing mainly books." She hesitated for the manager to interpret her comment, and to be sure they understood the word kleptomaniac. "The book, on Vladimir de Pachmann, belonged to Doctor Flemming, and was to be an important source of information for his own book he was writing on the life of the pianist. My brother is also writing a similar book, and I believe was keen to keep this new copy of the local de Pachmann book for himself, even though it will eventually be available for sale for anyone to buy." She paused as the manager translated. "It was a bitter disappointment for me to learn that the police had definite proof my brother was the thief. He has since left Italy, and Doctor Flemming has decided to drop charges. I discovered the truth a few hours before the boat left for the cruise, and my mood was one of anger, shame and sadness as we set off down the river. I think it was an important reason why I behaved the way I did, so my friends could not be in any way responsible. I blame my brother."

No one spoke as the officers continued to take notes. Olivetti sat down and finally spoke up. "Thank you Miss Lipska—that helps us a lot." He glanced at Inspector Bianci. "Do you wish to comment Artur?"

Bianci was a slightly overweight middle-aged man, dressed in street clothes. He was wearing a tie, and would never have aroused suspicion of being a policeman. He remained seated, and responded immediately in good English. "Those of you who are not Italians will not know the responsibilities of OVRA in ensuring safety on the river. We are always suspicious when boat accidents of this type happen to tourists. I too have read the details in the report. I conclude that the responsibility for the pianist's accident cannot be placed on any one of you. I believe Miss Lipska's version and explanation. No charges will be laid with anyone in this matter. It seemed to us more than coincidence at first that our police were involved with the two investigations involving the same tourists." He looked toward Charles, "Doctor Flemming, your visit to Rome has another twist which I would like to discuss with you alone. You will all be able to read a full explanation of the accident in the official party newspaper *Il Impero* tomorrow morning. No blame for the accident has been placed on the boat operators, who managed the events very well but have been cautioned about future excessive consumption of alcohol on board. I want to finish by saying that we wish you all a safe return to your homes, and hope you never have to deal with such events again."

Collina stood to conclude the meeting. "Thank you for coming and for your patience. We would like you to wait for a few minutes Doctor Flemming, as well as Mr. Mercanti." Charles was perplexed. He could feel a return of the anxiety that he had endured earlier, before Agnieszka's rescue. He helped her from her seat, and asked Teresa to escort her outside and to wait for him. He looked at his watch and discovered it was almost nine fifteen. The five were left alone. Artur Bianco was the first to speak.

"We needed to speak to you Doctor Flemming because in addition to being involved in the two cases we have just discussed, we have evidence you have broken the law since your arrival in Rome." Charles could feel his face flush and his heart rate increase. He was beginning to perspire as he heard the manager translate the sentence for the others. He could hardly believe what he heard Bianco say next. "The owner of the chemist shop on Via Andrea near your hotel has admitted that, at your request, he illegally sold you six condoms — presumably for the purpose of contraception. This occurred two days ago, but there is no paper proof of sale. Nevertheless, you were seen buying the goods by another customer, and the chemist has admitted guilt. Were you aware that the sale of condoms is against the law?"

Charles wiped his brow as he tried to regain his composure. "I was told it was not usual for condoms to be offered for sale to residents or tourists, and I take responsibility for buying them." There was an awkward pause as the three officers conferred in whispers. He wondered if he should offer to take them back to the pharmacy. Bianci finally spoke. "This crime occurs more often in Rome than suspicious falls from boats on the Tiber, Doctor Flemming, especially amongst visitors from other countries. We suggest when you visit our country again you bring such personal products with you. The state and the party have a policy, supported by the Catholic Church, to make contraceptives illegal so that our people may grow in numbers. The chemist who sold you the condoms will be interviewed again and likely fined."

CHAPTER TWENTY-TWO

"Maximus in minimis"
(Laying great stress on little things)

Agnieszka and Teresa were waiting in the lobby as Charles emerged from the room followed by the three police officers and the manager. The two women said nothing, choosing not to show their curiosity. He decided to say nothing about the mysterious police matter either. "Well I am glad we have finished with the police," he commented, as he watched the three officers leave. "Thank you for coming this morning Teresa and thank you for giving your version of what happened that night. I know you are making preparations for your trip back home. We will always feel a great amount of gratitude for what you have done. I should also mention how pleased I was that Agnieszka mentioned Dr. Mazzini and how helpful he was in Ostia." He gave Teresa a hug as she stood and prepared to leave. "I was glad to help," she replied, "and I hope the rest of your stay will be more pleasant." Turning to Agnieszka, she added, "I hope your press conference and recital go well. I wish I could stay to hear you play. I will say goodbye to you both now and give you a hug too."

"I hope the Atlantic cooperates on your trip back to the States, and your voyage will not be difficult. I look forward to seeing you again Teresa," Charles replied.

He watched her leave the lobby, and turning to Agnieszka gave her another, longer hug. "I expect you are curious about the business we discussed at the end. Believe it or not it was all about the condoms I bought several days ago. I bought them to avoid a pregnancy. Selling them is illegal in Italy. The chemist who sold them to me told me that, so he could be fined as a result of trying to be kind to a tourist. It is another example of the type of bureaucracy current in this country."

She looked amused as she stared into his eyes. "I am curious about those condoms. You will have to show me how they work!" They both laughed as they began to walk toward the elevator. "I will indeed. I did not have an opportunity to thank Mr. Mercanti for his patience and kindness, so come along with me while we do so." The manager was modest in his acknowledging his "small role," and said his secretary had finished typing the verses of the two national anthems in English as requested. He returned from his office with the typed sheets and was adamant in declining any fee for the service. They moved on toward the elevator.

"I see the time is passing quickly," Charles said as he checked the time. "It is almost nine thirty. What would you like to do now for the rest of the day?" He could tell she was thinking about her response as they walked slowly to the elevator. "I think I would like to practice again, at least in the morning—play the Beethoven sonata and perhaps the Haydn as well, and then have a rest—perhaps a nap. I think it would be worthwhile visiting the church after lunch to see if it is possible for me to try the piano"

"That seems a good idea. I will join you, and will read over the words of the national anthems as you play your pieces." They did not wait long for the elevator, and on arrival in Number 205, found the attendant was in the midst of cleaning the room. "I think it would be better if we went down stairs and had a coffee," Agnieszka suggested, and he agreed. They found their way back to the main floor using the stairs. The dining room was still serving late breakfasts to several guests. Over coffee she wanted to talk about some of the music on her programme—he thought perhaps in preparation for questions from the press. She had a lot of ideas about the Beethoven sonata. It was in three movements. Someone—she thought maybe it was the English musicologist Tovey—had written somewhere, in a recent edition of Beethoven's complete Piano Sonatas, that op. 31 No.1 was one of the seven sonatas that the composer had not dedicated to friends or sponsors.

"This sonata was also much less difficult to play than its larger immediate neighbours. I must be honest, and admit it is one of the reasons I chose it for tomorrow!" she admitted. "I could not dream of tackling the bigger sonatas without more preparation and I always find this one humorous in a way that is difficult to describe. It lasts about twenty minutes." They had finished their coffee, and decided that the chambermaid would be finished by the time they returned.

Agnieszka continued to talk as they proceeded upstairs. "I love the Haydn sonata very much. I remember practicing it when I was a teen, and played it at several recitals in Poland. It takes about eighteen minutes to play. Haydn seemed to be in a humorous mood when he wrote it. It has a beautiful *adagio* and a very brief *allegro molto*. I do not need to tell you anything about the Schumann as you know it very well."

The chambermaid was nowhere to be seen when they opened the door. The rooms looked spotless. Agnieszka said she wanted to use the bathroom, and after a few minutes emerged and settled immediately on the piano stool and played a few scales before beginning the Beethoven. Charles had found a comfortable chair, and began to scan the printed texts of the two national anthems. The manager's secretary had added a few details about authorship. She had written: 'The music for the official anthem, *Fratelli d'Italia,* (Brothers of Italy) was composed in 1847 by Michele Novaro, with words by Goffredo Mameli.

> Brothers of Italy
> Italy has awakened
> She has wreathed her head,
> With the helmet of Scipio, etc.

'Scipio is a famous family name from ancient Rome. The official anthem of the Fascist party, *Giovinezza* meaning "The Youth" is sung to words by Salvator Gotta and to the music of Giuseppe Blanc. It is a party song that has been sanctioned by Mussolini, who may have also contributed to the words. It is sung at all Fascist party gatherings and you will probably hear it sung this afternoon. Younger people know the words much better than the older generation:

> Hail, heroic people,
> Hail, immortal Motherland
> Your sons were born again
> With faith in the ideal
> Your warriors' valour
> Your pioneers' virtue
> Alighieri's view
> Today shine in every heart.

> Chorus:

> Youth, youth
> Spring of beauty
> Your song rings and goes
> Through the sorrows of life
> For Benito Musssolini
> *Eja, eja, alalà*
> For our beautiful Motherland
> *Eja eja alalà.*

'You may be curious to know who Alighieri was. Dante Alighieri was one of Italy's most famous poets who lived in the 13th Century. The line "*eja eja alalà*" means "hip hip hooray," as you would say in English. I hope these translations will be helpful.'

Agnieszka was starting the last movement of the Beethoven sonata as he laid the anthems aside. She was playing with assurance and finished the movement with a flourish. "I have just been reading the translations for the Italian anthems. Would you play me your national anthem before you play the Haydn?"

"I would love to. You will recognize it as a mazurka called after a man called Dabrowski who was a Polish General. The words of the anthem were written in the late 1700s by Josef Wybicki. The music was probably composed by a man called Oginski. No one is sure. I will translate the words in a moment. Here is the mazurka, usually played faster than I will play it. I suspect if I play this Polish mazurka as an encore, most people would not recognize it as the Polish national anthem!" She laughed as she began to play. It seemed a typical mazurka to Charles. She finished the piece and turned in his direction.

"The words in English can be translated as:

> Poland has not yet perished
> While we live,
> We will fight with swords, for all
> That our enemies had taken from us.

"There is a chorus that says:

> March, march Dabrowski

From Italy to Poland
Under your command,
We will reunite with the nation.

"The reference to this country goes back to the wars when Polish troops were in Italy fighting with the armies of Napoleon. Their hope was that Napoleon would come to the defence of my country and re-establish it as a free and independent country! You can see that most national anthems have war and fighting as their themes."

"I agree. While you played yours I wondered if you might be brave enough to improvise a few variations on the *mazurka* theme. That would make it less recognizable to the audience and the authorities and perhaps legitimize it. What do you think?" She pondered for a minute or so, and returning to the keyboard played the anthem in a different key and with a faster tempo. "Do you mean like this? I can think about it, but it depends on the decision of the ambassador too. We must be diplomatic! Now I will play the Bach encore before we break for lunch."

*** *** *** ***

After a brief lunch they set off for the church. The taxi drive took only ten minutes. Agnieszka had changed into more casual clothes. Charles had decided not to change. It was now one o'clock and the press conference was scheduled for two. "I am hoping the piano might be available to try so that we can judge the church acoustics," she said as they set off in the taxi. The church was deserted except for several men, presumably from Radio Rome, working on the microphones for the recital recording. The Pleyel piano was still wrapped but had been moved to the centre of the chancel. They introduced themselves to the two workers who seemed to recognize Agnieszka from her photograph at the entrance to the church. She indicated she wanted to try the piano, and they agreed, moving to remove the cover. For the next fifteen minutes the church was filled with the sound of brief fragments of Beethoven, Bach, Schumann and Haydn. She said she was satisfied.

"There is an echo with the loud passages, but it is not an obstacle. I have dealt with that before in certain halls." The sound engineers wearing earphones had adjusted with their tape equipment as she played. When she had finished, their smiles seemed to indicate satisfaction. The parish priest had quietly appeared and had found a seat behind them. He introduced himself and spoke briefly in Italian with one of the men. They both nodded approvingly as they discussed the sound reproduction. The priest's English was limited, but he indicated he would show them the Saint Paul Room where the press conference would be held. "The men are happy with the piano sound," he said as they walked to the front of the church.

"I think you will be comfortable in this room," said Charles, as he surveyed the arrangement of table and chairs. "Are there any topics which might come up that you would like to talk about?" They had been standing in the rear of the room near a statue of Saint Paul.

"There is always the issue of de Pachmann and the controversies he generated in the music world over the years," she whispered. "They may want me to comment on his method of performance and how he justified his mannerisms. I will need to think before I respond as there may be a representative of the de Pachmann Society of Rome present."

"I agree. You should tread carefully. You did of course dedicate your first recital to his memory. You might mention that. As well, you did visit his gravesite and laid flowers on his grave as a gesture of your esteem. If you avoid controversy there should be no adverse reaction from anyone. Anyone asking questions will be introduced by Elizabeth, so you should know who they are and what newspaper or group they represent. I am confident you will be aware of potential trouble-makers."

Several men had quietly entered the room and taken seats near the front. Elizabeth and the ambassador arrived next, and came forward to greet them both. They conferred with Agnieszka in Polish, and it was obvious that she had raised the issue of the Polish national anthem because Ambassador Radinski looked thoughtful, his hand under his chin. He spoke briefly with Elizabeth. "I have raised the issue of my encore," Agnieszka whispered to Charles, as she walked a few steps away from the discussion. Elizabeth gestured to them both to come closer.

"The ambassador and I agree that if you play the Dabrowski *mazurka* slowly tomorrow—as a theme and with improvisations or variations, there should be no repercussions. We doubt that anyone will recognize it if you announce the piece as a Polish mazurka of uncertain source—which would be true!" They were both smiling and Agnieszka was obviously thrilled to have that issue resolved. The room was slowly beginning to fill with a mix of men and women of varying ages. They saw Miss Rosso had arrived with Mr. deMilo, who both took seats at the rear.

It was almost two o'clock and Elizabeth, with Ambassador Radinski holding Agnieszka's arm, had moved slowly to the front and taken seats behind the table. Charles moved into a seat next to Miss Rosso. The ambassador looked at his watch, and spoke briefly to Agnieszka, who was wearing her dark glasses. He stood to address the audience. Speaking in Italian, he began with a brief welcome and proceeded to introduce both Agnieszka and Elizabeth, who acknowledged his comments with polite nods. The press conference was to begin.

CHAPTER TWENTY-THREE

"Hoc genus omne"
(And all others of the same sort)

Elizabeth Valentini stood and reminded the assembled group that she would be translating the audience's questions from Italian to English, and the responses back to Italian as the conference proceeded. "We had discussed earlier whether Miss Lipska would respond in Polish or English. She is fluent in English, and knowing that some of you understood English, we decided to begin with that arrangement. I would welcome your questions at this time. Please raise your hand and introduce yourself." She translated the suggested arrangement and scanned the room. Several hands were immediately raised. "I will choose the first hand I saw," she said in Italian, pointing to a man in the front row, who decided to present his question in English.

"My name is Lorenzo Marchesi. I teach piano classes at the Academy of Music. Miss Lipska, I heard your recital at the *Academia Filharmonica* last Sunday and enjoyed your playing of Chopin very much——a style that some suggest follows the tradition of the late de Pachmann. I would like to hear you speak of how your kinship with the composer's music developed over the years."

Agnieszka smiled broadly. "Thank you for your kind comments as well as your question, which I will try to answer. I have loved Chopin's music since childhood. When one grows up in Poland his music becomes part of you." She paused as Elizabeth provided a rapid Italian translation. "I have an affinity for him as a person too. He was a complex man—the product of a French father and Polish mother. You know he never married. His health was always precarious. He was always physically frail, and in his later years became a semi-invalid with a chronic cough, and eventually died of his chronic lung disease." She paused and looked at Elizabeth who summarized her comments. "So my affinity is the result of my Polish roots, my love for his romantic piano music, his perfectionist poetic style and not to forget, his choice of the Pleyel piano, which I also love. I think it was Thomas Carlyle who said that Chopin was a great artist and 'a noble and much suffering human being.' I believe that too."

Marchesi had a supplementary question, this time in Italian. "That was a very kind comment from Carlyle. I have read that, before he died, Chopin directed that all his unpublished manuscripts should be destroyed after his death. If that had happened, it would mean we would be without many wonderful nocturnes, mazurkas, waltzes, and the *Fantasie-Imprompu* Opus 66, which you will be playing yourself tomorrow afternoon, and the *Polonaise* Opus 71. Do you think his wishes should have been obeyed?" There was light laughter from the audience while the question was translated.

"Chopin spent half of his somewhat unhappy life away from Poland, and yet it did not detract from his patriotism," Agnieszka replied, earnestly. "His *polonaises* and *mazurkas* are good examples of his nationalistic creations. His physical health was terrible. I have no doubt he was angry about his fate, and he was unhappy about his failures in love. He would have been very depressed at the end." She paused for the translation.

"His reasons for wanting his unpublished music to be destroyed may never be found. I am glad someone saw there was a flaw in his judgement. Other composers have left similar directives. In some cases a lot of music went up in flames. In others, the compositions are still available for us to enjoy." Elizabeth summarized her response and pointed to another man in the back of the room who stood and continued on the Chopin theme in Italian.

"Thank you for your answer to the last question Miss Lipska. My name is Moretto. I work as music critic for a city paper. On the same theme of Chopin's solo piano music—considerable editing of his scores has occurred since his death—some controversial. It is not rare to hear Chopin's music played with excessive freedom. How much freedom do you feel is appropriate in playing and interpreting his music?"

Agnieszka waited for the translation; "My teachers taught me to play his music as it was written. The tempo I use is rarely faster or slower than he indicated in the score. I never add phrases or octaves that are not indicated. I am against the practice of splitting of the hands, as is popular with some pianists. De Pachmann himself did this sometimes. There are examples of piano music where that is acceptable because the composer indicates it. In the case of the opening movement of Beethoven's Sonata, Opus 31, number one, the uncoordinated hands add considerable delight to the work. You will remember he wrote it so the right hand is always too impatient to wait for the left!"

A woman near the front had raised her hand and stood. "My name is Nadia Rossi. I must speak in Italian. I am a member of the Vladimir de Pachmann Society here in Rome. I too enjoyed your recital last Sunday. I hope you continue to play Chopin as close to the de Pachmann tradition as you can. I see you will be playing a Beethoven sonata tomorrow. My question concerns the common belief that de Pachmann did not have the same affinity for the piano music of Beethoven as he did for Chopin. Simon Williams, the British critic, who introduced you at the recital has written a long article on this subject."

"Thank you for your question Miss Rossi. Elizabeth has just translated it. I am aware of Mr. William's views about de Pachmann's Beethoven performances but I have not read his paper on the subject, which also deals with his stage behaviour. In my view, de Pachmann did not always fail Beethoven. Some critics praised certain of his recital interpretations, but he was not always consistent. He was sometimes criticized for his idiosyncratic Chopin as well." She paused again for translation.

"My guess is that his poor performances of Beethoven—and sometimes Chopin—were influenced less by his lack of understanding of the composer's music and style, but more by his mood and level of anxiety at the time. Some critics thought he played Beethoven's piano music in an excessively romantic fashion—'not masculine enough', they wrote." She paused again for the translation to catch up. "But he sometimes played Beethoven's chamber works very well, as he would then have the score before him. Having the score would reduce performance anxiety or stage fright, as well as reduce memory lapses. He likely had an obsessive-compulsive disorder as well and was driven to act out some of the stage antics as a way of neutralizing his anxiety."

She paused and then continued, "It is not my style to talk to the audience as he did. But other pianists do—Francis Plante, the well-known French pianist is an example. He is now about ninety-six years old. Franz Liszt is another pianist who smiled and gazed at his audience as he played. Richard Strauss was said to make awful facial grimaces. I regret not having the opportunity to hear de Pachmann play the piano more than twice—and never heard him play Beethoven. I had hoped to meet him on this visit, but it was not to be. He did pass through Poland, visiting Kraków, while on his honeymoon in 1885, but that was long before I was born." She swallowed a glass of water as she waited for another question.

Another man had risen and said he had a question. "My name is Bruno Garavelli. I write organ reviews for the *Evening Post*. I sometimes hear blind organists play with amazing facility. I did not hear your recital on the weekend, but I did read the reviews, which were wonderful. I can see you are visually impaired and I do not want to be too personal about this question." He paused to allow Elizabeth to translate. "My question concerns your approach to the piano as one who is blind. How were you taught in your country? How do you practice? And what obstacles do you have to overcome when playing in public?"

Agnieszka smiled as she listened to the translation. "I anticipate this question every time I meet the critics in Warsaw or Kraków. I do not mind at all discussing the answers. Fortunately I was not blind from birth, and it was not until I was about five when my vision began to fail but in my early teens my vision rapidly failed. So I had some very good tuition before that happened. I attended the School for the Blind in Kraków until I was nineteen." She took another sip of water as she waited for the translation. "Since then, I have learnt to read scores with strong eye glasses but I cannot use a score at the piano to sight-read. My memory serves me well, and I have virtually no stage fright — perhaps that is because I am not intimidated by an audience that I cannot see." There was light laughter before she continued after the translation. "If you close your eyes or wear a blindfold at the piano, it will be obvious to you what a blind person feels. You mentioned blind musicians playing the organ. That is a much more challenging instrument than the piano, and I too am amazed when I see it played by someone who cannot see. I did hear the organ recital by Leszek Janinski on Sunday, and I enjoyed reading your review. People sometimes ask me if recording music in a studio is more relaxing than playing on stage. I do not sense there is a difference."

An unidentified male speaker asked a question in Italian that Elizabeth was compelled to repeat as only a few had heard it. "Have you recorded much of Chopin's music? I see there is recording equipment in the church ready for the recital tomorrow."

"I have recorded a small amount in Poland, and one recital last year in Vienna—some of his *mazurkas* and *études*. I would like to do more. Perhaps Radio Rome will broadcast this recital for more to hear—if it is good enough!" The audience laughed at her self-deprecation. "I think pianists and other musicians should have more involvement in creating recorded music. They have an obligation to the public who do not always have the opportunity to attend recitals".

After the translation another woman stood with a question. "I am Rosa Baylini, a freelance critic. I have a question about piano competitions. You were quoted in your printed programme on Sunday as being opposed to them and I am curious why. After all, the International Chopin competition in Poland has so far been very successful."

"You are correct. I do not see a great deal of merit in competitions, but I have had some pressure exerted from my friends in music to enter the Vienna International Piano Competition next year. The Fryderyk Chopin Competition began six years ago and we have now had two—the most recent was last year. The first, in 1927, attracted about twenty-five contestants. Last year, there were eighty-nine, if I remember correctly. The winners of the two competitions were Russians—last year it was Aleksander Uninski, an excellent pianist. He also won the Polish Radio prize for the best performance of a mazurka." As usual she paused and gave the cue to Elizabeth to translate and continued. "To win, one must have tremendous technical skill as well as exceptional artistry, and also be lucky with the jury! In 1927, the Chopin Competition jury was made up of all Polish musicians but last year it was international. That makes it fairer. Unfortunately, there are always more losers than winners. A competition can seem like a scaled down version of a war or battle. I think there should be a place for the audience to contribute to the judging as well. You are correct, it is not the way I wish to play music—as a competitor." She paused and added another comment; "I should mention that I have had very limited experience playing concertos with orchestras. I have no problem with the scores, but being unable to see the conductor well is a disadvantage. Most conductors are unwilling to allow a soloist to take the lead and follow you!"

There was a pause after the translation. Had the audience exhausted their curiosity? Finally a young woman stood and without introducing herself addressed herself to Agnieszka in English. "We have read in the newspapers and heard on the radio of your close call a few nights ago while on a cruise on the Tiber. You must be a good swimmer. You appear to have recovered very well, so we are very pleased you decided to go ahead with tomorrow's recital. None of us ever attempt to swim in the Tiber on a winter's night!"

There was general laughter as the comment was translated.

"Yes, it was a shock to find myself in the water in pitch darkness. I received great medical care from the staff at the hospital in Ostia, for which I am very grateful."

There was again applause after the translation. Elizabeth glancing at her watch commented that it was time to conclude. "I thank you all for coming and I hope you enjoy the recital tomorrow afternoon."

After saying farewell to Elizabeth and the Radinskis, Agnieszka and Charles found their way back to the hotel by taxi. It was a sunny afternoon and Agnieszka seemed excited and energetic. She was very pleased with the press conference and she said she was now in the mood to shop! Earlier in the week she had met a hotel receptionist whose name was Renato. She had offered to help Agnieszka with shopping at any time during Renato's work break. The shopping was said to be good in the commercial section of the hotel. Charles was very supportive. "Since I also have some shopping to do, why don't we both spend the rest of the afternoon at the shops?" They agreed and a call to the reception desk found that Renato would be available during a work break, at about four-thirty pm. He checked the time and found it was just past four. "I will leave you to find your way down to reception. You know the way by now and Renato will be waiting at the desk. Good luck with your shopping." He gave her a long hug, a kiss on the cheek and said goodbye. "I have my room key and money," she said. "We can meet later and discuss dinner."

CHAPTER TWENTY-FOUR

"Nec scire fas est omnia"
(We are not allowed to know all things)

Agnieszka Lipska was a slow shopper. She told Renata she knew exactly what she wanted but she insisted on examining each article carefully in good light. Her new friend was patient, however, and helped her select a formal pale blue dress for her mother, a white shirt and striped tie for her father. She wanted to buy a dress for her eleven-year-old sister, whose name she said was Clara, but she was not sure she had found the right size. She also wanted to buy a present for Charles. That took much longer as she could not think of something he seemed to need. He wore ties so that was her choice in the end—a red tie with white stripes. The presents were wrapped, the bill settled and they left to return to the reception area. Agnieszka was very pleased and grateful to Renata for her help. She said she would find her way back to Room 205 alone and set off toward the elevator with her purchases.

Charles had set off with several objectives in mind. He wanted to visit the friendly chemist nearby who broke the law and sold him condoms and he wanted to buy a watch for Agnieszka. He set off on foot confident that he would remember the location of the chemist's shop and he did. There were some customers before him who appeared to be obtaining prescriptions. When his turn came, he was recognized immediately by the owner, who introduced himself—for the first time—as Marcello Gaddi. The issue of the fine was uppermost in Charles' mind.

"I have some guilt about the situation in which you find yourself—and all because of me," he began. "I was reminded today by a member of the police that the sale of condoms was illegal just as you told me. They reminded me that you would be fined for what I consider to be your kindness and generosity. I would like to offer to pay the fine for you." Mr Gaddi slowly shook his head. "I would never agree to that. You would be amazed to know how small the fine was. The police have already been here. I put forward an argument that you were a doctor from Canada and were entitled to traditional Italian generosity. In fact, when I saw you enter the shop today, I thought you wanted more condoms. I was prepared to break the law again!" They both laughed at his sense of humour and now Charles shook his head. "I have a few left—enough for now—but I am very grateful for your offer." Looking over his shoulder he saw there were other customers waiting, so it seemed prudent to terminate the discussion. They shook hands and Charles departed with a final "thank you" to Marcello Gaddi, who resumed his essentially legal business of dispensing pharmaceuticals as if nothing had happened.

Emerging from the chemist's shop, he decided to turn right and to walk further down the street to look for a jeweller selling watches. The sidewalks were busy with people, many merely window-shopping. Within a few blocks he found a likely shop and was pleased to be served by a knowledgeable sales clerk who spoke some English and knew the trade. He said he wanted a lady's watch that a partially blind person would find easy to read. He examined several makes before choosing a Panerai with white face and wide black dials. The clerk assured him it would be suitable. The price seemed steep but the quality was high and he was told it would last a lifetime. They debated the price and found a common ground before he left the shop with Agnieszka's new watch in his pocket. He had accomplished all he set out to do—his final shopping mission before leaving Rome.

He walked back to the hotel using a different route and found himself gazing into several art shop windows along the way. There was a poster in a window advertising an exhibition of paintings of Caravaggio at a gallery called Galleria Doria Pamphlj, which he has visited in 1925. That was where he had seen the artist's painting of Mary Magdalene. Caravaggio was a wonderful painter of biblical scenes. The painting reproduced on the poster in the shop window was *The Murder of John the Baptist*. Charles remembered snatches of the story of Caravaggio's life. At an early age he had moved to Rome for painting lessons and had got into trouble with the law – with much more serious consequences than those that Charles had encountered. Carveggio took many chances, frequently broke the law and because of his short temper loved to defy the police.

In the 16th Century the police were possibly even more intolerant than now. It was after the painter had stabbed and killed a man, whose name was Rannucio Tomassoni, that he had to leave the city to avoid arrest, eventually reaching Napoli where he stayed for a short period. He was frequently on the move for the rest of his life.

For some reason, Charles could always remember the name of the unfortunate Tomassoni, who had paid a high price for his encounter with Caravaggio. Despite his troubles the painter made a great reputation painting. His works were masterpieces of light and contrast. Charles resumed his walk back to the hotel and remembered that Rome had always been a popular city for learning the art of painting. Goya had travelled there from Spain as a young man to study with an artist of Polish-German nationality.

Agnieszka was sitting in the reception area waiting for his return and talking to Renata, who was preparing to complete her evening shift. Introductions were made and he heard about the success of their shopping expedition. He decided to show her the watch. "I want to show you your present," he said, as he took the small package from his pocket and presented it to her. She was surprised and excited as she quickly opened the box and pulled out the watch. Holding it up to the light and moving the watch face to her right eye she exclaimed, "it's just right! I can now tell you the time. It's ten minutes to six. Am I right?" she asked as she showed him the watch to read.

"Yes, you are," he replied, as he looked quickly at the hands. "Let me put it on your arm." She watched him as he fiddled with the strap and secured it fast on her right arm. "Thank you very much. It is beautiful. Now I can throw away my water-logged one." She did a little dance as she held her right arm in the air while looking at her new gift, much to Renata's amusement. She did a complete turn and held out her arms to embrace him. "It will be a constant reminder of you and your kindness." She kissed him on the cheek and held her lips there for several seconds. They said goodbye to Renata, and Charles thanked her again for being so kind.

Charles turned to Agnieszka and asked, "Did your shopping go well? What did you buy?" She suggested they return to Room 205 together so that she could show him her purchases. He watched as she disappeared into the bedroom and returned with a mischievous grin on her face. She wanted to tease him today and decided to hide his gift behind her back. "I bought you a present with the help of Renata. Can you guess what I bought?"

He pretended to think intently as she stood her distance. "You have to give me some clues. Is it something I can wear? A pair of socks? A shirt? A tie? Or perhaps shaving cream?"

"You are almost right. It will be very easy to pack for your travels and you can wear it now if you wish." She revealed the neatly packaged present, which he moved forward to accept. "Open it and see for yourself," she suggested. The tie was just the right colour. He loved red. "Thank you for being so kind." He walked toward her and gave her a long hug and kiss. "I will not wear it now because I prefer to wear the one I have on today but perhaps I will wear it on the train." She said she felt like having a short walk outdoors and finding a place to eat. He agreed.

They walked back down the stairs to the reception area and spoke to Renata. They would be out for an hour, she told her. Renata seemed to have something for them as she produced some letters. "You have some mail here Doctor Flemming. It just arrived." she said and produced two letters, one readdressed from Hotel Splendide. He saw that one was from Lisa Johansen from the Southampton office. The other he placed with Lisa's letter in his inside pocket. He was curious to read Lisa's letter but he decided to wait until later.

It was a pleasant day but the sun was setting. They decided to take a short walk to look for a quiet café near the Piazza Della Republica. Dinner was being served in a small *trattoria* on Via Napoli. Some of the earlier clientele were leaving so there were lots of empty tables. A small group of musicians was playing light music at the far end of the room. "I feel like having a pint of beer," he said as they found a quiet table near the window. "I have never seen you drink beer. Do you like it?" he asked. She turned up her nose and shook her head. "It has never been a drink I have liked but a glass of white wine would suit me." The waiter was soon making suggestions for dinner and orders were taken for drinks. He was offered an Italian lager, which was new to him.

"This morning I spoke to my secretary at her home in Toronto. I needed to keep her up to date on my travel plans. She has given me details of the sailings of the Scantic Line and it will be easy to find accommodation later next week. There is a ship sailing from Gdynia on Friday, the 27th."

The drinks had arrived quickly and they toasted one another formally. "Here is to a successful and relaxing train trip back to Poland on Sunday," he said as he raised his beer stein. They decided to have a light lunch with a small order of spaghetti and meat sauce with a green salad.

"Are you curious to read what the letters are about?" she asked, "I noticed Renata had two for you." He was surprised to find her so curious. Reluctantly, he produced the two letters and opened the first with the Roma cancellation. He scanned the letter.

"This is a surprise—a letter from Mr. Pallottelli's Villa. His secretary writes: 'Dear Doctor Flemming: It has been brought to our attention that you have been staying in Rome for the past week attending a medical meeting. Madame Ruth Mosconi of the local de Pachmann society has kept us informed about the events surrounding the tributes to our dear friend, recently departed. We regret that arrangements for the funeral have precluded any contacts with the many friends of de Pachmann. Mr. and Mrs. Pallottelli have been deeply saddened by the death of their friend of many years and have spent an exhausting two weeks dealing with details of his estate. It has necessitated Mr. Pallottelli being away from Rome for a few days dealing with this business. Both of the pianist's sons have returned to Paris and London so that we now have found the time to write.

'We know that a local contact has made enquiries on your behalf about Mr. de Pachmann's latest edition of his memoirs. Unfortunately, the printers have not yet been able to assure us of the date of publication so we are still not able to tell you when it will be available. We had debated allowing your contact to have a copy of the final manuscript but the printer would not permit that. There were also delays in having the manuscript translated into English, as the original translator, Mr. Cook, was not available. We wish you the best of success with your own biography of our dear friend and look forward to reading it after publication.

'We apologize for not being able to extend hospitality during your stay and Mr. Pallottelli regrets he was not able to attend the recitals given by your friend Miss Lipska from Poland. We have read the reviews of the recitals in the newspapers and have been pleased to see the favourable responses from our local critics. Yours very truly, Sergi Mezzetti, Secretary to Mr. Pallottelli'."

Agnieszka had been listening attentively while taking sips from her wine glass. "I regret now we did not extend a personal invitation to the Pallottellis to attend any of my recitals. He especially had such a strong attachment to de Pachmann."

"My guess is he would not have been able to attend, based on the details about his travels in this letter. I know he have been very pleased how well the recitals were attended and received," Charles said. She nodded in agreement. He paused and hoped she would not ask him to open Lisa's letter, which he did not want to read to her. It was lying by his beer glass but she was obviously curious about it. "I am always interested in letters from away and the different stamps. Where is the other from?"

He knew the letter could not be bypassed. "It is from England, from the shipping company, Canadian Pacific, with which I travelled from Canada." He opened the letter and scanned the details quickly. It was signed by Lisa. She picked up the envelope and examined the stamp closely. He swallowed and quickly debated if he should read it aloud and decided he would – at least most of it. "It is from the wireless operator on the *SS Montrose*, which is the liner I sailed on from Canada."

"I like the stamp. What does she say?"

There was no way around the issue. He began, "She writes: 'Dear Charles,

We have recently arrived in Southampton after another trans-Atlantic trip. I am curious to hear of your travel plans for returning to Canada. I looked but did not see your name on the passenger list for our return trip. I had debated coming to Rome to spend a few days with you while we are in port but work obligations took priority'."

He paused briefly pretending to have difficulty with her handwriting, which was not the case. Not knowing what to leave out and not wanting to appear obviously selective in what he left out he made a quick decision to read the last part of the letter as written: 'We did not have time to discuss our experience on the crossing in December but I still remember the wonderful nights we spent together. I do not want our friendship to drift so we become merely strangers again. If you receive this letter before you leave Rome and have time to call me here at the Southampton office during the day, the call can be easily transferred to my cabin on board. The telephone number is on the letterhead. I look forward to seeing you again'."

She had signed the letter "Love, Lisa" but he decided to read "Sincerely, Lisa."

There was silence as he slowly folded the letter, returned it in the envelope and returned it to his jacket pocket. He looked at her expression and saw it was an unhappy one. She had removed her dark glasses and her eyes showed her disappointment. He immediately regretted having read the letter—it would have been easy to deceive her—skipping the sensitive parts. She had not commented yet and he took the opportunity to try to explain.

"I had not told you about my friendship with this woman on the crossing from Canada because I did not think it was important. We met the day after the ship left Halifax. One inevitably makes new friends on a ship especially if you find yourself at the same dinner table. She was seated at the Captain's table for dinner that evening and we started a conversation that established a relationship, which eventually lead to our eating dinner together every night. We found a common interest—in music. She was a fan of Edvard Grieg, her country's best-known composer, and so was I. So we spend many hours together discussing him and other composers. When the ship docked in Southampton we had discussed the possibility of her coming to Rome for a few days but she failed to communicate with me while I was in London and so our travel arrangements never connected." He found himself feeling defensive and knew he was treading on thin ice.

Agnieszka remained silent after he had finished his brief explanation. She kept looking at her wine glass. She finally spoke, her voice choked with emotion. "Perhaps I have had unrealistic expectations Charles. I should not feel annoyed but I do. I think you should have been more open about your previous relationships in the same way I have with you. We are about to set off on a two-day journey to Poland together in a few days and I suddenly hear about your sexual exploits on an ocean liner just a few weeks ago with a woman who appears to expresses her continued interest in you. Can you understand how I feel?"

She had raised her voice in a desperate fashion at the end so that he looked around to see it there were others within hearing distance. He was saved from producing an immediate response by the arrival of the waiter with the order for spaghetti. Neither seemed in the mood to eat immediately but he knew he had to respond. "I did not say we had a sexual relationship. Even if we did it should not change the way I feel towards you. You were not in the picture then. That brief episode on the ship is something in the past. I had decided long before this that there was no future in the relationship. We certainly did not express our love for each other. She is a nice young woman and she was lonely." He paused and hearing no response suggested, "I think we should change the subject and enjoy our lunch."

Agnieszka remained silent and Charles knew the issue was not forgotten. He watched as she slowly began to taste the spaghetti. In therapy he had always tried to have the patient talk while he maintained silence, remaining in the background.

He remembered what Freud had said about the art of psychotherapy: 'The doctor should be opaque to his patients and like a mirror should show them nothing but what is shown to him.' But was he now assuming the role of therapist with this beautiful woman whom he had professed to love and whom he had resolved from the beginning not to relate to as a therapist?

He watched and waited without touching his spaghetti. He sensed she was slowly softening her attitude of annoyance or anger. She seemed to be thinking about her response. "I agree—this is ridiculous. I really have no claims on you and I certainly have no right to judge you based on your past relationships. I am sorry I asked you to read that letter. It was your personal business and I made a mistake. I accept your explanation and I believe you when you say the affair has been closed." She placed her fork on her plate and shook her head. "I think the spaghetti is rather tasteless so please forgive me if I do not finish it. I like the wine though and would like another glass." She emptied her glass as she finished speaking and placed it on the table with a thump.

The conversation had blunted his appetite as well, but he made a gesture of eating around the edges of his plate. He found it difficult to make eye contact and knew there were still issues that had not been resolved. He was seeing this complex woman in a new light. The angry side had not previously shown itself and he was surprised that he had not seen it before. Was she unusually jealous? Perhaps this was simply premenstrual tension as he wondered if she was about to have a menstrual period. He had seen it before, at home and in some patients. He wondered if she would suggest that as an explanation but he was quickly realizing that he was dangerously close to analyzing his best friend, which he had sworn never to do. Just when an analyst needs some relief from dilemmas such as this a solution sometimes comes along.

The trio of musicians, a woman and man playing violins and another man with an accordion could be heard approaching the table. It seemed they were to be serenaded and their arrival was just in time to break the ice. He could see the expression on Agnieszka's face assume a picture of relaxation—the table tension suddenly lifting. He reached for her hand and squeezed. She returned the gesture. The female violinist spoke some English and asked if there might be a request. They looked at each other briefly in thought. "Shall I?" she finally asked. "Go ahead", he replied. "Can you play the tango called *Jalousy* by Jacob Gade, the Danish composer?" Agnieszka asked, using the Danish pronunciation of the work. After a brief discussion amongst the three musicians and without any further comment, they began the well-known piece, exaggerated somewhat by adding a distinctly Latin rhythm.

He knew the tune and he wondered if she would explain her choice at the end. She did not seem inclined to do so even as the three moved slowly to another table while continuing to play. "I liked that very much", was all he heard her say. She seemed more relaxed. He did not know how to respond. The waiter came to his rescue almost immediately after the musicians had left and enquired about their lack of enthusiasm for the meal. She explained she was not hungry— the spaghetti was fine but ... could she have another glass of wine? "We have been distracted," he explained. He would prefer a cup of coffee.

"We must not let this conversation spoil our travels together", he suggested. She looked at him and shook her head. "I feel ashamed that I behaved like that and I apologize. When we finish the wine and coffee we should go back to the hotel. I have been having odd stomach pains all day. They could be my monthly period, but the pain seems much different—more severe."

CHAPTER TWENTY-FIVE

"Oderint dum metuant"
(Let them hate me provided they fear me)

Angela Roscetti was not sorry to be missing piano lessons. On any other Saturday she would be heading off at eight-thirty with her older brother to the Conservatory of Music about three city blocks away—about ten minutes' walk. But today she and her mother had tickets for Agnieszka's piano recital at one o'clock at the Church of All Saints, and she was very excited. Saturday was not a workday for most at the people at the legation, and the ambassador, knowing there was considerable interest in the recital, agreed to excuse everyone from work in the afternoon even if they needed to be there. Sophie had spoken to Angela's music teacher about the recital, and her absence from piano lessons had been approved.

Angela had been awake early and saw it was a bright sunny day as she carefully dressed in the white dress she kept for occasions like this. After breakfast her mother had insisted she spend an hour practicing the piano, and Angela did not mind being reminded to do so at all. She had been trying to master the Bach preludes and fugues, as her teacher had placed a lot of emphasis on the keyboard music of Bach. They had an early lunch together. Her father never came home for lunch as he was employed at a large manufacturing plant about ten kilometres away. Before he left for work he had told her he wished he had bought a ticket too.

Now she was seated with her mother and several friends from the Polish Legation in seats very close to the front of the Church of All Saints. She had insisted they leave home early as she wanted to be sure of a front seat. But they were told the front row had been reserved for government officials who had not yet appeared, just fifteen minutes before the recital was to begin. She had never been in this church before. In the entrance she had seen a large picture of Agnieszka with details of her recital programme. She asked her mother if Agnieszka could get the poster for her after the recital. "We could probably ask for that after the recital," her mother had said. It was dark and cool inside the church. Two men from Radio Rome were checking their recording equipment.

The printed recital programme listed the pieces to be played with a brief description of each, in Italian, on the second page:

PIANO RECITAL
by
MISS AGNIESZKA LIPSKA of KRAKÓW, POLAND
1300 HOURS on JANUARY 21, 1933
CHURCH OF ALL SAINTS
PROGRAMME

SONATA in C Major, No.60   JOSEPH HAYDN
SONATA No. 16 in G Major, op.31 No.1   LUDWIG von BEETHOVEN

KINDERSZENEN, Op. 15   ROBERT SCHUMANN
                    Intermission
FOUR NOCTURNES   FRYDERYK CHOPIN
            op.27, No.1 in C SHARP MINOR
            No. 2 in D FLAT MAJOR
            op.48. No.1 in C MINOR
            No.2 in F SHARP MINOR
FANTAISIE – IMPROMPTU   FRYDERYK CHOPIN
            in C SHARP MINOR, op.66
            PLEYEL PIANO provided by "PIANOS of ROME"

The church seats were beginning to fill, and the Radio Rome technicians were back putting finishing touches on their sound equipment. Angela remembered that Agnieszka preferred to play on a dark stage. A number of men and women had emerged from a room at the front of the church, and were finding seats further in the rear. Among them Angela recognized the ambassador's wife, who had came forward and was sitting in a seat at the front. Her mother had said Madame Radinska was to introduce Agnieszka.

A middle-aged woman wearing a dark full-length dress had come from the audience, moved to the piano, seated herself and opened a music score. Angela's mother thought she might be the woman who often played the national anthems at state gatherings and concerts. Angela had never heard her play before, but she knew every word of both the anthems. They sang them every day at school. A murmur of voices could be heard from the rear of the church, and turning she saw several men and women were moving toward the front. The audience began to rise from their seats.

She had never seen Benito Mussolini before, except in the newspapers, but wasn't that him? She was positive it was. The man was dressed in military uniform, was of medium height and was accompanied by several men also in military dress, all with heads uncovered and wearing distinctive black shirts. She wanted to ask her mother if that man was really *Il Duce* but she decided she couldn't. No one had said *Il Duce* would be here today. She wondered if Agnieszka knew, and if it would make her nervous if she did. The official party had now found seats in the front row but everyone had remained standing. The pianist, without any hesitation, began to play a brief introduction to the first national anthem, and the audience began to sing several stanzas of *Fratelli d'Italia*.

There was pause while the pianist arranged the piano score for *Giovinezza*, which was then sung loudly and lustily until the last stanza. There was a light applause as the audience settled in their seats. The lights over the piano were dimmed and Mrs. Radinska moved to the centre of the church. She introduced herself in Italian, saying she wished to say a few words about the recital and to introduce Miss Agnieszka Lipska, an unusually talented Polish pianist, who had already impressed audiences with her special affinity for the music of Chopin.

"This afternoon Miss Lipska had chosen a programme of her favourite composers whom she had admired from her student years. We are pleased that

Radio Rome is recording the recital and we wish to express our thanks for their decision to undertake the project. Perhaps the recording will be broadcast at a later date for more to hear."

Mrs. Radinska was sure Miss Lipska would be honoured by the presence of representatives of the Italian government, the Minister of Culture and especially *Il Duce.* A loud applause erupted in response to this comment. They were told that a short intermission of fifteen minutes would occur before the Chopin selections in the second half.

There was a brief pause following the introductory comments as Mrs. Radinska returned to her seat. The lights over the piano had been dimmed even further. A door from the front of the church had opened, and Angela could see from the light of the room that Elizabeth had emerged, holding Agnieszka by the arm. The audience broke into applause as the women moved toward the piano. Agnieszka bowed several times before seating herself on the piano stool. She looked toward the audience, her dark glasses glistening, and smiled briefly. Angela remembered that she was a very beautiful woman. Now with her head bowed, her hands sought the keys as she played a brief chord to test the piano's acoustics.

She immediately launched with confidence into the Haydn sonata, the sounds completely filling the church. There was loud applause at the end, as Agnieszka rose to stand near the piano and bowed. The Beethoven sonata that followed also caught the mood of the audience, and it too was applauded with enthusiasm. Agnieszka stood again, bowed several times and returned to the piano. All was quiet as the audience waited for the Schumann. Angela loved this piece and she closed her eyes in anticipation. She soon sensed Agnieszka was playing with unusual feeling. She found herself self consciously wiping tears from her eyes at the conclusion of *Traumerei,* the longest piece in the work. She looked quickly at her mother whom she could see had tears in her eyes too. As the sound of *Der Dichter spricht* faded into the shadows of the old church, the audience erupted in shouts of "*Bravo!*" There was prolonged applause and repeated *Bravos!*

Angela found herself jumping to her feet as the audience rose in unison. Loud applause continued with Agnieszka standing at the piano, smiling, bowing repeatedly and raising both her hands in acknowledgement. The lights had been slowly increased, revealing Elizabeth approaching the piano and offering her arm to lead Agnieszka toward the front room. The applause continued as they both disappeared through the door leading into the bright lights of the Saint Paul Room. They were soon on their way back to the centre of the church where Agnieszka bowed repeatedly in acknowledgement. It was now intermission time.

Back in the Saint Paul Room and dazzled by the light, Agnieszka was suddenly aware that someone familiar had approached and had embraced her with a kiss on her cheek and a whisper, "You were wonderful, especially in the Schumann. I have not heard you play it better! I have to admit it gave me a lump in my throat." She returned his kiss and Charles could feel her cheeks were wet. "I was in a daze," she replied. "I really do not know how well it came across—but it did seemed to be somewhat special. The applause was deafening. Thank you for being so kind." He paused and thought *how modest!* Should he tell her about her special audience? He suspected she did not know. He was still holding her with his arms around her waist. "You should sit and rest before the second half."

"I would like a glass of water." she replied as Charles guided her to a nearby chair and sat beside her. He saw that Elizabeth had volunteered to go to the washroom for the water. "Did you know there were special visitors listening to you in the front seats?" he asked. She shook her head. "I certainly could not see them."

"Well I think they may be coming to meet you at this moment!" he replied as he suddenly stood. He had seen the door to the church had opened, and a group of uniformed men had entered and were approaching, followed by three men in ordinary clothes and a young women, whom he had seen entering the church with the other party members. "Be prepared to meet *Il Duce!*" Agnieszka heard Charles say, as she was suddenly surrounded by a group of strangers. Elizabeth had returned with the glass of water and explained to the uniformed visitors that she worked at the Polish Legation.

Mussolini needed no interpreter. He was known to be fluent in English and French, and was dismissive towards Elizabeth as he offered his personal respects to the Polish ambassador, and his congratulations to Agnieszka in English for "*signora's* brilliant performance."

A thickset man, with a heavy scowl from dark eyes that cast a perpetual glare about the room, he was an intimidating figure, and his smile seemed oddly out of place. He had reason to smile. The fascist leader had recently consolidated his hold on the government, reducing the liberal opposition to a minority, and set himself up as second only to King Victor Emmanuel as head of state – and the king could not oppose the black shirts without risking civil war.

Charles contented himself with staying in the background while the dictator and Agnieszka exchanged pleasantries. There were smiles all around, except from the small dark-haired woman who had accompanied *Il Duce*. She seemed jealous of Mussolini's attention towards Agnieszka.

The tone of Mussolini's voice suddenly changed as he glanced about the room, perhaps certain that the ambassador and Mrs. Radinska could not hear the conversation. "*Signora* will come to my rooms tonight … we will … play together."

The tone and the leer in his eyes made his intentions quite clear. Ambassador Radinski who had heard the comment was visibly embarrassed. Charles, who was nearby, had also heard and was furious, and quite forgetting how *Il Duce* handled his opponents, said aloud "I say …" moving towards Agnieszka protectively. The plain-clothed guards moved toward their leader.

Agnieszka held up her hand, motioning Charles back without looking at him, and without missing a beat, politely and calmly informed the dictator, "I am sorry, I have an engagement at my country's legation tonight, *Duce*, and my fiancée would not approve."

Mussolini glared at Charles, then without further comment turned on his heel and stormed out of the room. His entourage followed, only the dark-haired woman casting one last venomous look at Agnieszka. Ambassador Radinski was quickly apologetic. "I should have warned you, he is infamous for his womanizing. I do apologize."

Charles was shaking with anger, but quickly recovered. He had overlooked Agnieszka's introduction of him as her fiancée. "I apologize to you ambassador. I trust my reaction will not cause any diplomatic problems?" The ambassador had moved to the door, glancing out to see what reaction *Il Duce's* sudden reappearance had drawn from the audience. "He has resumed his seat. Miss Lipska, can you continue your recital?"

Agnieszka said she was ready, but Charles watched her hand tremble as she drank slowly from the glass of water Elizabeth—who had seemed completely terrorized—had offered. Charles' curiosity got the better of him. "Who was that woman?" he asked. Elizabeth offered the information. "She is Claretta Pettacci, *Duce's* mistress. She is ... not nice!"

Gathering their dignity, the group left the room and joined the audience for the start of the second half. Charles paused to give Agnieszka a hug and kiss before leaving. "I know you will play the Chopin well as you always do." Elizabeth paused for them all to be seated before escorting Agnieszka back into the sanctuary and to the piano, midst loud applause. Mussolini, his stare even more intense, was seen to sit through her performance without offering applause.

Agnieszka later acknowledged the experience had been overwhelming.

CHAPTER TWENTY-SIX

"Adaceo fortuna juvat"
(Fortune favours the bold)

Many in the audience said the second half was the highlight of Agnieszka's recital. The audience loved Chopin's music, and listened with rapt attention, as they did in the first half. The *nocturnes* were familiar to many who knew the composer's music. There was immediate applause after each group. The *Fantasy-Impromptu* was an ideal choice for the last selection. The programme notes mentioned that this work was published six years after the composer's death, and twenty years after its composition in 1835. Why Chopin chose to keep the work in manuscript is a mystery. There had been general agreement that all his posthumous works should be preserved and not destroyed. Agnieszka, with Elizabeth, was called back again from the Saint Paul Room in response to the continued rhythmic applause. There was an obvious wish for an encore.

Before resuming, she turned to the audience and said in a clear voice, "I would like to play *Jesu, Joy of Man's Desiring* by Bach—for Angela Roscetti, who is in the audience." After the encore there was prolonged applause. A second encore was imminent. She turned again to the audience, "Here is a *mazurka* with variations that I especially love. It is of course Polish but the composer is unknown". It was the Polish national anthem!—to be played, as she had promised—at a slower tempo than usual, but with considerable flourish and with several improvised variations. Would the audience recognize the work? Some musicologists and music teachers in the audience might, but it was unlikely that the government officials would. It was her personal statement, not of defiance but more an injection of Polish patriotism midst a sea of fascist propaganda. The audience enjoyed the work and after several acknowledgements of the applause from Agnieszka, the front row party representatives rose and smartly made their exit through the front door, as the audience stood and continued to applaud.

Charles knew that Agnieszka would like to speak to Nancy Holmes before she left to return to Ostia. Now he could see that Miss Rossi and Mr. deMilo were heading in his direction. He offered to shake their hands and they accepted. "Thank you for managing a very successful recital," he said, "I thought it went exceptionally well. Did you?"

Miss Rossi nodded and said she was thrilled with both the performance and the large attendance, especially on a Saturday afternoon. "Mr. deMilo and I will go now to congratulate Miss Lipska, and we will later come to your hotel—in the evening perhaps, to finalize the arrangements. We will have a cheque for her then. We are naturally very excited that our leader had decided to come as well. He is a lover of classical music and a musician as well. His presence has made the event complete." She was looking over his shoulder and added, "I see someone else would like to speak to you!" Charles turned and found that Nancy Holmes had sought him out from among the crowd as the audience slowly made its way outside. There were warm greetings, after which he was introduced to her husband, whose name was Karl. "With a K," he said. They had both loved the recital and wanted to thank Charles and Agnieszka for the tickets.

"Let me take you to see Agnieszka. She will be very glad to see you again Nancy. Follow me." Inside the Saint Paul Room there was much activity and a buzz of conversation. He could see a small group surrounding Agnieszka— Elizabeth, Ambassador Radinski and his wife, Angela and her mother Sophie, as well as several music critics whom he had seen at the press conference. He recognized Bruno Garavelli, the organ music critic, and the woman who had asked a question earlier, before the recital. He could not remember her name. He could see that Agnieszka, seated on a small chair, was in a daze and looked exhausted. It was appropriate to intervene, and he did. He gave her a hug and kiss, introduced her to Nancy's husband, and she listened to their brief comments about how well she looked, the beautiful recital and the thrill of being there—with *Il Duce*—before they said goodbye.

Charles heard Agnieszka tell Nancy she would never forget how well she had been treated at the hospital, and he endorsed her comment before the Holmes couple left. He knew he had to tell her what he had felt about the second half of the recital. "Give us a few minutes," he suggested to the ambassador, who seemed eager to leave. "I want to tell her how wonderful she was this afternoon." There was an empty chair next to hers, and Charles sat and reached for her hand. She listened as he described his feelings during the recital. She reached over and kissed him on the cheek. "I must thank you for everything. I could not have done it without you."

"Of course you could. I did only what was required—and all for you. It would be hard to say the second half was better than the first because the whole afternoon was such a great success. De Pachmann would have loved the programme, especially the Chopin, but he would have been envious of the way you played the Beethoven too." She laughed at his comment. "I can see the Mussolini episode did not affect your playing," he added. "Not enough to come between me and Chopin," she replied. "I wonder if Mussolini ever heard de Pachmann play Chopin."

Angela's mother, who was not far away, seemed to want to speak to her. "Do you think Angela can have the poster with a picture of you in the front of the church, Agnieszka?—I mean the poster with your recital programme?"

"I am sure she can Sophie. Do you think you can remove it without help? Perhaps Charles can help you."

"We can rescue it on our way out," he replied, "I sense that the ambassador is ready to leave." The group moved into the church and headed down the isle toward the entrance. The Radio Rome technicians were gathering up their equipment and microphones. Charles, who was escorting Agnieszka, turned to Elizabeth. "I wonder if the recording was successful. Can you ask them?"

Elizabeth moved toward the nearest of the two men and had a brief conversation before rejoining them. "He is very pleased with the sound recording, and is confident it will be very faithful to your playing," she said. "I am glad," Agnieszka replied with a smile. She walked toward the piano and gently moved her left hand over the keyboard. "The Pleyel was very faithful to me this afternoon. I assume Miss Rosso will be making the arrangements to have it returned to its home. Now let us find the famous poster for Angela." She reached for the young girl's hand as they walked slowly down the centre isle together. The church janitor was in the hallway and offered to remove the poster and to roll it up for Angela to carry. "I will hang it on my bedroom wall for the rest of my life!" the little girl declared, as she gave Agnieszka a long hug. "Thank you."

Charles took Agnieszka's arm again as they walked down the steps. "You must be very hungry, as you have not had any food since breakfast," he suggested.

"I am hungry, and also suddenly my legs are very tired. I feel I have used up all of my energy this afternoon!" She leaned toward him and whispered, "Perhaps we can spend no more than an hour at the legation—enough time to have tea—and some cake. I hope they will serve cake! Then we can go back to the hotel for a sleep. I have lost my sense of time. Is it past four yet?"

He looked at his watch and told her she was close—ten minutes to four. The drive to the legation was prompt. The ambassador's chauffeur knew how to save time moving through the busy streets. The legation kitchen staff had prepared a small buffet of cakes and sweet breads for afternoon tea. Agnieszka was helped to a chair and seemed relieved to sit down again. Mrs. Radinska was sympathetic and served her a cup of tea immediately. "You must try the Polish cake. Our chef made it this morning especially for you!"

Claudio Bianco, the legation attaché, had joined the party and after shaking hands gave a little speech in English, saying how much he had enjoyed the recital and how thrilled the staff had been to be able to listen to Agnieszka play their beloved Chopin on three occasions during the past week. His comments were acknowledged with a prolonged applause. Mrs. Radinska wanted to say something and asked for attention. "Agnieszka," she began to speak slowly in English. "This week, you have been as much an ambassador for our country as we have been or try to be. Poland will always be proud of you. We were touched to hear you play your improvisation of our national anthem a few hours ago. I felt like I should stand and sing along with you, but I would have been an embarrassment for *Il Duce!*" Enthusiastic applause followed her comments.

Charles was suddenly moved to say something. He walked to the centre of the room and raised his hand for attention. Someone tapped on a teacup to attract attention. "Some of you know me as Charles Flemming from Canada, and may have heard that I have been trying to be a tour guide for Agnieszka since her brother left Rome. If you read the newspapers or listen to the radio news you will know that I did a poor job several nights ago on the River Tiber." There was a murmur of laughter from the listeners. "But Agnieszka has forgiven me, and as you can see, has recovered in a miraculous manner. You have seen the proof in her ability to give this wonderful recital today. Tomorrow night we head back to Kraków. I have a feeling this will not be our last visit to Rome. So I want to thank you ambassador, Mrs. Radinska, Elizabeth, Mr. Bianco and all the legation staff, on behalf of Agnieszka, for your kindness and hospitality towards her—and to me as well—during the past week. Elizabeth was very kind in taking on the job of translating for the press conference—no easy task. Thank you Elizabeth."

His comments were followed by prolonged applause as he walked back to shake Elizabeth's hand and give her a brief hug; then moving to Agnieszka's chair, leaning over and kissing her on the cheek. "Thank you for doing that," she whispered, "It was just right." The cakes and sweet breads were very popular with everyone, and after two cups of tea and the speeches it seemed time to say goodbye. The ambassador insisted his chauffeur drive them back to the hotel, and they accepted. Hands were shaken all around before they left. Agnieszka was wiping tears from her eyes as she said her final goodbyes. In the limousine, she snuggled close and held Charles' hand tightly for the whole journey. He found a twenty-five lire note, which he pressed into the chauffeur's hand before he drove away.

*** *** *** ***

"We should check the hotel bill before we go up stairs," Agnieszka suggested, as they walked back into the lobby. As promised, the manager's secretary had prepared a detailed resumé of the costs, and after quickly reviewing the items no discrepancies were found in his or her accounts. Arrangements were made to settle both the accounts in the morning. They made their way back to the room and began to debate their evening plans. There seemed more sense to eat at the hotel dining room later. They were both tired and had little interest in going out. A telephone call confirmed that there would be a table in the dining room available for eight o'clock. Charles felt he needed a Martini cocktail, but Agnieszka wanted a glass of white wine.

A call to the bar resulted in a knock on the door and arrival of the drinks within ten minutes. They sat and toasted their good fortune and success. "Tomorrow we will be on our way back to Poland, so let us drink a toast to the future," she said with an air of triumph. She was looking much more happy as she raised her glass. "I will drink to that," he replied. "I am sure our journey will be relaxing and fun. I may not have mentioned it to you, but I love train travel." He remembered her relating the events at intermission and realized there was a nagging question about the recital he had not asked. "I know your conversation with Mussolini was disturbing but did he or the minister of culture comment on the music you had chosen, or your playing?"

She did not respond immediately and seemed in thought. "I cannot remember because both Elizabeth and I seemed somewhat overwhelmed with Mussolini's presence. I don't remember either he or the minister actually commenting on my playing, but the minister said a few words about the importance of Italian women making their mark in the area of culture. *Il Duce* said he especially liked the Schumann, which is interesting. He likes romantic music it seems and based on his proposition to me he is romantic in other ways!" She paused and laughed. "I can laugh at the episode now. It was quite ridiculous, wasn't it?" Charles did not respond as she continued, "He said he was looking forward to hearing the

Chopin pieces. As you saw, they did not spend a lot of time in the room and he seemed to make a quick exit when I declined his invitation to dinner." Charles sensed that she had not fully appreciated the fact that Mussolini had felt he had been rejected and insulted. There seemed no point in expanding on the possible implications of her refusal since he could sense Agnieszka had not felt as strongly about it as he.

She continued in her reminiscing; "I was bothered by their claims to be promoting culture. Everyone knows about their abuse of the liberties of people who disagreed with their philosophy." She was thinking while looking at her clasped hands holding her glass of wine. Without raising her head she asked him; "Do you think de Pachmann agreed with the fascist ideals and went along with the propaganda?"

"I do not think we will ever know for sure. His secretary, Pallottelli, may have been a party member and his wife as well, according to people to whom I had been introduced in Toronto. I think that de Pachmann would have been so single-minded and apolitical he would not want to concede any of his principles to the government. He was an Italian citizen, but likely remained silent about his beliefs. He would not have wanted to take any chances that might lead to reprisals."

"Do you know if Simon had any further run-ins with the members of de Pachmann Societies before he left?" Agnieszka sounded genuinely concerned.

"He did not mention it to me if he did," Charles replied. "Any plans they may have had to sabotage his visit to Rome seem to have fizzled. After de Pachmann's death they would have been obliged to honour his memory without any public demonstrations. An odd meeting at the train station and a few boos and hisses on mentioning de Pachmann's foibles during his introduction to your recital on Sunday was about all I heard as a statement of their anger." She looked surprised to hear about the train station episode, as she had not been told. He summarized briefly what had happened.

"I have not read Simon's paper on de Pachmann's Beethoven style, although we discussed earlier the possibility of your reading it to me tomorrow—perhaps on the train." He finished his cocktail and asked if she wanted another glass of wine. She said she would wait until dinner. "I feel I should relax in the bathtub before dinner. Could you run the water for me?"

She had settled in the tub just as a knock sounded on the hall door. It was a young man from the reception area announcing, "a letter for Miss Agnieszka Lipska. It was delivered about ten minutes ago, Sir," he explained. The envelope looked official with an elaborate logo of the Misericordia Eye Hospital in the top left hand corner. He returned to the bathroom, which had become very steamy from the hot water.

"You have an interesting letter which was just delivered. Would you like me to read it to you?"

"Of course, please do".

Charles pulled the small bench toward the tub and sat down before opening the envelope. Agnieszka watched as he removed a hand written letter on a single sheet of paper. Scanning the sheet he began; "At the top there is a letterhead of the Department Head of the Misericordia Eye Hospital here in Rome. Her name is Professor Maria Cagianno. She has written a short message in English. Here is what she says: 'Dear Miss Lipska; You may be surprised to receive this letter— handwritten in haste. We have never met, but I enjoyed very much your recital at the church today. At intermission a friend in the audience told me that your vision had been almost totally lost from retinitis pigmentosa. She knew where you were staying and I have taken the liberty of writing to you about my interest in RP.

'I have spent much of my medical career studying the natural history and current treatment of RP throughout the world. I have never met a professional pianist who suffers from this, and for that reason I would very much like to meet you before you return to Poland. If you were available for an hour tomorrow, I would be pleased to meet you in my clinic here at the hospital for an interview and a brief examination if you agree. There would be no charge for this, of course. The telephone numbers for my clinic and home are at the top of the page. Please feel free to call me any time today. I do hope you will forgive me for being so presumptuous but I would like to meet you because I am a lover of music lover as well as a doctor. Yours sincerely, Maria Cagianno'."

He looked up from the letter and tried to guess Agnieszka's reaction from her facial expression. He sensed she had been listening attentively, as her eyes had been focused in his direction while silently rubbing a bar of soap in her hands. All he could see was an expression of surprise. "What an unusual letter and equally unusual offer! I have never heard of Professor Cagianno. Have you?" He shook his head. "I have not. I agree, it is an unusual letter. You should decide today if you are willing to see her as we are leaving tomorrow. When was the last time you had your eyes examined?"

"It must be more than six years. Before then, I had regular examina- tions at the Kraków Eye Clinic, but I was eventually told there was no treatment they could offer me even if my sight continued to worsen—which it has." She had resumed her washing routine as she spoke. Charles thought he should give her some direction towards making a decision. "Professor Cagianno writes in very good English, so she must speak it well. I would be glad to call her at home and suggest we visit her in her clinic in the morning—that is if you agree. I am not trying to push you to decide, but she does seem genuinely interested, and you have nothing to lose and perhaps something to gain." He waited for her re- sponse and could see she was still puzzled. "I want to finish my bath first. I will think about it and we can discuss it after." He agreed and said he would leave her to finish her bath and to think about the offer.

Leaving her to finish her bath he returned to the sitting area and he re-read Professor Cagianno's letter, and noted she had several specialist degrees in oph- thalmology. She was the department head at the Misericordia Eye Hospital, and likely had impressive credentials. It was an unusual way though for a doctor to introduce herself to a stranger, especially one from another country. But Agni- eszka was different, and it was clear that Maria Cagianno was as well. Perhaps she had a new approach to management of RP that doctors in Poland had not tried. He would never encourage her to submit to any experimental treatment. On the surface he could see some potential benefit from meeting the professor.

He could hear sounds from the bathroom that suggested Agnieszka had finished her bath, and had pulled the plug. He slowly opened the door and found her sitting on the bench drying her legs. "Did you want to wash your hair? I can help you." She smiled and replied, "thank you, but I will wait until tomorrow in preparation for several days on the train. I find it is very difficult to wash my hair on a train." She stood and continued to dry herself. He took her towel and began to dry her back, giving her a kiss on the neck as he finished. He always found their bathroom encounters with her being naked very erotic, but he knew there were other priorities now. "You are so beautiful," he whispered in her ear, "and I do love you very much." She turned and they kissed. "That is so nice to hear. I love you too."

There was a brief pause and he wondered if she was preparing to remind him about his spending the night there, and making love again, but she wanted to talk about the letter. She reached for her dressing gown hanging on the door. "I have thought enough about Professor Cagianno's offer and agree with you. I would like to meet her. Can you call her now? She is not likely to be at the clinic on a Saturday afternoon."

He felt pleased and told her so. He put his arms around her. "I was hoping you would say that. I will call her at her home right away!"

"I will get dressed while you call."

They returned to the sitting room together and Charles dialled the operator. He gave her the number and listened as the phone rang through. A male voice answered *"buon giono."* Not daring to use his very limited Italian, he asked in English to speak to Professor Cagianno and heard *"un attimo per favour."* She came to the telephone immediately. "Professor Cagianno, my name is Charles Flemming, a friend of Agnieszka Lipska. We have just read your kind letter, and I am pleased to tell you she will be happy to meet you tomorrow, preferably in the morning as we leave late in the evening."

"That will be fine with me. Can you make it by ten o'clock? A taxi driver will know how to get you there from your hotel. I will be waiting for you. Please give Miss Lipska my best wishes." He said they could be there easily at ten, and thanked her for her kindness. Agnieszka had been listening as she searched for some clothes in her closet, and he saw she had eventually found something suitable.

"The professor sounds very nice and has sent you her good wishes," he said. He was surprised she did not look happy as she stood quietly near the closet door looking out the window in deep thought. He sensed she was not excited to hear the news. She must have read his mind, as he heard her say immediately, "I have lived with retinitis pigmentosa all my life, and I have to say it has been so long that I find it hard to feel much optimism—even from Professor Cagianno's letter. I have spoken to you about this before and I am ashamed to admit it. You know how I feel. You have been so supportive, and I know you are doing what is best for me. I appreciate it very much. Believe me." He moved towards her, reached out and gave her a long hug. "I understand how you feel, but you are also strong and have an exceptional talent. You have managed to live with this very well, and I am sure you will continue to do so."

He could feel her tears on her cheeks, and he moved to kiss her on the left eye, his lips staying there for several seconds. "I could kiss your eyes forever. If it could help you see better I would spend the rest of my life doing that. Maria Cagianno might have some new ideas, so we should visit her tomorrow with lots of hope. I think the word Misericordia means *heart of mercy*". He saw she had managed a smile. "I did not know that but it gives me hope," she replied.

"Of course it does. I see it is past seven o'clock and Miss Rosso said she would be here around seven-thirty to see you. When you have finished dressing we can go down to the lobby and wait for her, and then have dinner. Or perhaps we should begin packing some of your cases before she comes. How many did you bring?" She was scratching her head in thought. "I am sure there are four— one for the sheet music scores and the other three for my extensive wardrobe!" Her comment made them both laugh. "Can you help me pack?" she asked. He agreed and suggested he should pack the music scores, as that would be the easiest. The room soon became a scene of busy activity with them both moving to and fro. Within half an hour they had completed most of the packing, with the clothes closets and drawers virtually empty. He had watched her fill her three cases and commented, "You seem to travel surprisingly lightly for a woman!" She laughed and explained, "I never like to carry a lot of luggage on the train. In fact three of these cases could be checked as baggage. I can manage with one." She was interrupted by the ringing of the telephone. Charles answered and was told by the receptionist that Miss Rosso had arrived. He said they should ask her to come up to the room.

Miss Rosso was full of praise for the success of the recital. Almost all the seats had been sold, and she had heard many favourable comments as the audience left the church. "I have prepared a summary of the expenses for your records Miss Lipska. The costs are for rental and moving of the piano, for the use of the parish church, our fee and I have included an honorarium for the woman taking tickets and the caretaker. I hope you agree to that final item. The remaining amount is your fee, and I have written a cheque in your name for 12,550 *lira*. You will be hearing later from the people at Radio Rome about the recording. There should be a professional fee for that too, but you will need to negotiate that with them." They walked slowly together towards the entrance. "I will contact you sometime in the near future Miss Lipska, and hopefully you will agree to return for more recitals in Rome—perhaps even in Milan or Naples. I hope your experience on the river will not influence your decision." They all laughed and Agnieszka wanted to respond.

"I feel you have been an excellent agent Miss Rosso, and I will certainly consider coming back again. Goodbye until we meet again." She paused and added, "you must promise you will call me Agnieszka, and not Miss Lipska from now on." Miss Rosso agreed and added she felt the same about calling each other by first names. She shook hands with them both. Charles added his agreement regarding the success of the press conference and the recital and said goodbye.

CHAPTER TWENTY-SEVEN

"Suaviter in modo, fortiter in re"
(Gentle in manner, vigorous in action)

The dining room was unusually busy but the headwaiter had reserved a table in a quiet area of the room. Light dance music was being piped through the loud speakers and several couples on the dance floor were moving in time with the music. Their waiter had left menus and had taken an order for a half bottle of white wine. "I have been thinking that Miss Rosso was very professional with the arrangements", said Charles. "Yes," she replied, "all the planning was well executed. I was also very pleased with the press conference. The acoustics in the church could have been better but the Pleyel piano was a very good one. It seemed to be a new piano but the keyboard was very responsive. I will be waiting to hear the sound quality from the recording they made. I wonder what the critics will have to say in tomorrow's papers. We must ask the manager to have the reviews translated for us."

"I am sure he will do that. Mr. Mercanti has been very helpful. He has always been available to translate for us in the meetings with the police and I have asked his advice many times about issues that have come up. Perhaps we should make sure we give him a token of our appreciation when we leave tomorrow. Of course his staff has been very obliging too." The waiter had returned and was preparing to open the white wine. "What did you order this time?" she asked. "This white is not an exciting one," he replied, "it is an Orvieto, but it is from a well-known maker—Antinori. I think we may have had it before." He asked to see the vintage after the waiter had poured two glasses. "It is from the 1932 vintage, so it is very young." He swirled the wine and put his nose to the glass. "I like the bouquet and it is pleasantly fruity." He raised his glass. "I want to propose a toast—to our future. May it be a happy time for us both." She raised her glass and tasted the wine. "I will endorse that. It is a pity we cannot see into the future. I believe we must take one day at a time and deal with each as best we can!" He was watching her intensely. He could not see her eyes behind her dark glasses. "I love the way you look tonight and I will be very interested in what the Professor thinks of your vision tomorrow." She smiled and said, "thank you."

The printed menu was not very different from previous evenings. The waiter suggested they try the lamb shank, with mixed seasonal vegetables and mint jelly. There was also tenderloin of pork and a seafood selection of fried scampi in garlic, served with rice. Agnieszka said she wanted the scampi and Charles chose the lamb shank.

"I am pleased that we have made a start with our packing as tomorrow will be busy," she said as she sipped her wine, "are there things you need to do before leaving?"

"Not really. I have already found you a new watch as I promised and I have paid a visit to the chemist who sold me those condoms." He laughed as he mentioned the condoms.

He could see she was also amused. "I love the watch but those mysterious condoms—I have not seen them yet! When do you plan to give me a demonstration?" She was trying to keep a serious face.

"If you fall asleep tonight before I get to join you in bed it may be another twenty four hours before you see how they function." He could not help laughing at the conversation. They were teasing one another.

"Perhaps I should have mentioned the condoms to *Il Duce* at intermission", she replied. "I suspect he could have dealt with it very promptly and got you off the hook!"

He was surprised to hear her use a common English expression, but he did not mention it. "I was disappointed that you did not introduce me at intermission. I could have asked him myself! He does speak English, but Elizabeth might have been uncomfortable with the topic of condoms."

She did not respond immediately and he could see she was briefly lost for words. She had decided to be serious. "Elizabeth has been very kind, hasn't she? I could not have gone through the press conference without her. Should we send her something in appreciation? Perhaps we could send her flowers."

"I think that would be a great idea," he replied. He produced his diary from his jacket pocket and made a few notes to remind him. The waiter had arrived with the two courses and they both began to eat in earnest. Both choices were well prepared and they decided to order another half bottle—this time a Barolo from 1928. After a second course of Italian cheeses and two coffees they were ready to leave. The waiter had looked tired, but had been attentive so they left a generous tip.

The wine and food had combined to make them both mellow. Arriving in her bedroom, they decided it was not too early to get undressed and to climb into bed. They were in the mood for love and both naked. In a few minutes he discovered that Agnieszka's single-size bed was not generous in size—meaning they were very close together—almost as one. She gave him her glasses for safe keeping on the bedside table. She was eager to be shown how a condom was designed and how it was slowly rolled on. She found it amusing and wanted to be involved, which added to the eroticism. "I think it will feel different", he heard her say some time later, as they came to the end of their exploring and experimenting with hands and kisses. She was as eager as always to find out the difference. They were able to last for only a few minutes before coming together.

He was more out of breath than he had expected as he rolled on his back onto the narrow bed. She had cuddled into his side with her free arm over his chest. "That was the best yet I think—even considering that the condom did feel strange. What do you do with it now?" He was surprised she would not have known and responded by telling her most people in hotels flushed them down the toilet. "If we were at home they could be thrown out. In Rome I suppose it will eventually end up in the Tiber. Since condoms seem to be so little used in this country, ours will be a rare sight to the fish in the river." They had another laugh over that idea before she muttered she was sleepy and wanted him to turn off the lights. It was almost eleven thirty. They kissed good night and tried to reach an agreement over bed space. It was not easy.

*** *** *** ****

Charles was awake early on Sunday morning. He felt stiff and his back ached. He could not turn over easily in the small bed. He was able to raise his left arm to peer at his watch, but could not see its face, as the room was still dark. He thought it must be well before seven o'clock. He did not want to wake Agnieszka by turning on the bedside table light. Should he get up, go to the bathroom, and turn on the light? He resisted, as he did feel warm and cosy. During the night she had again snuggled up to his back, and he could feel the warmth of her naked body, and hear her breathing. Last night there never seemed to be enough room in the bed for both of them, and that seemed the most likely reason why he was tired. He had slept poorly. They had made love after dinner and with unusual intensity. He tried to remember if he had used a condom. Yes, he had, as he remembered that he had got up and flushed it in the toilet before he returned and fell asleep. He thought of the guilty chemist down the street, and of his visit yesterday. This was their last day in Rome, and there was a medically important mission at ten o'clock. The two issues had been on his mind and probably combined with the narrow bed to make him feel fully awake.

It was not the first time Charles had decided he was not sorry to leave Rome. Yet he knew he had hardly scratched the surface of this fabulous city, with its many churches, cemeteries, museums, fountains, monuments and catacombs—a blend of religious and secular. He had seen some of the highlights before, but could see another visit was very likely—to allow them to see what they had missed. The fascist presence was another matter. He had become drawn into their world of policing and surveillance as well as becoming at least once— with Agnieszka—a reluctant tool of the state propaganda machine. Did he have excessive expectations from the consultation at the eye clinic? Maria Cagianno claimed considerable experience with retinitis pigmentosa, and might have some suggestions for improving Agnieszka's vision. He had now reached a level of urinary urgency.

When he returned from the bathroom he found Agnieszka was awake and aglow with smiles. "Good morning! How did you sleep in this bed?" she asked. Before he could answer she added, "Come back in bed for a few minutes." He climbed back beside her and felt her warm body heat. He snuggled towards her and kissed her neck. "Yes, there were moments when I wondered if I should go back to my own bed, or move onto the sofa in the next room!" He was conscious of a strong sexual urge again, and she was encouraging him. "Let me put on another condom," she whispered, "We have lots of time." He needed no encouragement and she was as eager as earlier in the night. They both stayed together longer this time. Later, she said having sex had made her hungry and she was thinking of food. They should get up, have a bath together and then go down to eat. He helped her run the bath water and they both shared the fun of being together in the big tub again. She had not mentioned the odd abdominal pain since yesterday and had not yet had a menstrual period.

As Charles dried he suggested that they could have a relaxing breakfast there in the room, in private rather than using the dining room. He would call and ask for room service. What did she want to eat? "Fresh orange juice, croissants, marmalade, cheese and coffee," she said. He phoned in the order and in fifteen minutes it arrived.

They had planned to allow lots of time to travel to the hospital, so they went downstairs thinking of seeking a taxi by nine thirty. The drive to the hospital— which was in the Aventine area of the city—was prompt. They were there by nine-fifty, and after asking directions were told that Professor Cagianno's office was on the ground floor. The hospital receptionist had been told to expect them, and an elderly male attendant was prepared to accompany them. Maria Cagianno was a short, somewhat stout woman, who looked about fifty years old. Her hair was grey, and she wore it tied in the back in a bob. She greeted Agnieszka with enthusiasm, holding both her hands in a warm handshake. "You must be Charles Flemming," she said, turning her head and reaching to shake his hand too. "We feel very privileged to have you see us Professor Cagianno, and Agnieszka is interested in learning what you think about her eyes," he replied.

"It is a pleasure to do this for you and please call me Maria. I will use your first names too. I very much enjoyed your recital Agnieszka. Let me first look at your hands." She proceeded to examine Agnieszka's hands carefully. "Wonderful hands! Now I know at least one reason why you play so beautifully," she concluded. They were ushered into the professor's office, and directed to chairs near her desk. "I want first to get a brief history of how your vision has changed since you were a child, and what other doctors have told you." Agnieszka paused before proceeding to relate details of her family history and the events that lead to the diagnosis of RP, and how her vision had progressively deteriorated. "That gives me a good background of the situation," the professor concluded, "now I would like to give you an eye examination."

"I will stay here while you have your examination," Charles said, as it seemed an appropriate suggestion. He saw no benefit in being there during the session. Maria Cagianno, with Agnieszka by the arm, headed out of the office, turning left in the direction of the clinical examination rooms. Professor Cagianno's status in the medical hierarchy of Italy was impressive. He walked around her office examining the numerous certificates hung on the walls. In a country like Italy, he had heard that a woman was less likely to move to the top position in a hospital such as this. Her experience and reputation would account considerably for her current position as head of an eye disease hospital. He had studied eye diseases for a month during his internship in Toronto, and had always found the ophthalmoscope a challenging instrument. The findings his teachers claimed to see in their patient's eyes were sometimes completely lost to him.

He was puzzled why the eye clinic seemed quiet today, until he suddenly realized it was Sunday. He picked up a magazine and flipped slowly through the pages. It was full of advertisements in Italian, which he could not understand. There were interviews with celebrities, colour photos of movie stars and some politicians. He found himself yawning and realized he was sleepy. Trying to sleep in that bed last night was a disaster. He must have slept only a few hours. He looked at his watch. It was ten twenty-five and he wondered why Agnieszka was taking so long to return. What time was the train leaving? Where had he placed the train tickets? He came back to reality with a start; his head jerked downward, and knew he had been awakened by a loud snore. He looked about and realized he was still alone in the professor's office. His magazine had fallen to the floor. Perhaps it would help if he stood up and walked down the corridor. He had reached the office door at the same time as Agnieszka and Maria Cagianno appeared hand-in-hand around the corner.

"I have some interesting news," he heard Cagianno say. "Sit down and I will describe my findings. I have not told Miss Lipska yet what I found." He helped Agnieszka to her chair and sat himself down beside her. He gave her a quick kiss on the cheek and reached for her hand. Agnieszka was quiet and he saw she seemed puzzled. Maria Cagianno, now behind her desk, had found some blank paper and was writing notes as they waited. She finally raised her head and addressed them both, "First of all, you have the classic changes of retinitis pigmentosa, Agnieszka. There is no doubt about the diagnosis, but you also have cataracts—posterior capsular cataracts that are affecting your vision in a major way. That means that surgical removal of these could greatly improve your vision." She paused and seemed to anticipate their reaction. Agnieszka was quiet and Charles was the first to respond. "That is very interesting Maria. What do you feel are the chances her vision could be improved with cataract surgery?"

"That depends where she wishes to have the surgery. There are several speciality areas in the world. I do not know how good the surgery for cataracts is in Poland, but it would be a logical place to investigate. I have a good friend at the Warsaw Eye Clinic whom I could contact for an opinion. I would be pleased to write Professor Zelichowski about my findings. If you agree, he could contact you when you get back home."

"I have heard of Professor Zelichowski," said Agnieszka, "and I would be very pleased to see him on my return. You have my address in Kraków."

Cagianno rose from her chair and walked around to her visitors' chairs, "before you leave, I want to say again how much joy your recital gave me yesterday. I enjoyed the Schumann *Kinderszenen* especially. I think you have great talent and will continue to have a successful career."

Agnieszka thanked her for taking the time to see her. They rose and shook hands. Cagianno accompanied them back to the front entrance of the hospital, arranged for the telephone operator to call a taxi, and said her final goodbye to them both.

A taxi back to the hotel was easily found and Agnieszka was full of enthusiasm about the prospect of improvement in her vision. "I am very pleased to hear the news," Charles said. "We must arrange to see the eye surgeon next week if he is available."

CHAPTER TWENTY- EIGHT

"There is wisdom of the head,
and wisdom of the heart" (Charles Dickens)

Although it was a Sunday, and not a working day for his staff, Mr. Mercanti had arranged for his secretary to come to the hotel and translate the critics' reviews from the morning's newspapers. The English translations were ready when they returned from the hospital just before noon. Gathering the two typed sheets from the reception area Charles and Agnieszka decided to seek coffee and a light snack in the dining room. The room was almost deserted, except for an elderly couple having a delayed breakfast, likely because they had slept late.

"There are two reviews here," Charles said as they settled at a table near the window, "and there may be more in the afternoon papers. Let me start with the longest, which begins with the title: *Il Duce Attends Recital of Blind Pianist."* He looked in her direction. Agnieszka could not hold back a laugh. "With a title like that it must be from the official party newspaper, *Il Popolo d'Italia!"* He found the headline amusing as well. "You are probably right. Let me see if I can find the name of the newspaper," he added, as he scanned the typed sheet. He shook his head. "No, the secretary seems to have forgotten to type the source of this one! But let me read the review: 'The Church of all Saints was the location of an interesting recital yesterday afternoon, which attracted a capacity audience including *Il Duce,* himself a musician and a patron of the arts as well as representatives of the Ministry of Culture. Miss Agnieszka Lipska, a blind pianist from Poland, had already given a recital of the piano music of Chopin last Sunday afternoon at the *Academia Filharmonia,* which she had dedicated to the memory of the recently deceased pianist, Vladimir de Pachmann. Yesterday's recital programme allowed this very talented pianist to prove that she has a repertoire beyond that of her country's most famous composer. She had programmed a selection of composers of Germanic origin, Haydn, Beethoven and Schumann, in the first half, followed by compositions by Chopin in the second. Miss Lipska chose to play on a grand piano from the firm of Pleyel, Chopin's favourite instrument maker while he lived in Paris. The acoustics of the church were not always kind to Miss Lipska's choices of repertoire. The Chopin selections especially would have benefited from a more intimate room. In the Beethoven sonata the pianist made good use of the right pedal to enhance the sound of the upper registry.

'The first choice for the beginning of the recital was a particularly attractive one, the Sonata Number 60 in C Major by Joseph Haydn. This may have been the composer's last sonata composed for solo piano, written during his sojourn in London and dedicated to his pupil, Therese Jansen Bartolozzi, whom he met during his stay in that city and who had also been a pupil of Clementi. Miss Lipska played the sonata in her own manner—sometimes with astonishing results—while giving full sway to the composer's constantly changing and amusing musical thoughts.

'The Beethoven Sonata No. 16, opus 31, Number 1 in G Major is one of the few sonatas of the composer's output that was not dedicated to one of his admirers or benefactors. It has been said that it is an expression of Beethoven's oft-scarce sense of humour. The composer's pupil Carl Czerny described the first movement as "full of energy, capricious and wittily vivacious". The right hand always seems impatient to wait for the beat. Miss Lipska's interpretation throughout displayed ample virtuosity combined with emotional understanding of the work.

'Robert Schumann's *Kinderszenen* seldom fails to provoke sentiments that can sometimes approach sadness. Clara Wieck once wrote to her lover Robert that he was "a child at heart". The interpretation we heard yesterday afternoon left this listener with the impression that he was hearing these pieces for the first time. Every scene was especially well played in an affectionate manner that revealed the childlike mood the composer had intended. The seventh scene, *Träumerie*, was especially well played in a most dreamlike manner. Schumann does not appear to have indicated strict tempo markings for this composition, and pianists tend to choose tempos of considerable variation. Miss Lipska adopted just enough freedom of imagination, resulting in most tempos being just about right to these ears.

'Her interpretations of Chopin's piano works have won Miss Lipska considerable praise in her own country, as well as in Vienna, where she played last year for the first time. After intermission, she returned to play a selection of popular Chopin pieces including four nocturnes from opus 27 and 32, each played in a slow sentimental manner with an appropriate amount of *rubato*. The final selection was the composer's Fantasy Impromptu opus 66 in C Sharp Minor, which was not published until about twenty years after his death. We do not know why he chose not to publish while he was alive, as it is a masterpiece. It was played with considerable virtuosity and flamboyancy. The pianist was generous in playing two encores; the first, a transcription by the pianist Myra Hess of the choral from J.S. Bach's Cantata Number 147, known as *Jesu, Joy of Man's Desiring*. Miss Lipska added a short piece at the end, which was announced as being by an unknown Polish composer but seemed to have been of her own creation. This was in the style of a Polish *mazurka*, but it was unfamiliar to this reviewer. Miss Lipska added several clever variations on the theme to the delight of the audience.

'On Friday, prior to the recital, a press conference allowed the artist to expand on the obstacles faced by a professional pianist who has lost much of her vision, as well as on her special attachment to the legacy of Vladimir de Pachmann. We look forward to the return of this remarkable pianist'."

Charles looked up from his reading and glanced at Agnieszka. He knew from her expression she was happy, and he waited for her to speak. She finally broke the silence; "I am overwhelmed with that review—so well written and the reviewer is obviously knowledgeable about the music. He did seem excessively enthusiastic though, don't you think?"

"Not at all! I agree with everything he wrote," Charles said cheerily. "Are you ready for the review from *La Republica?*'

"Yes, of course. I hope it is not as flowery."

The waiter, who had been discreetly waiting until their discussions had come to a close, had approached and provided a lunch menu. They both quickly agreed that a ham sandwich would do, along with a cup of coffee.

Charles was scanning the second review. "This second review was signed with the initials ESV, and I do not know who that might be. Here is what ESV wrote. The title is *Miss Lipska's Piano Recital*: 'Miss Agnieszka Lipska, a pianist from Kraków, Poland, gave a piano recital yesterday afternoon at the Church of All Saints, which was fully attended. Special attendees included *Il Duce*, who has always supported the arts and is a musician himself. Also in attendance were the Minister of Popular Culture and his staff. During a press conference in the St. Peter's Room on Friday, prior to the recital, Miss Lipska discussed with candour a variety of subjects including her early tuition, the effect of progressive loss of vision, her love of Chopin's music, her special attachment to the pianist de Pachmann, her views on fidelity of the performer to a composer's intentions and other matters.

'Her programme in the first half included the last sonata by Haydn (No. 60 in C Major), Beethoven's Sonata opus 31, No. 1 in G Major and Schumann's *Kinderszenen* (Scenes from Childhood), opus15, written in 1838, before his marriage to Clara Wiek. The Haydn sonata is full of the composer's fun and humour, with irregular phrases and deceptive cadences. In the first movement she chose a somewhat slower disciplined tempo than usual. The third and final movement, *allegro molto*, is brief (about two minutes) and full of surprises and jokes. Miss Lipska manoeuvred expertly through each of the three movements with the necessary accommodation for the composer's constantly changing and nonsensical musical thoughts.

'Beethoven's sonata must have been selected to maintain the sense of wit and humour established with the Haydn work. In the first movement, the hands find themselves unable to play together! This adds to the fun of the work. The second movement assumes an expansive lyrical quality. The final movement allowed the performer complete freedom to display her abundant virtuosity.

'Throughout history composers have often paused to return to the fun and games they remember from childhood to express their memories as musical works—often with true simplicity. Robert Schumann's journey back to his childhood in the early part of 1838 resulted in what he described to Clara Wieck, who was not yet his wife, as "thirty droll little things" from which he selected the thirteen he clearly loved the most. The collection was published as *Kinderszenen*, opus 15. Miss Lipska took us through Schumann's poetic masterpiece with a virtuoso's mastery. Particularly appealing for this reviewer were her renditions of *Träumerei* and *Der Dicter spricht*. There were moments when her playing transported this listener into a world where he cannot recall having been before. The audience response was appropriately enthusiastic.

'The second half was devoted to Chopin. The nocturnes from opus 27, in C sharp and D flat as well as from opus 32, in B Major and A flat major were played in the tradition of de Pachmann. The *Fantasy-Impromptu* opus 66 in C Sharp Minor, played with amazing virtuosity, concluded a very rewarding recital by this talented pianist. The recital was recorded by Radio Rome for future broadcast. We look forward to hearing the recital again on radio.

'Encores played by Miss Lipska were JS Bach's *Jesu, Joy of Man's Desiring* and Variations on a Polish *mazurka* by an anonymous composer'."

Agnieszka laughed. "It seems he could not identify my national anthem, which is what we wanted."

"Indeed," Charles agreed, "Both reviewers will now be searching through their scores for the composer of that mysterious mazurka. I thought both reviews were fair, and likely reflected the view of the audience. I am very pleased for you. This is a fitting end to your visit to Rome." He reached over, put his arm around her shoulder and placed a lingering kiss on her cheek. "We should do some last minute checks of our rooms to be sure every thing has been packed after we finish our sandwiches."

The waiter was prompt and after they had finished their sandwiches, coffee and signed the bill they rose and moved toward the exit. Charles could not help noticing Agnieszka's slow rise from her chair. She seemed to be uncomfortable and in pain. The hotel receptionist was waiting at the door holding several envelopes addressed to Charles. "This one was dropped off a few minutes ago Doctor Flemming," she explained. "Thank you," he replied and turning to Agnieszka, "I will wait until we are upstairs to open these." He examined the envelope the receptionist had said had recently arrived. "The name on this envelope is one I do not recognize but the others I do."

Before they could leave, the receptionist added, "the manager would like to see you both in his office. He says it is very urgent."

Charles looked at Agnieszka in surprise. "Not more trouble with the police I hope!"

Mr. Mercanti appeared to be in an agitated state. Before explaining the reason for his concern, they heard him exclaim, " I am afraid you must call the Polish ambassador immediately Doctor Flemming. The ambassador will explain. I will put the call through for you."

Charles was put through without delay. "Ambassador Radinski...." he thought it best to begin with another apology concerning his outburst towards Mussolini, "I do hope my conduct has not caused you...."

Radinski was unusually abrupt. "Not you Doctor Flemming. This concerns Miss Lipska's recital and her choice of the Polish national anthem in her programme. We had thought it would go unnoticed, but it appears a music critic from one of yesterday's late evening papers had discovered the truth, and the Ministry of Culture is not pleased ... not pleased at all."

Charles could sense the ambassador's tension over the telephone. "I think it best if you and Miss Lipska settle your account with your hotel as soon as possible and move to the legation. You can stay here for the rest of the day until your train leaves. We can arrange an escort to the station."

Charles agreed. He had not consulted Agnieszka who would have overheard his comments. The ambassador continued, "prepare to leave immediately Doctor Flemming. I can send a car right away."

Agnieszka was aghast when he told her the news. "Are we in danger?" she asked, her hands at her mouth. "I don't think so," he tried to sound reassuring. "The ambassador wants to avoid any problems with our travel plans. Of course, one never can tell with the Black shirts. It only takes one to decide to take the law into his own hands, and we might have some ... difficulty."

His memory went back to the threatening young men he and Simon had seen stalking the station in Genoa and on their arrival in Rome. Would they be questioned when they went to the station in the evening? Agnieszka would certainly be identifiable, not merely her attractive features, but her photograph had been posted all over Rome to advertise her last recital.

Despite his earlier good will Mr. Mercanti seemed almost relieved they would soon be leaving his hotel and he hurriedly settled the accounts. The luggage was retrieved from their rooms and the manager offered a fleeting "Arrivaderci" as Charles and Agnieszka quickly left the lobby to find the car sent by the ambassador. Charles could not relax and was feeling distinctly vulnerable as the driver—perhaps too casually given the circumstances—carefully negotiated the traffic. Clearly the chauffeur was not a typical Italian motorist!

It felt as if eyes were watching their every move, perhaps prevented from striking because they were under some sort of diplomatic immunity in the legation limousine. Agnieszka clutched his hand all the while but remained silent. They were both physically relieved to pass through the gate into the legation grounds, where the ambassador was waiting to meet them, concern obviously etched on his face.

"I am hopeful this will turn out to be— what do you call it Doctor Flemming—a tempest in a teapot?" the ambassador told them as they were ushered into the adjoining suites. "I have not received an official complaint from the government, but I will not be surprised to receive a diplomatic notice tomorrow to appear before the Minister of Culture, if not Mussolini himself, to explain why Miss Lipska chose that encore."

Agnieszka had been preparing her own defence. "But, it's a traditional Polish *mazurka*, surely in the name of cultural exchange they cannot...."

The ambassador cut her short. "Miss Lipska, it is far more than that. I have been considering my decision to suggest you play the mazurka assuming no one would know. The truth is—had you played the anthem here, at the legation, on sovereign territory of the Polish government, there would have been no objection. But they will argue that you played it in a church, on Italian soil, in front of the most powerful man in the country. He was unaware of the nature of the piece. The fact that a provincial newspaper would announce it might make him appear ignorant. He is very sensitive to such things. He likes to be considered a musician and this could be perceived as an insult, not just to him, but to the Italian people, at a time when nationalism is a powerful political force."

Charles walked to the window and glanced outside. He almost expected to see a riotous mob gathering outside the gate, screaming their heads off but the street was quiet, dampened only by a slight rain.

"You must rest," the ambassador suggested. "My wife and I will make you both at home until the time you leave. Your luggage has been taken care of and we will escort you to the train station, after dinner."

Charles felt relieved and he could see Agnieszka was as well. "Thank you ambassador. You have made it very easy for us."

He turned to Agnieszka as the ambassador left the room. "I thought you might be having the stomach pain again during lunch at the hotel". She nodded, "yes, it seemed to creep up on me just before we left the table. I have some aspirin left".

He was not completely assured but suddenly remembered the envelope he had been given by the receptionist. He drew Agnieszka aside and opened it.

CHAPTER TWENTY-NINE

"Totidem verbis"
(In those very words)

Charles opened the envelope, and after a quick scan of its contents exclaimed, "You will be very surprised to hear what this letter says," he was suppressing a smirk. "It is from a Mister Alfredo Crepaldi, whom I have never met, but he seems to be the person who was to find the new de Pachmann book for me. Listen to what he says: 'Dear Doctor Flemming; By now you will know that the book, which I left for you last week was not the new edition of the original biography of de Pachmann published in 1916. My secretary was unable to obtain a copy of the new edition because Mr. Pallottelli's office advised her that it had not yet been released from the printers. It is to be published later this month in the January edition of *La Nuova Italia Musicale*. I hope her decision to leave you the 1916 copy has not delayed your plans for researching your book on de Pachmann'."

He paused and looked at her. He could see she had already dissolved into laughter. "I realize what this means. Alexei's plan to get the new book has backfired!" she exclaimed. "Yes, it appears so. Let me read the rest: 'I did not telephone you about this earlier as I have been away from Rome on business. Also my English is very poor, so I arranged for my secretary, who is better in English, to prepare this letter while I was away. If you are leaving Rome soon, I would be pleased to obtain the new version and send it to our mutual friend in Toronto. I wish you a safe return to Canada and hope your stay has been successful. Yours Sincerely, Alfredo Crepaldi, Attorney at Law'."

"He is a lawyer and his address is on the envelope, so I will write to thank him for this. Do you think Alexei realizes that he did not get the new edition?"

Agnieszka still sounded a little angry at the thought of her brother's misdemeanour. "I don't care. It is ironic that it happened this way. He deserves what happened. But I do not want to talk about his problem any more. I just feel relieved that we are safe here in my country's legation." She paused as if in thought. "I have just remembered that I had wanted to shop to buy one more thing for my family before leaving. I wonder if it would be possible."

"I will ask the ambassador if he will allow his chauffeur to drive us there and drop us off somewhere where you can shop. It should only take a few minutes."

After some thought and with some caution, the ambassador agreed provided they kept a low profile and were efficient in their shopping. "My wife knows of a dress shop that is open for a few hours on Sunday afternoon—by appointment only of course," he added. "I am sure she can call and arrange for Miss Lipska to visit." After the phone call had been made, Charles and Agnieszka set off in the legation car.

The clothing store was easily found. The manager welcomed them warmly and introductions were made in English. Agnieszka told the manager she was a

slow shopper, so Charles suggested he leave her under the guidance of a very
pleasant clerk, promising he would return in fifteen to twenty minutes. When he
returned she was waiting with a small shopping bag over her arm. She had found
what she wanted.

They were soon back at the legation car and he could see the driver was
much relieved. They had been gone longer than expected and Charles apologized. He knew the ambassador would be worried. Within ten minutes the driver
had them back in the safety of the legation grounds. The ambassador's wife met
them at the door and ushered them inside. The staff had prepared a meal in anticipation of their arrival and while they sat and sampled a light fare of mush-
room soup and shrimp salad Mrs. Radinska announced she had discovered the
review of Agnieszka's recital that had precipitated their rapid exit from the hotel. "Let me read it to you," she said.

"*Ambitious Polish Pianist Performs in Sunday Matinee* is the title of the review," she read aloud. "Here is what the critic—whose initials are RFV—says:
'The Polish pianist Agnieszka Lipska gave a recital at the Church of All Saints
yesterday. The church was filled to capacity to hear this young pianist, who had
already given a successful recital in the city the previous week. The programme
was eclectic and generally successful. The event was highlighted by the appearance of *Il Duce* accompanied by members of the Ministry of Popular Culture.
Miss Lipska played sonatas by Haydn and Beethoven, as well as pieces by
Schumann and Chopin. Her best renditions were in the Schumann *Kinderszenen*
and the Chopin selections. The Chopin pieces demonstrated why she is considered the successor to de Pachmann as an interpreter of Chopin *par excellence.*
Her approach to the Schumann was very personal, in which she demonstrated a
warm tone with the required virtuosity and an understanding of the emotion and
drama of the scenes from childhood. The sonatas by Haydn and Beethoven,
which opened the program were generally well-played with only occasional
wrong notes, especially in the rapid passages of the final movement of the Beethoven, where the artist seemed to display a sense of keyboard abandonment.
Playing wrong notes was a fault of which Beethoven himself was sometimes
accused. Her rendition of Bach's *Jesu Joy of Man's Desiring,* a transcription by
Myra Hess, as an encore was an example of exceptional attention to the spiritual
aspects of the piece. The final encore, A Polish mazurka, not from one of the
more than fifty from Chopin's hand, was played in a unique style with dance
like improvisations. The composer was not announced but to this reviewer's ears
the mazurka in question was the Polish national anthem in disguise. There was
no explanation why this distinguished pianist would choose this as an encore.
Was it an act of defiance? Perhaps a show of Polish patriotism? The Pleyel piano chosen by the artist did not always meet the challenges of the church acoustics so that the piano sound in quiet passages seemed all too frequently to disappear into the ceilings.

'Playing the piano without perfect vision is a challenge, but Miss Lipska's
background and solid training in classical repertoire allowed her to easily sur-

mount any obstacles. Apart from some technical flaws this was a most enjoyable recital by a talented artist'."

Charles looked at Agnieszka and could see she was not finding the review to her satisfaction. "He enjoyed the programme and identified the *mazurka,* but I do not remember wrong notes, did you?" she asked.

"I am not sharp enough to say if there were or not," Charles confessed. "It really doesn't matter, as the critic wrote, "playing wrong notes was one of Beethoven's faults—one that he probably did not feel ashamed of."

"I agree and I do not feel ashamed either," Agnieszka was mollified. "Wrong notes may become apparent when I have a chance to hear the tapes. I was surprised to hear that the visit of Mussolini and the Minister of Popular Culture was the highlight of the recital, but our critic must be a loyal member of the party. Or perhaps his editor insists that he toe the party line." Mrs. Radinska nodded in agreement. "My husband will see that the matter of our national anthem is settled to their satisfaction. He has dealt with the Ministry of Culture before." Agnieszka stood and stretched. "Thank you for the very enjoyable lunch. I would like to rest for a few hours. May I use one of your bedrooms?"

Mrs. Radinska was eager to provide a room for them to rest. Charles and Agnieszka found themselves in a very cosy bedroom suite on the second floor with a lounge and comfortable chairs and a chesterfield. Agnieszka wanted to stretch out on the bed. She had decided to take two more aspirins to help with her stomach pain. He noticed she was soon asleep. He soon found himself dosing on the comfortable chesterfield. The quiet of the room was interrupted by the telephone.

Agnieszka answered before he could leave the chesterfield and spoke briefly to the caller in Polish. "Yes, we can be ready for dinner at seven o'clock. Thank you for your kindness." Agnieszka hung up the telephone. "It was Mrs. Radinska," she said. She sighed and fell back on the pillow and closed her eyes. He could see she was worried. "This Mussolini business has been a worry for me. We have not yet managed to leave Rome and there is still a threat of interrogation at the station."

"We must not let this Mussolini affair spoil our travels together," he suggested in his best conciliatory tone. We should try to get some more sleep."

The *wagon lit* to Milan was to leave Rome at 22:30 hours and passengers were expected to be at the train station forty-five minutes before departure. Agnieszka had decided she needed another nap so Charles retreated to the adjoining lounge area to check on the items he knew were essential to be done before they left. Fortunately, before their impromptu exit from the hotel in the afternoon they had made sure several important items were not forgotten. Arrangements were to be made for the piano to be moved back to the dealer on Monday. Mr. Mercanti had been left a generous tip for his attention. On Monday morning flowers were to be delivered by a near-by flower shop to Elizabeth Valentini at the legation. Agnieszka had already written a thank-you note for Elizabeth, which she had asked the Ambassador to give to her at work on Monday. The Ambassador had been given a note for the legation staff thanking all those involved in arranging her tour, catering for the receptions and for providing the Pleyel pianos. The expenses for the brief hospital stay in Ostia had been paid earlier by bank money order through the hotel.

They had a compartment reserved on the night train to Milan. Train connections from Milan to Vienna, and onward to Kraków meant no excessively long waits in crowded train stations—as long as there were no delays along the way. Passports had been packed in an overnight bag and the rest of their luggage although substantial was manageable. On Saturday he had ordered a case of Italian wine for the Lipska family. The wine merchant had recommended a Chianti Classico from the 1929 vintage made by Rufina and promised to deliver it to the train. He would be no more than three days in Poland as the date for the sailing of the liner *S.S. Scanyork* from Gdynia was the 27th. He had read in the brochure that had arrived with the tickets that the *SS Scanyork,* close to 5200 tons, had been built in Philadelphia in 1919 and for some time was called the *S.S. Schenectady* but was sold to other interests and had been refitted in 1932 to be more suitable for the type of passengers who travelled the Gdynia-Copenhagen-Halifax-Philadelphia run.

The few days in Kraków would allow time to arrange Agnieszka's medical appointments—with a gynaecologist and perhaps with the ophthalmologist, Maria Cagianno, had promised to write to in Warsaw. That would mean a journey to that city. It seemed unlikely they could arrange all of the medical visits before he left for Gdynia.

How would he deal with Alexei? Agnieszka had said he would not be returning until after he had left. He had taken the de Pachmann book from the hotel and by now must realize his folly. He and his sister obviously had a much poorer relationship than he had earlier assumed. Such difficulties had not been apparent for the first few days he had spent with them in Rome. He seemed to be genuinely interested in promoting her career and undertook to facilitate her tour arrangements.

His free time in Rome after the meetings had been spent in a different manner than he had anticipated. He had hoped to visit some of the Roman fountains, the Vatican, especially to view the art collection again, to visit St Peter's Cathedral and to visit the house where John Keats had spent his last days. He had seen the Keats grave on his first visit in 1925 and had read the inscription on the tombstone: *'Here lies a man whose name was writ on water'* – the dying comment of a disillusioned and despondent man. The day they had visited de Pachmann's grave had been marred by his revelation of Alexei's guilt and the subsequent near-tragedy on the Tiber. Agnieszka had been very convincing in her explanation for the accident but had she been depressed enough to impulsively jump into the river? He was now seeing a more impulsive aspect of her personality. His visits to the statue of Moses had made up for the other sites that had been impossible to visit.

The sea route home from Poland would mean he would not see Simon as they had hoped. Simon was a good friend. He knew they would keep in touch but he had doubts about how his own relationship with Alexei would evolve. His kleptomania was not under his control but it was possible he may consider the issue of such a minor nature that did not need resolution. He looked at his watch and saw it was close to seven o'clock.

Agnieszka was still asleep when he walked into the bedroom. She woke quickly, sat up, wanted a hug and said she was feeling better. Her pain had almost gone. After a quick fix-up they were ready to meet the ambassador and Mrs. Radinski in the dining room. Dinner was very informal. Agnieszka ate very little. Charles could see she was still having cramps. Their hosts were convincing in their assurance that the Mussolini affair would not likely come to a head until Monday. By then they would be safely out of the country en route to Poland. The legation car was made available to take them with their luggage to the station in time to make the train but with no unnecessary waiting. Mrs. Radinska and the legation staff said goodbye with best wishes for a safe journey. The ambassador kindly offered to accompany them to the station to be an interpreter and to be sure their arrangements for leaving were uncomplicated.

No complications were encountered at the station, and as the ambassador prepared to leave they both expressed their warm appreciation. Ambassador Radinski was now in a relaxed mood. His last words were, "I hope you will find Rome a safer city on your return." They were all laughing as he turned and began walking back to the legation car.

CHAPTER THIRTY
"Amos caecus est"
(Love is blind)

Charles suspected he would not sleep well—he seldom did on trains. Their compartment was warm and cosy and the porter had already turned down the beds before they had boarded and informed them they should arrive in Milan about seven o'clock. Did they need a wake-up call at about six perhaps? It would allow them time to have breakfast before they arrived. "Yes," he said, "it is a good idea." Agnieszka seemed more interested in turning in than planning for the next morning. So she was ready for bed soon after the train had left the station. Her stomach pains had become a nagging issue again so to help with sleep she had taken a few more aspirin tablets. He decided a Scotch and water would help him sleep. She was not interested in a night cap, gave him a kiss, said "good night", and was almost asleep by the time the porter had returned with his drink—a double Scotch and water. He was soon feeling more relaxed. The rhythm of the carriage wheels on the tracks and periodic distant short toots from the locomotive whistle were the only sounds he heard as Agnieszka's breathing was very quiet.

At the station, they had decided to check most of their luggage in the baggage car. A twelve-bottle case of Italian Amarone from the Bolla vineyards for the Lipska family had been delivered to the train and it had also been checked. The wine merchant had attached an explanation: the Chianti had not been in stock but Charles was assured that this wine was perhaps better. Before leaving the hotel, Radio Rome had delivered a package of tapes of the last recital, which had made her very happy. The Lipski family had an up-to-date tape playback unit.

Before the train left he had bought an illustrated travel book about Poland written in both English and Polish and had become engrossed in the first chapter. It was about the early history of the country but he found that part uninteresting and soon moved on to the second chapter about its geography and agriculture. He realized he was unfamiliar with details of the geography of Poland and was surprised to see on a well-illustrated map that the city of Kraków was just inside the Polish border with Czechoslovakia. He finished his drink, got up to wash and brush his teeth, returned and settled on his bunk. His watch said it was almost midnight—time to turn off the light. A faint glow from a night light near the door made it possible to see the outline of Agnieszka's head. She was sleeping peacefully. Again he was reminded of how beautiful she was. With her eyes closed in sleep one would never suspect she was virtually blind. The human face was a mysterious terrain that Charles never tired of exploring. He lifted the window shade and saw only darkness outside except for reflections of a few carriage windows. They were now well into the country, away from the city lights. He was reminded again how he always felt such complete trust in the locomotive engineer to make their journey a safe one.

Sleep was slow in coming. His imagination was very active. How would Freud have made similar return journeys from Rome after his many visits to the city? Did he take the overnight *wagon lit* such as this or travel by day? His fear of train travel might dictate that he avoid travelling at night. He would find it difficult to sleep. There would be very little to see out the windows. He could find much more pleasure in daylight conversation with his daughter Anna or some other travelling companion. During the day he could read, write and smoke cigars—unless fellow travellers in the same compartment complained. He felt sorry for Freud—living and working in Vienna today was said to be increasingly difficult. The city was no more hospitable, perhaps less, to Jews than in the past and his psychotherapy practice was not well patronized.

Agnieszka had earlier hinted that there was considerable prejudice against Jews in Poland, where they made up about ten per cent of the population and were very active in the economic and cultural life of the country. In some towns (she said they were called *shtetls.*) Jews could make up a majority of the population. Kraków had a thriving and prosperous Jewish community. The book he had bought briefly described how Jews had found refuge in Poland over the centuries after being expelled from many countries of Europe including Great Britain. There were also about 500,000 Jews living in Germany.

His thoughts turned to de Pachmann and how events had turned his writing project into one of disinterest. He had wanted to visit de Pachmann's country home, Fabriano, but that gradually became a potentially useless exercise since the pianist had died but they had at least visited his grave in Campo Verano Cemetery. De Pachmann's secretary had left Rome on business and the new edition of the 1916 biographic manuscript had not materialized. There were many aspects of the pianist's life that he had hoped to explore. What had the Danish King, Christian IX, said about him when he presented him with the Order of the Danebrog during the pianists visit to Copenhagen in 1885? He had tried but had never been able to find a transcript of the King's formal presentation. This Order of the Danebrog was an ancient one presented only to those who had made a significant contribution to Danish society. He had obviously been as popular a pianist there as in other countries throughout the Continent.

Charles turned with his face to the window but sleep was still not within reach. Was de Pachmann as good a keyboard artist as he claimed? Some critics thought he was a virtuoso. What was Liszt's true assessment of his art? Stories of their association and friendship that had originated from de Pachmann were sometimes highly embellished and perhaps mythical. The stories were based on his belief that Liszt, from their first contact, had concluded and sometimes declared that his young friend was the one true interpreter of the piano music of Chopin. Did Liszt really kiss the young man after his student performance of his piano concerto in Vienna—just as Beethoven was said to have kissed the young Liszt years before?

Was there truth in the story that Liszt had once declared that de Pachmann played Chopin's music better than Chopin himself? De Pachmann cherished his memories of Liszt and always promoted him as the finest pianist, living or dead.

He declared that he was the 'king of pianists' and of course he was right. De Pachmann often played Liszt's compositions and on several occasions devoted a complete recital programme to his works. He did this despite a prevailing opinion amongst critics and some of the public that the music had little merit. When de Pachmann auditioned for the beginning of studies at the Vienna Conservatory at the age of seventeen he played the Liszt *Rigoletto Fantasy* with the highest approval of Professor Joseph Daks. He often played it as an encore while on tours in later years. It was as a student in Vienna, that he had played the Liszt Piano Concerto No.1 at a Conservatory concert where the composer was in attendance. Despite lack of critical approval of his music, Liszt did not lack for promotion from a circle of professional pianists of the day especially those who had spent time with him in Weimar. Those loyal students included the pianists Walter Bache, Frederick Lamont, Arthur Friedheim and others. In later years, after the composer's death, de Pachmann openly copied many of Liszt's styles: some aspects of his demeanour at the piano and his distinctive hairstyle.

Charles had accepted the fact that the book he had planned to write on the life of de Pachmann would never materialize. But the thought made him feel sad. His plan was to give it the title *Understanding de Pachmann*, which was to be an assessment of his life from a psychological view rather than as a complete biography. Now if he were to choose a title, it might be *Mourning de Pachmann* but he really had not felt much grief over his death. He wondered why he had not felt more. The man was not easy, and stories of his short temper left a certain unpleasant flavour.

Now his mind was a muddle. He had loved so many things about Rome: little Angela Roscetta's playing of the Mendelssohn *Songs Without Words* popped into his head; Agnieszka's final recital. He hated the fascist political philosophy and was glad to leave it behind. He had revived with pleasure images of the chemist who sold him the contraceptives and the understanding owners of the Tiber Queen. His life had changed in a little more than a week. The organ and piano music he had heard had left him moved—changed. He would never be the same. Agnieszka had left him in a stew on more than one occasion—triggering his anxiety, disappointment and temporary grief—as well as her anger and jealousies. He had been tempted to leap deeper into those depths—to fish in those waters but he had not. Slowly he realized the train had come to a stop and the sudden silence was what he needed. He was asleep in a minute.

*** *** *** ***

He awoke feeling hungry. He opened the blind and noted it was still dark outside. They had both been deeply asleep when the wake-up call had come. She had said "good morning", and said she had slept surprisingly well. The abdominal cramps had almost disappeared but she seemed unusually quiet. He sensed that all was not well with her. She had said, "I won't be long", in the middle of a kiss, before retreating to the toilet, emerging after what seemed like ages looking refreshed and more relaxed. He did not take long to do his toilet, deciding to skip shaving until the train reached Milan.

The dining car was not far and they were soon seated before a well-laid table covered with white linen. Daylight was appearing over the horizon and the train was making good time. She was not hungry but he ordered a full breakfast with juice, cheese, ham, coffee and toast. She said she remembered a dream, which she wanted to tell him about. She had been somewhere—perhaps in Rome—but it could have been in Poland. She had prepared for an evening solo recital. The problem was she had mislaid the programme notes and was unable to remember the order of the pieces. "Here I was seated at the piano before a hushed audience but feeling very anxious. Was it the Bach Partita or the Sonata by Scarlatti I had chosen as the opening number?" She had quickly decided on the Bach and that seemed to have had no adverse reaction from the audience, so she followed with the Scarlatti number. "I remember which Scarlatti Sonata because it is my favourite, the one in B Minor. During the applause, which followed, my memory again failed. I was sure a Beethoven Sonata was to follow but which of the thirty-two? I was sure it was not a late one. It would be best and make sense for me to exit the stage now, after the Scarlatti and seek help back stage.

"A male stage-hand whom I thought I recognized approached me and was kind enough to help me find my way but I suddenly found myself outdoors in almost total darkness. Fortunately the evening was warm and there were faint lights visible across the square. I had obviously chosen or been shown the wrong door, which seemed to have locked when it closed. It would not yield.

"It was then I woke with an urge to use the toilet. The train had stopped so it was easy to navigate my way in the dark. You were sleeping. To my relief the dream did not continue after I fell asleep again."

She smiled weakly as she finished the story. She had been toying with her fork as she described the dream. He reached for her left hand and she dropped her fork. He felt her squeeze his hand in response. He smiled in return. "It isn't always possible to interpret dreams. My patients sometimes tell me about theirs and I always try to have them sort out the meaning themselves." The waiter had reappeared. "But here is your juice, so we can discuss your dream later, if you wish." She ate lightly and he avoided discussing her abdominal pains. Through the window he could see the sun had now appeared over the horizon. The lights from distant farm house windows passed quickly by in a faint low-lying fog. There was a light covering of snow in the fields. Black coloured birds could be seen swooping over the flat land in search of food.

He was surprised to hear her say she wanted to talk about her dream again. He had buttered her toast but he could see she had taken only two bites. "I don't often have those sorts of dreams."

She paused to drink some coffee and returned his gaze. "I think that dream was telling me something about my recital career—possibly about my confidence and my concerns about the future. In the last two days, I have felt poorly. It has given me more time than usual to think about where my future is going. I have some important engagements that Alexei has booked in several cities in Poland and likely in Paris but I feel very ambivalent towards him for what he did to you—and to us both—in Rome. I feel strongly I should ask him to relinquish his role as my manager. I think the man in my dream was Alexei. But if I do release him from his obligations, I do not know where I will turn to find someone who is capable of taking on that job. My sight is so poor that my manager would have to be a person with many talents—someone willing to see that all my professional needs were attended to. You know what it involves—you did it for several days last week and did it very well too!" She smiled and squeezed his hand, which she had not released. The waiter had returned and refilled their coffee cups.

"I am so appreciative for what you have done at some sacrifice too. I will never forget you. But I will not have you any more when you leave in a few days. I will be completely in the dark – on the outside, as in my dream. I have wondered if my mother could possibly undertake the task. Father could never do it. When you meet her you will see she is very capable and she has always been totally supportive of my career. I tell you as well—and it will be no surprise—that my professional success has meant my family has benefited significantly. We have been able to improve our home and last year we were able to afford a new car. I feel very excited to be returning home and bringing you with me to meet them."

Charles had not interrupted her while gradually feeling himself fill with pity for her situation. He hoped he had not shown it in his expression. But he remembered she would not likely see well enough to read his face or even to sense his mood. He had followed her analysis of the dream carefully and was uncertain whether he should endorse her conclusions or to leave what he thought unsaid. But he sensed she was waiting for his opinion as she fixed her gaze at his face in a quizzical fashion.

"I mentioned earlier that dreams are probably best interpreted by the dreamer rather than by someone else. I thought you gave a reasonable interpretation but at the same time you must not let the content of that dream determine your future and chart the professional route you will follow once you get back home. Alexei has been mean—I admit. He has acted in a somewhat predictable fashion for a kleptomaniac. I predict that he will not mention the affair when we see him again, just as he seemed to ignore the episodes at school many years ago. Your mother had to deal with those. You will have an opportunity to connect with your parents again—and we must not forget those tapes. We will have fun listening to them. Then you can judge if the critic who spotted your wrong notes was correct."

They both laughed at that idea. "I'm sure he was right about that", she added.

"Perhaps you should seriously consider learning to play the organ. Your new friend, Janinski from Warsaw, could introduce you to an experienced organ teacher in Kraków. He would likely have contacts. I am also optimistic that your vision will improve with cataract surgery." He paused and decided not to mention the other medical problem—the mysterious pelvic complaint—a possible explanation for her pain. There were possibilities that he did not want to think about or discuss with her.

"I am also very interested in exploring Kraków with you to see if everything you have said about it is true." That made her laugh as well. She finished her toast and coffee while he waited for his ham and cheese.

She had certainly assumed a more relaxed look after their conversation. "I am curious about your cramps. Have they gone?" She shook her head. "I took some more aspirin before we came to the diner so it is a lot better. It is not bad now."

His cheese and ham plate had arrived and he knew they should soon return to their compartment. "I am almost finished, so we can get back so you can relax before Milan. We should be on time and we should not have to wait long to connect to Vienna." He looked at his watch. "We should be there in about an hour."

CHAPTER THIRTY- ONE

"Amor est vital essential"
("Love is the essence of life")

The train connection in Milan was easier than either Charles or Agnieszka had anticipated. The train had arrived on time. The baggage items had been transferred. Charles had time for a shave in the station washroom. A newspaper stand at the station had several recent editions of the London *Times.* He had not read an English newspaper for the past week, so he chose two recent editions— Friday and Saturday, January 20th and 21st, to read later. He was amazed to see the dimensions of this grand railway station, the largest in Europe he had been told. He had walked with Agnieszka through the magnificent booking hall, with its glass covered roof, leaded windows, grand staircases, marble walls and sculptures. He had been aware of the possibility that their identity might trigger an encounter with OVRA agents or Black Shirts, but no one had approached them so he assumed the news of their departure had not yet reached the authorities.

They were now seated in a carriage compartment close to the dining car. Their train, pulled by a large steam locomotive, had left for Vienna almost an hour ago. Agnieszka, who had been sleeping briefly before the train arrived in Milan, had again settled for another nap. She had told him she still felt sentimental about de Pachmann, and regretted she had not seen him before he died. After all, de Pachmann and his legacy — as well as the spirit of Chopin — had been the main reasons why she, and in a sense both, had travelled to Rome. If he could find Simon's paper on de Pachmann's Beethoven style would he read it to her? Charles found it in his brief case and began to read against a rhythmic background of the noise of wheels on the tracks.

She interrupted him on several occasions to tell him about some of the Polish and Russian pianists she had heard play in her youth—Paderewski, Friedman and on one occasion Josef Lhévinne, the Russian. "They were all very good, but I would have loved to have heard my countryman, Carl Tausig play. It is sad that he died at age thirty of typhoid fever! One of my teachers told me about his prodigious talent. I read that de Pachmann, when he was young, after hearing Tausig play a recital in Odessa, had decided it was necessary for him to retreat from the stage, to study and practice for several more years. He did not feel he had reached the level of keyboard technique that Tausig had shown at that recital. Tausig was then considered one of Liszt's most accomplished students."

Charles had resumed reading Simon's paper, but before he had finished page six, Agnieszka was sound asleep again. They were scheduled to arrive in Vienna after dark. The train was sometimes late, so it might be close to midnight. Their tickets said the connection to Kraków would necessitate a wait of two hours, but a sleeper had been booked, so they should arrive on Tuesday, in the morning or early afternoon.

The outside temperature had dropped significantly, and he could sense that winter was in the air. In fact, outside the window he could see occasional snowflakes. The temperature in the carriage had been turned up, and the steam in the pipes could be heard intermittently grumbling in the background. He had slept poorly on the night train from Rome and, without much warning, he too was asleep, the London *Times* falling to the floor.

He dreamed he was back in Canada—in Toronto. It was snowing. He sensed he had earlier taken Toby for a walk and now he had just given the pup his dinner of commercial dog food. As always, within a few minutes the dish was empty and Toby was looking for more. A telephone, somewhere in the house, probably in the kitchen, was ringing. When he answered, he recognized the voice. The dean of medicine was calling to ask about his travels, his presentation at the congress and his impressions of Rome. How had Charles' research into the odd pianist gone? Poorly, Charles replied—too many distractions. He was tempted to mention Agnieszka, but he decided against that. Yes, he would be back to work on Monday and would be glad to give a seminar later in the week on the talks he had attended at the convention.

The train had come to a stop with a sudden jerk at a station, and he was awakened from his dream. Agnieszka, slumped in her chair with her head on a collection of pillows, slept on. He needed a drink—something alcoholic. He looked at his watch. It was almost time for lunch, and Agnieszka would likely be hungry soon. He remembered the half-empty bottle of Scotch in his brief case, which he had forgotten he had. He poured a generous amount with a dash of water, sat back in his seat again and gazed out the window at the people wandering by on the platform. This was likely Verona—he had missed the station sign, so he could not be sure. He picked up the *Times* and found where he had left off. The train gave a gentle jerk and slowly moved off again. He soon realized he had been engrossed in the newspaper and had missed the station sign again. It was almost certainly Verona.

They were soon out of the city passing farmlands now white with snow. Scattered vineyards were visible in the distance—deserted for the winter. The view was quickly changing as the train moved into mountainous country—the panorama of mountains and valleys of the Dolomite range of the Alps—'the most beautiful mountains in the world' according to an Italian travel brochure. The train would soon be passing through some of the longest railway tunnels in the world, on what was sometimes called the Brenner Railway, so called because of the famous road tunnel. He had read that somewhere near these mountains was the site of one of the most terrible battles of the war—on the mountains of the Cortina d'Amprezzo—between the armies of Italy and Austria. The Austrians had treated their Italian prisoners very badly.

In a small village somewhere in these mountains the painter Titian had been born, and lived to be more than ninety years old. His relaxed, creative life style must have been an important factor in his longevity. The next brief stop, Bolzano, where no one seemed to leave the train and only a few passengers boarded, was brief. There was more snow on the ground and on the platform paths. He could see the breath of the railway attendants and passengers as they moved past the window. The next stops were to be Chiusa and Bressanone, then on through the mountains into Austrian to Innsbruck, the capital of Tyrol. He had read that the train line beyond Brennero was now electrified. There was to be a change of engines and crew before proceeding to Innsbruck. The train would then be pulled by a Class 1670 electric locomotive with a different wheel arrangement, according to a railway brochure in their compartment. He would have an opportunity to examine the engine in Innsbruck, as there was a longer than usual stay. Electrification of the Austrian Federal Railways was still in progress. The advantages of electric engines over this terrain were obvious: better traction on steep grades, the elimination of smoke and cinders in the long tunnels, and less need for artificial ventilation systems.

Agnieszka was awake before they reached Bressanone, and said she wanted to change into something less casual for lunch. She noticed his glass of Scotch, said she was ready for a drink, and accepted his offer to find her a glass of wine. He knew she was not a fan of whiskey. He set off to the lounge car while she changed. The speed of the train had slowed, and Charles could see snow swirls outside the window as they climbed further into a land of winter. He found the choices of wine were limited to Italian varieties, but he knew she had liked *Est! Est! Est!* There were half-bottles available and the bar tender had given him two wine glasses to bring back to the compartment.

"You are looking refreshed after your sleep," he commented as he opened the door of the compartment. She was in a different mood, which she volunteered, was because her abdominal pains had almost gone. She had changed into a skirt with a wide belt and a sweater. He looked at her admiringly. "I am so glad you feel better. I found a half-bottle of that quaint Italian wine we drank one afternoon in Rome." She looked at the label and laughed. "I remember how the waiter explained the reason for the name. I liked it a lot," she added. There would be another thirty minutes before lunch, so they settled with their drinks and watched the white countryside pass by. "I want to hear the rest of Simon's paper—but after lunch. I am sorry I fell asleep as you were reading to me!" Charles laughed at her genuine regret, and shook his head. He promised to read her the rest later.

Agnieszka was silent for several minutes before bringing up a topic that seemed to be foremost on her mind. "I have been thinking of Simon and the business of music criticism as my mind goes back to our Rome experiences. You know I have issues with music critics, and our Welsh friend Simon is no exception. The quality of their critical writing certainly varies. I thought the reviews of my recitals in Rome were generally fair. Of course, I sometimes wonder how much of their reactions were subjective, and how much objective, and how much my being virtually blind influenced their judgement. Sometimes I feel that my poor vision gives me an advantage. I can hear them say, 'considering she is blind she does very well with the difficult Schumann or the Beethoven piece'." She laughed at her comment. "I wonder how Simon has written about my first recital in his *Musical Muse*. He promised to send me a copy."

"I do not think an honest critic would comment in that way on your blindness," Charles replied. "It is possible that an artist's unusual stage personality, such as de Pachmann's, for example, would provoke more adverse criticism than a comment about a disability. If a recital is recorded, it means that unusual physical histrionics that can provide a certain atmosphere in a live performance become hidden. I am looking forward to listening to your tapes of the last recital at the church. If I were a critic I would try to be impartial, be totally open." He thought for a moment. "The music critic's capacity to judge the merits of a performance surely must depend mostly on his general musical education and his capacity to be sensitive. Simon is an example of a music critic who has a good background of keyboard training with seemingly good teaching. Music critics have performance standards that are looked for in artists, which are expected to be met, but these can be no more than the authority of tradition. Simon makes that point in his Beethoven paper. The critic should also be a good writer—able to express and justify what he feels and thinks." He could see she was listening attentively. "Do you think that critical judgement of an artist's piano performance should take into consideration the quality of the piano as well?" she asked. "I believe if the piano is one of exceptionally high quality it deserves to be noted," he replied. She nodded her head in approval.

He decided to change the subject. "Would you like me to read the news in the *Times* to you before lunch? There is likely something about Poland that would interest you." She said she would like that. Charles looked quickly through the middle pages. "There is no political news from Poland, but lots from Berlin, where Hitler is still causing a stir. I see there is an announcement of a London concert on January 17th at the Queen's Hall. A Polish pianist, whose name is Jan Smeterlin, will play the Szymanowski Concerto for Pianoforte and Orchestra. Have you heard of Smeterlin?"

"I have, but have never heard him play. He comes from Bielsko, and he is about forty years old now. He was a child prodigy. I believe he has left Poland and settled in London." Agnieszka seemed deep in thought as she gazed out the window. Turning away she added, "Poor Szymanowski has had health problems. I was told he has tuberculosis –like Chopin. I have not heard the concerto, which I think is new." She paused again. "I wonder why pianists like Smeterlin leave Poland and develop their career elsewhere. Perhaps it is for the money. I admire him for tackling that concerto as I have heard it has a lot of virtuoso passages. I am sure I could never play a piano concerto with orchestra now. I could not see the conductor well enough or get the important entry clues." She looked out the window again and seemed lost in thought.

Charles looked at his watch. "Perhaps we should finish the wine and look in the dining car now to see if lunch is being served. I am feeling hungry."

*** *** *** ***

They enjoyed a light lunch in the dining car while watching the winter scene pass by. They ordered another half-bottle of the *Est! Est! Est!* with their spaghetti and shrimp sauce. Agnieszka said she wanted to talk about music criticism again, so he immediately lost interest in the passing scene outside.

"I keep thinking of Simon and critics again. I have always been surprised at the influence some critics have had over the years—especially in the last century—in regard to new compositions. Instead of being champions of new music of composers such as Brahms, Wagner and Bruckner, they frequently allow their radical and narrow opinions to sway and shape public opinion against them with resultant neglect of their new works. As a result of that attitude the prestige of certain critics fell, and their role in the world of music became questionable." She looked out the window and he wondered how much she could see. "Before long we will be passing through Vienna, the home of the critics Edward Hanslick and Julius Korngold. What a contrast between them! Hanslick liked Brahms but was an anti-Wagnerite, while Korngold was a Wagner promoter. G.B. Shaw in England was another one who could often see little value in the new music of certain composers. Overall, he was not very helpful to his readers, and often failed as an advocate of the composer and artist."

She drank some of her wine as she waited for a reaction from Charles. She decided to continue. "So, do you feel that any critics—of music or of the theatre—have a useful role? People who buy newspapers seem to read what they write—although it is probably a minority. You said earlier if the critic is a good writer as well as being a good judge he deserves to be read."

Charles had been thinking of de Pachmann and the pianist's on-and-off battles with certain American critics as she spoke. "De Pachmann certainly had a low tolerance for critics. Those in New York seemed to be much less accepting of his style than those critics in Boston. Mind you, some Canadian and British critics could be equally cruel. Simon's theory is that when de Pachmann played Beethoven, he played the notes correctly but it did not always sound like Beethoven should. It was Beethoven recreated by de Pachmann—but not in the wonderful way that Liszt was said to have recreated Beethoven. The performer sometimes tries to become more important than the composer!"

The train was slowing as it navigated the curves and the high grades, finally stopping at a small station. "I think they will change engines here at Brenner," he said, as he gazed though the window but he could see she was not interested in railway talk. They would soon be in Innsbruck and he would have a chance to see for himself. They finished the wine, he paid the bill and they made their way back to their compartment.

*** *** *** ***

Days later, on the train from Warsaw to Gdynia, Charles tried to remember the events on the rest of their journey and was surprised that he had seen or noticed so little of the countryside from Innsbruck to Vienna. Much of the Vienna-Kraków section was at night, so they had been sleeping. *En route* to Vienna the train had gone through monotonous tunnels, always emerging into the fading light of the afternoon with panoramic views of snowy mountains and plains—dotted with coniferous trees covered with heavy snow. Perhaps he had forgotten the details because he had been too tired to notice. They were late arriving in Vienna. The train had been delayed for almost an hour in Linz because of a rail switch malfunction. They had spent several hours in the Vienna station but there had been no time to see the city. Agnieszka's mother had been envious—it was her favourite city, and she had been waiting for years to visit again. He had been surprised that border customs and immigration delays had been kept to a minimum. The porter had taken their passports and papers and dealt with the officials while they slept.

Kraków station had been busy at 11:30 in the morning. Snow had been falling for hours before the train arrived. Another train, pulled by a noisy steam locomotive, puffing grey smoke high into the air, was leaving on another track as they arrived. The Lipska family was easy to spot. An excited young blond haired girl embraced Agnieszka as soon as she had stepped onto the platform. Clara was introduced first, then Elizabeth and Adam. Charles was puzzled by Clara, as he was sure Agnieszka had never mentioned having a sister. Perhaps she was a cousin? She looked to be about twelve, and must have skipped school that morning to meet them. It was cold and there was a chilly wind stirring up drifts. Small piles of snow had already collected along the platform. While Agnieszka and Clara walked up the platform toward the station, chattering in Polish, each holding Adam's arms, Elizabeth had come to his rescue, taking his arm and saying, "I want to speak to you—in English of course."

First, she told him he must call her Elizabeth—not Mrs. Lipska! She wanted to tell him how grateful they were that he had agreed to accompany their daughter home. "She could never have done it alone." Elizabeth turned to him and smiled. "I was glad to help under the circumstances," he told her. He had returned her glance and remembered thinking she was just as beautiful as her daughter—just about the same height as Agnieszka, as she gripped his arm. She was wearing a long, heavy light grey winter coat with a fur collar. She had deliberately chosen a slower pace along the platform than the others. "You may have noticed how naïve Agnieszka is, considering her age. Apart from her professional career, she has lived a somewhat solitary life. Did she tell you she was thirty one?" He decided to lie. Yes, she had told him, and he agreed she was naïve but that was an attractive characteristic and had not presented any barriers.

He had replied without thinking. If there were a possible message in his answer, Elizabeth had not reacted. If she had he had missed it. "I think she has lost weight and looks more tired. Did you find her a burden?" No, he hadn't. But he told her of his concern when she fell overboard in the dark. She wanted to hear more about that later. He had not mentioned she had been missing for hours after. He decided he should mention that she had been unwell for several days— seemingly the start of an unusually painful menstrual period. Elizabeth had nodded her head, silently suggesting she understood. He decided not to mention the cataracts. He was curious to know about Clara, and was told she was indeed Agnieszka's younger sister. As what seemed like an afterthought, Elizabeth expressed surprise that neither Agnieszka nor Alexei had told him about their little sister.

They had almost reached the open station door. As they passed the large, grumbling locomotive, its nose pointed toward the station at the end of the track

Charles commented, "I love locomotives, so I want to look at this one for a minute." He noticed she was amused. "I do not mind—we have lots of time," she replied, "the baggage will not be there yet." After they had caught up with the others the baggage did arrived in a few minutes on a carriage pushed by a railway platform employee. Elizabeth led the way to the car park, this time taking her husband's arm.

The brief wait had given him an opportunity to examine the family. Alexei, based on his memory, looked more like Adam, who was tall and slim. Charles had noticed Elizabeth's dark grey eyes and her dark brown hair lightly touched by grey. Her complexion was darker than either of her daughters. Clara looked more like Elizabeth and Agnieszka, than her father. Outside the station it had stopped snowing. A short drive through the old city via Szpitaina Street lead up a snow covered street called Kanonicza, leading eventually to a charming two story Renaissance house set well back from the street and lined by coniferous trees, many laden down with snow. He was in the front seat of the Mercedes and heard Agnieszka say from the back, "this is it—our home, Charles. I hope you will feel welcome." He turned and replied, "I already feel at home with you all. This is wonderful—I am thrilled."

CHAPTER THIRTY-TWO

"Amicitiae nostre memoriam spero sempiternam fore"
"I hope the memory of our love will be everlasting" (Cicero)

The Lipski family seemed determined to make his stay an enjoyable one. At the same time they were occupied in welcoming Agnieszka home, and they did that as well. The luggage had been taken upstairs to the bedrooms. Charles was given Alexei's former bedroom, a spacious room with two of the walls covered in photographs of contemporary pianists, mainly of Polish origin. There was a photo of the pianist Jan Smeterlin as a young man. He was not surprised to find a collection of books Alexei had left behind. He spent some time examining the titles and wondered how many really belonged to Alexei, and how many had been "borrowed".

Within an hour, even before fully unpacking, Agnieszka was downstairs in the lounge, seated at the Pleyel practicing scales and playing fragments from her Rome recitals. He later went to join Clara in the lounge, where she was sitting very attentively in a nearby chair listening to her sister play. She had put on a new dress that Agnieszka had bought for her in Rome. He told her she looked lovely, and she seemed to understand, but her command of English was limited. Elizabeth and Adam could be heard being busy in the kitchen. Agnieszka had asked her father to play the tapes of her last recital for the family, but Adam suggested they do that in the evening when they were less busy, and when their guests had arrived.

Agnieszka's enthusiasm surprised Charles, and she seemed overwhelming at times. She told him she was determined to maximize every hour of his stay in Poland. "You will be leaving in three days!" she reminded him. "I want to show you my beloved Kraków. Perhaps after a few days here you will want to stay!" In fact by Wednesday—after two busy days of sightseeing—Charles remembered thinking perhaps he should stay longer, but it was of course out of the question. He assured them all he would return again—perhaps next year—if he could get time off. He had also been introduced to Olga who was busy in the kitchen helping to prepare dinner. She was the servant woman he had heard about, who came during the day and had a reputation for being an excellent cook.

After a light lunch they decided to shop in the town for snow boots. Charles had not come prepared for snow like this. They had a tasty soup of yoghurt and beetroot called *chodnik litewski,* and then set off by car to a clothing store with Elizabeth at the wheel, stopping *en route* to let Clara return to her school.

Later, while seated on the train to Warsaw early Friday morning, Charles remembered waking early on Tuesday with a headache. He knew why—he had consumed too much wine and vodka the night before. They had listened to the tapes of the final recital before dinner, and everyone was full of praise for Agnieszka's performance. The quality of the tapes was very good, and no one seemed to hear the wrong notes the anonymous Italian critic had heard in the

Beethoven sonata. They were all amused to hear the story of Mussolini's visit to the church and to learn how the Minister of Culture was to be told about the Polish National Anthem on the following day.

Olga and Elizabeth had prepared a veritable feast, which had gone on until close to eleven o'clock. Elizabeth had worn her new dress, and Adam his new shirt and tie. Olga had prepared a hot cucumber soup, called *zupa ogorkowa* to start, followed by *fasolka po bretonsku,* a bean and sausage stew. Finally came Elizabeth's speciality, *sernik,* a desert of raisin-covered, orange-flavoured cheesecake. Charles had earlier suggested the wine he had brought from Italy would go well with the meal, and it did. Three guests had been invited to dine with the family—one of Agnieszka's former music teachers, Alfred Morzychi, and his wife, as well as a young woman called Anna, one of Agnieszka's friends from school. Morzychi appeared to be about seventy years old, but he could still play the piano, and he demonstrated how well he could play Chopin when he gave in to pressure after dinner. Anna, a friend from the school for the blind was able to see to some extent. She was fluent in English, and she and Charles had a long discussion about the pleasures of Rome. She would love to visit some time soon.

Clara and Agnieszka had both retired about ten thirty, as Clara had school in the morning and Agnieszka had said she was very tired. After dinner, he and Elizabeth sat and talked about some of the Kraków sights she and Agnieszka thought he should see. Adam had offered vodka—served ice-cold and neat. He remembered being told by one of them that the city had once been the royal capital of Poland in the Sixteenth Century. "It is without a doubt the most beautiful city in Poland!" one of them had declared. Since Charles had sensible footwear and wearing apparel, it seemed possible they could walk to most of the usual sites they had pointed out to him as they passed in the car in the afternoon. He had decided to buy a warmer winter jacket as well.

Because of the headache, he had gone downstairs to look for some aspirin. He found Elizabeth alone in the kitchen making coffee. She found him some aspirin and began to made toast for breakfast. Clara had already had breakfast, and had left for school. The others were still in bed. They sat in the kitchen at the table and Elizabeth talked about how wonderful Vienna had been to visit, and how much she wanted to see Rome some day. She wanted Charles to describe again in more detail how Agnieszka had fallen into the river, but he tried to abbreviate how she had been treated for her bruises at the hospital in Ostia. The important detail was that the medical staff had been very attentive. The picture he painted was merely a shadow of the real drama, and he hoped his version was not dissimilar to Agnieszka's. It seemed that it was not. Agnieszka had also told her mother about the river incident, as well as her visit to the eye hospital and meeting Professor Cagianno. The professor was to contact her and hopefully she would travel to Warsaw for another opinion.

Elizabeth nodded approval and added, "I have not heard of Professor Zelichowski, but I assume he has a good reputation." She was curious to know if cataract operations were successful in Canada. Charles admitted he had no experience with eye surgery, so he could not say. Elizabeth was also curious about the prolonged abdominal pain. "I know it is not your speciality, but what do you think of the doctor's finding at the hospital, and Agnieszka's unusually painful menstrual period?" She looked worried as she asked. He paused before answering and drank the last of his coffee. He was deliberately vague but tried to be reassuring. "I think she will need to consult her doctor here, who might refer her to a specialist for another opinion. It may be a common fibroid of the uterus or an ovarian cyst." Elizabeth looked at him now with an amused expression. "Did you find it odd that the doctor thought she might be pregnant?" He smiled back, and told her about his initial reaction of surprise, but being assured by Agnieszka that she had not missed a period. "The doctor did not do a complete examination, so he likely guessed that a pregnancy was the most common cause of such a swelling in a young woman!"

Elizabeth had offered him another cup of coffee, which he accepted. She rose and walked to the coffee pot. He noticed she was wearing a snug dressing gown that displayed her youthful figure and attractive legs. He had dreamed about a woman like her last night, and it was the woman's beautiful legs that he seemed to remember most. He had wondered earlier about her age when he first saw her at the train station. She walked back to the table, stood and poured coffee into his cup. He could sense her close presence and caught a trace of the cologne she was wearing. He was thinking again how attractive she was, and wondered if she was being deliberately seductive. She touched his shoulder lightly with her free hand and said in a soft voice, "I think you were very kind to Agnieszka. I like you and I understand why Agnieszka was attracted to you." He could feel himself flush, and heard himself say, "I think you are a very beautiful woman Elizabeth. Adam is a very lucky man." She had not moved her hand from his shoulder and had replied in a whisper, "unfortunately, Adam is not interested in me—not sexually, I mean. He is almost ten years older than me, his health is poor and that is why he withholds his libido from me." Charles was surprised. He was aware of feeling aroused, and temporarily speechless, but he knew what he should say in response—something he suspected she would want to hear.

He looked up and fixed his eyes on hers. "I am sure that Adam loves you. You are a very attractive woman and very hospitable." He could now feel her left hand pressing more intensely on his shoulder. Later he had doubts about what she had said as she lowered her voice; "Perhaps some night before you leave—I can visit you, or perhaps we can go for a ride outside the city—alone." She removed her hand, slowly moved away and sat across from him at the table. She was looking more serious as she leaned forward fixed him in the eye and whispered, "I would like that very much—would you?" He looked toward the kitchen door to be sure there was no one near. "I must think of Agnieszka—it would not be fair. She would be devastated if she knew we had...." He did not finish his response. Elizabeth made a face, sighed and stood to leave. "I know. It makes me feel guilty suggesting that to you. I hardly know you. Now I must get dressed. We have some sight seeing to do today." She smiled again and walked toward the door. She turned and he heard her ask, "And how is your headache?"

*** *** *** ***

Agnieszka had not been feeling well. Her abdominal pain had kept her awake for part of the night. She did not want breakfast because she felt bloated and nauseated. Charles had gone up to her room at Elizabeth's request, and had carefully examined her abdomen while she lay on the bed. The hard mass, which he had not felt before, was easily palpable. It seemed to be fixed, and she said the area was tender. She looked paler than usual too, but her pulse was normal and she had not seemed febrile. She said her menstrual period had started yesterday, but he suspected this pain was not simply dysmenorrhea. He looked at her in silence, thinking about the best advice he could give. She had reached for his examining hand and held tight. "What do you think Charles? Is it serious?" she asked. "I am frightened—afraid of the unknown. I have never had a period like this before. That swelling worries me too." He was conscious of how tightly she was gripping his hand and how anxious she looked. He turned to look at Elizabeth who had been standing at the foot of the bed. She was looking very worried.

Turning back to Agnieszka and looking her in the eye he replied, "Yes, I am worried about this swelling, so I think your mother should call your family doctor to see if arrangements can be made for you to be seen soon by a gynaecologist—perhaps today." He heard her mother say, "I agree. I will call doctor Runowski's office right away. She is always very obliging," as she left to go down stairs. He was left alone to deal with Agnieszka's obvious anxiety. He was seated on the bed, and leaned forward to kiss her on the nose. She had released his hand and he felt her arms encircle his neck and hold him tightly. He did not speak for a moment. "I am very worried," she had whispered. He could see there were tears in her eyes.

"I know you are. I promise to stay with you through all this. You will not be alone. We do not know the cause of the pain or how serious this swelling is. It is a concern, and it is important for you to be examined properly at the hospital, but you must try to be strong and not be alarmed. Your mother is calling your family doctor to arrange the visit." She reacted in a loud voice; "I do not like Doctor Runowski much. She has seen me numerous times in the past and always seems to be more interested in my eyes than in me as a person." Charles smiled and responded, "That is a common complaint that patients make of doctors and there are many explanations. You can be sure today that your illness will be treated not simply as a disease. We will make sure you are kept informed of the findings." Elizabeth had appeared again with the news that the doctor was not in the office but her secretary had promised to contact the chief of gynaecology at the hospital and request an early appointment. "I think you should stay in bed for a while longer," Charles suggested. "Have you taken any aspirin for pain lately?" She shook her head.

He looked at Elizabeth. "Can you find some more aspirin? If you do not have many left, we may need to go to the chemist for more." Elizabeth said she did have a bottle in the kitchen, and went to find it.

Charles stayed with Agnieszka for hours awaiting the telephone call from Doctor Runowski. She was able to sleep for almost an hour. Finally, just before noon the doorbell rang, and Runowski was escorted upstairs to Agnieszka's room. Charles had decided to stay in his bedroom and await the verdict. As he suspected, a decision had been made to have her seen today at the hospital. A consultation had been arranged with the head of the gynaecology service at three thirty. Doctor Angèle Runowski, an efficient, slim, middle-aged woman with a short-cut blond hairdo, had been introduced before she left again for her office. Charles followed Elizabeth into the kitchen and she summarised briefly the doctor's opinion. The doctor had been mystified and agreed about the need for an urgent opinion.

The next two days had been stressful for the family. Agnieszka had been seen that afternoon, examined, and a decision had been made to have an exploratory operation on Friday, the day he was to leave for Gdynia. She was admitted to the hospital. He had not met the gynaecologist but Elizabeth—who had stayed with Agnieszka—had been told by the specialist that the swelling was likely an ovarian tumour or cyst, and must be removed. Agnieszka's spirits were low and knowing the decision, she spent a lot of the afternoon in tears. She said she was very disappointed to be missing the organ recital on Thursday evening, but she was glad they would be going. Finally an injection of morphine had settled her pain and she fell asleep again. Charles and Elizabeth both stayed in her hospital room and offered whatever comfort seemed appropriate. Adam was waiting at home when they arrived. He needed a drive to the academy of music, where he had arranged earlier to examine three pianos that were out of tune.

The gynaecologist's differential diagnosis had seemed a pessimistic one— possible ovarian cancer — but he had told Elizabeth her daughter was unusually young for that diagnosis. That did offer some hope, and a decision had been made between the two that Agnieszka not be told the possible diagnosis.

Charles and Elizabeth had spent many happy hours talking about de Pachmann, Alexei's problem, Agnieszka's wish to travel to Canada, and who would now manage her professional career. Elizabeth had told him she had found the conversations helpful in keeping her mind off Agnieszka's surgery. A lot of snow had continued to fall and the roads were often slippery, but on Thursday morning and afternoon the two of them had managed to see some of the sights on foot—the Town Hall, the Sixteenth Century Gothic Basilica of the Virgin Mary, the Jewish Quarter—the two of them slipping and crawling while holding one another arm-in-arm. In the evening, he had seen Agnieszka alone, and said an emotional goodbye. They agreed to meet again before long—perhaps in Canada—and to write often.

Before he left she had something to say. She had remembered Helen Keller's famous comment about dying. Charles had been surprised to discover the theme of the quote after she had recited it to him. She seemed to remember every word. He had not heard it before. He could remember how she had fo-cused her grey eyes on his face, and had gripped his hand as she had slowly and softy spoken the words. The message had left him speechless and he had been aware of a lump in his throat that had refused to go away until he had left the hospital.

In the evening, Elizabeth had driven him and Adam to the organ recital in the nearby suburb, the name of which he could not remember. He could not con-centrate on the music, as wonderful as it was. They all agreed on the way home that they had felt the same. Early on Friday morning there had been a short drive to the railway station. Before leaving the house he had said goodbye to Clara and Adam, who were still in pyjamas, and a final emotional farewell to Eliza-beth—in the car outside the station—before he collected his bags from the trunk. Charles insisted Elizabeth not come to the ticket office or the train platform with him and she reluctantly agreed. It was a very cold morning. As he was leaving she handed him a letter and suggested he not read it until after reaching his ship in Gydnia. He was curious but placed it in his jacket pocket. As he prepared to walk to the train he turned to return the kiss that Elizabeth had thrown him through the open car window.

At that moment he was again struck by her beauty—so like her equally beautiful daughter. He suspected this to be merely a small part of this unique woman's character.

CHAPTER THIRTY-THREE

"Est amantium irae amoris integration?"
(Are the quarrels of lovers the renewal of love?)

Friday, January 27th. Maria Pilchner, one of two pursers on the liner *S.S. Scanyork* of the American Scantic Line, had been assigned to cabins on the second deck for this voyage. She had just finished recording in her logbook the list of the thirty-six occupants in the deluxe staterooms on her deck. She glanced at her wristwatch and noted it was almost 19:30 hours and remembered that the single occupant of Cabin 266, a middle aged man named Flemming—a doctor, according to his Canadian passport—had requested a wake-up call before dinner. He had arrived on the ship looking exhausted and had told her in English that he needed a nap before dinner. The ship, already at sea, had left Gdynia two hours ago bound for Copenhagen, Halifax and Philadelphia. She could hear the familiar throb and feel the vibrations of the engines under her feet as she made her way down the corridor to 266. She heard no response to her two knocks and tried the door, which was unlocked. The cabin was in darkness. She pressed the switch for the nightlight and could see her passenger was still lying on his berth. She called his name softly and he immediately raised his head with a start.

"Doctor Flemming, this is Maria. You asked to be called before dinner. It is now almost 19:30 hours." She added, "Is there anything I can get you before dinner? Or perhaps you would prefer dinner in your cabin?"

He did not respond to her questions; his head had fallen back on the pillow. Maria had worked with the American Scantic Line for almost ten years and had seen many passengers in various stages of seasickness and sometimes alcohol intoxication from excesses at dinner or at the ship's bar. She decided it was best to turn on the cabin light to allow better examination of her guest and she did. She raised her voice. "I hope you do not mind the light sir but you seem unwell." The extra light allowed her to see immediately that although he was awake and staring at the ceiling, his eyes were red and swollen from crying. Without turning his head he replied, "I am sorry Maria but I do not feel like eating dinner tonight." He paused and added, "I am not seasick and will be fine in the morning. Thank you."

She wondered later why she had been so personal as to ask him the reason he had been crying. It was not unusual for her to see passengers cry after leaving family and friends behind on the wharf but this man's look of extreme sadness seemed to go beyond a few tears of separation from friends. He was travelling with a Canadian passport so he would not likely be leaving family behind. She remembered that she had quietly sat down on a chair near his berth while waiting for his next response, which was not immediate. She had waited patiently—perhaps too long—and had wondered if he might think she was being too inquisitive. She had considered asking him the same question again. But she did not have to ask again. She watched as he slowly sat up and moved his bare feet over the side of the berth onto the floor. He was wearing the plain white dressing gown with the Scantic Line logo on the pocket—provided to occupants of first class cabins. His hair was a mess and her immediate thought was that she should later suggest he visit Boris, the barber, tomorrow on the third deck. He moved with ease from his bed and she decided he was not intoxicated.

He ran his fingers through his hair as if he had read her mind. "You are very kind and I apologize for looking such a mess. I have received a letter today with some information that has made me very depressed."

For the next ten minutes she had listened as he related an obviously abbreviated story of his travels over the past two weeks: his meeting a Polish woman in Rome and how they had become lovers. He had just spent almost three days in Kraków with her parents. He already knew there were some things about the family, which were different. However, there was one he had not suspected. An older brother had a reputation for stealing books, which he knew about before. There was also a much younger sister whom he had not heard of before arriving at the train station in Kraków. She remembered he paused several times to blow his nose before continuing. "Before leaving Poland, this woman and I agreed to meet again—in Canada. She is a professional pianist and I had offered to help arrange a concert tour in my country. It seemed like such a logical arrangement. Her mother handed me a letter before I said good-bye. She had suggested I read the letter after settling on the ship." He shook his head and looked directly at her. "It was bad news. I do not want to tell you what it said. In fact, I have read the letter three times already and still cannot fully fathom what it means."

There was an awkward silence and Maria Pilchner knew it was time to leave. "I understand. I will bring you a light dinner from the galley. It will save you having to get dressed and having to face the other passengers." He smiled and nodded his head. "Yes, perhaps that would be best – in about an hour. A glass of red wine would be nice." She rose from her chair, promised to return in about an hour and quietly left the cabin.

He looked about the room and spent a few minutes getting his bearings. He was suddenly aware that he needed to use the toilet and for a brief moment was not sure where he had seen the toilet door. He had not unpacked his suitcases, which he had hastily parked in the far corner. He needed to find his toothbrush and paste. He had not brushed his teeth since having breakfast with the Lipskas in Kraków. He was aware of the gentle movement of the ship as she moved further into the deeper waters of the Baltic Sea. Looking briefly in the toilet mirror he was shocked at his appearance. His hair needed cutting and he looked old and depressed. He decided he needed a shower. It might clear away the cobwebs and help sort out his state of mind.

A warm shower and shampoo did have a therapeutic effect and he returned to the stateroom, in the dressing gown, found a chair and began to think. He could not rid his mind of that wretched letter. He had left it in the inside pocket of his jacket. Perhaps if he read it again more slowly it would make more sense. He got up, retrieved it and returned to his chair. He regretted not asking Maria for a cocktail before dinner but he remembered he had bought a bottle of Scotch in Kraków and had stowed it somewhere. But where had he packed it? A brief search was successful and he had soon settled again with a generous glass of Scotch and water.

He opened the letter and began to read. It had been hand written by Agnieszka's mother yesterday, the day before he had left on the train: 'Dear Charles; I hesitated for a long time before writing this letter. Adam and I discussed the matter on several occasions and finally agreed that it was important to give you more background information about our unfortunate family. You will find some details upsetting and we apologize for that. It seemed easier to write the details in a letter than to give you the details face to face. I know Agnieszka has told you about Alexei's problem and you know about her unfortunate malady. The blindness has been a challenge to both Adam and Agnieszka but they have coped very well I think. Agnieszka in particular has risen above the blindness and has made a great success of her musical career. But our lives have been challenged by yet another problem—one you know nothing about and this is the subject of my letter.

'When you arrived at the train station in Kraków, I could see you were surprised to meet Clara and now I know that Agnieszka had not told you about her. That was an error in judgement but no surprise to us. Clara has been raised from birth as our daughter but the truth is she is Agnieszka's child. Agnieszka does not seem to remember this and we feel it would be better if she forgot forever. When Agnieszka became pregnant with Clara she was almost twenty-one years old, still surprisingly naïve and obviously vulnerable despite her age. She had by then lost a lot of her vision and was struggling to develop her career in music with the help of her music teachers. Without our knowledge she became easy prey to one of her teachers and became pregnant at a weekend party. She had become intoxicated and remembered very little of the event. It was our belief that intercourse occurred only on this one occasion. If so, she was very unlucky. It was four months later that we discovered the pregnancy. Agnieszka did not realize herself what had happened. We considered laying a rape charge but it was too late and it would have caused a lot of agony for us. An abortion in our religious community was out of the question. Agnieszka has lived in a state of denial over the past ten years. I think she really believes now that Clara is our daughter.

'As a psychiatrist you will know more about the dynamics of such situations than we do. You may have a plausible explanation for her failure to tell you about "her little sister". She did buy Clara a dress in Rome and I think you were aware of that. We saw that you have a very close relationship—a loving one it seems—one that we hope will develop further if that is your wish. There was talk of you helping to arrange a concert tour of Canada for her sometime in the future. We would be very supportive of your plans. We also appreciate your interest in her health—her gynaecological problem. The cause will hopefully be clarified in a day or two. Thank you for being so helpful when she became ill and had to be taken to the hospital. The possibility of surgery for the cataracts will have to wait. I will keep you informed about any decisions.

'Needless to say, we have not told Agnieszka about this letter and I suspect you will want to keep it a secret. As a psychiatrist, you will use your clinical judgement here. When Clara was born we arranged for Agnieszka to see a family friend—a retired psychiatrist. He advised us not to attempt to have her assume the role of mother of Clara because she was in a state of denial. Those were his words. She did not help chose her baby's name and we have insulated her from any decisions regarding Clara's upbringing. Coming from the Freudian school of psychiatry our friend believed that the subconscious mind could not distinguish between memories and imagination. He hoped her memory of the events would remain repressed. We are not sure they have.

'Again I want to apologize for the manner we have chosen to tell you these things. We certainly enjoyed your brief stay with us and we hope to see you again before too long. Thank you again for bringing the wine from Italy. We enjoyed it very much and since there are still a lot of bottles left we will continue to do so. Thank you especially for the precious but all too short moments we spent together. May you have a safe and smooth crossing to Canada. Sincerely yours, Elizabeth.'

He folded the letter and leaned back in the chair and closed his eyes. He could now make more sense of the letter than he had before. He no longer felt a need to cry. Elizabeth had given him the letter that morning as they said goodbye at the train station. She had suggested he read it on the ship. He sipped his Scotch and began the process of analyzing what he had read now for the fourth time. He was not very familiar with child psychiatry but he remembered that memory loss in survivors of early sexual abuse, in contrast to simply forgetting, could reflect a strategy of dissociation—of avoidance—developed to reduce distress over the event. In such cases, avoidance behaviour became virtually permanent so that traumatic memories remained totally hidden and profoundly inaccessible to ordinary memory. He had heard of cases of what was known as psychogenic amnesia. The subconscious defence mechanisms were likely the same.

He found himself regretting this type of analysis. The constancy of love was being challenged here—as it had in Kraków—such as he had never experienced before. He was struggling to salvage some understanding out of this new information about the woman he was convinced he loved. There had been times on the train to Warsaw earlier in the morning when he believed his relationship with Elizabeth had been a dream but it had not.

The Scotch was having a relaxing effect and he decided to put the letter aside and to unpack his suitcases. This cabin would be his home for the next week. Running his fingers through his hair he realized it was still not dry so he returned to the toilet to find a dry towel. Within fifteen minutes he had emptied his cases, hung up his clothes and was feeling at home. The cabin had the look of being recently refurbished. The ship, built in 1919 had been converted to a cargo and passenger vessel just a year before, with accommodation for seventy-two passengers. The walls looked recently painted in an orange colour; the carpet looked relatively new and the toilet fixtures also. There were twin beds and two portholes but when he pulled the curtain and looked out all he saw was pitch darkness. The moon was not visible. The ship was now rolling noticeably more than it had before and the vibration of the engines was just perceptible. He had no concern about seasickness. On the crossing from Halifax on the *SS Montrose* there had been high seas but he had not had any problems with seasickness, appearing at the dining room for every meal even when many of the passengers were unable to leave their rooms.

Within an hour he was feeling very much more relaxed and was toying with the idea of writing a response to Elizabeth. If he wrote it now along with a letter to Agnieszka he could mail it in Halifax in about two weeks. His plans were interrupted by a knock on the door. He answered and found Maria standing in the corridor holding a tray covered with a white napkin. "Please come in Maria. You are very kind and just in time too."

She had laid the tray on his desk and removed the napkin. He could see on a plate a small green salad with sliced tomatoes with a glass of red wine but nothing else. She could tell he was surprised. "I did this on purpose Doctor Flemming. I brought you only a salad because I want you to finish the rest of your dinner in the dining room with the others. The first serving has just about begun. So have your drink and eat your salad before you join the other passengers."

His first reaction was to put up a stubborn refusal to do any such thing, but he slowly saw her strategy. He smiled and laid his hand on her shoulder. She was not more than five feet tall. "You are right. I will do just that. Thank you. I will be there in about half an hour."

Maria made a quick exit and Charles realized he did have an appetite. The salad was tasty and the wine was dry and fruity. He changed into a suit and tie, drank the last of the wine as he moved toward the cabin door to find his way up the corridor to the dining room on the main deck. He was surprised to find that a large number of passengers had already assembled there and appeared ready to start the first course. There was a noisy buzz of conversation, some in English but mostly in what he assumed was Polish. A man who seemed to be the head waiter greeted him with a friendly smile, asked in English for his cabin number and directed him to a table set for six.

There were already two couples who appeared to have completed their first course. Introductions were made. One women and her husband were Canadian, returning to Halifax and the other couple Polish. They were travelling to Winnipeg to live. He had enjoyed their conversation. The main course had been a *Pierogi*—a dumpling filled with potatoes, meat and cheese—followed by a desert called *Babka*, a raisin-covered sugary cake. A red wine from Bulgaria, which Maria had brought him earlier, went well with the main course. He had begun to feel tired again and apologized for not staying to talk after coffee. The ship was rolling more than earlier as he walked back to his cabin. Maria had been back, tidied his things and turned down his bed sheets. He sat in the easy chair and closed his eyes. He remembered he had decided to write a letter to the family. In his desk he found writing material and envelopes:

"Friday, Jan. 27/1933

"Dear Agnieszka, Elizabeth, Adam and Clara;

"I am writing this on the high seas about four hours out of Gdynia. I have just returned to my cabin after an excellent dinner of typical Polish fare.

"I have addressed the letter to you all and expect Elizabeth will translate it and read it to Adam and Clara. By the time you receive it, you should have some good news to report after Agnieszka's operation.

"I wish I could describe in detail my many impressions of your country, viewed from the window of my train today, but that will have to wait for another occasion. The views were fascinating. A large part of the countryside looked asleep under a heavy blanket of snow. It was a long journey but not at all unpleasant. The train was comfortable, the staff very efficient and kind. I had lots of time to read, to think and to sleep. I decided I should write a paper for publication based on my talk I gave in Rome so I spent several hours on that. I developed a taste for vodka while staying with you and the bar on the train was well supplied. I enjoyed my brief stop in Warsaw with a good onward connection. It is a city that from the train window pales in comparison to Kraków. You will not be surprised to hear that.

"The ship was late leaving port tonight, partly because stormy weather had delayed its arrival from Helsingfors earlier in the day and also because our train had been delayed by a heavy snowfall between Warsaw and Gdynia. I am hoping the winter weather will not mean a stormy crossing to Halifax. I am pleased to report that I have been well cared for by the ship's crew. A young Polish woman, whose name is Maria Pilchner, has made sure my stateroom is neat and tidy. It has two portholes but there is nothing to see at this hour—just pitch darkness.

"I will always have fond memories of my brief stay with you all in Kraków. You could not have been more hospitable. I enjoyed meeting and getting to know the family. Thank you for showing me the sights of your beautiful city. I am sorry Agnieszka could not share the visits we made to the sites. I would hate to have missed the organ recital last evening, even though my thoughts were with her. Combined with my stay in Rome and my travels with Agnieszka, the experience has been truly wonderful. Thank you once again."

He paused to read what he had written. He reread it twice and decided not to finish it now but to sign it later. He checked the time and found it was after eleven thirty. It seemed time to turn in.

*** *** *** *** ***

Over the next few days he realized despite his earlier determination to remain completely non-clinical in his dealings with Agnieszka, the woman to whom he had professed his love, he saw his efforts had come to naught. His present state of mind did not allow him to do anything other than accept the truth. She had not been a virgin as she said—or perhaps believed. Their relationship could have and should have been much less complex. He felt helpless to do anything about it at this time. He had written a letter but he had taken care to be discreet. Here he was at sea—far removed from the loving but also tragic family he had learnt to know in Kraków. He remembered the strong bond he had felt with her mother, Elizabeth. Perhaps it had been their similarity in age—the wisdom of experience—but he had sensed something stronger—a sexual attraction that in the beginning had seemed inappropriate to pursue.

His contacts with Adam had been more intellectual than emotional. His English was limited but he and Elizabeth had spent hours discussing Polish politics, the poor state of their economy, the rise in anti-Semitism in Poland as well as in Germany and the threat of resurgence of German aggression. Adam had told him that the Polish Catholic Church appeared to legitimize prejudice towards Jews and it was not an isolated phenomenon but a reflection of overall Church attitude in other Catholic countries in Europe. Church leaders were also concerned about the rise of Communism, Liberalism and Free Masonry. He had not seen Alexei who had not returned from France and for that he was thankful.

He found Clara to be a dear little girl, who had seemingly escaped the retinitis pigmentosa family scourge of failing vision, but was totally in the dark about her true parents. That should forever remain a secret. He was now finding it easier to judge the Rome experience as a disaster, which he could have avoided. How easily we rationalize events when we look back over our life's journeys, casually passing by the largely invisible road signs along the way. His had been a journey with excessive emotional baggage, sometimes with difficult travelling companions.

Somewhere along the way he had become lost – made the wrong turn. Charles Flemming, Professor of Psychiatry, was now leaving the shores of Poland thinking more like an analytical psychiatrist than a tempestuous and committed lover he had seemed to be days before.

EPILOGUE

"Death is no more than passing from one room into another. But there's a difference for me you know because in that other room I shall be able to see."
(Helen Keller 1950)

The *SS Scanyork* took almost two weeks crossing from Gdynia to Halifax, Nova Scotia, at no more than twelve knots per hour. There had been a brief stop in Copenhagen to take on several passengers and freight. The winter Atlantic was sometimes stormy—stormy enough to reduce his enthusiasm for the dining room. But Charles was proud to say he had not been seasick. Most of his hours during the day were spent seated at his desk in Cabin 266. He read, wrote several drafts of his paper on the differential diagnosis of the Obsessive-Compulsive Disorder and the Obsessive-Compulsive Personality and he set time aside to think and meditate. There were some important references that he needed for the paper but he could find those before giving the draft to his secretary for typing. His plan was to submit the paper to the *Canadian Medical Association Journal*. He re-read the travel book on Poland as well as the issues of the London *Times* again in considerable detail—the court circular, marriages and deaths, books of the week reviews, weather forecasts, the concert schedules, shipping news and other insignificant details. He noted the *SS Montrose* was to sail from Southampton on the 27th! He could have caught it if he had left Rome earlier.

Many hours were spent ruminating about his life experiences and rehearsing recent and past encounters and their effects on his present attitude to love and relationships. He dredged up his recent dreams and tried to relive those of Agnieszka's that she had told him about but he could not always interpret the symbolism in hers or his based on Freud's theories. Their details seemed to fit real life events but at the time were sometimes complex. He retraced more than once his visits to Moses and the Church of Saint Peter in Chains in Rome because it drew him closer to Freud and his work on analysis. He resolved to read again Freud's paper *Observations on Transference Love*. His recent experience had led him to suspect that he himself had fallen in love with Agnieszka because of transference. But didn't most love relationships arise from transference? Perhaps—but with the exception of love of parents—especially his mother and dear sister, Sarah. His love for Anne seemed to be different too—no memory of transference there. He promised himself when he got back to Toronto he must do something he hadn't done for several years—visit Anne's gravesite. It had been thirteen years since she died. For that matter he should drive to Farmington to visit his family's graves as well. He could not remember the last time he had visited.

On January 29th, the first Sunday at sea, he found himself that morning after breakfast in the ship's chapel seated alone with his head bowed, quietly saying a prayer for Agnieszka. It was she who monopolized his thoughts. At her hospital bed on Thursday, the day before he left, she was sleepy from the sedation but he had tried to make the point that all our lives have their share of disappointment, pain and sickness. Although pain and discomfort can be unrelenting, for many it was fear that was worse to bear. She told him again that she was afraid of what the surgeon would find but he could tell she had found the morphine injections a great relief for fear and pain. They had each shed tears before he said a final goodbye. He was going to attend the organ recital that evening. She had told him she was sorry they had not made love since leaving Rome. He had said that he would relive what they had shared and there would be other times. As he finally rose to leave, she surprised him by wanting to recite a quotation of Helen Keller, whom she knew something about.

He remembered how she had held his hand, opened her eyes wide and in a slow voice whispered, "Helen Keller once said, 'walking with a friend in the dark is better than walking alone in the light'. " He knew what she meant and he was choked with emotion and moved closer leaning over the bed to grasp her in his arms—for what seemed like ages. He could feel her try to return his hug as well, but she did not have the same strength. He remembered kissing her on the lips and whispering in her ear, "I am so glad I could walk with you in the light and the dark—even if only for a few days. I love you and will never forget you. Everything will be all right." As he walked down the stairs to the ground floor he tried to justify the rightness of his comments. He feared he would never see her again. His strong suspicion was that she might have a malignant tumour of the ovary. If she did, her prognosis would depend on the degree of spread. In his meditations in the quiet of his cabin he remembered those very last moments and often found himself saying a prayer for her recovery and for her family. He later reread his unfinished letter to the family, added only a few words at the end, put it in an envelope and sealed it. He would mail it from Halifax.

He made new friends at different dining tables and in the lounge. Sometimes they exchanged addresses. After dinner, he enjoyed sitting in the music room where he listened to the elderly black American gentleman named Oscar play popular tunes and some classics on a white piano— with remarkably few wrong notes. Sometimes he would have too many drinks of Scotch and would doze for brief periods in his chair. He would finally say good night and slowly make his way back to Cabin 266. He always slept well. On calmer days, he put on his new winter coat and ventured on deck—usually walking alone but sometimes with his new friends. When he was walking alone he could meditate—sometimes on a single thought. Sometimes he tried to remove all thoughts from his head completely. He spent hours gazing over the horizon and was always surprised that he had seen no other ships passing at a distance. But he knew it was a large ocean.

Maria Pilchner became a good friend. She attended to his needs with a surprising commitment. She saw that the cabin was neat and tidy. She liked to talk during her visits and even after her chores had been completed. In their conversations he found her very affectionate. Did she understand his issues based on the first night on board? He sometimes wondered if he was interested in her as a lover. But he suspected the Scandia Line would have strict rules about that. She told him she had been married but her husband, an officer in the Polish army, had lost his life in the 1920 war with Russia. They had no children, so she was alone. He was amused to hear her say she found Halifax rather uninteresting but she said the ship did not often stay in port more than twelve hours. Philadelphia was another matter. There she had found Polish friends with whom she spent time ashore.

The SS Scanyork docked in Halifax on the afternoon of February 11th, and after saying goodbye to Maria and other crew he had met, he cleared Customs and Immigration and walked with his luggage to the Nova Scotia Hotel, where he checked in for the night. It was cold with snow on the ground. At the nearby Canadian National Railways' station he was able to book a sleeper on the Ocean Limited for the next morning. He would be in Montreal on the following morning. He attempted to telephone Kraków from his room but he was reminded by the operator that there was a seven-hour time difference—meaning the family would now be asleep. He and Elizabeth had exchanged telephone numbers when they said goodbye at the railway station. Perhaps in the morning he would try again.

After dinner he felt he needed a walk. The temperature had dropped considerably. He remembered his way around the docks from the day he had left last year. He found a mailbox and posted his letter. It would take a few weeks to reach there. He set off on foot and made his way along Lower Water Street. He could see the docks were busy. The SS Scanyork had not yet finished unloading. Passing Pier 27, he was surprised to find his old ship, the SS Montrose, loading freight at the floodlit wharf. A stevedore taking a break for a smoke told him she had arrived today from Saint John, New Brunswick. She was preparing to leave for Glasgow and Liverpool in the morning—leaving with Lisa Johansen—his exciting wireless operator friend!

He walked slowly to the foot of the ship's gangplank and debated for several minutes if he should ask permission to come aboard and ask for her. He knew what would happen. But hadn't he had enough of impulsive love making for a while? The words of a respected and elderly clinical psychiatrist friend, that he often directed to his perplexed patients, echoed in his head: 'Take cognisance of reality and postpone gratification!' Somewhat reluctantly, he made a decision to walk away. Turning his head once more to take a final glance in the direction of the gangplank, he made his way slowly back to the hotel.

The train to Montreal was almost an hour late arriving because of snowdrifts in northern New Brunswick. He barely made his train connection to Toronto, finally arriving home about four o'clock in the afternoon. He was exhausted. Uppermost in his mind was the telephone call to Poland, which he had not been able to make before leaving Halifax, or in Montreal. Elizabeth answered the telephone and he knew immediately she had sad news. Their connection was poor but he was able to hear her news. The pathology report had confirmed the diagnosis of ovarian cancer. Unfortunately, the tumour had spread so the prognosis was very poor.

He had been listening with increasing dread to the details of the medical report: "Agnieszka has not been told the truth at this stage. She is still in hospital being treated for a peritoneal infection. Her gynaecologist has assured her that the treatment will allow her to come home very soon. We are devastated, as you can imagine. Adam has been very quiet—not talking and looking depressed. Clara has been kept in the dark but feels very sorry for her sister's problem. I try to keep a level head and see her every day. I wish you were here but that is unrealistic. She has written you a letter with my help. It should reach you in a few weeks."

He was waiting for an opportunity to comment. "I feel terrible Elizabeth. I wish I could be there too. Your letter was a great shock. It made he rethink the meaning of my love for her but please believe me, I still do. Please tell her you have spoken to me and I will be writing to her as often as I can. Please tell her I miss her and I love her."

"I will do that. As you can imagine, she has been thinking a lot about her future. We called Professor Zelichowski's office in Warsaw and explained the situation. She plans to have the consultation as soon as she recovers but ... we shall see. Alexei has returned from Paris and has cancelled the recitals he had planned for her in March. That is about all the news—not happy news I am afraid." The telephone reception was getting worse so he briefly said goodbye and promised to write. She said she would do the same.

He did keep his promise and wrote a letter every week—usually on Sundays. Agnieszka wrote often as well—letters full of optimism and memories—especially memories. She had now returned home but was spending most of the days in bed. She was taking medication for pain. She never mentioned her prognosis. Some days she was able to go down stairs to play her piano. Her favourite piece was the Myra Hess arrangement of Bach's *Jesu, Joy of Man's Desiring*. He loved to read her letters but soon the letters were always from her mother's hand.

On the morning of May 23rd, he answered the telephone and heard Elizabeth's voice with the final news—he had lost his dear friend. He was not surprised.

"At about three in the morning she stopped breathing and died peacefully in her sleep. On the previous evening she had been lucid and knew she was dying. She told us she wanted you to have the tapes of her final recital. Before going back to sleep she had said to me, 'tell Charles'."

He found it hard to speak but offered his sympathies to her and the family and said he would write soon. He replaced the receiver and tried to remain calm. He looked at his schedule for the day, called his secretary at the office and told her the news. She suggested he cancel all his appointments for a few days. He did not object. He wondered how to deal with the tapes. Perhaps a local record company would be interested. But he had a burning urge to keep them himself until he had listened to them again and again until he had memorized each piece. Then perhaps he would publish them in memory of Agnieszka.

Two weeks later, he received a long letter from Elizabeth written after the funeral with more details of Agnieszka's final days, a comment on the cold weather and how they were coping. Inside was a copy of Agnieszka's obituary from the local newspaper. Elizabeth had written a translation for him:

"**Lipska, Agnieszka Maria.** 1900-1933, well known pianist and composer. Elizabeth and Adam Lipska announce with profound sadness the death of their eldest daughter on May 23 after a short illness. Agnieszka was born in Kraków on September 12, 1900. At an early age she had shown signs of a promising musical talent but by the age of five had already shown early signs of failing vision from retinitis pigmentosa. Nevertheless, at the age of seven, she was enrolled at the Academy of Music under Madame Maria Zimmerman and made her local debut at age ten at the Academy playing a programme of music of Liszt, Chopin, Brahms and Szymanowski to considerable acclaim. She enjoyed composing miniature pieces for piano and at her debut played her 'Polonaise' as an encore. Over the years, she studied under several other prominent music teachers at the Kraków School for the Blind, including Alfred Morzychi. In 1929, at the peak of her career, she was awarded the Chopin Gold Medal from the Polish Friends of Chopin. Although she had been encouraged to enter the Warsaw International Chopin Competition she never did because she did not believe in the philosophy of piano competitions.

"Despite her marked loss of vision, Agnieszka's piano repertoire was extensive and included Bach, Scarlatti, Haydn, Beethoven, Mozart, Brahms, Schumann and several contemporary Polish composers. However, her first love was the solo piano pieces of Chopin and her idol was the now deceased Ukrainian pianist, Vladimir de Pachmann, at one time the undisputed greatest interpreter of Chopin's piano music. In January of this year she gave a series of recitals in Rome, one of which was an all-Chopin programme, which she dedicated to the memory of Mr. de Pachmann. Her final recital was recorded by Radio Rome and may be released on recordings in the future.

"Agnieszka is survived by her parents, brother, Alexei, younger sister, Clara and a number of distant relatives living in Poznan. She will be greatly missed by many close friends including Simon Williams of Cardiff and her dearest Canadian friend, Charles Flemming of Toronto. The funeral is scheduled for May 25 at 1400 hours with celebration of Requiem Mass at the Polish Orthodox Church of Polish Martyrs in Kraków. The Lipska family will receive friends at their home in Kraków, 206 Kanonicza Street, between 1200 and 1600 hours on May 24.

"Interment will be at the Orthodox Cemetery in Kraków after the Mass."

The funeral had been well attended. In the morning the weather had cleared—the sun was shining and by the afternoon the remnants of the winter's snow had virtually melted away.

*** *** *** ***

Although spring was a welcoming visitor to Toronto, Charles' memories of his winter in Europe were not easily erased. He wrote to the Lipski family whenever he found the time—most weekends when he was free from hospital call duty. He toyed with the idea of travelling to Poland again. Elizabeth was encouraging. He knew an Atlantic crossing in summer would be more enjoyable. He loved to read the letters from Kraków and saved every one of them in a bedroom drawer, where he would sometimes retrieve them to read again late at night.

His Rome experience had left a lasting impact on his attitude to life and death—and to love as well. His friends noted the change in his personality. He paid a visit to Anne's grave and left fresh cut flowers near her headstone. On a long weekend he drove to Farmington to visit the cemetery where his parents and Sarah had been interred. He took Toby along and they stayed overnight in a local B&B establishment where the manager had two dogs and he did not object to Toby sharing the bedroom for the night. A stroll through the cemetery brought back memories of his visit to the de Pachmann gravesite in Rome with Agnieszka. He later tried to understand why, but he knew on that Saturday afternoon in the Farmington cemetery—for the first time—as he walked out the gate, that he finally felt a genuine grief for the man. Was it the realization that it was de Pachmann, the pianist with the magic touch and startling eccentricities, whom he had not greatly admired, had been in large part responsible—even in death—for bringing Agnieszka ever so briefly into his life?

BIBLIOGRAPHY

Huneker, James: *Old Fogy: His Musical Opinions and Grotesques,* Theodore Presser Co. Philadelphia 1913.

Husson, Adèle: *Reflections: The Life and Writings of a Young Blind Woman in Post -Revolutionary France, s.*n. 1825.(Translated and with commentary by Catherine J. Kudlick and Zina Weygand, New-York and London, New York University Press, 2001.)

Perry, Edward Baxter: *Descriptive Analysis of Piano Works,* Theodore Presser, Philadelphia, 1902.

Remarque, Erich Maria: *All Quiet on the Western Front,* s.n. 1829 Vienna Masterworks, Vienna Austria, 1999.

Symons, Arthur: *Plays, Acting and Music: A Book of Theory*, Jonathan Cope, London 1928.

West, Rebecca: *The return of the Soldier,* The Century Co., New York 1918.

BIOGRAPHY

Born in 1936, Carl Abbott received his diploma in medicine from Dalhousie University in Halifax, Nova Scotia in 1959. He practised for two years at Botwood Cottage Hospital, Newfoundland before returning the Victoria General Hospital in Halifax, Nova Scotia to study internal medicine for two years and then for another two years worked as a Fellow of the Medical Research Council of Canada at the Toronto General Hospital.

From 1966 to 1967 he was the travelling Fellow of the Medical Research Council of Canada at St. Mary's Hospital medical school in London, England, and some years later served as honourary consultant in Clinical Pharmacology at the Royal Post-Graduate Medical School in London.

In 1965, he became a Fellow of the Royal College of Physicians and Surgeons of Canada specializing in internal medicine. Dr. Abbott served on the staff at the General Hospital and St. Clare's Mercy Hospital in St. John's Newfoundland before returning to Halifax to work and teach in the city's hospitals and at Dalhousie University. In 1989 he became a Fellow of the American College of Physicians, and is a specialist in Hypertension of the American Hypertension Society.

He has authored and co-authored more than one hundred papers on medicine, including his 1989 paper *Gille de la Tourette Syndrome in a performing artist: The case of Vladimir de Pachmann*, presented at the Royal College meeting that year, and which became the foundation for his first novel *Mourning de Pachmann*.

His interest in music and medicine also allowed him to author *Patterns of morbidity and mortality in the 18th Century: The case of W. A. Mozart (1756-1791)*, published in the supplement to the journal *Clinical & Investigative Medicine* in 1991, and *The Mozart family's physicians and their treatments*, published in *The Dalhousie Review*, in 1994. In 2010, he published an article *Marguerite de Pachmann: a forgotten woman pianist and composer* in the *Musical Times, Vol.151, No.1913*.

Married, with three children, Dr. Abbott is now semi-retired and intends to occupy his time with more writing projects, and in the pursuit of his hobbies of travel, watercolor painting, tennis and wine tasting.